th

Books by Kerry Greenwood

The Phryne Fisher series
Cocaine Blues
Flying Too High
Murder on the Ballarat Train
Death at Victoria Dock
The Green Mill Murder
Blood and Circuses
Ruddy Gore
Urn Burial
Raisins and Almonds
Death Before Wicket
Away with the Fairies
Murder in Montparnasse
The Castlemaine Murders
Queen of the Flowers
Death by Water
Murder in the Dark
Murder on a Midsummer Night
Dead Man's Chest

The Corinna Chapman series
Earthly Delights
Heavenly Pleasures
Devil's Food
Trick or Treat
Forbidden Fruit
Cooking the Books

Short Story Anthology
A Question of Death:
An Illustrated Phryne Fisher Anthology

Introducing the Honourable Phryne Fisher

Become addicted to Phryne's
first three riveting mysteries

Kerry Greenwood

Poisoned Pen Press

Poisoned Pen Press

Copyright © 2011 by Kerry Greenwood
Cocaine Blues © 1989 by Kerry Greenwood
Flying Too High © 1990 by Kerry Greenwood
Murder on the Ballarat Train © 1991 by Kerry Greenwood

First US Edition 2011

10 9 8 7 6 5 4 3 2

Library of Congress Catalog Card Number: 2011927731

ISBN: 9781590589724   Trade Paperback

Poisoned Pen Press
6962 E. First Ave., Ste. 103
Scottsdale, AZ 85251
www.poisonedpenpress.com
info@poisonedpenpress.com

Printed in the United States of America

Contents

Foreword

Thank you for buying this book. I have a wizard and three cats to feed. Picture the scene. There I am, in 1988, thirty years old and never been published, clutching a contract in a hot, sweaty hand. I have been trying for four long and frustrating years to attract a publisher and now a divinity has offered me a two book contract about a detective in 1928. I am reading the ads as the tram clacks down Brunswick Street. They are not inspiring posters. I am beginning to panic. This is what I have striven for my whole life. Am I now going to develop writer's block? When I never have before?

Then she got on the tram and sat near me. A lady with a Lulu bob, feather earrings, a black cloth coat with an Astrakan collar and a black cloche jammed down over her exquisite eyebrows. She wore delicate shoes of sable glace kid with a Louis heel. She moved with a fine louche grace, as though she knew that the whole tram was staring at her and she both did not mind and accepted their adulation as something she merited. She leaned towards me. I smelt rice powder and Jicky. "Why not write about me?" she breathed. And, in a scent of Benedictine, she vanished. That was the Honourable Phryne Fisher. I am delighted to be able to introduce you to her.

Kerry Greenwood
September 2010

Cocaine Blues

Chapter One

Will go, like the centre of sea-green pomp
...upon her irretrievable way.
'The Paltry Nude Starts on a Voyage',
Wallace Stevens

The glass in the French window shattered. The guests screamed. Over the general exclamation could be heard the shrill shriek of Madame St Clair, wife of the ambassador, '*Ciel! Mes bijoux!*'

Phryne Fisher stood quietly and groped for a cigarette lighter. So far the evening had been tedious. After the strenuous preparations for what was admittedly the social event of the year, the dinner had been a culinary masterpiece—but the conversation had been boring. She had been placed between a retired Indian Colonel and an amateur cricketer. The Colonel had confined himself to a few suitable comments on the food but Bobby could recite his bowling figures for each country match for two years—and did. Then the lights had gone out and the window had smashed. Anything that interrupted the Wisden of the Country House matches was a good thing, thought Phryne and found the lighter.

The scene revealed in the flickering light was confused. The young women who usually screamed were screaming. Phryne's father was bellowing at Phryne's mother. This, too, was normal. Several gentlemen had struck matches and one had pulled the bell. Phryne pushed her way to the door and slipped into the front hall, where the fuse box door hung open, and pulled down the switch marked 'main'. A flood of light restored everyone except the most gin-soaked to their senses. And Madame St Clair, clutching melodramatically at her throat, found that her diamond necklace, reputed to contain some of the stones from the Tsarina's collar, was gone. Her scream outstripped all previous efforts.

Bobby, who had a surprisingly swift grasp of events, gasped, 'Gosh! She's been robbed!' Phryne escaped from the babble to go outside and scan the ground in front of the broken window. Through it she could hear Bobby saying ingenuously, 'He must have broken the jolly old glass, hopped in, and snaffled the loot! Daring, eh?'

Phryne gritted her teeth. She stubbed her toe on a ball and picked it up—a cricket ball. Her feet crunched on glass—most of it was outside. Phryne grabbed a passing gardener's boy and ordered him to bring a ladder into the ballroom.

When she regained the gathering she drew her father aside.

'Don't bother me, girl. I shall have to search everyone. What will the Duke think?'

'Father, if you want to cut out young Bobby from the crowd, I can save you a lot of embarrassment,' she whispered. Her father, who always had a high colour, darkened to a rich plum.

'What do you mean? Good family, goes back to the Conquerer.'

'Don't be foolish, Father, I tell you he did it, and if you don't remove him and do it quietly the Duke will be miffed. Just get him, and that tiresome Colonel. He can be a witness.'

Phryne's father did as he was bid, and the two gentlemen came into the card room with the young man between them.

'I say, what's this about?' asked Bobby. Phryne fixed him with a glittering eye.

'You broke the window, Bobby, and you pinched the necklace. Do you want to confess or shall I tell you how you did it?'

'I don't know what you mean,' he bluffed, paling as Phryne produced the ball.

'I found this outside. Most of the glass from the window was there, too. You pushed the switch, and flung this ball through the glass, to make that dramatic smash. Then you lifted the necklace off Madame St Clair's admittedly over-decorated neck.'

The young man smiled. He was tall, had curly chestnut hair and deep brown eyes like a Jersey cow. He had a certain charm and he was exerting all of it, but Phryne remained impervious. Bobby spread out his arms.

'If I pinched it, then I must have it on me. Search me,' he invited. 'I won't have had time to hide it.'

'Don't bother,' snapped Phryne. 'Come into the ballroom.' They followed her biddably. The gardener's boy erected the ladder. Mounting it fearlessly (and displaying to the company her diamanté garters, as her mother later informed her) Phryne hooked something out of the chandelier. She regained the floor without incident, and presented the object to Madame St Clair, who stopped crying as suddenly as if someone had turned off her tap.

'This yours?' Phryne asked, and Bobby gave a small groan, retreating to the card room.

'By Jove, that was a cunning bit of detection!' enthused the Colonel, after the disgraced Bobby had been allowed to leave. 'You're a sharp young woman. My compliments! Would you come and see m'wife and m'self tomorrow? A private matter? You could be just the girl we've been looking for, bless my soul!'

The Colonel was far too firmly married and full of military honours to be a threat to Phryne's virtue, or what remained of it, so she agreed. She presented herself at 'Mandalay', the Colonel's country retreat the next day, at about the hour when it is customary for the English to take tea.

'Miss Fisher!' gushed the Colonel's wife, who was not a woman generally given to gushing. 'Do come in! The Colonel has told me how cleverly you caught that young man—never did trust him, reminded me of some of the junior subalterns in the Punjab, the ones who embezzled the mess funds...'

Phryne was ushered in. The welcome exceeded her deserts and she was instantly suspicious. The last time she had been fawned over with this air of distracted delight was when one county family thought that she was going to take their appalling lounge-lizard of a son off their hands, just because she had slept with him once or twice. The scene when she declined to marry him had been reminiscent of early Victorian melodrama. Phryne feared that she was becoming cynical.

She took her seat at an ebony table and accepted a cup of very good tea. The room was stuffed to bursting with brass Indian gods and carved and inlaid boxes and rich tapestries; she dragged her eyes away from a very well-endowed Kali dancing on dead men with a bunch of decapitated heads in each black hand, and strove to concentrate.

'It's our daughter Lydia,' said the Colonel, getting to the point. 'We are worried about her. She got in with a strange set in Paris, you see, and led a rackety sort of life. But she's a good girl, got her head screwed on and all that, and when she married this Australian we thought that it was the best thing. She seemed happy enough, but when she came to see us last year she was shockingly pale and thin. You ladies like that nowadays, eh? But all skin and bone, can't be good…er ahem,' faltered the Colonel as he received a forty-volt glare from his wife and lost his thread. 'Er, yes, well, she was perfectly all right after three weeks, went to Paris for a while, and we sent her off to Melbourne brisk as a puppy. Then, as soon as she arrived back, she was sick again. Here is the interesting thing, Miss Fisher: she went to some resort to take a cure, and was well—but as soon as she came back to her husband, she was sick again. And I think…'

'And I agree with him,' added Mrs Harper portentously. 'That there's something damned odd going on—beg pardon, my dear—and we want some reliable girl to find out.'

'Do you think her husband is poisoning her?'

The Colonel hesitated but his spouse said placidly, 'Well, what would you think?'

Phryne had to agree that the cycle of illness sounded odd, and she was at a loose end. She did not want to stay in her father's house and arrange flowers. She had tried social work but she was sick of the stews and sluts and starvation of London, and the company of the Charitable Ladies was not good for her temper. She had often thought of travelling back to Australia, where she had been born in extreme poverty, and here was an excellent excuse for putting off decisions about her future for half a year.

'Very well, I'll go. But I'll go at my own expense, and I'll report at my leisure. Don't follow me with frantic cables or the whole thing will be U.P. I'll make Lydia's acquaintance on my own, and you will not mention me in any of your letters to her. I'll stay at the Windsor.' Phryne felt a thrill at this. She had last seen that hotel in the cold dawn, as she passed with a load of old vegetables gleaned from the pig-bins of the Victoria Market. 'You can find me there, if it's important. What is Lydia's married name and her address? And tell me—what would her husband inherit if she died?'

'Her husband's name is Andrews, and here is her address. If she dies before him without issue, he inherits fifty thousand pounds.'

'Has she any children?'

'Not yet,' said the Colonel. He produced a bundle of letters. 'Perhaps you'd like to read these,' and he put them down on the tea table. 'They are Lydia's letters. She's a bright little thing, you'll find—very canny about money—but she's besotted with this Andrews feller,' he snorted. Phryne slipped the first envelope and began to read.

The letters were absorbing. Not that they had any literary merit, but Lydia was such an odd mixture. After a dissertation on oil stocks that would not have disgraced an accountant, she indulged in terms of such honeyed sentimentality about her husband that Phryne could hardly bear to read it. *My tom-cat has been severe with his mouse because she was dancing with a pretty cat at supper last night*, read Phryne with increasing nausea.

And it took two hours of stroking before he became my good little kitten again.

Phryne ploughed on while the Colonel's wife kept refilling her tea-cup. After an hour she was awash with tea, and sentiment. The tone became whining after Lydia reached Melbourne. *Johnnie goes out to his club and leaves his poor little mouse to pine in her mouse-house...I was ever so sick but Johnnie just told me I'd over-eaten and went to dinner. There is a rumour that Peruvian Gold is to start their mine again. Don't put any money into it. Their accountant is buying his second car...I hope that you took my advice about the Shallows property. The land is adjacent to a church right-of-way and thus cannot be overlooked. It will double in value in twenty years...I have transferred some of my capital to Lloyds, where the interest rate is half a percentage higher...I'm trying baths and massage with Madame Breda, of Russell Street. I am very ill but Johnnie just laughs at me.*

Odd. Phryne copied out the address of Madame Breda in Russell Street and took her leave, before she could be offered any more tea.

Chapter Two

Or old dependency of day and night
Or island solitude, unsponsered, free
Of that wide water, inescapable.
'Sunday Morning', Wallace Stevens

Phryne leaned on the ship's rail, listening to the sea-gulls announcing that land was near, and watched for the first hint of sunrise. She had put on her lounging robe, of a dramatic oriental pattern of green and gold, an outfit not to be sprung suddenly on invalids or those of nervous tendencies—and she was rather glad that there was no one on deck to be astonished. It was five o'clock in the morning.

There was a faint gleam on the horizon; Phryne was waiting for the green flash, which she had never seen. She fumbled in her pocket for cigarettes, her holder, and a match. She lit the gasper and dropped the match over the side. The brief flare had unsighted her; she blinked, and ran a hand over her short black cap of hair.

'I wonder what I want to do?' Phryne asked of herself. 'It has all been quite interesting up until now, but I can't dance and game my life away. I suppose I could try for the air race record in the new Avro—or join Miss May Cunliffe in the road-trials of the new Lagonda—or learn Abyssinian—or take to gin—or breed horses—I don't know, it all seems very flat.

'Well, I shall try being a perfect Lady Detective in Melbourne—that ought to be difficult enough—and perhaps something will suggest itself. If not, I can still catch the ski season. It may prove amusing, after all.'

At that moment there came a fast, unrepeatable grass-green flash before the gold and rose of sunrise coloured the sky. Phryne blew the sun a kiss, and returned to her cabin.

Still wrapped in her robe, she nibbled a little thin toast and contemplated her wardrobe, which was spread out like a picnic over all available surfaces. She poured a cup of China tea and surveyed her costumes with a jaundiced eye.

The weather reports promised clear, mild conditions, and Phryne briefly considered a Chanel knitted silk suit, in beige, and a rather daring coat and skirt in bright red wool but finally selected a fetching sailor suit in dark blue with white piping and a pique collar. The waist dropped below her hips leaving five inches of pleated skirt, which even the parochial taste of Melbourne could not find offensive.

She dressed quickly and soon stood up in cami-knickers and silk stockings which were gartered above the knee, and dark-blue leather shoes with a Louis heel. She examined her face in the fixed mirror as she brushed ruthlessly at her perfectly black, perfectly straight hair, which fell into a neat and shiny cap leaving the nape of her neck and most of her forehead bare. She pulled on a soft dark-blue cloche, and with dexterity born of long practice, sketched her eyebrows, outlined her green-grey eyes with a thin kohl pencil, and added a dab of rouge and a flourish of powder.

She was pouring out her final cup of tea when a tap at the door caused her to dive back into the folds of the robe.

'Come in,' she called, wondering if this was to be another visit from the First Officer, who had conceived a desperate passion for Phryne, a passion which, she was convinced, would last for all of ten minutes once the *Orient* docked. But the answer reassured her.

'Elizabeth,' announced the caller, and Phryne opened the door and Dr MacMillan came in and seated herself on the stateroom's best chair, the only one free of Phryne's clothes.

'Well, child, we dock in three hours, so that affected young Purser told me,' she said. 'Can you spare the rest of that toast? That blighted woman in steerage produced her brat this morning at three of the clock—babies seem to demand to be born at benighted hours, usually in a thunderstorm—there's something elemental about babies, I find.'

Phryne passed over the tray—which still bore a plate of bacon and eggs and more toast than Phryne could possibly eat after a long day's famine—and surveyed Dr MacMillan affectionately.

She was forty-five if a day, and having had the formidable determination to follow Dr Garret Anderson and struggle to become a doctor, she had had no time for anything else. She was as broad and as strong as a labourer, with the same weatherbeaten complexion and rough, calloused hands. Her hair was pepper-and-salt, cut ruthlessly into a short Eton crop. For convenience, she wore men's clothes, and in them she had a certain rather rugged style.

'Come up, Phryne, and watch for the harbour,' said Dr MacMillan. Phryne slipped the sailor suit on and joined her in the climb to the deck.

Phryne leaned on the rail to watch Melbourne appear as the *Orient* steamed steadily in through the heads and turned in its course to find the river and Station Pier.

The city was visible, the flag on Government House announcing that the Governor was at home. It appeared to be a much larger city than Phryne remembered, though admittedly she had not been in any position to see it clearly when she had clung to the rail on the way out. Dr MacMillan, at her side, threw a foul cigar overboard and remarked, 'It seems to be a fine big city, well-built stone and steeple.'

'What did you expect? Wattle-and-daub? They aren't savages, you know, Elizabeth! You'll find it much like Edinburgh. Possibly quieter.'

'Ah well, that will be a change,' agreed the doctor. 'Are your trunks packed, Phryne?'

Phryne smiled, conscious of three cabin trunks, two suitcases, a shopping bag and a purse in her cabin, and seven large trunks in the hold, no doubt under a lot of sheep. Her dangerous imports into her native land included a small lady's handgun and a box of bullets for it, plus certain devices of Dr Stopes' which were wrapped in her underwear under an open packet of Ladies' Travelling Necessities to discourage any over-zealous customs official.

They leaned companionably into the wind, watching the city come nearer. The little book in the cabin had informed Phryne that Melbourne was a modern city. Most of it was sewered, had water and in some cases electricity laid on, and there was public transport in the form of trains and trams. Industry was booming, and cars, trucks and motorcycles outnumbered horse transport thirty to one. Most streets were macadamized and the city was well served with a university, several hospitals, a cricket ground, the Athenaeum Club, and a Royal Arcade. Visitors were urged to attend the Flemington races or the football. (Collingwood were last year's premiers, the pamphlet claimed, to Phryne's complete bemusement.) Ladies would appreciate a stroll around the Block Arcade, the shopping highlight of the city, and would admire Walter Burley Griffin's interesting addition to Collins House. The Menzies, Scott's, or the Windsor Hotel were recommended for first-class passengers. Phryne wondered where the steerage passengers were advised to stay. 'Elevator House, I expect,' she said to herself. 'You can always rely on the Salvation Army.'

'Eh? Yes, splendid people,' agreed Dr MacMillan absently, and Phryne realized that she had spoken aloud. Had she been at all used to blushing, she would have blushed, but she wasn't, so she didn't.

Clearing customs required less expenditure of charm than Phryne had feared, and within an hour she and her mountain of baggage were through into the street and waiting for a taxi. Dr MacMillan, lightly encumbered with a Gladstone bag full of

clothes and a tea-chest of books, hailed vigorously, and a motor swerved and halted abruptly before them.

The driver got out, surveyed the pile of impedimenta, and remarked laconically, 'Y'need another cab.' He then yelled across the road to a mate, Cec, who was lounging against a convenient wall. Cec vanished with a turn of speed which belied his appearance, and returned in charge of a battered truck which had evidently once belonged to a grocer. 'Cox's Orange Pippin' still decorated the flaking sides.

So these are the natives, thought Phryne. Cec was tall and lanky, blond with brown eyes, young and ferociously taciturn. The other driver, who was apparently called Bert, was short, dark and older. Both were strikingly attractive. I believe they call it 'hybrid vigour', Phryne mused.

'Load up,' said Bert, and three porters obeyed him. Phryne observed with amazement that at no time had the hand-rolled cigarette moved from its place on the driver's lower lip. Phryne distributed tips with a liberal hand and took her place in the taxi. With a jerk they started off for Melbourne.

It was a fine, warm autumn day. She doffed her moire coat and lit a gasper, as they left the wharf area with a great smoking and roaring of engine and proceeded to take a series of corners at alarming speed.

The driver, Bert, was examining Phryne with the same detached interest as she was examining him. He was also keeping an eye on the traffic, and the following grocer's van driven by Cec. Phryne wondered if she would ever see her expensive baggage again.

'Where we goin' first?' yelled Bert. Phryne screamed back over the noise of the labouring engine, 'First to the Queen Victoria Hospital, then to the Windsor Hotel, and we aren't in a particular hurry.'

'Nurses, are you?' asked Bert. Dr MacMillan looked resigned.

'No, this is Dr MacMillan from Scotland, and I'm just visiting.'

'You staying at the Windsor, Miss?' asked Bert, removing his pendant cigarette and flinging it through the rattling window

of the taxi. 'Toffy, are you? The time will come when the working man rises up against his oppressors, and breaks the chains of Capital, and…'

'…then there won't be any more Windsor,' finished Phryne. Bert looked injured. He released the steering wheel and turned his head to remonstrate with the young capitalist.

'No miss, you don't understand,' he began, averting death with a swift twiddle of the wheel that skidded them to safety around a van. 'When the revolution comes, we'll all be staying at the Windsor.'

'It sounds like an excellent idea,' agreed Phryne.

'I saw enough of such things during the war,' snorted Dr MacMillan. 'Revolutions mean blood and murder. And innocent people made homeless.'

'War,' said the driver sententiously, 'is a plot by Capital to force the workers to fight their battles in the name of economic security. That's what war is,' he concluded.

'Is Cec still following?' Phryne asked, hoping to divert this fervent communist.

'Yeah, Cec is on our tail. He's a good driver,' said Bert. 'But not as good as me.'

The city was flying past, halated behind them in the cloud of exhaust and dust generated by the ex-grocer's van, and they stopped suddenly at an unimposing entrance. As the air cleared, Phryne saw the legend of the main door and realized that she must part with Elizabeth MacMillan. She felt an unexpected pang, but suppressed it. The doctor kissed Phryne on the cheek, gathered her Gladstone bag and her coat, and Cec unloaded the tea-chest onto the pavement without actually endangering the lives of too many passers-by. Elizabeth waved, the driver hauled his unwilling motor into gear and, avoiding a clanging tram by inches, belted down to Collins Street, described a circle around the policeman on point duty, and groaned up the hill. They inched up, past the Theosophical building and the Theatre, past two churches, some rather charming couturières, and brass plates by the hundred, until Phryne saw a large and imposing grey

building dead ahead, and entertained a momentary apprehension that her driver might try his steed on the majestic flight of steps that fronted it.

Her fears were unfounded. The driver had done this journey before. Bert hauled the motor around in another three-point turn and stopped, grinning, in front of the austere portals of the hotel. The doorman, not blanching in the least at this outlandish vehicle, stepped forward with dignity and opened the door by its one remaining hinge. Phryne took his gloved hand and extracted herself from the car, brushed herself down, and produced her purse.

The driver abandoned his vehicle and handed over Phryne's coat, grinning amiably. He was wearing a new cigarette.

'Thank you so much for the interesting ride,' said Phryne. 'How much do I owe you and—er—Cec?'

'I reckon that five shillings will do it,' grinned Bert, avoiding the doorman's eye. Phryne opened her purse.

'I think about two-and-six will do it, don't you?' she said artlessly.

'And a deener for Cec,' Bert bargained. Phryne handed over the extra shilling. Cec, a gangly man with more strength than appeared to inhabit his bony frame, transferred Phryne's trunks and boxes into the care of a small army of porters, all in the livery of the hotel. Then, with a whoop and a cloud of dust, the drivers vanished.

'I'm Phryne Fisher,' she informed the doorman. 'I made my reservation in London.'

'Ah, yes, Miss,' replied the doorman. 'You're expected. Come in on the *Orient* this morning? You'll want a cup of tea. Come this way, if you please.' Phryne surrendered herself, and stepped up into the quiet, well-ordered, opulent world of the Windsor.

Bathed, re-clothed, and hungry, Phryne came down into the hotel dining room for luncheon. She cut a distractingly fashionable figure in pale straw-coloured cotton and a straw hat, around which she had wrapped a silk scarf of green, lemon and sea-blue. She chose a table under the cluster of marble cupids,

selected clear soup and a cold collation from the menu handed to her by a neat girl in black, and considered the inhabitants.

The women were well-dressed, and some quite beautiful, though admittedly a little behind the mode. The men were dressed in the usual pin-stripe and the occasional dark suit, solicitors or bank managers, perhaps. A few bright young things in flannel bags and sports jacket or Fugi dresses swinging braid, and caked make-up livened things up. One actress was in grease-paint, wearing a set of beach pyjamas in gold cloth and a turban. Her fingers dripped with jewels, and a leopard-cub on a strong chain sat at her feet. The Windsor took them all in its stride.

The soup was excellent; Phryne demolished it and her collation and three cups of tea, then returned to her room for a rest. She fell asleep, and didn't wake up until the dressing-gong sounded for dinner.

While she had been asleep, her clothes had been unpacked, pressed, and hung up in the massive wooden wardrobe. The room was decorated in excellent, if subdued, taste, though she would have preferred a less aggressive pink for the lampshades and fewer statues of nymphs. Phryne had a grudge against nymphs. Her name, chosen by her father, had been Psyche. Regrettably, at her christening he had not been himself, due to a long evening at the Club the night before. When called upon for her name, he had rummaged through the rags of a classical education and seized upon Phryne. So instead of Psyche the nymph, she was Phryne the courtesan.

After some investigation, Phryne had been comforted. The courtesan had certainly been a spirited young woman. In court, her case going badly, her Counsel had torn down the front of her robe and revealed her beautiful breasts to the Court. They had been so in awe of such perfection that they had acquitted her. And it had been Phryne who, having amassed a pile of ill-gotten gold, had offered to rebuild the walls of Thebes if she could have placed on them an inscription, 'The walls of Thebes: ruined by time, rebuilt by Phryne the courtesan'. But the sober citizens of Thebes had preferred their ruins.

And serve them right, thought Phryne Fisher, donning silk undergarments and a peacock-blue gown by Patou. I hope that the Romans invaded them. Now, shall I wear the sapphires or the enamels?

She considered the long sparkling earrings, pulsing with blue fire, and hooked them through her ears. She swiftly tinted and arranged her face, brushed her hair vigorously, and threaded a fillet through the shining strands. Then she gathered a sea-green cloak and her purse, and went down to dinner.

She restored herself with a cocktail and an excellent lobster mayonnaise. Phryne was devoted to lobster mayonnaise, with cucumbers.

It was a fine night, and none of her companions looked to be in the least interesting, except for a humorous gentleman with a large party, who had smiled very pleasantly at her, in apparent admiration of the gown. He, however, was occupied and Phryne needed to think. She ascertained that the Block Arcade was still open, it being Saturday, and returned to her room to change into trousers and a silk pullover, stout shoes, and a soft felt hat. In such garments, she was sufficiently epicene to attract no attention from the idle young men of the town but she could make her femininity felt if she wanted to.

Since she wanted to think and to walk, she donned her sub-fusc garb and went into the warm dusk.

Trams passed with a rush and a rumble; the city smelt of autumn leaves, smoke and dust. She walked, as the doorman had directed, straight down Collins Street. In case it turned cool, she had put on a reefer jacket, box-pleated, with pockets, and as she was unencumbered with a purse, her hands were unusually free. Forests of brass plaques decorated the sober buildings of Collins Street; it reminded her of Harley Street, and London, though the crowds were noisier here, and cleaner, and there were fewer beggars. Phryne felt the crackle of leaves under her shoes.

She passed the Presbyterian Church, the Manse, the Baptist Church, and paused on the other side of the road to stare at the Regent Theatre, a massive pile, decorated to within an inch of

the stress-tolerances of concrete. It was so unashamedly vulgar that Phryne rather liked it.

A group of factory girls, all art-silk stockings and feathers, bright with red and blue and green shifts and plastered with a thick veneer of Mr Coles' products, jostled past Phryne in the harsh street, shrilling like sparrows. Phryne resumed her even pace, passing through the crowd under the Town Hall eaves and across Swanston Street.

Chapter Three

She said, 'My life is dreary, dreary,
Would God that I was dead!'

'Mariana', Tennyson

Cec cocked a thumb at a girl drooping in a tall man's arms on the pavement in Lonsdale Street.

'Tiddly,' commented Bert as he came to a halt. 'And only eleven in the morning. Cruel, innit?'

'Yair, mate?' he yelled to the man, who was hailing him, 'where ya goin'?'

'Richmond,' replied the man, hauling the girl forward by the waist and packing her ungently into the cab next to Cec. 'She'll give you the address. Here's the fare.' He thrust a ten-shilling note into Bert's face and slammed the door. 'Keep the change,' he added over his shoulder, and he hurried away, almost breaking into a run as he rounded the corner into Queen Street. The crowd swallowed him, and frantic honking and personal remarks from the traffic behind as to Bert's parentage made him move on.

'He was in a bloody hurry,' Bert commented. 'Beg pardon, Miss. What's the address?'

The girl blinked and rubbed her eyes, licking cracked lips.

'I can go home, now,' she whispered. 'I can go home.'

'Yair, and the fare paid, too. Where's home?' asked Bert in a loud voice calculated to pierce an alcoholic fog. 'Carm on Miss, can't you remember?'

The girl did not reply, but slid bonelessly sideways until she was leaning on Cec's shoulder. He lifted her gently and said to Bert, 'Something wrong, mate. I can't smell no booze. She's crook. Her skin's hot as fire.'

'What do you reckon?' asked Bert as he rounded into Market Street and stopped to allow a dray-load of vegetables to totter past.

'Dirty work,' said Cec slowly. 'She's bleeding.'

'Hospital, then,' said Bert, avoiding a grocer's lorry by inches. The overwrought driver threw a cabbage at the taxi, and missed.

'The hospital for women,' said Cec with ponderous emphasis. 'The Queen Victoria Hospital.' The girl stirred in Cec's arms and croaked, 'Where you taking me?'

'To the hospital,' said Cec quietly. 'You're crook.'

'No!' She struggled feebly and flailed for the door handle. 'Everyone'll know!' Bert and Cec exchanged significant glances. Blood and foul-smelling matter were pooling in the lap of the blue, cheap-and-showy dress she had worn to her abortion. Cec grasped the hand firmly and pressed her back into the seat. She was panting with effort and her fingers seemed to brand his wrist. She was only a child, Cec realized, perhaps no more than seventeen. Haggard and fevered, her dark feathery hair escaped from its pins and stuck to her brow and neck. Her eyes were diamond bright with pain and fever.

'No one'll know,' soothed Bert. 'I know one of the doctors there—you remember, Cec, the old Scotch chook with all the books who came with the toffy lady? She won't say nothing to no one. Just you sit back and relax, Miss. What's your name?'

'Alice,' muttered the girl. 'Alice Greenham.'

'I'm Bert and that's Cec,' said Bert as he skidded along Exhibition Street, dragged the taxi into Collins Street and gunned the failing engine up the remains of the hill to Mint Place.

They dumped the cab outside the hospital, and without apparent effort Cec carried Alice Greenham up the steps to the front door. Bert hammered with clenched fist and pounded on the bell. Cec stepped inside as the door swung open, while Bert turned on the nurse who had admitted them and barked. 'We got an emergency. Where's the Scotch doctor?' Nurses are constitutionally incapable of being daunted. The woman stared him in the eye and was silent.

Bert, at length, realized what she was waiting for.

'Please,' he snapped.

'Dr MacMillan is in surgery,' she announced. Bert drew a deep breath, and Cec spoke while offering the girl in his arms to the nurse.

'She fainted in our cab,' he explained. 'We came for help,' he added, in case he had not made his meaning clear. Cec did not talk much, finding in general that words conveyed nothing of what he wanted to say.

Alice Greenham moaned.

'Bring her in here,' the nurse relented, and they followed her into a bare examination room, painted white. Cec laid her down on a stretcher bed.

'I'll fetch the doctor,' said the nurse, and vanished. Bert knew that nurses did not run, but this one walked very fast. Bert and Cec looked at each other. Cec was striped with blood.

'I spose we can't just go and leave her,' faltered Bert. 'Jeez, Cec, look at you!' Cec brushed fruitlessly at the bloodstains. He sat down next to Alice and took her hand.

'She's only a kid.'

'She's in some grown-up trouble.'

Bert did not like hospitals, and was about to suggest that they had done their duty and could now leave, when Dr MacMillan bustled in.

'Well, well, what have we here? Fainted, did she?' she demanded. 'Is she known to you?'

Cec shook his head. Bert piped up, 'A bloke put her into our cab in Lonsdale Street. Gave me ten shillings to take her to

Richmond. Then she keeled over, and Cec noticed...the blood, and we brung her here. She didn't say much, but her name's Alice Greenham.' Dr MacMillan smiled unexpectedly.

'Sister will give you a cup of tea,' she announced, 'and you will wait until I come back. We must talk about the man in Lonsdale Street. Sister! Give these gentlemen tea in the visitor's room, and send Sister Simmonds to me immediately.'

∽∽∽

Phryne reached the Block Arcade, from which shone a soft, seductive light, out past the severe, dark stone Athenaeum Club with its pseudo-Roman decoration. The Arcade, by contrast, was entered by charming portals fringed with delicate iron lacework, and the floor, such of it as could be seen beneath the scuffling feet of thousands of loafers, was tiled most elegantly in black and white. Phryne drifted along with the crowd, observing with detached amusement the mating habits of the locals; the young women in shocking pink and peacock blue, dripping with Coles' diamonds (nothing over 2s.6d.), painted, and heavily scented with Otto of Roses. The young men favoured soft shirts, loose coats, blinding ties and Californian Poppy. With the reek of burning leaves drifting in from some park, motor exhaust and the odd salty ozone tang produced from the trams, the Arcade was suffocating.

The shops, however, were engrossing, and Phryne purchased a pair of fine doeskin gloves, and a barrette for her black hair, sparkling with diamantés and formed in the shape of a winged insect.

She arranged that these purchases should be wrapped and delivered to the Windsor, and decided that she could cope with a cup of tea. She caught sight of herself in the mirror-shiny black pillar of the glove shop, and paused to tidy her hair. In the reflection she noticed the set, white face of a girl, standing behind her, unaware of Phryne's regard, who was slowly biting into her lower lip. The horror on that face gave Phryne a start, and she spun about. The girl was leaning on the opposite pillar. She was dressed in a light cotton shift of deep, shabby black, and her

legs were bare. She was innocent of gloves, hat or coat and had scuffed house-slippers on her feet. Her long, light-brown hair was dragged back into an unbecoming bun, which was coming adrift from its pins. Her blue eyes stared out of what would have been a fresh, milk-maid's complexion, if she had not been tinged heliotrope by some illness or internal stress. On impulse, Phryne crossed the Arcade and came up to the girl, wondering what it was she held concealed in her hands close to her body. As she approached, she identified it—it was a knife.

'Hello, I was just going to get some tea,' she said casually, as though meeting an old acquaintance. 'Would you like to come too? Just over here,' she added chattily, leading the unresisting girl by the arm. 'Now, sit down, and we'll order. Waitress! Two teas, please. Sandwiches?' she asked and the girl nodded. 'And sandwiches,' added Phryne. 'I think that you'd better give me that knife, don't you?'

The girl handed over the knife, still mute, and Phryne put it in her pocket. It was an ordinary kitchen knife, such as is used to chop vegetables, and it was razor-sharp. Phryne hoped that it would not slit the pocket-lining of her new coat.

Tea was brought. The Moorish arches, hung with artificial flowers and lanterns, were soothing, and the light was not harsh. Phryne dispensed tea and sandwiches, and watched her companion becoming more lively with each mouthful.

'Thanks, Miss,' said the girl. 'I was famished.'

'That's all right,' said Phryne easily. 'Some more?'

The girl nodded again, and Phryne ordered more food. A jazz orchestra was damaging the night somewhere, but not near enough to preclude speech. The young woman finished the sandwiches, leaned back, and sighed. Phryne offered her a gasper, and she refused rather indignantly.

'Nice girls don't smoke,' she said trenchantly. 'I mean...'

'I know what you mean,' smiled Phryne. 'Well, what about it? What are you doing here?'

'Waiting for him,' said the girl. 'To kill him. I come from Collingwood, see, and I got a job as a housemaid in this doctor's house. The doctor's missus, she was a very good woman.'

Phryne had a feeling that she had heard this story before.

'But her son, see, he kept following me about, mauling me, and he wouldn't leave me be. Tonight, it all got too much for me, and I told him what I thought of him, and that I'd tell his mum if he didn't leave me alone. He came back when the old lady was having her afternoon nap, and threw me down. I donged him one, and he gave me such a belt I could hardly see, but I got my knee into him, and he let go, and ran away. Then the missus calls me in after dinner and tells me that I've been "shamelessly pursuing her son", and that she was putting me out of the house, "a low, vulgar wench", that's what she called me. And she gave me no character and no wages. And him sitting there grinning like a dog, being a good boy. So I took me things to the station and I stole the peeling knife out of the kitchen and I was going to kill him. 'Cos I can't go home. Me mum's got seven others to keep, and she depends on my wages, see? So I'll never get another job. He's made me into a whore, that's what he's done. He deserves killing.'

'So he does,' agreed Phryne. Her companion was a little taken aback. 'But there are better ways to do it. Did you expect him here tonight?'

'Yair, he's a knut—one of them dandies, he always parades up and down here.'

'Have you seen him yet?' asked Phryne.

'That's him there,' said the girl. A young exquisite, clearly bung-full of conceit, sauntered past.

'What's your name? I'm Phryne Fisher, from London.'

'Dorothy Bryant. Ooh, look at him! I wish I could get my hands on him!'

'Listen, I need a maid, and I'll employ you. I'm staying at the Windsor, I'm quite respectable,' she added. 'Now, if I revenge you on that young hound, can you keep a quiet tongue about my activities?'

'If you can do it, I'm yours,' swore Dorothy. Phryne smiled. 'Watch, and don't move from here,' she said, then slid out into the crowd. The young man was accompanied by several fellows, equally expensive and excruciatingly idle. Phryne listened to their conversation as she stalked the young man.

'Then I laid her on the floor of the manse, and she'll never dare complain—not the vicar's daughter!' crowed the young man, and his companions guffawed. Phryne insinuated herself close to the youth and with a swift and skilled slice, cut his braces through the loose coat, and then slit up his undergarment, so that all below the waist was revealed. By the time he realized what had happened he was standing, perfectly dressed as to coat and shirt and hat, and quite bare down to his sock-suspenders.

It happened quickly; but the crowd in the Arcade appreciated it at once. The young man was surrounded instantly by the more unruly half of Melbourne's fashionable society, all of them howling with mirth. When he took a step forward and tripped, sprawling on the floor, the mob crowed with delight, as did the young man's companions. And when a large policeman hoisted him to his feet and hauled him, suitably covered by his helmet, off to the watch-house to be charged with indecent exposure and conduct likely to cause a breach of the peace, the vaulted ceiling rang with raucous comments and shrieks.

Phryne slipped back into her place and ordered some more tea, and Dorothy put one small warm hand on her wrist. The girl's eyes were shining with tears.

'I'm yours,' affirmed Dorothy.

'Good. We'll pick up your bundle tomorrow, and I've a maid's room attached to my suite at the Windsor; you'll be comfortable there. And you wouldn't really want to go on the streets, Dorothy; it isn't at all amusing, really.'

Dazed, Dorothy followed Phryne out of the Arcade and back up the hill to the hotel.

తార

As soon as Bert and Cec were safely gone, Dr MacMillan took the large scissors and cut off the blue silk dress, bundling it

and the underwear together and slinging them into a corner. A quick examination assured her that her patient had undergone a criminal abortion, performed by an amateur with only a sketchy knowledge of anatomy.

Sister Simmonds, who intended to undertake medical studies as soon as she could earn the fees, arrived and Dr MacMillan explained her diagnosis.

'Clean all that matter away, Sister—you see? Some foreign body introduced into the womb—a knitting needle or syringe of soapy water, perhaps slippery elm bark. Butchers! Mind, Sister, an abortion done under ether with proper asepsis is not perilous—better, usually, to clear the contents of an incompetent womb before the third month, than coddle a near-miscarriage to term and birth a monster or a sickly bairn which dies as a neonate. But this is butchery. Look, the cervix is widely dilated and all the vaginal bacteria have rushed in and started colonies.'

'How long ago did this happen, Doctor?' asked Sister Simmonds, taking up another carbolic-soaked cloth.

'Two days, maybe three. Criminals! They perpetrate this outrage on nature, and the girl begins to miscarry—this one was four months gone, perhaps—and they usually send them home to cope with the results. Septicaemia is the least they can expect. Well, how would you diagnose her?'

Sister Simmonds picked up Alice's hand and felt for a pulse. It flickered so fast that she could not distinguish the separate beats. The girl's temperature was 104 degrees. She was alternately sweating and shaking with cold, and dried out and burning with heat. Her belly, breasts and thighs were patterned with a scarlet-fever like rash.

'Sapraemia,' she announced. Dr MacMillan nodded.

'Treatment?'

'Salicyclates and anti-tetanus serum.'

'Good. Tell them to prepare a bed in the septic ward, and the theatre as soon as you can. If I remove the source of the infection she will have a better chance. Arrange for ice-water sponging and paraldehyde by injection.

'Poor mite,' added Dr MacMillan, touching Alice's cheek. 'But a bairn herself.'

❦

Bert sipped his tea suspiciously. It was hot and sweet and he drank it quickly, burning his tongue. He did not like this at all. He suspected that Alice was going to lead them into trouble and fervently wished that the tall man in Lonsdale Street had chosen another cab to deposit the poor little rat into. Cec was staring at the wall, his tea untouched.

'Drink your tea, mate,' suggested Bert, and Cec said, 'She's only a kid,' again. Bert sighed. He had known Cec for many years and was aware that his heart was as soft as putty. The rooming house in Carlton where they both lived presently lodged three cats and two dogs which had all been found *in extremis* and nursed back to aggressive, barking, scratching health by his partner. After all, Bert thought, I seen him sit up all night nursing a half-drowned kitten. Plain nutty on anything weak and wanting, that's Cec. And what Mrs Browning is going to say if he wants to bring a stray girl home, I don't know. She created something chronic about the last puppy. The thought made him smile and he patted Cec on the shoulder.

'Tails up, Cec. She'll be apples,' he encouraged, and Cec took up his cup.

He had barely raised it to his lips when Dr MacMillan entered the room, and they both stood up. She waved them to their hard hospital chairs again and sat down heavily in the only easy chair. Cec poured her tea.

'How is she?' he asked anxiously. Dr MacMillan shot him a quick look, and saw the brown eyes full of concern, without the inevitable fear which would have marked the man responsible for Alice's condition or for her operation. She sighed.

'It is not good. She waited too long to come to us. She has blood poisoning and I don't know if we can save her. It will be touch and go. It depends upon how strong her will to live is.'

'Can't you do anything?' demanded Bert.

'No. Even modern medicine can do very little. She must fight her own battle, and maybe lose it. Now, tell me all about the tall man in Lonsdale Street.'

'About six feet, lofty beggar, with dark hat and suit, looked like a gentleman. He was worried, but. Gold signet ring on the left little finger with a diamond in it big as a hatpin.'

'Was he a pimp?'

'Nah, and she's no whore,' objected Bert. 'I should know, I've carried enough. Only people who can afford taxis, almost.'

'No, she's not one of them,' agreed Cec, 'she made a mistake, that's all. Some bloke ain't acted square. He's podded her and then left her, and she must have a respectable family, because she said she could go home now. You remember, mate? She wouldn't have said that unless she came from a good home, and they didn't know.'

'Yair, she was frantic,' said Bert. 'We said that you wouldn't tell 'em.'

'Nor shall I,' agreed Dr MacMillan. 'I shall tell them that she is here, but not what brought her here. One can get blood poisoning from any breach in the skin. A rose thorn would do. What else can you recall about the man who brought her to you?'

'Nothin' much else. Black hair, I reckoned, and a toffy look. Eh, Cec?'

Cec, overcome by his unaccustomed eloquence, nodded.

'Yair, and I reckon we've seen him before.'

'Where?'

'Might have been in the cab, might have just been on the street—have a feeling that it was somewhere around Lon. or Little Lon....Cec, does that toffy mug ring a bell?'

'Nah, mate. You musta been on your pat.'

'We don't usually work together, see. Cec has a truck. But she's laid up with piston trouble so we're doing a double shift. Nah, I can't remember. Why do you want to know?'

'To inform the police, of course,' stated Dr MacMillan quietly. 'He must be found and put in jail. If she dies, he is a murderer. Butchers! They batten on the respectability of these

stupid girls—it's always the innocent and deceived that get caught—and they mutilate them, charging ten pounds for the savagery that a cannibal wouldn't stoop to, and then they dump them like so much garbage to bleed out their lives in the gutter. Nothing is too bad for such men—nothing. If I could but lay a hand on them myself I'd inoculate them with bacteria, and watch how they liked trembling and shrieking their lives away down to an agonizing, filthy death.'

'Not the jacks, though,' mumbled Bert. 'Not the cops...'

'And why not? You are essential witnesses.'

'Yair, but Cec and me don't have no cause to love the jacks.'

'I am not asking you to love them, nor will they be concerned with your petty crimes. You will come down to Russell Street with me this afternoon and you will tell them everything you know, and I will answer for it that you will walk out again. Do you understand?'

They understood.

❦

At three o'clock in the afternoon, Bert and Cec tailed Dr Mac-Millan into the police station, under the red brick portal, and came before the desk-sergeant on his high pedestal.

'I am Dr Elizabeth MacMillan, and I have an appointment to see a Detective-Inspector Robinson.'

'Yes, Madam,' said the desk-sergeant. 'He's expecting you. These are your people, Sir,' he added to a soberly dressed young man sitting beside him. They followed him along a corridor and into a small, bleak office painted institution green. It contained a desk, a filing cabinet, and four hard chairs. The cable-car clanged outside. At his signal, they all sat down and there was a moment's silence while he took down a folio ledger and unscrewed a black fountain pen.

'Your names, please,' he said in a carefully unmodulated voice. The man was colourless, with mid-brown hair, mid-brown eyes, and nothing noticeable about him at all. They gave their names. When he heard 'Albert Johnson' and 'Cecil Yates' he grinned.

'The red-raggers, eh? Still fighting the capitalist menace? Been to Russia yet? With a lot of property reasonably suspected to be unlawfully obtained?'

Cec stared mournfully at Dr MacMillan.

Bert, glaring at the policeman, snarled, 'Your time will come. Oppressor of the widow and orphan, upholder of the exploiter...'

'That will do,' interposed Dr MacMillan. 'I spoke to you, officer, if you recall, about these gentlemen. They behaved, in relation to this wretched girl, with notable gallantry and gentleness. I have assured them that they are required only to state what they have observed about this butcher of an abortionist, and I would not be forsworn.'

She fixed the uncomfortable detective with her eye, and he flinched.

'That's right, Madam, you are quite correct. Now, tell me all about the man.'

Bert, assisted by Cec, repeated the description, and the detective lost his indifference. He flicked over the pages in the ledger and read aloud, 'Six feet tall, cropped hair, swarthy complexion, signet ring on his left hand.'

'Yair,' agreed Bert. 'We couldn't see his hair because he had his hat on, but I reckoned that it was black, or very dark brown, like shoe polish. And a little smear of a moustache, just a line on the upper lip.'

'That's him,' said the detective. 'He's been involved in this racket for three years—or that's as long as we've known about it. We call him Butcher George. The first victim was a girl called Mary Elizabeth Allen, found dead in the Flagstaff Gardens, dumped out of a car by a man of that description. Good girl, by the way. The next was a common prostitute known as Gay Lil, real name Lillian Marchent, found dying in a gutter in Fitzroy Street. She said that the job was done by a man called George Fletcher and gave a similar description. Course, you can't rely on the word of a girl like that...'

'O can't ye?' demanded Dr MacMillan, her accent becoming more Scottish as she lost her temper. 'I've worked with enough

of 'em to know you can trust 'em just as fine as anyone—they're human women, for the Lord's sake! Lil's death is just as much a tragedy as the good little girls—they all die the same, Detective-Inspector.'

Dr MacMillan saw that Bert, Cec, and the policeman were all regarding her with the same puzzled stare. She concluded that men were all alike, one side of the law or the other, and held her tongue. The detective-inspector read on.

'Third was a married woman—eight kids she had—and she got home before she bled to death. Left her husband a note saying that George had charged her ten pounds and she was sorry. Man answering to that description seen leaving the house. That was six months ago. And now your girl—when do you reckon it was done?'

'Two or three days ago.'

'And will she live?'

'I hope so. I can't tell,' sighed Dr MacMillan. The detective-inspector leaned back in his chair.

'We don't know enough. It's always hard to find 'em, because their victims protect 'em. To a girl in that situation, even death seems better than continuing pregnant, with social ruin staring her in the face. And some of them are quite competent. Some even use ether and have an operating room. Some like this bastard—beg pardon, Madam—force themselves on the girls before they do the procedure.'

Cec growled, and Bert demanded, 'If you've got all this proof, why don't you catch him?'

'No clues, he gets rid of the ones who die.'

'And the ones that live won't say a word. They committed a crime by having the abortion, I understand,' said Dr MacMillan. 'We see enough of them at the hospital. Bleeding like pigs, infected, mutilated, torn and sterile for life, they all insist that it was a hot bath, or a horse-ride, or a fall down some steep stairs. Very well, officer. Thank you for seeing us.'

'Here, you're going to do nothin'?' protested Bert. The detective-inspector turned a weary face towards him.

'Why don't you mobilize the comrades?' he suggested tone-lessly. 'This George is somewhere in the city, near where you picked up this poor girl. Keep your eyes open, you may see him again.'

'I tell you what, mate,' called Bert as he was ushered out, 'if I do see him, I'll run the bastard down!'

Back in the taxi Cec drove and Bert asked questions.

'Is she going to live?'

'As I said to that policeman, I don't know. I've cleared the womb of its remaining contents so the source of infection is gone. I've stitched up the damaged flesh and disinfected every bit I could reach. She will decide her own fate now. And I must get the almoner to find her relatives, and I have a surgery at four—so shall we stop dawdling?'

Cec ground gears and they picked up speed.

Dr MacMillan was decanted at her hospital and Cec and Bert resumed their rounds. They did not speak, but patrolled up and down the city, picking up fares, and watching for the tall man with the moustache and the signet ring with the huge diamond. Cec followed Bert and Bert succeeded Cec, until they went home to Carlton at about three in the morning.

'Wouldn't it rot your socks!' exclaimed Bert, kicking at a passing fence. 'Wouldn't it!'

Cec said nothing, but that was normal for Cec.

Chapter Four

When this yokel comes maundering
Whetting his hacker
I shall run before him
Diffusing the civilest odours
Out of geraniums and unsmelled flowers.
It will check him.
'The Plot against the Giant', Wallace Stevens

'You ain't one of them white slavers, are you?' demanded Dorothy, stopping dead in Collins Street, and causing a gentleman directly behind her to swallow his cigar. Phryne reached into her pocket, chuckling.

'If you're really thinking that, then accept this ten quid and go home to your mother,' she suggested. The idea of scouting for white slaves in the Block Arcade tickled her fancy. Dorothy looked at the ground so intently that Phryne wondered if she was surveying for the gold which was popularly supposed to pave Melbourne's streets.

After a little while the girl took Phryne's hand.

'I don't think that really,' she said in her flat, harsh drawl. 'Not really. But it was in the *Women's Own*, see, and they said that lots of working girls gets took by them.'

'Indeed. Come on, Dorothy, it's not far now.'

'Slow down, Miss, you walk so fast. I'm wore out.'

'Frightfully sorry, old dear,' murmured Phryne, slowing her swift pace and patting Dorothy's hand. 'We'll soon be there; just around the corner at the top of the hill. You shall have a bath, and perhaps—yes, a cocktail, and…'

Phyrne led Dorothy up the steps into the Windsor and past the magnificent doorman, who did not so much as flicker an eyelash at the sight of the miserable and underclad Dorothy. His only private comment was to the effect that the aristocracy did have singular tastes.

Phryne conducted Dorothy to the bathroom and shut her in, instructing her to wash herself and her hair thoroughly, pointing out the products to be used for various surfaces. She left her confronting, rather dubiously, the array of jars, unguents, boxes and wash-balls which were laid out upon the skirted table, next to a very naked nymph in gunmetal. Phryne sighed. Clearly the nymph had aroused all of Dorothy's latent suspicions. However, a certain splashing and puffs of scented steam from under the door indicated that her doubts did not extend to either hot water or Phryne's cosmetics. The smell of 'Koko-for-the-Hair' (as used by the Royal House of Denmark) made itself palpable.

Phryne had few really ingrained fears, but lice was one of them. The very idea made her skin crawl. In her early youth she had spent a miserable day with her head wrapped in a kerosene-smelling towel and she was not going through that again if she could help it. She rummaged in her fourth trunk, and found a very plain nightdress and a dressing gown in a shade of orange which did not suit her at all, and sat down to check off her visiting list.

She had some twenty people to leave cards upon in the morning, and the prospect gave her no pleasure. She sorted out a suitable selection of cards and wrote, on each, the name of the person who had referred her to the householder. This took about twenty minutes, and at the end of it Phryne began to wonder at the silence in the bathroom. She crossed the room and knocked, the garments over her arm.

'Are you all right, old thing?' she called, and the door opened a crack.

'Oh, Miss, I've tore my dress, and it's the only one I got!' wailed the hapless maid.

Phryne stuffed the nightwear through the gap in the doorway and ordered, 'Put those things on, Dorothy, and come out! I'll advance you enough for a new dress.'

There was a muffled gulp, almost a sob, from the room, and a moment later, Dorothy emerged in a sweep of orange satin.

'Oh, ain't it fine! I love pretty clothes!' she cried. It was the first spontaneous exclamation of pleasure Phryne had heard from the girl, and she smiled. Dorothy, bathed and revenged, was unrecognizable. Her fair skin was flushed, her hair appeared darker because it was wet, and her eyes shone.

Phryne opened a little door and said, 'Would you like to go straight to bed? This is your room, and here is the key—you can lock yourself in, if you like.'

'I'll sit up a little, Miss, if I may.'

'Very well. I'll order tea.'

Phryne picked up the house phone and did so, then returned to her seat at the desk, while Dorothy paraded up and down, enjoying the swish of her gown.

'Did you mean it, Miss, about me being your maid?' asked the girl, turning when she reached the wall to parade back.

'Yes, I need a maid—you can see the mess my things get into...' Phryne indicated the sitting room, which was liberally strewn with her belongings. 'But only if you want the job. I'm here on confidential business, inquiring about a lady on behalf of her parents, so if you want to work for me you must never gossip or tell anyone anything about what you might overhear. I need someone of the utmost discretion. We may be staying in grand houses, and you must not, on any account, say anything about my concerns. You're free to talk about me,' she added, grinning. 'Just not my business.'

'I promise,' said Dorothy, solemnly wetting her forefinger and inscribing a careful cross on the breast of the satin gown. 'Hope I may die.'

'Well, then, all you have to do is to look after my clothes, find things that I've lost, answer the phone if I'm not in, and generally look after me. For instance, tomorrow someone has to take a taxi and deliver all those cards to people I'm supposed to meet in Melbourne. How about it?'

Dorothy's chin went up.

'If I've a new dress, I can do it.'

'Good stuff!'

'What about wages, Miss?'

'Oh. I don't know what the going rate for a confidential maid and social secretary is. What were you getting?'

'Two-and-six a week and me keep,' said Dorothy. Phryne was shocked.

'No wonder they've got a servant problem here! What were you doing for that?'

'Everything, Miss, but cooking. They kept a cook. And the washing was sent out to the Chinese. So it wasn't too bad. I had to go out to work. We can't live on what Mum earns. Of course, you wouldn't know about that. You don't know what that's like, no disrespect meant. You ain't never had to starve.'

'Oh, yes I have,' said Phryne grimly. 'I starved liked Billy-o. My family was skint until I was twelve.'

'Then how...?' asked Dorothy, folding a dressing gown. 'How...?'

'Three people between Father and the Title died,' Phryne said. 'Three young men dying out of their time, and the old Lord summoned us out of Richmond and onto a big liner and into the lap of luxury. I didn't like it much,' she confessed. 'My sister died of diphtheria and starvation. It seemed too cruel that we had all those relatives in England and they hadn't lifted a hand until Father became the heir. But don't tell me about poverty, Dot. I ate rabbit and cabbage because there was nothing else, and I confess that I've not been able to face lapin ragoût or cabbage in any form since. Oh, you've found the blue suit, I had forgotten I bought it.'

The tea arrived on a silver tray. There was also a teacake, which Phryne cut and buttered immediately.

'Never mind my history, come and help me eat some of these cakes,' said Phryne, who hated teacake. 'White tea, is it? And two lumps?'

Dorothy sniffed, was about to wipe her face on her gown, then remembered herself and retreated to the bathroom to find her handkerchief. While she poured the tea, Phryne reflected that Dorothy must be very tired. Revenge and release is just as much of a strain as hatred and murder. She palmed a small white pill and dropped it into the tea. Dorothy needed the sleep.

The girl returned and made a promising inroad into the tea-cake before she took up her cup.

'I'll ring an agency in the morning and find out how much I ought to pay you,' said Phryne. 'And tomorrow we shall buy you some clothes. The uniform will be paid for by me, and you can have an advance to buy your own clothes. We shall also pick up your box from the station.'

'I think I'd better go to bed now,' observed Dorothy thickly, and Phryne helped her to the small room, tucked her in, and before she closed the door, noted that the girl was fast asleep.

'Two-and-six a week and her keep,' said Phryne. She poured another cup of tea and lit a cigarette. 'The poor little babe!'

⚭

Alice Greenham woke in a white bed, strangely docile, and floating above her tortured body on a cushion of morphia. Women clad in big white aprons came by, periodically, to do things to the body, which Alice felt belonged to someone else. They soaked it with cold water and laid a wet sheet over it. This looked comic, and she giggled. The baby, at least, was gone, and she could go back to her church-going, respectable home, unburdened of proof of her shame.

She had not believed that five minutes could change someone's life. She had gone to a church-run dance, and had been enticed out into the bike shed by a boy she had always thought nice, a deacon's son. They had leaned against the creaking wooden wall while he had fumbled with her clothes and whispered that he loved her and would marry her as soon as his father gave him a halfshare in the shop. From that joyless, clumsy mating had come all this trouble. He had not seemed to know her when they next met, avoiding her eyes and when she had told him about the baby he had shouted, 'No! not me! You must have been going with plenty of blokes!' And he had struck her across the face when she had persisted.

The nurses—she had identified them by their caps—were gathered around the body now. A woman in trousers was filling a syringe. Alice sensed that this was a crisis. She was sleepy and airy and light, and they were trying to drag her back to that suffering, twisting thing on the bed below. Well, she wouldn't go. She had been hurt enough. That oily man, George, and his foul hands all over her. No, she wouldn't go back, they couldn't make her.

Now they were holding the body down. It struggled. The woman in trousers was injecting something into the chest. The body slumped, and the nurses clustered around it.

She was unable to avoid a shriek as the body dragged her back and her poisoned womb convulsed. She opened her eyes, looked directly into Dr MacMillan's face, and whispered, 'It's not fair...I was all light...' before her words were extinguished in a long, hoarse scream. The fever had broken.

Chapter Five

'All people that on earth do dwell
Sing to the Lord with cheerful voice...'
'The Old Hundredth',
Church of England Hymn

Phryne was poring over the newspaper's society columns at breakfast when she heard Dorothy in the bathroom. Presently the young woman emerged, looking much refreshed. Phryne selected a knitted suit in beige and handed it over, together with a collection of under-garments and a pair of shoes. Dorothy dressed biddably enough, but Phryne's shoes were too big for her.

'Put on your slippers again, for the moment, and we'll get you some shoes tomorrow—today's Sunday. Listen to those bells! Enough to wake the dead!'

'I s'pose that's the idea,' observed Dorothy, and Phryne looked up from her paper, reflecting that there was more to Dorothy than met the eye. The girl had ordered herself a large breakfast on Phryne's instructions, and now sat placidly absorbing a mixed grill at eight of the morning as though she had never lain in wait with murder in her heart.

'What do I have to do when I deliver them cards, Miss?' she asked, painfully swallowing a huge mouthful of egg and bacon.

'Just tell the man to wait, walk up to the front door, ring the bell, and give the card to the person who answers. You don't need to say anything. I've put my address on the back. Can you manage it?'

'Yes, Miss,' agreed Dorothy thickly, through another mouthful.

'Good. Now, I am lunching with Dr MacMillan at the Queen Victoria Hospital, and to fill in the time I shall go to church. So when you get back, see if you can introduce a little order into the clothes, eh? I shall return in the afternoon. Order whatever you like for lunch, but perhaps it would be better if you didn't leave the hotel until I get back. We don't want any trouble from your erst-while employer, do we? Here's the money for the taxi; pay what's on the meter and two shillings tip, no more, and don't forget to pick up your bundle from the station. I say, that suit does things for you, Dorothy! You look quite stylish.'

Dorothy blushed, accepted the money, which was more than she had seen in her life before, and gulped down the last of her tea. She stood up, smoothing the beige skirt, and said haltingly, 'I'm ever so grateful, Miss…'

'Consider whether you still think so after you've tackled the mess,' Phryne said briskly. 'Got everything? Good, off you go now.'

Dorothy left, and Phryne smiled to herself, tossing up whether she would ever see the girl again, once set loose in possession of five pounds and a new dress. She mentally slapped herself for such cynical thoughts and reflected that it was indeed high time that she went to church.

An hour and a half later, the strollers in Melbourne would have noted a slim, self-possessed and beautifully groomed young woman sauntering down Swanston Street to the cathedral. It was a crisp, cool morning, and she was wearing a severe dark blue silk suit, with a priceless lace collar, dark stockings and black shoes with a high heel. She had pulled a soft black cloche down over her hair, and the only note of eccentricity was her sapphire earrings, which glinted brighter than stained glass. She ascended the steps of the cathedral as if faintly surprised that the great west door had not been opened for her, and took her place in a back pew with economical grace. She accepted a service card and a hymn book from a jovial gentleman, and unbent sufficiently to smile her thanks. He looked familiar.

He was stout, ruddy and pleasant looking, tailored to the nth degree, with a shirt whiter than snow. As the organ struck up the 'Old Hundredth', Phryne recognized him as the man who had smiled across the dining room last night.

She stood up to sing, and heard at her side a thundering bass to her light soprano, easily rising over the sheep-like bleating which passes for singing in most Church of England congregations.

All people that on Earth do dwell
Sing to the Lord with cheerful voice…

Her neighbour was certainly adding a cheerful and forceful voice to the anthem. Phryne approved. She saw no reason to sing in church unless one meant to really sing. By the end of the hymn they were attracting a certain amount of attention from the polite citizens in the front pews, and Phryne smiled at her neighbour.

'I do love a good sing,' he whispered. 'Can't stand all that moaning!'

Phryne laughed softly and agreed. The gentleman slipped a card onto the open page of her hymn book, and she reciprocated with one of her own. It had been engraved, not printed, on heavy cream card, and merely said, 'The Hon. Phryne Fisher, Colling Hall, Kent'. She knew it to be in the best of style. His card was also engraved, and stated that the rosy gentleman now listening devoutly to a reading by a clerical person with the snuffles was Mr Robert Sanderson, MP of Toorak. Phryne recalled that he was on her list of noteables and she slipped the card into her purse, giving her attention to the sermon.

It was not long, which was a mercy, and dealt mostly with Christian duty. Phryne had heard so many sermons on Christian duty that she could almost predict each word, and amused herself for some time in doing just that, as well as admiring the stained glass, which was catching the morning sun and blazing like jewels. The sermon passed into the general confession, and Phryne admitted with perfect frankness that she had done those things which she ought not to have done and left undone those things which she ought to have done. The service went on as she reflected on her time in Paris, on the Rive Gauche, where she had done many things which she ought not to have done but which nevertheless proved very enjoyable, for a time, and reminded herself that she had seen Marcel Duchamp checkmated by a child in a Paris café. That, Phryne thought, must be worth a certain number of small sins. She stood hurriedly for the final hymn, and the church began to clear. Mr Sanderson offered her his arm, and Phryne accepted.

'I believe that I have a left a card with your wife, Sir,' she smiled. 'I'm sure that we shall meet again.'

'I hope so, Miss Fisher,' said the MP in a deep, rich voice. 'I'm always disposed to like a young woman who can sing. Besides, I believe that I knew your father.'

'Indeed, Sir?' Phryne showed no sign of horror that her working-class past was to be revealed, and the MP admired her courage.

'Yes, I was introduced to him when he was leaving for England; some little trouble with the fare. I was delighted to assist him.'

'I trust, Sir, that he remembered to repay you?' asked Phryne frigidly. Mr Sanderson patted her arm.

'Of course. I regret mentioning the matter. May I escort you, Miss Fisher?'

'No, Sir, I am going to the Queen Victoria Hospital. But perhaps you could remind me of the way?'

'Straight up the street, Miss Fisher, and turn into Little Lonsdale Street and thus into Mint Place, just past the Town Hall. A matter of half a mile, perhaps.'

'Thank you, Sir,' smiled Phryne. Then she released herself, and walked away, a little offended and saddened. If her father had left debts of honour all over Melbourne, then establishing herself in society was going to be difficult. However, she was inclined to like Mr Sanderson, MP. He had a hearty voice and an open and unaffected manner, which must be an asset to any politician. And perhaps he could give her lunch at the Melbourne Club, the bastions of which Phryne had a mind to storm.

She climbed the hill to the Museum, located Mint Place with a certain difficulty, and announced herself at the desk in a ramshackle building, smelling rather agreeably of carbolic and milk.

It was partly wood and partly brick, and seemed to have been built rather on the spur of the moment than to any pre-arranged plan. It was painted buttercup-yellow and white inside.

Dr MacMillan appeared, dressed in a white overall which became her well, and gentleman's trousers with a formal collar and tie showing above a tweed waistcoat.

'This way, dear girl, and I'll show you a consulting room, a ward, and the nursery, and then we'll go to luncheon,' said Dr MacMillan over her shoulder as she took a set of oilcloth-covered stairs like a steeplechaser.

For all her age and bulk, Dr MacMillan was as fit as a bull. They reached the top in good order and Dr MacMillan opened a painted door and disclosed a small white room, windowless, equipped with couch and chair and desk and medicine cabinet.

'Small, but adequate,' commented the doctor. 'Now to the nursery.'

'Tell me,' asked Phryne, 'how did this hospital for women come about? Was it a charitable endowment by the old Queen?'

'It was a surprising thing, Phryne—could only have happened in a new country. Two women physicians began a practice here in Melbourne, and the medical establishment, being what they still are, blighted and hide-bound conservatives, would not allow their femininity to sully the pure air of their hospitals. Nurses, yes. Doctors, no. So they set up in the hall of the Welsh Church—the only hall that they could get, I've felt kinder toward the Welsh ever since—and they had one tap and one sterilizer and, pretty soon, more patients than they could cram in. They were sleeping on the floor, and there were deliveries on the hour. But they didn't want only a lying-in hospital, and they petitioned for a general hospital. Parliament refused them any funds, of course. So they petitioned the Queen, and every woman in Victoria gave her shilling, and the old Queen (God bless her) gave them their charter and the right to call it the Queen Victoria Hospital. Unfortunately the fabric of this building is none too good. We shall be moving in a few years to a new home, and then we can raze this tenement to the ground. It used to be a governesses school. In here, Phryne, is the nursery. Do you like babies?'

Phryne laughed.

'No, not at all. They are not aesthetic like a puppy or a kitten. In fact, they always look drunk to me. Look at that one—you'd swear he had been hitting the gin.'

She pointed out an unsteady infant with a wide and vacant smile, repeatedly reaching for and failing to seize a large woollen ball. Phryne picked up the ball and handed it to the child, who waved his hand and gurgled. Elizabeth lifted the baby and tickled him while he cooed. 'Not the faintest spurt of maternity?' she asked slyly.

'Not the faintest,' Phryne grinned, and shook the baby by its small, plump hand. 'Bye, baby. I hope your mother loves you better.'

'She may,' replied the doctor dryly, 'but she abandoned him all the same. At least she gave him to us, and not some baby farmer who'd starve him to death.'

'How many are there?' asked Phryne, covering her ears as one baby began to cry, which set all the rest of them off so that the nursery resounded with little roars of fury.

'About thirty; it's a quiet night,' replied the doctor. She replaced the child in his cot and led the deafened Phryne out of the nursery and down a flight of stairs to a ward.

Rows of white draped beds stretched to infinity. There were moveable screens in yellow around some of the beds, and on most of the white painted lockers were small traces of individuality;

pictures or books or flowers. The floor was polished and dustless and down the length of the room was a long trestle table loaded with linen, and trays and equipment.

'Here's a remarkable man, you know,' she added, stopping at the seventh bed from the door. 'He brought this poor lass in—she collapsed in his cab.'

Cec stood up, laying Alice's hand gently down, and ducked his head. Waking up, Alice saw an elegant lady standing before her, and smiled.

'Hello, how are you?' Phryne asked, feeling a wave of affection for the girl.

'Better,' whispered Alice. 'I'm going to get better,' and Cec said slowly, 'Too right.'

'Sleepy,' murmured Alice, and floated off again. Cec sat down and took up her hand.

'What's wrong with her?' Phryne asked as they moved on.

'Criminal abortion—the monster nearly killed her with his unskilful butchery—and from what she says, raped her as well.'

'Police?' asked Phryne, wincing.

'Say they can do nothing until someone locates the bastard. I believe that yon cabbie and his mate are looking for him. They were much concerned. You recognize him, Phryne?'

'Of course, he's Bert's mate, Cec. You don't think that he's responsible for her condition?'

'I thought that, naturally. But I don't believe so. His mate says that he's never seen her before until the man put her into their taxi in Lonsdale Street.'

'Will she live?' asked Phryne.

'I believe so,' said Dr MacMillan. 'Now, I've found a pleasant place for lunch, so let us go, otherwise I'll get distracted again, and won't have lunch until next week.'

She led the way at a fast trot to a small but clean dairy with scrubbed pine tables and stone walls, and pulled out a chair.

'Ah, what a place,' sighed Dr MacMillan. 'The missus makes excellent pies and the coffee is all that the heart can desire. Mrs Jones,' she bellowed through a serving hatch, 'lunch! Coffee! And that right speedily!' An answering 'All right, Doctor, hold your horses!' from the room behind indicated that Dr MacMillan had made her presence felt before. Phryne put down her purse and lit a gasper.

'I see that they have accepted your trousers, Elizabeth,' she commented.

'Aye, they have, and without a murmur.' Dr MacMillan ran a broad hand through her short pepper-and-salt crop. 'And they've a fascinating collection of patients. Ah, coffee.'

The coffee arrived in a tall jug, accompanied by hot milk and granulated sugar. Phryne poured herself a cup and sipped. It was indeed excellent. Dark and pure.

'And what have you been doing, m'dear?' asked the doctor.

'Establishing myself. I've hired a maid,' answered Phryne, and told Dr MacMillan all about Dorothy. 'And I think I shall buy a plane. A new Avro perhaps.'

'I always meant to ask you, Phryne, how did you come to be answering my call for help in the 'flu epidemic? You could have knocked me over with a feather when I sighted you climbing down out of that plane.'

'Simple,' said Phryne, sipping coffee. 'I was at the airbase when your call came in, and there was only me and a mechanic there. And a choice of two planes, both of 'em rather war-weary. There was a dance in the village and all the men had gone to it. So I persuaded Irish Michael to swing on the propeller of the old Bristol, and off I went. It seemed like the right thing to do. And I got you there, didn't I?'

'Oh, aye, you got us there all right. I was never so frightened in all my life; the wind and the storm, and the sight of the waves leaping up to drag us into the water. What a journey! I swear that my hair turned white. And you as cool as a cucumber, even when the compass started to spin.'

'No point in getting upset in the air,' said Phryne. 'Very unforgiving element. No use changing your mind about it, either. Once you're up, you're up, so to speak.'

'Aye, and once ye're down, ye're down. I can't imagine how we found the island, much less how we landed on it.'

'Ah, yes, that was a little tricky, because I couldn't see very well, what with the spray and the wind, and there's only one long beach to land upon, and I was afraid that our approach was too fast, but I couldn't count on finding the beach again, the wind was so strong, so I just put her down; that's why we ran along the shore for such a long way. But it was a good landing; we had at least ten feet to spare when we ground to a halt.'

'Ten feet,' said Dr MacMillan faintly. 'Pour me some coffee, there's a dear.'

'The real courage in that jaunt,' observed Phryne, 'was yours. I couldn't have gone into those cottages, with all that filth and stench and corpses, not for anything, except that you swept me along in your wake. I still have nightmares about the cottages.'

'Crofts,' corrected Dr MacMillan. 'And they need not cause you grief. As my highland grandmother said—and she had the Sight—"Tis not the dead ye have to be concerned about! Beware of the Living!" And she was a wise woman. The dead are beyond your help or mine, poor things. But the living need us. Thirty souls at the least, Phryne, are still on that island to praise God who might now be angels—or devils. And speaking of courage, m'girl, who crept up the hill onto that Lord's land and led away and slaughtered one of his beasts to make broth?'

Phryne, recalling the thrill of stalking highland cattle through mist and over bog in company with a handsome young gillie, laughed, and disclaimed any virtue in the feat.

They lunched amiably on egg-and-bacon pie, then Phryne strolled back to the Windsor in an excellent mood.

She inspected the hotel's lounge, found a copy of Herodotus, and took it with her to her suite.

The rooms were transformed. Dorothy had returned, and had evidently put in a good two hours' work, folding and hanging and sorting clothes, pairing shoes, and repairing ripped hems. A small pile of neatly mended stockings lay over the arm of the sitting room chair, and a petticoat decorated the other; the long rip in the hem, made by some partner's heavy foot, was put together like a suture, so the rent could hardly be seen. Phryne dropped into the only unoccupied chair, a little dazed. Dorothy came in from her bedroom, where she had been combing out her hair.

'Did you have a nice lunch, Miss?'

'Yes, thank you, and you have evidently been busier than a beaver! How did you manage with the cards?'

'Very well, Miss. And I got my bundle, and all. Here's the change from the taxi.'

'Keep it, Dorothy, a woman should have a little extra money. Did you remember to have lunch?'

'Oh yes, Miss. And there's a note for you, brought by hand about an hour ago,' she said, handing Phryne a folded letter.

'Thank you, Dorothy. I don't want anything for the moment, so why don't you finish your hair. You mend beautifully,' she added. 'Why did you become a house-maid?'

'Mum thought it best,' replied Dorothy. 'It ain't nice to work in factories or shops.'

'I see,' said Phryne. Factory work was still considered low.

Phryne unfolded the note. It was headed in gold with the name 'Cryer' in a tasteless and flamboyant script, and the address underneath; Toorak, of course. The hand-writing was also lacking style, being scrawled across the page in purple ink.

'Please honour a little dinner party tomorrow night. Melanie Cryer'. It boded ill; purple ink and no directions about time or dress. There was a telephone number below the gold heading. Phryne picked up the instrument and spoke to the operator.

'Toorak 325,' she said and there was a buzzing and a few odd clunking noises. Then a woman's voice said, with an accent which was pure Donegal, 'Cryer's. Who did ye want?'

'This is Phryne Fisher. Is Mrs Cryer at home?'

There was a muffled squeak as the maid transferred the message to someone obviously standing next to her, and Phryne heard the experience violently displaced. A shrill voice exclaimed, 'Why, Miss Fisher, how kind of you to call!'

Phryne hated the voice instantly, but replied cordially, accepting the invitation and asking at what time and in what habiliments she should present herself at the mansion Cryer. The hour was eight and the clothing formal, 'Though you will find us very rustic, Miss Fisher!' Phryne politely disagreed, which took a certain resolution, and rang off. If this was the social pinnacle of Melbourne, she reflected, this was going to be a grim investigation indeed. She sat back in the chair and addressed her maid.

'Dot, I've got a question to ask, and I want you to consider it carefully.' Phryne paused before going on. 'Do you know *an address?*'

Dot dropped the jewellery box she was holding, and earrings spilled out all over the carpet.

'Oh, Miss!' she breathed. 'You haven't been…caught?'

'No, I'm not pregnant, but I'm looking for an abortionist. Do you know an address?'

'No, Miss, I don't,' said Dot stiffly. 'I don't approve of such goings-on. She ought to marry him and have it proper. It's dangerous…that operation.'

'I know it's dangerous. The man nearly murdered a friend of my cab-drivers, and I want to put him out of business. He's in the city somewhere near Lonsdale Street. Is there anyone you can ask?'

'Well, Miss, if that's what you're doing, I'm all for it. There's my friend, Muriel Miller. She works in the Pickle Factory in Fitzroy. She might know. They're not all good girls in the factories, that's why Mum didn't want me to work there…'

'Good. Is your friend Muriel married? Is she on the phone?'

'No, Miss, she lives at home; her Dad's got a lolly shop. There will be a phone there. I don't know the number,' said Dot dubiously, crawling in search of earrings. She secured and paired the last one as Phryne searched the telephone directory and found the number.

'Will she be at home now?'

'Probably. She helps in the shop in the afternoon.' Phryne dialled, then held out the phone to Dot.

'Mr Miller? It's me, Dot Bryant. Can I speak to Muriel? Thank you.' There was a pause, and she said breathlessly, 'Hello, Muriel? It's Dot...I got a new job and I'm staying at the Windsor!...Yes, it was a stroke of luck! I'll tell you all about it tomorrow, I'm going home to see Mum, can you come over then?... Good. M-m-muriel, have you got *an address*?...No, it isn't for me, I promise. It's for a friend....No. I can prove it. Well, can you find out? All right. I'll see you tomorrow. Thanks, Muriel. Bye.'

'She says that she'll find out, Miss. I'll see her tomorrow. But how do we know that it's him?'

'There can't be that many abortionists in Melbourne,' said Phryne grimly. 'But if necessary, I'll call them all. Now I'm going to dinner.'

Chapter Six

Made one with Death
Filled full of the Night
'The Triumph of Time',
Algernon Swinburne

The following morning, Phryne took Dorothy on a shopping tour of Melbourne. She found that the young woman had excellent taste, though inclining to the flamboyant. Dorothy was also most anxious to save Phryne's money, which was a pleasant change from the bulk of Phryne's acquaintances, who were over-eager to spend it.

By luncheon time, they had acquired two uniformlike dresses in dark-blue linen, stockings, shoes, and foundation-garments in an attractive shade of champagne. As well as an overcoat of bright azure guaranteed to cheer the winter days, and a richly embroidered afternoon dress, bought over Dorothy's protests by Phryne, who was adamant that the possession of pretty clothes was the second-best sustainer of a young woman's morale in the world.

Phryne had presented her credentials at her bank, and had opened an account at Madame Olga's in Collins Street, in case some trifle might attract her. This she rather doubted, considering Melbourne fashion, until she was trying on evening gowns in Madame's sumptuous parlour. Madame, a gaunt, spiritual woman who looked upon the mode as a remote and harsh deity requiring great sacrifices, observed Phryne's lack of interest in the available gowns, and snapped an order to a scurrying attendant.

'Fetch *cinq a sept*', she ordered.

The acolyte returned carrying with nervous tenderness a garment bundled in thin white silk. This was unrolled in reverent silence. Phryne, clad lightly in camiknickers and stockings, waited impatiently for the rite to be completed; she was sure that ice was forming on her upper slopes.

Madame shook the dress out and flung it over a stand, and stood back to watch Phryne's reaction with restrained pleasure. Dorothy gasped, and even Phryne's eyes widened.

It was deep claret, edged with dark mink; evidently a design by Erté, with few seams, the weight of the garment depending entirely from the shoulder. The deep decolleté was artfully concealed with strings of jet beads, which served the function of preventing the dress from sliding off the wearer's shoulders, but leaving a gratifying impression that this was, indeed, what it might at any moment do.

'Would Mademoiselle wish to try?' asked Madame, and Phryne allowed the dress to be lowered over her head. It had a train, but not so long as to be inconvenient, and the huge sleeves, inspired by an Imperial Chinese robe, slid gracefully together at the front to make a muff for her hands. The deep colour contrasted effectively with Phryne's pale skin and black hair, and as she moved, the liquefaction of the satin flowed over her limbs, moulding her as if in gelatine. It was a perfectly decent but utterly erotic dress and Phryne knew that she must have it.

'I have not shown this to any one in Melbourne,' observed Madame with quiet satisfaction. 'There is no lady in Melbourne who could wear it with sufficient panache. Mademoiselle has style, therefore the gown is made for Mademoiselle.'

'It is,' agreed Phryne, and accepted, without turning a hair, a price which made Dorothy gasp. This was the gown of the year, Phryne thought, and would make exactly the right impression on the Cryers, and hence on the rest of Melbourne. She mentioned the Cryers to Madame, who winced.

'Madame Cryer has much money,' she said, 'and one must live; *que voulez-vous*! But taste of the most execrable; *des parvenus*,' she concluded, shrugging her shoulders. 'I will have the gown conveyed to Mademoiselle's hotel?'

'If you please. I am at the Windsor,' said Phryne. 'And now I must tear myself away, Madame; but I shall return, you can be assured.'

She wondered if she should ask Madame, who was evidently well-informed, about Lydia, the subject of her investigation, but decided against it. The fashion houses of Europe were the primary base of all gossip in the world and she had every reason to believe that Melbourne, being smaller and more incestuous, would be as bad, if not worse.

Dorothy and Phryne lunched lightly at the Block Arcade, and called upon a domestic employment agency to inquire as to the proper wages for a ladies' maid. Dorothy was astonished to learn that she was to earn at least a pound a week, plus uniforms, board and washing, and was even more taken aback when Phryne promptly doubled it to two pounds a week with all clothes thrown in. Dorothy rushed off to see her mother and explain her changed circumstances, while Phryne visited an Elizabeth Arden beauty parlour in Collins Street. There she spent a luxurious couple of hours being massaged, steamed, and pomaded, with an ear alert for gossip. She heard nothing useful except the interesting comment that cocaine had become the drug of choice for the dissolute upper class.

She emerged glowing, after fighting off assistants with various tonics and beauty powders which they felt that she stood in need of. She returned to the hotel, walking briskly, and slept for three hours. By then, Dorothy had returned, and was unpacking the Erté dress with appropriate delicacy.

'Well, what did your mother say?' demanded Phryne, sitting up and sipping her tea. 'Have you found my jet earrings in your searches, Dorothy?'

'Yes, Miss, they were in the bottom of that trunk. Mum said that you sounded rather worldly, but I told her that you went to church on Sunday, at the cathedral, and she said that you must be all right, and I think so too. Here's the earrings.'

'Thanks. I need the black silk stockings, the black camiknicks, and the high-heeled black glacé kid shoes, and otherwise just a touch of "le Fruit Défendu". Call down to the desk and ask for a taxi to the Cryers' house, will you, Dot? Do you mind me calling you Dot?'

'No, Miss, that's what me sisters call me.'

'Good,' said Phryne, arising from her bed and stretching. She shed the mannish dressing gown as she moved toward the bathroom. 'I intend to impress Melbourne in that dress.'

'Yes, Miss,' agreed Dorothy, picking up the telephone. She was still unused to it, but no longer regarded it as an implement of incipient electrocution. She gave the order with passable directness, and rummaged for the underwear which was to be the foundation of the amazing gown.

An hour later, Phryne surveyed herself in the mirror with great satisfaction. The satin flowed like honey and above the flamboyant billowings of the dress her own small, self-contained, sleek head rode, painted delicately like a Chinese woman's, with a red mouth and dark eyes and eyebrows so thin that they could have been etched. The jet earrings brushed the fur, longer than her skillfully cut cap of dark hair, which was constrained by a silver bandeau. She threw a loose evening cape of silk-pile velvet as black as night over the whole ensemble and took a plain velvet bag shaped like a pouch. After a little thought, she put into it the small gun, as well as handkerchief and cigarettes and a goodly wad of currency. Phryne was not so used to wealth that she was comfortable without a monetary bulwark against disaster.

She swept down the stairs with Dot in anxious attendance. The doorman unbent sufficiently to help this lovely aristocrat into a waiting cab, and to accept without change of expression a thumping tip; and he and Dorothy watched her as she was carried magnificently away.

'Ain't she beautiful!' sighed Dot, and the doorman agreed, reflecting again that the tastes of the aristocracy weren't so odd after all. Indeed, Dorothy in her new uniform and her own shoes was very easy on the eye herself. Dot recollected herself, blushed, and retreated to Phryne's room, to listen to the wireless playing dance music and to mend yet more stockings. Phryne usually bought new ones as soon as the old developed holes, and this extravagance shocked Dorothy profoundly. Besides, she liked mending stockings.

Phryne leaned back and lit a cigarette. She was smoking Black Russian cigarillos with gold-leaf tips; not really as palatable as gaspers, but one must be elegant, whatever the sacrifice.

'Do you often go to the Cryers?' she asked the driver.

'Yes, Miss,' he said, pleased to find that someone who looked so like a fashion plate actually had a voice.

'They has lots of these do's, Miss, and mostly I takes people there, 'cos old Ted is a mate of mine.'

'Old Ted?'

'Yair, the doorman at the Windsor. We were on the Somme together, we were. A good bloke.'

'Oh,' said Phryne. The Great War had so sickened Phryne, while the rest of her school was possessed with war fever, that she avoided thinking about it. The last time that she had cried had been as she sat dropping tears on the poems of Wilfred Owen. She wanted to change the subject.

'What are the Cryers like? I am a visitor, you know, from England.'

She saw the taxi-driver's eyes narrow as he calculated what would be safe to say to this woman reclining on his back seat and filling his taxi with exotic, scented smoke. Phryne laughed.

'I won't tell,' she promised, and the driver seemed to believe her. He took a deep breath.

'Mean as a dunny rat,' he opined.

'I see,' observed Phryne. 'Interesting.'

'Yair, and if they found out I said that, I wouldn't be driving no cab in Melbourne ever again, so I'm trusting you, Miss.'

'You may,' agreed Phryne, crushing out her Sobranie. 'Is this the place?'

'Yair,' said the driver disconsolately.

Phryne surveyed the iced-cake frontage of a huge house; the red carpet and the flowers and the army of attendants awaiting the guests; and cringed inwardly. All this display, while the working classes were pinched beyond bearing; it was not wise, or tasteful: it smacked of ostentatious wealth. The Europe from which Phryne had lately come was impoverished, even the nobility; and was keeping its head down, still shocked by the Russian revolution. It had become fashionable to make no display; understatement had become most stylish.

Phryne paid for her taxi, extracted herself and her gown without damage, and accepted the escort of two footmen to the front door of the Cryer mansion. She took a deep breath, sailed inside, and delivered her velvet cloak to a chambermaid in the ladies' withdrawing room. This was draped with silk in a distressing pattern, and constituted a pain to the eye, but Phryne gave no sign of her opinion. She tipped the chambermaid, tweaked every luscious fold into place, shook her head at the image in the full length mirror, and prepared to greet her hostess.

The hall was painted a subdued green, which had the unfortunate effect of casting a deathly shade into every face. Phryne announced her name and braced herself. Madame Cryer, she was convinced, was an embracer.

Sure enough, there was a scatter of feet, and a skeletal woman in black and diamonds threw herself at Phryne, who submitted philosophically to the disarrangement of her hair and the painful imprint of facets on her cheek. Mrs Cryer smelt strongly of Chanel, and was so thin that Phryne wondered that she did not slit seams with what seemed to be the sharpest hips and shoulder blades in Melbourne. She made Phryne feel unduly robust and healthy, an odd sensation.

She allowed herself to be drawn forward by bony hands, glittering with a burden of precious stones, into a brilliantly lit ball-room. It was domed, huge, and full of people; a long buffet was laid along one wall, and a jazz band was conducting their usual assault on the five-bar stave in the musicians' gallery. Hideously expensive and overblown tuberoses and orchids were everywhere, lending a heavy and exotic scent to the hot air. The effect was somewhat tropical, costly, and vulgar. Mrs Cryer stated that, having heard they'd met, she had seated Phryne next to Mr Sanderson, the MP at dinner, which allowed Phryne the luxurious idea that there might be a human being in this assemblage despite appearances. Then her hostess dropped a name that caused Phryne's painted mouth to curve in a private smile.

'You may know the Hon. Robert Matthews,' shrilled Mrs Cryer. 'We're all so fond of Bobby! He's playing for the gentlemen, in the cricket match. I'm sure that you'll get on terribly well.'

Phryne, who had been the cause of Bobby's banishment to this foreign shore, was tolerably certain that she would not get on terribly well with him; and that moreover when she had known the young man, he had not been an Honourable. She caught the eye of that gentleman across the room at this point in her hostess' discourse, and he sent her a look in which pleading and fury were so nicely mingled that Phryne wondered that her hair did not catch fire. She smiled amiably at him and he looked away. Mrs Cryer had not intercepted the glance, and bore Phryne with her across the floor, which had been polished to the slipperiness of ice, to introduce her to the artistic guests.

'We are fortunate to have snared the Princesse de Grasse,' said Mrs Cryer in a far-too-loud aside. 'And she sponsered the *premier danseur* and *danseuse* of the *Compagnie des Ballets Masqués*—they are all the rage this season, perhaps you have seen them?'

Phryne caught up with her hostess and managed to free her hand.

'Yes, I saw them in Paris last year,' she said, recalling the strange, macabre charm of the dancers performing a *ballet masqué* in the tattered splendour of the old Opera. It had been primitive but spine-chilling—they had performed the mystery play of Death and the Maiden. Paris had been intrigued, but the *Compagnie des Ballets Masqués* had vanished, just as they were becoming the rage. So they had come to Australia! Phryne wondered why. She slowed her pace, smiling at Mr Sanderson, MP, as she passed him, and receiving a conspirational grin in return. The artists were solidly established at the buffet, as artists generally are, and only abandoned eating when Mrs Cryer was at their elbow.

'Princesse, may I introduce the Hon. Phryne Fisher? Miss Fisher, this is the Princesse de Grasse, and also Mademoiselle...er...'

'De Lisse, and this is my brother Sasha,' put in the young woman. She and her brother, evidently twins, were tall, long-legged and graceful, with similar features; pale, elegant, high cheekbones and deep, expressive brown eyes. They both had curly brown hair, identically cut, and were dressed alike in leotards and tights of unrelieved black. Sasha bent over her hand with a flourish, and declared: 'But Mademoiselle is *magnifique!*'

Privately, Phryne agreed with him. There was no one in the gathering who surpassed her in style and elegance, unless it was these two dancers in their plain garments which proclaimed the essential beauty of their bodies. The Princesse de Grasse, about whose title Phryne had serious misgivings, was small and wizened and Russian, dressed in a flaming red gown and a sinfully lengthy sable cape. She laid a chill claw on Phryne's wrist and smiled a sardonic smile; wonderfully expressive, it seemed to take in their hostess, the room, the food, and the unlikelihood of her title, plus a generous admiration of Phryne, all without a word. Phryne's answering smile deepened, and she pressed the small hand.

'I cannot remove the cloak,' whispered the Princesse in Phryne's ear, 'since I have no back to my gown. You must come and visit me. You are the first person in this God-forsaken place with an interesting face.'

'I will,' agreed Phryne. She had no time to say more, for her hostess was waiting with manifest impatience to show her off to some other parvenu. Phryne went placidly, carrying her head high, and deriving a certain amusement from Mrs Cryer. That lady was expounding social theory, a subject for which she was not qualified.

'All of these horrid communists,' wailed Mrs Cryer. 'I live in no fear, of course. All my servants love me,' she declared. Phryne did not say a word.

Faces and hands—the night was full of them. Phryne nodded and smiled and shook hands with so many people that they began to blur. She was becoming fatigued, and was longing to sit down, obtain a strong cocktail and light a cigarette, when her attention was recalled.

'This is Lydia Andrews, and her husband John,' Mrs Cryer was saying, and Phryne perked up and inspected her subject.

Lydia Andrews was well-dressed and had been made up by an expert, but was so limp and lifeless that she might have been a doll. She had fluffy fair hair and pink ostrich feathers curled childishly over her brow. She wore a beautifully beaded gown in old rose and a long string of pink pearls that reached to her knees.

It was only the momentarily sharp, penetrating glance that she gave Phryne as she was introduced that recalled the girl of the letters at all. This young woman could not be as languid as she seemed, not with a mind that could collect information on a grasping accountant. Phryne was wary. If this was the pose Mrs Andrews decided to affect, then who was she to interfere?

Lydia exuded deep apathy, boredom and a strong desire not to be where she was, which Phryne found curious. This was said to be the social event of the season. Behind her, her husband loomed, a portly young man, his corpulence straining his well-made evening clothes. He had thinning dark hair, balding toward the crown, and a large, unpleasantly warm and damp handshake. His eyes were a particular pale shade of which Phryne had always been suspicious, and he urged his wife forward with a hidden but painful tweak of the upper arm. Even then, she did not particularly react, though a look of surprised hurt crept into her china-blue eyes. Phryne disliked them both at sight, particularly John Andrews, whom she recognized as a domestic tyrant. But that did not make him a poisoner.

After the rest of the introductions had been completed and she had freed herself from her hostess, she found Lydia Andrews, according to her brief, and began assiduously to cultivate her, suppressing her private predeliction for Sanderson or the dancers.

Lydia proved difficult to separate from her husband, to whom she clung with the perversity of a limpet attaching itself to an ocean liner, where it knows that it is both unwelcome and unsafe. John Andrews finally undid his wife's fingers from their clutch on his arm with no great gentleness, saying abruptly, 'Talk to Miss Fisher, there's a good girl. I want to see Matthews, and you know you don't like him!' and then deserted Lydia, disregarding her little cry of pain. There was something very odd indeed in this relationship, thought Phryne, and possessed herself of Lydia's hand and such of her wavering attention as she could command.

'John's right, I don't like that Matthews boy,' she said suddenly. Her voice was flat and stubborn. 'I know that he has grand relatives in England but I don't like him and I don't like John having any business dealings with him. I don't care how plausible and charming he is.'

Phryne could not help but agree, though she could see that the stubborn repetition of the words, over a few days, could cause the kindest man to lose his accustomed suavity. She doubted that John Andrews was ordinarily in possession of many manners, as he favoured the 'I'm a common man, I am' stance of those born to wealth inherited from several generations of land-snatching squatters.

Phryne found a couple of chairs and sat Lydia down, collecting a brace of cocktails from an attentive waiter on the way. Her feet ached to dance—it was one of her best accomplishments— and she had marked out the dancer Sasha as a partner. He was presently dancing with his hostess, who moved with the rigidity of a museum specimen, and he was contriving to do impressive things, even with such a companion as Mrs Cryer. However, she had come to cultivate Lydia. Phryne lit a cigarette, sighed, and asked, 'What brings you to this gathering, Mrs Andrews? Evidently, it does not amuse you.'

Lydia's eyes took on an alarmed look. She clutched at Phryne, who fought an urge to free herself as urgently as John Andrews had; too many people had been seizing her for one night.

'No, no, I'm sure it's perfectly delightful; I'm not very well, but I am enjoying it, I assure you.'

'Oh,' said Phryne politely. 'I'm not. Such a crush, is it not? And so many people whom I don't know.'

'Oh, but everyone is here—it's the social event of the season,' parrotted Lydia. 'Even the Princesse de Grasse. She's fascinating, isn't she? But alarming, such bright eyes, and I'm told that she's very poor. She escaped the Revolution with only the clothes she stood up in. Since they came with the *Compagnie des Ballets Masqués* everyone has been inviting them, but they wouldn't accept—the Princesse brought them, so now Mrs Cryer owes her a favour. They'll dance for us later.'

Phryne was shocked. This was very bad. One invited artists to social events, but only for the pleasure of their company. To invite singers or dancers to perform for their supper was inexpressively vulgar, and deserved a prompt and stinging rebuke. Phryne wondered whether the Princesse would deliver it, and if so, whether Phryne would have the pleasure of hearing it.

'Yes, it's very bad,' agreed Lydia, reading Phryne's thoughts. 'One would not do such a thing at home, but things are different out here.'

'Manners are the same all over the world,' said Phryne, sipping her cocktail, which was agreeably powerful. 'She should not have done it. However, I shall be enchanted to see them dance again. I saw them in Paris, and they were strangely compelling. They danced Death and the Maiden; did they do that here?'

'Yes,' said Lydia, a trace of animation creeping across her features. 'It was very strange, full of meanings which I just couldn't grasp, and the music was odd—almost off key, but not quite.'

'I know what you mean,' agreed Phryne, reminding herself that Lydia was not of such profound stupidity as she chose to appear. She offered her a cigarette, and lit another for herself. The dancers had completed their foxtrot, and Sasha was making for Phryne. Lydia pressed close to her.

'I like you,' she said confidingly in her little-girl voice. 'And now that Russian boy is coming to take you away. Come to luncheon tomorrow—will you?'

The little powdered face turned up with a pout to Phryne. She felt a sudden sinking of the stomach. She had met women of this cast of mind before—the clingers, fragile and utterly ruthless, who wore down friend after friend with their emotional demands, always ill and exhausted and badly treated, but still retaining enough energy to scream reproaches at the retreating friend as she fled, guilt-stricken, down the hall. And the next week to replace that friend—always female—with another. Phryne recognized Mrs Andrews as an emotional trap, and had no choice but to throw herself in.

'Delighted,' she said promptly. 'What time?'

'One o'clock,' sighed Lydia, as the Russian boy emerged from the sea of people as sleek as a seal, smiling enchantingly. He took Phryne's hand, kissed the knuckle more lingeringly than was necessary, and gestured at the dancing. The band were essaying a tango, with shuddering atonal shriekings added to make the sound modern, and Phryne smiled on her companion. The tango was a dance she had learned in Paris from the most expensive gigolo on the *Rue du Chat-qui-Pêche*, and she had not had an opportunity to dance it in polite society. They attracted general attention as he led her out on the floor; both slim and pure of line, and the young man so unadorned that he could have been naked.

The whole room had stopped to watch them as they began to dance, so fluid their movements, so highly charged the sacramental caresses. Sasha slid, moved, turned, with the effortless grace expected of a dancer, but there was more in his tango than mere practice. The more impressionable of the ladies in the audience were reminded of a panther; and one of the serving-maids, clutching her silver spoon to her bosom, whispered to her companion, a waiter, 'Ooh, he's a sheik!'

The waiter was unimpressed with Sasha, but Phryne's dancing, as the satin and fur flowed ahead and behind her, affected him profoundly. She could combine the grace of a queen with the style of a demi-mondaine, and he had never seen anything like her in his life.

'Oh, if I could 'ave 'er!' he whispered, and the serving-maid rapped him sharply with the spoon.

Dancing with Sasha, Phryne decided, was almost as exciting as doing a loop-the-loop in a new plane in a high wind. He was graceful, and she could feel the ripple of excellent muscles beneath the leotard which fitted him like a second skin; he was exceedingly responsive to her slightest movement, but he led with confidence; she had no fear that he would drop her, and he smelt sweetly of a male human and Russian Leather soap. Her emotions were stirred but she could not afford to become infatuated with him. She was explaining patiently to herself that she was not infatuated, but merely sensibly attracted to one who was personable, graceful and an excellent dancer, when they swept to a synchronized stop, and bowed to the applause which broke out all around them.

Sasha was holding her hand and drawing her down into yet another bow. Phryne woke up, resisted the pull, and removed her hand from his, not without an inward pang. The boy turned her gently by the shoulders as the band lurched into a foxtrot, and Sasha said his first words.

'You dance very well,' he commented. 'I have seen you dance before.'

'Oh?' asked Phryne, resisting the urge to move into his embrace. He had the muscular nervousness of a highly-bred horse; intensely alive, and reacting to every touch.

'Yes, in the *Rue du Chat-qui-Pêche*,' continued Sasha, 'with Georges Santin.'

'So it was,' agreed Phryne, wondering if the young man was attempting to blackmail her. 'It was Georges who taught me to tango, and it cost me a pretty penny, I can tell you. I saw you in Paris too, with the *Compagnie des Ballets Masqués* in the old Opera. Why did you leave so suddenly?' she asked artlessly.

If the young snake was intending to ask embarrassing questions, then he would learn that Phryne had a fair battery of them too.

'It…it was expedient,' said Sasha, missing a step and recovering instantly. He spoke thenceforward in French, in which he was fluent, but with a heavy Russian accent. Phryne's French was suitably Parisian, but in her Left Bank days she had picked up a number of indelicate apache idioms, and used them with alarming candour.

'I find you very attractive, my beautiful boy, but I cannot be blackmailed.'

'The Princesse told me that it would not work,' admitted Sasha ruefully. 'And I should not have persisted against her wisdom, but I did, and see what a fool I am revealed to be? Beautiful, charming lady, forgive your humble suppliant!'

'Before I forgive you, tell me what you wanted,' said Phryne.

Sasha paused, quivering, then led her to where the old Princesse sat perched on a golden metal chair, nibbling caviar russe and surveying the dancers with a sardonic eye, like an old parrot on a perch. She eyed Sasha and Phryne, and cackled.

'*Et puis, mon petit,*' she cackled. 'Next time you will listen to me. Always I am right—infallibly right. It runs in the family; my father told the Tsar to attend to Rasputin and not declare war, but he did, and came to a bad end. As did poor Russia. And now I come to think of it, me. And you. Foolish boy! Is Mademoiselle still speaking to you, worthless one? I told you she is not one to yield to pressure! But she might have reposed in your arms and agreed to your every wish had you used what charm the lord God saw fit, for some reason, to endow you with!'

Phryne, observing that her partner was thoroughly chastened, and rather at a loss as to how to react, claimed a cocktail and some of the Princesse's caviar russe, and resolved to wait until the old woman's attention could be diverted from the hapless Sasha to explain.

'I still might—they are very pleasant arms to repose in,' she agreed placidly. 'But I need more information. What do you want? Money?'

'Not precisely,' said the old woman. 'We have a thing to do, and we believe that you can help us. You are investigating the strange illness of that female in Rose, are you not? Colonel Harper—'e is an old friend of mine.'

'I can give you no information until you reciprocate,' temporized Phryne through a mouthful of the excellent caviar. The old woman cackled again.

'*Bon*. You suspect the snow, do you not?'

'Cocaine?' asked Phryne, thinking that it was a surprising question. It had not entered her head that Lydia was a drug-fiend.

'We came from Paris in pursuit of the trade,' stated the old woman calmly. 'We of the *Compagnie des Ballets Masqués* are chasing the king of the trade. We believe that he is here—and you will help us find him. You cannot approve of it?'

Phryne, recalling the haggard cocaine-addicts, twitching and vomiting to an early grave through torments not surpassed by the Inquisition, shook her head. She did not trust her interlocutor, and she had difficulty believing anything which she was hearing, but both of them seemed serious.

'Is this a personal vendetta?'

'But yes,' said the Princesse. 'Of course. My daughter died of it. She was these children's mother.'

'What do you want me to do?' Phryne asked.

'Tell us if you find anything. And come with me, in the morning, to Madame Breda's Turkish Bath.'

'But I do not suspect snow,' said Phryne.

'Perhaps you should,' said the Princesse.

Phryne agreed. The Princesse pierced her down to the undergarments with her old, needle-sharp eyes, nodded, and clipped Sasha affectionately across the ear.

'Go, fool, and dance with the mademoiselle again, since your feet are better on the floor than in your mouth,' she chided. Sasha held out his arms, and Phryne walked into them, where she fitted comfortably, and they danced until her attention was claimed for dinner. Sasha faded away with a backward glance to join his sister and the Princesse high up on the left-hand side of the table. Phryne was seated between Lydia and the affable Robert Sanderson, MP, two seats from their hostess.

⌒

It was hours before they would allow her to sit up, and even then she was so tired by the movement that she drooped over her tray. Cec had visited, bringing chrysanthemums, and he had spoken kindly to her, unlike some of the nurses, who were abrupt, cold, and disapproving. She liked Cec. Her mother had come to weep over her narrow escape from death, and marvel that such damage could be wrought from a grazed knee.

Alice wondered what she looked like. They had cut off her hair, which she thought her best feature, and it was short and curly around her head, but she had got so thin that she could almost see through her wrists.

She had talked to the policeman who had taken down everything she had falteringly said, in a black notebook. Unfortunately, she did not know much. She had been taken from the railway station in a vehicle with blacked windows—some sort of van, and she had been so hustled into the house that she had not been able to identify the street. It was narrow and cobbled, badly lit and noisy. She could smell cooking sausages and beer, as well as a chemical smell. She had given a description of the room, but it was so ordinary that it could have been one of a thousand innocent parlours, with piano and fireplace and antimacassars. She could not remember how she got out onto Lonsdale Street, after spending two days in a spare stretcher bed in the corner of the room, along with another girl, who said nothing, but moaned in a foreign language.

She did not know why they had kept her so long, except that the foul George had seemed to want her there. He had only become panicky when he felt how hot she was.

A pale, well-dressed lady had looked into the room once, and then hastily shut the door. She had been dressed entirely in dark blue and had been very pretty.

The policeman had seemed disappointed and had gone away, begging her to call him if she remembered more.

Meanwhile, she had nothing to do but drink her egg-and-milk and sleep. All of her life she had worked. Being idle was a strange sensation.

Having been brought back to life, she had no temptation to give up again, although she was so tired and thin and listless. Besides, Cec visited her every day and sat by her bed. He was silent for the most part, but there was something comforting about his silence and he held her hand as if it was an honour. Alice was not used to this.

Chapter Seven

Oh, what can ail thee, Knight at Arms,
Alone and palely loitering.
'La Belle Dame Sans Merci', John Keats

The first course, a delicate asparagus soup, passed politely enough, with Lydia offering timid comments on the Melbourne weather, to which Robert Sanderson responded in hearty agreement.

'They say, if you don't like the weather, just wait half an hour and it changes. Makes matters of dress dashed difficult, I can tell you.'

'Not so much for gentlemen,' observed Phryne. 'You are forced to wear the same uniform whether it is hot or cold, wet or dry; I believe it has been described as the "Assyrian Panoply of the Gentleman". Do you not get tired of it?'

'Yes, perhaps, Miss Fisher, but what would you have me do? I can't go about in old flannel bags and a red tie, like those artist chaps up in Heidelberg. The people who have done me the honour to entrust me with the exercise of sovereign power expect a certain standard, and I am delighted to follow their wishes. In this, at least, I can please them. Not, alas, in much else.'

Phryne digested this speech along with the asparagus soup. Anyone who could clothe a trite statement in such orotund

periods was obviously born to be a politician. The soup passed, and the entrée, whitebait with accompaniments of lemon and buttered toast, made its appearance. The food was delicious, but the conversation was beginning to bore Phryne. Mindful of her task, she could not divert the company with anything shocking, which was her usual method of gaining either interesting conversation or sufficient silence to eat in comfort. Mrs Cryer was holding forth on the insolence of the poor.

'A dirty man—I mean, really smelly—opened the door of my taxi, and had the nerve to ask for money! And when I gave him a penny, he almost threw it at me, and called me a most insulting name.'

Phryne diverted a few entrancing moments wondering what he had called her. A mean bitch, perhaps, which would seem to meet the case admirably.

'A similar thing happened to me,' reminisced Sanderson. Phryne looked at him. She was hoping that her good opinion of him was not about to be spoiled. 'A grubby fellow polished the windows of my car, with a villainously dirty rag, so that I could hardly see out of 'em, then asked me for a sixpence—and offered to clean 'em again for a shilling, with a new rag.'

Sanderson chuckled, but Mrs Cryer bridled.

'I hope that you did not give him anything, Mr Sanderson!'

'Of course I did, ma'am.'

'But he would only spend it on drink! You know what the working classes are!'

'Indeed, ma'am, and why should he not spend it on drink? Would you deprive the poor, whose lives are bad and miserable and comfortless enough, of the solace of a little relief from grinding poverty? A sordid, sodden relief perhaps, but would you be so heartless as to deny the poor even that pleasure in which all of us indulge at your generous expense?' He looked meaningfully at the glass of wine at Mrs Cryer's place—it was her third, yet she had eaten very little. An unbecoming flush mounted to her hostess' hairline, and Phryne leapt in the conversational breach, her opinion of the MP confirmed. She had a feeling that she had heard the speech before—Dr Johnson, was it?—but it did him credit. However, Phryne wanted to gain a few points with Mrs Cryer, and this seemed to be a good time to earn some.

'Tell me, Mr Sanderson, what party do you belong to? I know so little about politics in Melbourne.'

'I am, and always have been, a Tory, and I am pleased to say that we are presently in an excellent position. At the moment I have the honour to represent the electorate in this area; I was born here. My father came from Yorkshire, but I have never been home. Never had the time, somehow. There are many things that keep me here. At present, for example, we are setting up soup-kitchens, and a measure of work will be provided for the unemployed, for which they will receive sustenance wages.'

'Won't that be very expensive?'

'Yes, probably, but we cannot allow the working men to starve.'

'What about the working women?' asked Phryne artlessly. There was a shocked silence.

'Why, Miss Fisher, don't say that you're a suffragette!' giggled Mrs Cryer. 'So indelicate!'

'Did you vote in the last election, Mrs Cryer?' asked Robert Sanderson, and his hostess glared at him. Phryne thought that she had better leave politics alone, and changed the subject.

'Any of you gentlemen interested in flying?'

To Phryne's great relief, one Alan Carroll piped up from across the table with an enthusiastic summary of the latest Avro, and the conversation went on to a discussion of scientific miracles, the telephone, the wireless, the car, the electric train, the flying machine, and the chip-heater.

The roast chickens were brought in, and the conversation flagged. Lydia, however, continued to speak to her husband in vicious undertones. Phryne was unobtrusively attentive and what she heard confirmed her opinion that despite Lydia's vapid appearance she had a whim of iron.

'I tell you that Matthews is crooked. He's laughing at your naivety. You must not believe him, that gold mine is fake. There

was an article in the *Business Review* about it—did you not read
it? I marked it for you. You will lose every penny we own, and
then you'll come crying to me. I told you, you have no business
sense. Leave the investing to me! I know what I'm doing.'

Mr Andrews took his tongue-lashing meekly.

Dinner concluded with ices and custards and fruit, and the
ladies withdrew to take coffee and gossip. Lydia clung to Phryne
but did not speak, and Phryne had no further chance to talk to
the Princesse, who was holding her own court in a corner, along
with a flagon of orange liqueur and a samovar. Phryne sipped
coffee, then shook off Lydia for ten minutes. She re-emerged to
find the ballroom in darkness. She understood that the dancers
were to begin, and found the Princesse attached to her elbow.

'You have decided?' she whispered.

'I agree, provided that you tell me what you find,' Phryne
answered without turning her head. The old woman cackled
disconcertingly.

'Quiet, now. They are going to perform.'

The guests were silenced by a painful mixture of Schoenberg
and Russian folk-song, derived from musically obtuse Styrian
peasants who had absorbed their atonality along with their
mother's milk. The sound hurt; but it could not be ignored.
Too much of it, Phryne was convinced, would curdle custard.

The music gave a sudden screech, and the young woman,
whose name Phryne had discovered was Elli, leapt into the ring
of people. She was dressed in her leotard, with the addition
of an apron and a long fair wig, done in plaits. She was both
comic and rather touching, as she skipped along, occasionally
pausing to pick flowers, which she gathered in her apron. She
danced a little childish, almost clumsy dance, indicating that it
was spring and a lovely day. She knelt to dip water from a pool,
then caught sight of her reflection. She made a few grimaces,
and unplaited her hair, trying out the effect and smiling through
the long tresses.

Creeping, silent as a cat, came Sasha, almost invisible in his
unrelieved black, with a white mask in his hand. The maiden

caught sight of him, bridled, and dimpled coyly. Sasha smiled, a guileless grin, and they danced a clumsy *pas-de-deux*, while the music hooted and roiled in peasant fashion. They circled the room once, tripping over each other's feet, and the audience began to laugh. Then the maiden twirled away on her own, apron flaring as her invisible flowers scattered in her path.

Sasha stood still, and donned the mask, immediately seeming taller, thinner and infinitely more alarming. His clumsiness became sinister when topped with a death's head. Even the mask was primitive; not a full skull but the bony frontal ridges and hollow eyesockets, cracked and broken and grey, as if he had been long buried. Under the half-mask was Sasha's own smooth jaw and soft red mouth, which somehow made it worse. The maiden danced her rustic little dance a few more steps, and Death followed her, now not at all clumsy. Without seeing him, she moved and dodged, eluding his grasp, until she turned and beheld him, and fled with a shriek.

Death pursued her, slowly, then faster, blocking and obstructing her course, until she ran into his arms. His feral grin chilled Phryne's spine, especially as she recalled her own wish to kiss that mouth. The maiden shuddered in the arms of Death; her knees gave way, and he bore her into the same peasant *pas-de-deux*, her feet trailing, her head lolling, pitiful as a scarecrow. Then, as they circled the room, she grew more alert; her hands rose and smoothed back her hair; she began a dance which grew wilder and wilder, until she subsided in Death's arms. Their close embrace was charged with an energy which was frankly sexual as the light dimmed, and the dancers left the floor, entwined like lovers. The last glimpse Phryne had of them was Death's mask, grinning back over the maiden's shoulder as she melted into him.

It was comic and savage, and frightening as Balanchine or any of the Russians; it seemed to bear many significances which were necessarily unspoken. The company was rather relieved when a large opera singer took her place next to the grand piano and began an ambitious piece by Wagner.

Phryne felt the Princesse's cold, monkey-like hand on her arm.

'They have something, no?' asked the Princesse proudly, '*Un petit air de rien, hein*? A little bit of something.' Phryne agreed and the large lady continued to murder Wagner.

Near two in the morning, and past time to leave, thought Phryne, rendered restless by the company and the boy Sasha, and mindful of her need to arise early and accompany the Princesse to the Bath House of Madame Breda—which sounded a dubious proposition at best. She glanced around for Lydia, but she had gone. Then she looked for Sasha and Elli and the Princesse, but they were nowhere to be seen. She took leave of her hostess, collected her wrap, and refused an offer of a taxi. She felt like walking; it was not far to the city. The streets were still cold, and slick with moisture which would soon be frost, and she had her little gun in her bag in case there should be any trouble from the hungry unemployed.

There was no one on the streets. Phryne loved the sound of her high heels clicking on the pavement and echoing back to her. She walked briskly up Toorak Road, where she remembered seeing a taxi-stand. It was a clean, pleasant night, and the air was just cold enough to sting, a contrast to the orchid-scented hothouse of Mrs Cryer.

She turned the corner into the road which would lead her back to the city. There were no taxis. No matter, she did her best thinking on her feet, at night. She sorted out her impressions as the street signs fled past. She had covered almost a mile in complete silence and contemplation when she heard the first disruptive sound. Feet running; many feet. There was a shout, and then a shot bruised the peaceful Melbourne night in a most unexpected fashion.

Well, thought Phryne, continuing at her even pace, she had walked unharmed through Paradise Street, Soho, and the Place Pigalle; should a small night affray bother her unduly?

There were more sounds of feet from a side street, then a body almost cannoned into Phryne, who leapt aside to present any attacker with a sight of her small gun. It was cocked and loaded.

'It's Sasha,' gasped the body. *'Pour l'amour de Dieu! Aidez-moi, Mademoiselle.'* He was still dressed as Death, with mask and leotard. Phryne dropped her aim so she should not shoot him through the heart, handed him the gun, stripped off her wrap and enveloped him in it. She tore the fillet out of her hair and forced it on his head, removing the mask and stuffing it in her muff. She repossessed herself of her gun, linked arms, and instructed him. 'You're tipsy. Lean on my arm and giggle.'

'Giggle?' asked Sasha blankly, staggering a little, then understanding.

The feet caught up with them, slowed to a walk, and approached from behind. Phryne threw back her head and crowed with mirth, nudging her companion, who reeled a little more than was theatrically necessary, and giggled a creditable high-pitched giggle. The feet passed, one on either side, and two men stopped in front of them.

'Have you seen a running man?' asked the smaller of the two in an aggressive Australian accent. 'He must have passed you.'

'Ooh, cheeky, stopping a couple of ladies on their way home!' replied Phryne in the same accent, after a certain excursus into cockney. 'We're a couple of decent girls, we are, and we ain't seen no running man. Though we 'ave seen a few of 'em lying down, eh, blossom?' and she laughed again, bearing Sasha up with considerable effort.

She was eyeing the two men keenly, so as to know them again. The speaker was a short, thick, bullet-headed individual, with a voice like a file and an aggressive moustache, waxed, and with rather more crumbs in it than fashion dictated; the other was taller and thinner, with patent-leather hair, a supercilious expression, and a thin moustache like a smear of brown Windsor soup. Both had suggestive bulges in their pockets which told of either huge genitalia or trousered pistols. Phryne inclined to the handgun theory.

Sasha said in French, 'Who are these rude men, my cabbage?' and to Phryne's surprise, the tall one answered in that language.

'*Mademoiselle, pardon, avez-vous vu un homme en courant d'ici?*' It was not exactly French as Phryne (and presumably Sasha) knew it, but it argued that some education had been wasted on Thug Two.

'*Non, non,*' protested Sasha with another giggle. '*Les hommes me suivent; je n'ai pas encore rencontré un homme qui me trouve laide.*'

'Carm on, Bill, these tarts don't know nothing!' exclaimed Thug One, and he and Thug Two crossed the road and retreated down a side alley. The last scornful comment of Thug One followed them up the street.

'And they're tiddly, too!'

'Sasha, what is wrong? Are you really tiddly?' asked Phryne, getting her shoulder under his armpit as he began to sink. She heaved him along to a high front step and lowered him onto it.

'One of them,' said Sasha with perfect clarity, 'had a knife.'

With that he sank gracefully into Phryne's arms and his head lolled on her shoulder.

'Oh, Lord,' said that young woman ruefully. 'Now what shall I do?'

At that moment she heard a car approaching, and stood irresolutely, gun in hand, awaiting it. Blessing on blessings, it was a taxi, though the sign was turned down, and she stepped out onto the road to intercept it.

'Here, you crazy tart, what's the idea?' demanded a familiar voice, and Phryne had to restrain herself from hugging the driver. It was Bert and Cec.

'Oh, Bert, it's about time you arrived, I've been waiting for hours. My friend has fainted. Help me get her into the car, and take us to the Windsor. I'll give you ten pounds.'

'Twelve,' bargained Bert, dragging the car back on its haunches and flinging open the door.

'Ten—that's all I've got on me.'

'Eleven,' offered Bert, gathering up Sasha and loading him into the back seat. Phryne followed, and the silent Cec climbed in. Bert started the cab with a certain difficulty, and said, 'What about twenty not to tell your Dad what you've been doing?'

Phryne produced the little gun and touched the back of his neck with the cold barrel.

'How about nothing at all? I thought we were mates,' she suggested silkily. Her patience with this pair of opportunists was wearing thin. Ten pounds would buy this cab, and have enough change for a packet of smokes and a glass of beer.

'We'll just leave it at the round ten, eh, shall we?' said Bert, not turning a hair. 'Lucky for you that Cec and me was passing by.'

Phryne, who was concerned about Sasha's condition, and moreover was perched uncomfortably on a pile of what was probably stolen property, was tight-lipped. They made the journey to the Windsor through empty streets, and Bert rang the night bell while Cec and Phryne supported Sasha, who had recovered enough to stand.

Phryne produced the ten pounds.

'How is the girl you brought into the hospital? Are you looking for this George?'

Bert spat out the cigarette in disgust.

'Yair, we're looking for him, but not a sniff. Cec reckons he's seen him before, but he can't remember where. The Scotch lady doctor took us to the cops and they said they'd do something but they don't know where he is either. But I've been collecting numbers—and a mate of mine is givin' me the drum about another one tomorrow.'

'Numbers?' asked Phryne, supporting Sasha with difficulty.

'Yair, phone numbers. All we need is a sheila to make the calls.' Phryne smiled, and Bert backed a pace.

'You got your sheila,' said Phryne in a flat Australian drawl. 'Call here, and we'll have a council of war—no, better, I'll find myself a car, and we'll do the phoning from a public phone where there is no operator. Meet me at the corner of Flinders and Spencer at noon, day after tomorrow. Goodnight,' she added, as the night porter opened the door and she swept Sasha inside and up the stairs. The two men stared at the closed door for a while, then made off on their own errand.

'You reckon she can do it, mate?' asked Cec after a long silence.

'Reckon,' agreed Bert.

Phryne succeeded in getting Sasha up to her room without much noise and found that Dot had gone to bed. She lowered the young man on to the couch, removed her fillet and cape, and surveyed the damage. The lassitude was explained by the fact that a razor-sharp knife had slit a long thin wound down the bicep, slicing through the leotard, and although it was minor compared to the wreckage produced by, say, an apache brawl, it was bleeding freely.

Phryne, aware that blood could not be removed from satin, threw off the beautiful dress, and found a towel and a newly washed stocking in the bathroom. She rang room service and ordered strong coffee and a bottle of Benedictine. Sasha returned to full consciousness to find himself being offered a drink by a young woman clad in black camiknicks, black stockings, high heels, and a towel. There was a long smear of bright red across her breast, which he felt was just what the costume needed.

His arm hurt. He looked down, alarmed at the amount of blood, anxious that the muscles might be damaged; there was a stocking bound tightly around it.

'You are not badly hurt, but to judge from the state of that jerkin you have lost a lot of blood. Your arm isn't crippled; bend your fingers, one at a time. Good. Now clench your fist. Good. Now bend your elbow. Put your fist on your shoulder and keep it there, and you might stop bleeding. Now, drink more coffee, please, and keep your arm and side still. A young man in one's hotel bedroom is capable of being explained, but a corpse is always a hindrance.'

Phryne, noting the young man's eyes upon her and realizing that her costume might be considered scanty, wiped the blood off her breast and wrapped herself in her mannish dressing gown. Then she poured a cup of coffee, lit a gasper, and waited for an explanation.

Sasha, feeling strength creep back into his weary body, drank coffee, sipped Benedictine and began to talk in French. That language came more easily to him than English.

'It was the Snow,' he said, investing the term *neige*, usually connected with French skiing lessons, with solemn horror. 'I heard that there was to be a drop of the stuff at a certain place, so I went there, without telling my sister or la Princesse. They will skin me alive! Though there is little necessity, I have effectively punished myself. You are sure about the muscle? It is very tender.'

Phryne reassured him. She recalled that she had some styptic powder, fetched it from the bathroom, and applied it to the arm. She could not help noticing how muscular he was, his skin as smooth as marble. She slit the side seam of the leotard and removed it, wrapping him in the gown which she used as a *peignoir*. It was of dark green cotton and suited him well. Although he resembled his sister very strongly, Phryne had no difficulty in remembering that Sasha was male, even when clad in female garments. His charm was not at all androgynous. As the Princesse had said, had he exerted all of the charm which God gave him, she would have lain down in his arms and given him anything he wanted.

He leaned his head back against her thigh as she sat behind him on the arm of the chair, and she ran her hand through the curly hair.

'Continue,' she ordered. 'So what did you do?'

'I hid myself outside the gate,' sighed Sasha. 'And the car drew up as they had arranged, and a packet was exchanged. Then they saw me, and I ran, like a fool! Two of them chased me, on foot, luckily. I don't know what became of the car. Then I realized that the one who had first seen me, who had lunged at me with a knife, he had wounded me...I was failing...then I saw you, and flung myself at your feet, and with great wit and a speed of thought to be marvelled at, you hid me and contrived to convey me here. Where is here?'

'The Hotel Windsor. I think that you had better stay here tonight. The Princesse is coming in a few hours to take me to the Turkish bath of Madame Breda. I can smuggle you out with us. What is your address?'

'We are staying at Scott's; a good hotel, but not luxurious, as this one is. I should like to live here,' said Sasha artlessly, reaching out his unwounded right hand for the coffee cup. Phryne laughed.

'I daresay you would. But you would shock my maid,' she added, wondering what Dot would make of the visitor.

She dragged the quilt off her bed and made Sasha comfortable on the sofa, despite his preferred wish to sleep with her, 'Like brother and sister, you know.' Phryne knew that her will to resist temptation was weak. She turned off the lights, pinned a note on Dot's door that said, 'It's all right, he's a visitor and anyway he's hurt. Call me at eight with tea and aspirins, P.'. Then she put herself to bed, resolutely turning the key in her door more as a warning to herself than any suspicion of Sasha's motives.

In any case, as soon as the lights were off, she slept like a baby.

Chapter Eight

Come down and relieve us from virtue
Our Lady of Pain
'Our Lady of Pain', Algernon Swinburne

Phryne awoke, feeling unhuman. Dot was tapping on her door. She lurched out of bed, accepted the tray and sat down to swallow aspirins and tea at top speed.

'Run me a bath, Dot, please, with lavender salts.'

Dot stayed put.

'What about 'im?' She jerked a thumb back over her shoulder. Phryne had forgotten Sasha. It was very early in the morning.

'Sasha? He was attacked in the street, and I brought him back here because it was too late for him to get back into his hotel. He's hurt, Dot, and I want you to be nice to him.'

She joined her maid at the door and saw that Sasha had thrown off the covers as he slept and now sprawled, like a youthful faun wearied with one orgy too many, naked to the waist, fast asleep and heart-stoppingly beautiful. Phryne sighed.

'But not too nice. Let him sleep, and if he's still asleep at lunch, leave him here. He won't do any damage,' she added. Her private papers were on her person and most of her jewels were in the hotel safe. As for her other possessions, well, this might be a good way of ascertaining if Sasha was a thief. Phryne Fisher had a taste for young and comely men, but she was not prone to trust them with anything but her body.

'Run my bath, please, Dot, and remember this is your afternoon off. Are you doing anything interesting?'

'I'm going home,' said Dot, receding in the direction of the bathroom. 'Then to the flicks. There's a new Douglas Fairbanks.'

Phryne sat down to drink her tea, adding a judicious measure of Benedictine. She decided upon severe black trousers, a white shirt, and a loose, bloused, black jacket as suitable dress for a visit to a Turkish bath, and she loaded the capacious pockets with the usual accessories. Finding the pouchy velvet bag of the night before, she removed the little gun, surveyed it thoughtfully, and added it to her accoutrements. Her headache began to ease. Sasha rolled over, fast asleep, and moaned. Phryne laid a hand on his forehead, but it was cool. He did not seem to have sustained any lasting damage.

Dorothy returned with the news that her bath was run, and Phryne subsided into the steam with a deep groan. All of her muscles hurt. She resolved to take more exercise before she danced with Sasha again, and applied some cream to her face. 'Too many nights like that, m'girl, and you'll be getting haggard,' she reproved herself, lathering her pale slender arms and breasts with Parisian soap. Despite the creaking of the tendons, she remained slim as the gunmetal nymph and completely unblemished. She sluiced herself down, dried and dressed, and accepted a light breakfast which Dot had ordered. The coffee completed her recovery. After further deep thought, she gave the small gun to Dot and ordered her to hide it. One cannot take much except intelligence and religious convictions into a Turkish bath, and one's garments are available to be searched.

The Princesse arrived at half-past eight, dressed in a shabby linen outfit evidently made for someone who was much taller and stouter. She said little, but stalked off down toward Russell Street, and Phryne followed.

The streets were windswept and chilly. The only sign of life appeared to emanate from Little Lonsdale Street, where the late-night revellers were eating eggs and bacon in the company of girls far too skimpily clad for the climate. The Bath House of Madame Breda was but a hop, skip and jump from these scenes of bacchanalian fervour, and Phryne, cold and disgruntled, felt that the neighbourhood was hardly salubrious.

The Bath was a large building, running the width of the block between Russell and Little Lonsdale. The stone was respectable and the doorway imposingly austere. Phryne was regretting her bed, possibly with Sasha in it, when the door was opened by a severe maid in black with a white cap. She ushered them in without a smile, and they entered a hall scented with the most ravishing, oriental steam. Phryne, after a little thought and several deep sniffs, analysed it as a heavenly compound of bergamot orange, sandalwood and something rare and precious—frangipani, perhaps, or orchid—a seductive, slightly sour scent, quite ravishing to the unprepared senses. The Princesse nudged Phryne in the ribs with an elbow evidently especially sharpened for the purpose of compelling attention.

'Smells like a brothel, *n'est-ce-pas*? A Turkish brothel.' Phryne's experience of brothels was not extensive, and her knowledge of Turkish ones was non-existent; but this was certainly how a Turkish brothel should have smelt. She nodded.

Madame Breda was advancing on them with an outstretched hand. Phryne stepped back a pace, for Madame was enormous. She stood a full six feet high and must have weighed fifteen stone; blonde and muscular, she could have walked on as a Valkyrie and gained nothing but applause. Her eyes were blue, her cheeks red, her complexion excellent, and her hair luxuriant; she was as strong as a goddess and very intimidating. And she was completely wrong for the part of King of Snow. She was the last person in the world whom Phryne could imagine selling any sort of drug. She was so oppressively healthy.

They were led into a pink-tiled room, filled with the overpowering scented steam, and divested of their clothes. The actual swimming bath was a full fifteen feet long, about four feet deep, and half-filled with Nile-green water.

'The demoiselles will begin in the steam room,' suggested the maid. She was unruffled, not a hair out of place, though the heat was reddening Phryne's cheeks and slicking her hair to her skull. They followed the maid into the Scandinavian bath, where the air was suffocatingly hot. There they shed their towelling robes and sat naked on rather spiky cane chairs. Phryne noticed that the Princesse, though wizened, was as straight of limb as a woman of twenty, and was as healthy as a tree.

'This reminds me of India,' remarked the Princesse. 'I was there with the Tsar's entourage, you know.'

Phryne was unaware of the visit of the Tsar to India, an imperial dominion which had every reason to be suspicious of the intentions of Russia. She doubted the story but nodded politely.

'This is the distribution centre,' remarked the old woman. 'The maid will deliver the snow to me as we recline at the massage and hydro-bath. Watch.'

And thereafter she chatted amiably of her extensive travels and her improbable amours. 'I danced the dance of the seven veils for the Prince and Rasputin—such eyes that man had, like our Sasha, he could command a woman in all things—and when I get to the fourth veil, the Prince, he can stand it no longer, and he...'

Just when the Princesse had Phryne's undivided attention, the maid interrupted, and moved them to a cooler room, where they were supplied with bitter herb tea 'to cleanse the system'. Phryne examined the maid. Her name, it appeared, was Gerda, and she was Madame Breda's cousin. Gerda had a washed-out, bony countenance and a pale, whispering voice, spiced with a little venom as she described her employer and relative.

'Her! She works me to death! Gerda, clean the bathing-pool! Gerda, serve the tea! And I had a young man in Austria, and an eligible *parti*. She offered me employment here, and I came hoping to amass enough for a useful dowry, and now my young man has married someone else, and I stay here, my heart broken.'

Phryne wondered how old this young man was, and how long Gerda had been in Australia. She was forty if she was a day, and a cold, sour forty, at that. Her iron-grey hair was dragged back into a vengeful bun, and her figure was not one which would attract the attention of any bathing-belle judges. She was built like a box; so much so that Phryne wondered if she might still have 'Cox's Orange Pippin' stencilled on her bottom. She decided that nothing could induce her to tip Gerda up and look.

An attendant entered with unguents, and the ladies reclined for a massage. The masseuse was Madame Breda herself, and after a certain initial impression that all her bones were being torn loose from their sockets, Phryne relaxed and began to enjoy the pummelling of the hard, skilful fingers. She felt the knots in her calf muscles soothed and coaxed away, and the rubbing oil, which was of sandalwood, imparted an agreeable pungency. On the next bench, the Princesse grunted with pleasure. Phryne was wrapped in her towelling robe again, and sat to watch her companion undergoing the treatment, with the enjoyment of one who has already come through.

Madame Breda clapped Phryne on the shoulder and boomed, 'Now you have warm bath with oatmeal, to take out the oil, and then the cold plunge. You have been walking far lately? Or dancing? Yes, it would be dancing in one so young and beautiful. Next time, do not dance so hard. You may do damage to a muscle. I have not seen you before. You are a friend of the Princesse?'

'My name is Phryne Fisher,' said Phryne carefully, not at all sure that she was a friend of the Princesse. 'I'm a visitor from England.'

'You shall come again,' declared Madame Breda, her rosy cheeks shining and her red mouth parting in a most daunting manner. 'You will find yourself most refreshed.'

This sounded like an order, but Phryne smiled and nodded. She was escorted to a luxurious bath, milky with oatmeal. The small attendant, a pretty girl only marred by a flat burn scar on one cheek, instructed her to lie back and be washed. Phryne felt like a Princess of Egypt being bathed in ass' milk, while the girl rubbed her gently all over with a soft muslin bag containing more oatmeal. When she seemed to be concentrating a little too markedly on the nipples and then the female parts, Phryne did not open her eyes, but murmured, 'No thank you,' and the girl desisted. So that was one of the offered entertainments of Madame Breda's. Pleasant, but not to Phryne's taste. Possibly, however, to Lydia's taste, thought Phryne, remembering how Lydia had looked at her. What an excellent opportunity for a little polite blackmail.

She was assisted out of the milk-bath, rinsed with warm clean water, and led to the green pool. Madame Breda was there.

'Jump!' she instructed, and Phryne jumped.

The water was cold enough to stop the heart.

After gasping, choking, and uttering a small shriek, Phryne duck-dived the length of the pool, turned, and swam back. Madame Breda had gone; the Princesse and Gerda were entering the room. Phryne, though she strained her ears, could not hear what they were saying, but she saw a packet change hands, and Gerda tucked a considerable wad of currency into the dark recesses of her costume.

The Princesse flung herself into the pool, climbed out, and shook herself briskly. She and Phryne reclaimed their robes and went back to the dressing room. The package was square, done up in white with sealing wax, like a chemist's. As they dressed, Phryne asked, 'Is that the stuff?'

'Of course,' said the Princesse. Phryne put her hand in her pocket, and encountered a folded piece of paper which had not been there before, and a wadded something, containing a crystalline substance of the consistency of salt. She did not take either object out into plain sight, and she did not think that the Princesse had noticed anything.

Dressed, they adjourned to Madame's parlour to partake of more bitter tea. Gerda was there, with a large and loaded tray.

'I will send your account to your hotel, Mademoiselle,' she observed respectfully. 'But I am instructed to offer you our treatments. Here is the mud pack, the bain effervescent, tea for complexion and vitality, and beauty powders. Madame Breda is famous for her powders.'

Phryne was familiar with this practice. Most beauty parlours made up tonics and headache cures and sold them when the customer was at her most relaxed. In view of the transactions which she had just seen, however, she was not willing to risk anything.

'No, thank you—but I shall come again. Ready, Princesse?'

'Certainly. Give Madame Breda my compliments,' said the Princesse with rare grace, and they left the Bath House.

'Tell me, Princesse, what is your real title? And why do you use de Grasse?'

'It is simple. I am the Princesse Barazynovska. When I came first to Europe they could not pronounce it. So I changed it. I have always liked Grasse. It is the centre of the perfume industry, you know, and has fields of lavender…and you, mademoiselle. You have not been born to the blue, eh?'

'Purple,' corrected Phryne. 'No, I was born in very poor circumstances. Bitterly poor. Then several people died, and I was whisked into fashion and wealth. I enjoy it greatly,' she said honestly. 'There's nothing like being really poor to make you relish being really wealthy.'

'And are you?'

'Which?'

'Really wealthy?' asked the Princesse, with every appearance of personal interest.

'Yes. Why? You said last night that you did not want money.'

'A little money would be pleasant, but I was speaking the truth.'

'Good. Now, give me that packet.'

The Princesse's hand went protectively to her bag.

'Why?'

'I want it,' explained Phryne hardly at all. 'Shall I make you an offer for it? Or are you an addict yourself?'

'No!' exclaimed the old woman. 'No! Make me an offer.'

Phryne reflected that it was fortunate that Melbourne was not a French-speaking country, or this conversation would have unduly interested the policeman whom they happened to be passing. She said abruptly, 'Twenty pounds.'

'Done,' agreed the Princesse, and handed over the packet. Phryne pocketed it, and stuffed notes into the Princesse's shabby purse.

'Well, I have shown you what you needed to be shown,' declared the old woman. 'And here I shall leave you. Farewell for now, dear child. I will send you my address. You interest me.'

And with that, she left, trotting away into the crowd. Phryne immediately inquired her way to a post office, purchased brown paper and string, and, on the way, dropped into the ladies' public toilet, where she hoped to be unobserved. She emptied her pocket, and found the little crunchy package and the note.

The package was full of a white powder, and the message written in greasy black pencil—perhaps eyebrow pencil—merely said 'Beware of the Rose'.

There was no signature and Phryne had no time to puzzle over it. She included the small package in her larger one, wrapped them up and addressed them to Dr MacMillan, with a brief note asking for an analysis, and only breathed a deep breath once the parcel had been stamped and consigned to the mercies of the post office.

Wondering about the Princesse and if she were trying to frame her, Phryne went into a cash chemist and bought a packet of bicarbonate of soda wrapped in white paper and sealed with red wax.

It was only ten in the morning, and Phryne was at a loose end. Eventually, she decided to see a newsreel as a painless way of passing the time, and spent a blameless hour learning about sterile dairies. One never knew when such knowledge might come in handy.

*

At twelve Phryne walked back to the hotel, to dress for Lydia Andrews' luncheon party. The weather was brisk and cool, and she chose a linen suit and draped herself in a loose cloth coat in dark brown, and called a taxi, all without waking Sasha, who was sleeping very deeply. Phryne wondered about this slumber, which seemed unnaturally profound, and was minded to jab her hatpin into him to see if it had some effect—but decided against it. One did not jab fauns with hatpins and she expected it to be a trying afternoon; it was not a good idea to begin it with a bad deed on one's conscience.

She arrived at the Andrews' address at ten past one, and saw that two chauffeur-driven cars were waiting outside. This pleased her. A tête-à-tête with Lydia was not an attractive proposition. Three ladies were seated at the luncheon table as she entered the neat, pastel-coloured house and gave her coat to a very small maid in pale blue. Phryne recognized only Lydia, sitting at the table with her back to Phryne. The two *inconnues* stared at her levelly. One was short and plump; one was short and thin. Their combined heights would not have reached the ceiling. They were both of indeterminate colouring, clothing and style, and Phryne had to keep saying to herself, even after they had been introduced, 'Ariadne is the thin one, Beatrice is the fat one.'

Lydia was overdressed in a pink Fuji dress, silk stockings, and a tasteless costume brooch in the shape of a flying bird that was enamelled in dark green and studded with stones so large that they must have been paste. She was tapping a pink pencil on a row of figures in a small notebook.

'Tell your husband that I disagree with him,' stated Lydia firmly. 'There is no profit to be got from these chancy gold shares. He can obtain three per cent from the companies on this list and I will advise you further should you decide to invest. I put seven thousand into Greater Foodstuffs and the dividends are excellent. I recommend it. And don't touch any share promoted by Bobby Matthews. He's a confidence man if ever I saw one.'

'You've always given me good advice,' murmured Beatrice. 'I put my little savings into the Riverina scheme and I've been very pleased with the result. If you say the Greater Foodstuffs is good, I'll tell Henry to invest.'

'You won't regret it,' said Lydia. 'Look at these accounts.' Beatrice scanned the list of figures. 'That's not much of a profit,' she commented. Lydia glared pityingly at her innumerate friend.

'Beatrice, that's the telephone number.'

Phryne coughed, and watched Lydia melt into a poor little girl in front of her very eyes.

'Oh, Miss Fisher!' simpered Lydia. 'Meet my guests…'

A cocktail was provided for Phryne, though the others were taking sherry, a drink which Phryne abominated. She attributed this to having got drunk for the first time at the age of fifteen at a dormy feast on cheap sweet sherry; the memory of that hangover would have caused a girl with less courage to swear off alcohol for life. The smell of sherry still made her faintly nauseous.

'Tell me about your family, Miss Fisher,' gushed Lydia, and Phryne tried the cocktail—it had been made with absinthe, which she did not drink—and obliged with a full description of her father's inheritance, his land-holdings, his title, and his house. Ariadne and Beatrice remained resolutely unimpressed, but Lydia was ecstatic.

'Oh, then you must have met my father—the Colonel. He's invited everywhere.'

'Yes, I believe I may have,' agreed Phryne. It was never wise to swear that one had never met a person when this could easily be checked.

'But you are not drinking—is the cocktail not to your taste?' added Lydia, and Phryne murmured that it was excellent. She was beginning to feel a little dizzy, and decided that one really needed to be in good athletic standing to indulge in Turkish baths. Phryne pulled herself together with an effort; the ladies had changed the subject, and were now discussing the social event at Mrs Cryers' last night.

'They said that those Russian dancers were there,' said Ariadne breathlessly.

'And that one of the ladies danced a most abandoned tango with the boy,' confided Beatrice, oblivious of Lydia's attempts to catch her eye. 'Disgustingly indecent, but skilful, I heard. I always think that too great a proficiency in dancing shows that a girl is really fast. Who was it, Lydia? Some flapper, I suppose.'

Lydia, at length managing to capture her friend's attention, pointed circumspectly at Phryne. Beatrice did not turn a hair.

'I expect that you learned to dance on the Continent, Miss Fisher,' was her only comment, and Phryne agreed that this was so. To Lydia's relief, the luncheon was now announced. Lydia led the way into a charming breakfast room with potted plants and ruffled curtains. Phryne, carrying the cocktail, decanted it unobtrusively into a potted palm against which she had no personal grudge, and hoped that it would not give her away by dying too rapidly.

The luncheon was excellent—light and cool, salads and ham and meringues—followed by cup upon cup of very good coffee. The ladies lit cigarettes and the conversation became personal.

All three of them, it seemed, had unsatisfactory husbands. John Andrews was cruel, crushing, and often absent, Ariadne's husband was persistently unfaithful, and Beatrice's a habitual gambler.

Lydia hinted, dabbing at her unreddened eyes with a perfectly white, perfectly dry handkerchief, at sexual perversions too grim for words. Phryne pressed a little, hoping that words might be found, but Lydia just shook her head with a martyred expression and sighed.

Phryne attempted to ascertain John Andrews' nature, but the picture of him gleaned through Lydia's sighs was curiously unconvincing. Phryne knew that he was crude, cruel, and a man who relished power; but she could not envisage him as intelligent enough to invent the complex tortures at which his wife hinted. Mr Ariadne was a banker; Mr Beatrice was an importer and stock-jobber. The litany of misery went on until Phryne could bear it no longer. She was sleepy, after the bath, and it was four o'clock. She stood up.

'It is my turn next, Lydia,' she said, patting the stricken woman on the shoulder and receiving that disagreeable frisson one gets from touching a fish. 'Come to lunch with me at the Windsor tomorrow.'

'Oh, not tomorrow—I can't come tomorrow. Besides, I expect that you are very busy. I'll call you, shall I?'

'Yes, do,' agreed Phryne, rather bewildered by this abrupt unclinging of one whom she had diagnosed as an inveterate clinger. 'Nice to meet you, ladies. Good day!'

She resisted the impulse to run. The three women had seemed to be watching her closely. What was this all about?

'Do you have any advice as to stocks I could buy?' she asked, conscious of her speech blurring. She was tired; and Lydia was watching her narrowly.

'Oh, Lydia is the person to advise you,' gushed Beatrice.

'My husband says that she has a mind like a man when it comes to money. Of course, she's made her fortune in her own right—it's all her own money, so she can spend it or invest it as she likes.'

This was not in accord with Phryne's briefing at all. She wondered where Lydia had got her money. From her husband? It did not seem likely. Feeling increasingly unwell, she left.

Chapter Nine

To hunt sweet love and lose him
Between white arms and bosom
Between the bud and blossom
Between your throat and chin.

'Before Dawn', Algernon Swinburne

Phryne returned to the hotel feeling sleepy out of all proportion to her exertions. She wondered what had been in the bitter tea (of which she had drunk three cups), at Madame Breda's. She sent a boy down to the kitchen for mustard and mixed herself an impressive emetic. She began to be sure that she had been poisoned. Calmly and coldly, she drank down a large quantity of the revolting mixture, sat quietly until it worked, then dosed herself again.

Phryne began to shiver, and drank down a glass of milk in small sips. Her digestion settled down, after its rude shock, and she was suddenly very awake, purged and cold.

She decided that she was not going to be sick again, cleaned up carefully, and opened the bathroom window to freshen the air. She inhaled several breaths of smoky normality before she shut the window, and decided that the best thing to do was to go to bed until she was back to human temperatures again.

She undressed, dropping her clothes on the floor, and padded barefoot to the huge bed, heaped with covers, dived in and snuggled down. She wanted to think, but fell asleep in a moment, exhausted.

Waking about two hours later to voices in the sitting room, she heard someone say clearly, 'That'll fix her!' and the outer door shut. The lock clicked. Phryne tiptoed out to the doorway and surveyed the room. Only one thing had been moved: her coat. She picked it up and shook it. Out of the deep pocket flew the third small crunchy packet of the day, and this time Phryne was taking no chances. She opened it, and shook out some powder; touched to the end of her tongue, it had a powerfully numbing effect. She flushed packet and powder down the water-closet.

She surveyed the room helplessly. Nothing else appeared to have been moved. She was sure that the voices had not been there long; she usually woke easily. Perhaps they would not have had time to secrete any more little packages. She noticed that her main door had a bolt, and she threw it, then put herself back to bed, puzzled. The bed was heaped with bolsters and could have slept a regiment.

It was when she rolled over to the centre of the massive bed and encountered a warm human body that she realized Sasha had not gone.

He woke as she touched him, and enfolded her in a close embrace; feeling her instant resistance, he released her and fumbled until he found a hand. This he began to kiss, delicately, only stopping in his passage up her arm to answer her questions.

'Sasha, what are you doing here?'

'Waiting for you.'

'Why are you waiting for me?'

'I want you,' he said in surprise. 'You are magnificent. I, also, am magnificent. We shall be magnificent together,' he concluded placidly, reaching her shoulder and burying his face in her neck.

This accorded with Phryne's idea of the situation, and as far as she could see Sasha did not constitute a danger to her life. Her virtue, she felt, could take care of itself.

'Were you asleep when I went out to lunch?' she asked, relaxing into his arms and running her hands down his muscular back with pleasure.

'Certainly. I can sleep anywhere and I had not slept for three nights; therefore I sleep like a dog.'

'Log,' corrected Phryne absently, as the skilful mouth crept down toward her breast, and she felt her body beginning to react. 'Kiss me again,' she requested, and Sasha kissed her mouth. By the time she came up for air three minutes later, she was so aroused by the beautiful, amoral boy, his well-taught hands and the touch of his soft mouth that she would not have cared if he had lain down with her in Swanston Street.

He rubbed his face across her breasts, catching at the nipples as his mouth passed, and his hands caressed her as she drew him towards and over her, and locked her strong thighs around his waist.

As Sasha sank towards her, she abruptly recalled that his other persona was death, and joined with him in an odd mixture of ecstacy and horror. Their love-making was an encounter of strength. Phryne caught glimpses of them in the long mirror, like small bits cut from an erotic French engraving; Sasha's mouth coming slowly down onto a nipple which strained to meet him; a flash of thighs conjoined as if welded; the curve of her breast against the upper muscles of his arm, scored across with a long red line.

They finally collapsed, quite spent, into each other's arms.

'You see,' observed Sasha contentedly, 'I told you. Magnificent.'

'Yes,' agreed Phryne.

'Perhaps you will bear my baby,' commented Sasha. Phryne smiled. Carried away by passion she certainly was, but her diaphragm had been in place since last night. She had always had a realistic view of her ability to resist temptation. She did not reply. Sasha, having slept so long, was now awake. She threw him a gown and said, 'Do you wish to bathe? Dot will be back soon.'

'You are anxious not to offend your maid?' asked Sasha, puzzled. 'But I do not wish to bathe. I wish to keep the scent of you on my skin. My sister will be jealous! She wanted you, also.'

'I'd rather have you,' said Phryne, and leaned across the bed to kiss him. He really was a darling.

Sasha pulled on the tights and leotard, which Dot had mended and washed. Phryne donned a lounging robe and ordered tea. The tray came, and with it an anxious manager.

'Excuse me, Miss Fisher, but there's a policeman below, and he has a warrant to search your room for...for...drugs! I don't know whether we can stop him from coming in. So I will bring him to your door in about ten minutes. Perhaps you will arrange matters, if you will be so kind, by then.'

With an economical gesture, which indicated Sasha and the mess of garments, the manager left. Phryne poured a cup of tea.

'What would you have me do?' asked Sasha. He was lounging back in his chair, seemingly unmoved by the imminent invasion. 'Are you still concerned that my presence will shock your maid?'

'No,' said Phryne. 'And here she is at last.'

Dot opened the door, closed it behind her, and leaned on it, as if prepared to defend the portal with her body.

'The cops!' she gasped. 'That snooty manager said the cops are waiting! He's having a real ding-dong go with 'em in his office. Oh, Miss, what are we going to do?'

'First, we calm down. Next, we search the rooms for anything that might have been hidden.'

'What kind of thing?' stammered Dot, staring wildly around.

'Small packets of white powder,' said Phryne. 'Where would you hide one, in this room, Dot?'

In answer, Dot took a straight-backed chair, stepped up onto it, and scanned the top of the wardrobe. She leaned at a dangerous angle, reached and clutched, and showed Phryne her hand. Another small packet, crunchy and made of muslin.

Phryne lost no time in flushing it, also, into the plumbing, reflecting that if the storm-water mingled at all with the drinking water, the whole of Melbourne would be out on a jag of truly monumental proportions.

'Dot, you are a brick! Now, quick, a little tidying, so that we shall not shock the policeman.'

'What about 'im?' demanded Dot.

'He stays where he is,' stated Phryne. 'I am not going to be involved in a French farce.'

This went right over Dot's head, but she flew into action, sweeping up armloads of clothes, making the huge bed with a few economical movements, and hanging up coats and dresses. In five minutes the rooms presented a thoroughly respectable facade, belying the frantic activity needed to produce it. Sasha drank tea and smiled.

When the expected knock on the door came, Dot responded. She swung the heavy oak aside, and greeted the manager and his attendant policeman with freezing hauteur. Phryne was impressed.

'This is the Honourable Phryne Fisher. Miss Fisher, these gentlemen have a search warrant. I have had it checked and there is no doubt that they are policemen, based at Russell Street, and that their warrant is valid,' said the manager, his eyes darting about the room, seemingly pleased by the transformation from bohemianism.

Phryne uncoiled herself from the sofa, in a stiff tissue brocade which whispered as she moved. She bestowed a nod of appreciation on the manager, who had provided this breathing space on the pretext of checking the warrant and the policemen. He smiled frigidly.

'Well, gentlemen, might I have your names, and inquire what you are looking for?' she asked pleasantly.

The taller and older of the two said stiffly, 'I'm Detective-Inspector Robinson, and this is Senior-Constable Ellis.'

'We have a warrant to search this room for drugs. Woman Police-Constable Jones is available to search the ladies, and we will search this gentleman. Your name, Sir?'

'Sasha de Lisse,' said Sasha politely. 'Delighted.' This appeared to disconcert Detective-Inspector Robinson. He shook Sasha's outstretched hand, and then did not quite know what to do with it.

'What are you looking for?' asked Phryne again.

'Drugs,' answered the senior-constable importantly. 'On information received...' He desisted as his chief elbowed him in the ribs. Robinson hesitated, but Phryne waved a hand.

'By all means search everywhere,' she smiled. 'Shall I order some tea?'

'That is not necessary,' said Robinson. He and the senior-constable began to search, watched by Phryne, Dot, and Sasha. They were self-conscious, but they were thorough.

The senior-constable was older than Robinson, whom Phryne assumed to be about thirty. Ellis was short and plump, he must just have cleared the minimum height. He had black hair, slicked back from a low forehead, and something about his eyes made Phryne anxious. He seemed to be too happy and too smug for one who did not know that he would find anything. She summoned Dot to her, and instructed her to keep a very close eye upon Senior-Constable Ellis. Dot nodded, her teeth biting into her lower lip. Phryne patted her hand.

'Calm yourself, old dear; I don't take drugs,' she whispered, and Dot released her lip long enough to flash her a small, tense smile.

They had searched all of the clothes, the bathroom, and the bedroom, and had found nothing. Sasha laughed quietly at some private joke. The manager stood stiffly by the door. Dot and Phryne had accompanied the searchers into the bedroom, and emerged as they began to rummage through Dot's room and the sitting room.

As a last move, Constable Ellis took Phryne's cloth coat down and shook it. A package, done up in white paper with sealing wax at each end, shot out and broke on the parquet flooring. The manager stared. Sasha sat up, his jaw dropping. Phryne therewith acquitted him of any knowledge of the attempted plant. Dot gasped. Only Phryne seemed unaffected.

'Just as she said!' exclaimed Ellis, diving for the packet and scooping the powder into his hands. The detective-inspector looked at Phryne.

'Well, Miss, what is the explanation of this?'

'If you taste it, you'll see,' replied Phryne, composed. 'I have been attending too many dinners lately. It's bicarb, man,' she urged. 'Taste it!'

The detective-inspector wetted his finger and dipped it in the powder. There was a hushed silence as he conveyed his finger to his mouth. He smiled.

'It's bicarb all right,' he told Ellis. 'Now, Miss, there's just the personal search, and then we'll be on our way.'

'On one condition,' said Phryne, standing up. 'I'll be searched, and so will Mr de Lisse and Miss Williams, but only if you will be searched, too.'

'You want me to be searched?' asked the detective-inspector, puzzled. 'Why?'

'Just a whim,' said Phryne lightly. 'Come, won't you allow this small liberty? You have found no drugs, although your information received said that you would. This visit has caused the worthy Mr Smythe, the manager of this excellent hotel, a lot of trouble. He is waiting for you to leave before he asks me to follow, so I shall have to remove to some lesser hostelry.

'I might also say,' Phryne continued, 'that I have never used drugs. Proper investigation beforehand would have told you this. I detest the stuff, and to be accused of using it is wounding to my feelings. Unless you accede to my request, I am going to complain, and I shall continue to do so until I have had you both put back on the beat, directing traffic in Swanston Street. Well?'

'I've got nothing to hide,' said Robinson. Ellis drew his chief aside by the sleeve.

'But, Sir, we're policemen!' he stuttered.

'I know that,' agreed Robinson. 'So?'

'We could arrest them and take them down to the station; search them there,' suggested Ellis. 'It isn't right, us being searched.'

Phryne unbuttoned the brocade robe.

'If you try to take me to any station,' she declared in a cold, remote voice, 'you will have to take me like this.' She dropped the robe and stood revealed, quite naked, pearly and beautiful. The manager, averting his eyes, allowed a small smile to cross his lips. You couldn't out-manoeuvre the Windsor's clients that easily. The policemen were taken comprehensively aback.

'Very well, Miss,' agreed Robinson. Ellis was gaping at Phryne open-mouthed, and his chief nudged him in the ribs.

'Call WPC Jones,' said Robinson, admitting defeat.

'The ladies can have the bedroom, and we'll stay in here. Mr Smythe can search us. If you will, Sir?'

Jones accompanied Phryne and Dot to the bedroom. She was a tight-lipped young woman with black hair dragged back into a bun. Dot went first, stripping off each garment with sullen fury, then reassuming them in cold silence.

Phryne had merely to remove the robe again. Outside, they heard Mr Smythe ask politely, 'What is this, then, Senior-Constable?' A rending noise followed. All three women were pressed to the bedroom door.

'What do you think has happened?' asked Dot.

'They've found a little packet of white muslin and paper on Senior-Constable Ellis,' reported WPC Jones. 'I never did like him, smarmy little hound. But what could have possessed him to do such a lame-brained thing?'

'Money,' said Phryne quietly.

'I thought so.' The police-woman looked Phryne in the face. 'We haven't got many rotten apples,' she observed. 'It's a good clean force, on the whole. If you've winkled out a bad'un, we owe you some thanks.'

Surprised, Phryne shook hands with Jones, something she would have given good money against ever happening, some ten minutes ago.

'Can we come out?' asked Jones through the door, and Detective-Inspector Robinson assented, gruffly. Dot, Phryne and WPC Jones emerged to be confronted with an unusual sight. The manager and Robinson were holding a semi-naked constable by the arms, and brandishing a small packet of the type with which Phryne had become wearyingly familiar. Colloidium plaster still hung from the packet in two long strips.

'You see? He had it attached to his chest by this plaster. And the next time you seek to execute a search warrant in my hotel, Detective-Inspector, I shall have every policeman searched before they come in. I never heard of such a thing! Innocent guests have been persecuted and the reputation of the Victorian police has been fatally compromised!'

Phryne agreed. 'Yes, what Mr Robert Sanderson, MP, is going to say when I tell him, I can't imagine. A most shocking thing. My guests and my confidential maid have been stripped and searched in a way only felons usually experience, not to mention myself. What are you going to do about it?'

Detective-Inspector Robinson shook his colleague ferociously. 'Speak up, you silly coot! Who paid you? Why did you do it, Ellis? You violated your oath, you'll be flung out of the Force, you've got a wife and four children, how are you going to live? Out with it, man!'

Ellis strove to speak, choked, and shook his head. Robinson struck him hard across the mouth. Dot watched unmoved. WPC Jones sat down, composed. Sasha watched amusedly, as though it were an indifferent show put on for his benefit. Mr Smythe released the arm he was holding and retreated a little. He neither liked nor approved of physical violence.

Ellis spat blood and said, 'It was a woman.'

'Old or young? Any accent?'

'Can't tell, it was on the telephone. No accent that I heard. She said, fifty pounds to plant the stuff.'

'Where did you get it?' asked Phryne, sharply.

'She sent it. Just the one little packet. I picked it up, with the fifty pounds, from the post office.'

'What post office?'

'GPO, Sir, she said…'

'She said what?'

'That if I didn't do it, she'd kill my wife and kids.'

'And you believed it?' spat Robinson. Ellis seemed surprised.

'Not at first, Sir, but she said she'd give me a demonstration. You recall those children, found with cut throats, dead in the beds, with their mother dead beside them? That was her work, she said, and you know we don't have a motive or a suspect for that.'

'Fool,' snapped Robinson. 'The victim's husband did it. He's down at Russell Street this moment, spilling it all.'

'You're sure, Sir?'

'Of course. I told you so at the time, you cretin.'

'I…I believed her…' stammered Ellis, and began to cry.

Detective-Inspector Robinson dropped the arm he was holding and turned away in disgust.

'Christ have pity,' he exclaimed.

'Pour the Senior-Constable some tea, Dot. Now, take my hanky and blow. That's right, now drink this,' and Phryne administered tea and a small glass of Benedictine. The young man drank and blew.

In a few moments, he was recovered enough to speak.

'So I got the packet and I was going to plant it. I did believe her, Sir. I needed the money, my wife has to have an operation… please, Sir, don't sack me. We wouldn't be able to live.'

He was now crying freely. Phryne took the Detective-Inspector aside. He accompanied her, still fuming.

'Need this go any further?'

'Of course it does, he's taken a bribe.'

'Yes, but under great duress. Could you make a confidential report, not actually sack him, but keep him on? You see, if he is thrown out on the street, it will be a sign to whoever is doing this that the plot has failed, and I don't want that to happen. Twig?'

'Yes. But what have you done to attract this kind of trouble?'

'A good question. I don't know. But I shall find out. Can we co-operate? Don't sack Ellis yet, and I'll let you in on the arrests, once I am in a position to be sure.'

'Dangerous, Miss.'

'Yes, but only I can do it, and it's better than being bored. Come on, be a sport. Think of getting your hands on a prominent local coke dealer.'

'Well…Only for a short time,' he temporized, 'a week, say.'

'Two,' bargained Phryne.

'Split the difference. Say ten days.'

'Done. You'll take no action for ten days, and I'll let you in on the kill. A deal?'

'A deal,' agreed Robinson. 'I'll have a word with WPC Jones, too. Ellis is a fool, but until now I would have said that he was as honest as the day. Here's my telephone number, Miss Fisher. Don't get in too deep, will you?'

'I am already,' said Phryne. 'Mr Smythe, I have accepted Detective-Inspector Robinson's apology, and I think that we can declare the matter closed. Good night, gentlemen,' she breezed, as Robinson, Ellis, and the manager exited. She closed the door on them and sank down onto the sofa, where Sasha put an arm around her.

'Dot,' called Phryne, 'order more tea, and come and have some yourself. That concludes the entertainment for the night, I hope.'

Phryne said no more until Dot came reluctantly and sat beside her, brushing down her uniform jacket as though the touch of the hapless constable had soiled it.

Sasha poured her some tea and leaned back again, encircling Phryne with a strong comforting arm. The young woman was trembling; Sasha wondered if the Princesse had over-estimated Phryne's strength. Dot sipped her tea suspiciously.

'Well,' said Phryne, her voice vibrant with excitement. 'They are now after me, as well as Sasha. This is excellent, is it not?'

'Oh, excellent,' murmured Sasha ironically. 'Excellent!'

'What do you mean, Miss?' asked Dot, setting down her tea-cup with a rattle. 'Who is after you? The person what hid the little bag on the wardrobe? I'd like to lay my hands on 'im, I would,' she continued, biting vindictively into a tea-cake. 'E'd know e'd been in a fight.'

'Him, indeed. Sasha, it is now time to tell us all that you know about this *Roi des Neiges*. Begin, please,' ordered Phryne. She was quite cool. The tremor had been hunting arousal, not fear. Phryne was enjoying herself.

Obediently, Sasha settled himself into the curve of Phryne's side.

'We were visiting Paris, before the end of the Great War; I was only a child, and I do not recall much about it; just the sound of the big guns, coming nearer and nearer, and Mama being frightened, and we could not sleep. I do not remember Russia, which we left in the winter—though perhaps the cold, that I remember from very small, the snow and the cold wind. Paris was cold, too. Mama and Grandmama came to Paris in 1918, just before the Peace was being signed. They had accomplished a great journey in escaping to Archangel, where the English were; they had gone most of the way on foot.'

'All very affecting, make a good film, but *revenons à nos moutons* if you please,' snapped Phryne, resisting the hypnotic attraction of the brown eyes and the honeyed voice.

'Patience,' smiled Sasha, not at all crushed. 'If you interrupt me, I shall lose my memory. So. We were all in Paris, my father having been killed by the Revolutionaries, and Mama sold some of the family jewels to keep us fed. The Tscarnov emeralds, and many other beautiful stones she sold in that winter.

'We sought a protector, and not Mama but Grandmama found one—an Englishman, a Lord, and he found us a flat and nurtured us as if we had been his own, for love of Grandmama—how we laughed about it, Mama and me!'

'Yes, and so?' asked Phryne impatiently. Dot was staring at Sasha as though he had dropped in from another planet.

'So, we lived with the English Lord until we were sixteen, then we were sent away to school in Switzerland. We were away for a year, Elli and me, and Grandmama wrote that all was well in Paris, so we did not inquire any more. Then we returned, two years ago, and found that the old Lord was dead—it was sad, he was a generous man—and that Mama was dying. We could see that she was dying. She had become habituated to the cocaine, and since the old Lord had left Grandmama a great deal of money, she could buy what she liked. She was sniffing it by the handful, and after the dose she would become bright and happy, like the Mama of yesterday, then morose, then bitter, then screaming and falling into fits. So the cycle. She did not sleep. She begged us to kill her.

'This was not necessary, for the saving of my immortal soul, as after a few weeks I might have done it,' admitted Sasha. Tears ran unchecked down his cheeks. 'She died. Before she died, we besought her to tell us who had done this to her, who had introduced her to this deathly drug. She would only tell us that the King, *Le Roi* of Snow had given it to her for free. She thought him kind—then the price had gone up, and then up. She had sold all her jewels. But Grandmama knew that some of the jewellery had not gone to pawnbrokers. This King had a taste for fine stones, we heard, and the great necklace of the Tsars, at least, had gone to him intact. And the Princesse's pearls.'

Something that Sasha had said hit Phryne's intuition like a lance through the solar plexus. He paused, feeling the tightening of her muscles, but she could not pin down the thought. She waved him on.

'And a collar of diamonds made, it was said, for Catherine the Great. Grandmama said that if we could survey Parisian society, then we would one day see the necklace, and then we would have our man. Thus was born *Le Théâtre Masqué*. Both my sister and I had danced together since we were children; also we had no profession. We danced the old story of the Maiden and Death, and Paris was intrigued. Night after night we played to packed houses in the old Opera, and night after night we scanned the jewelled ladies, looking for the necklace of Catherine. We even began to make a profit,' observed Sasha with artless astonishment. 'Always we looked. Then, at last, we saw it. On the bosom of a demimondaine, a worthless woman. I called upon her, and she said that it was only lent; the owner was an American parvenu. Him I spoke to, and at last he told me from whom he had bought it; and I came here to find that man, and to kill him...May I have some more tea?'

'The name, Sasha, the name?'

'But if I tell you the name, you may warn him, and thus my revenge will be lost,' complained Sasha. 'Also the Princesse will skin me.'

'Ah, but if you do not tell me the name, I will skin you, and I am closer than the Princesse,' said Phryne, baring her teeth and reaching for a fruit knife, as though willing to begin the skinning instantly. Sasha shrugged fluidly.

'His name is Andrews,' he said dismissively. 'We saw the man at the soirée where I had the delight of meeting you. He does not seem to be clever enough to be our *Roi*. But that is what the American told me. And I saw the sale note. A mere fortune, he paid for that necklace, when it was priceless.'

'Are there any more of your mother's jewels left unaccounted for?' asked Phryne.

Sasha nodded. 'Some. A great diamond cluster, and a brooch in the shape of a flying bird by Fabergé, in diamonds and enamel; a long string of pink pearls. We have not seen them yet.'

'I cannot believe that it is Andrews. He hasn't the brain!' exclaimed Phryne. 'Go on. Why did the Princesse take me to the Bath House of Madame Breda?'

'To show you the system. That night I met you, being under the special protection of *Notre Dame de douleur*, I was being pursued by the minions; I had been at a drop.'

'In Toorak?' gasped Dot. Phryne considered this.

'Yes, it does seem very odd and unlikely, Dot, but stranger things have been known, though not many. Go on, Sasha.'

Sasha obligingly provided the address, which Phryne wrote down in a small, leather-covered notebook.

'How did you know that the drop was to take place there?'

'The maid from the Bath House of Madame Breda told the Princesse; Gerda, I believe, is the name. With a stupidity which I cannot emphasize enough, I allowed myself to be seen.'

'Who was the carrier?'

'Madame herself, it seems. Two men were following her, at a distance; it was they who pursued me. Madame pays calls at the houses of her most favoured customers with Gerda, to massage them; she disposes of her "beauty powders" while there.'

'These men know you?' asked Dot, concentrating.

Sasha nodded. 'Indeed, they know me. They seem to be Madame's guardians while she carries the snow; most of the time, they are not with her. Luckily, they are not very intelligent.'

'Possibly not,' agreed Phryne, recalling Thug One and Thug Two. Sasha stood up and stretched.

'Now, Milady, shall I leave you?'

Phryne stretched out a hand to Sasha. She was very attracted to him but did not trust him out of her sight.

'No. Stay until morning,' she said, smiling. 'It's too late to be wandering the street. Won't your relatives be worried about you?'

'No. My sister will know that I am well. We are twins.' He bowed slightly to Dot and went into the bathroom, collecting Phryne's mannish dressing-gown on the way. Dot and Phryne eyed one another.

'Well, are you going back to your mother, now that my true depravity has been revealed?' asked Phryne with a smile. Dot grinned.

'I reckon you're different, Miss—outside the rules. And he's a sheik. Lucky to get 'im, p'raps. I'm for my bed, it's late.'

'So it is—good night, Dot.'

'Goodnight,' replied Dot as she closed her door. Phryne retired to her bed, to fortify herself with Sasha and philosophy against the coming trials of the new day. She did not doubt that there would be some.

Chapter Ten

Take a whiff, take a whiff, take a whiff on me
Ever'body take a whiff on me…
'The Cocaine Blues',
Traditional American Song

The coming trials announced themselves at eight of the morning in the person of Dr MacMillan. Dot, who was awake, let the agitated woman in, and knocked discreetly to rouse Phryne, who rolled over with a sleepy curse into Sasha's arms and spent an engrossing five minutes in extracting herself therefrom. Finally Dot entered, carrying two cups of tea, and Phryne gulped hers, rumpled her black hair into order, and staggered into the bathroom.

Twenty minutes later she emerged, respectably clothed, demanding aspirins and forestalling Elizabeth MacMillan with a languid wave.

'Elizabeth, I can't possibly attend to anything intellectual yet,' she groaned. 'Dot, get some black coffee.'

She lit a gasper and sank back into the sofa. The doctor surveyed her sternly.

'If you will gad about all night, and begin the day with black coffee and cigarettes, you'll be on my hands in a month, young woman,' she observed. 'And you'll be a hag before your time. I have something important to say and I've a woman in labour waiting for me to return; attend, if you please!'

Phryne drank her coffee. Her eyes lost their glaze; she was awake and alert.

'I apologize, Elizabeth, how foul I am being! Go on, of course!'

'Those packets you sent me. What are you playing at?'

'Why? What was in them?'

'This one,' said Dr MacMillan, laying down the chemist's package sealed with red wax, 'is sodium chloride: common salt. This one,' she laid down the muslin package, 'is pure cocaine. Where you got them is not my concern, but I'd advise you to have a care, my dear. These people have a reputation for being over-hasty in their actions.'

'So I'd heard...' murmured Phryne. The little packet had appeared in her pocket while she was at Madame Breda's, and it was real cocaine. But the big packet which she had obtained, as real cocaine, from the Princesse de Grasse was salt.

'Interesting salt,' added the Doctor, dragging herself to her feet. 'Traces of all sorts of elements in it. I reckon that it is Dead Sea salt—they use it for salt water baths in some beauty establishments, you know. Well, I must be off.'

'Stay at least for a cup of tea, Elizabeth!' protested Phryne, but the older woman shook her head.

'Biological processes won't wait for tea,' she observed, and was gone. She passed Mr Smythe, on her way out.

The manager was polite, but firm. He realized that Miss Fisher had been totally innocent of any wrongdoing in the matter of the police visit on the previous evening. He was delighted that it had all ended so amicably. But there must be no more of it. Another such episode and, for the good of his hotel, he would be reluctantly compelled to ask Miss Fisher to find alternative lodgings. Phryne smiled and assured him that she did not anticipate any such contingency, and that a sizeable *douceur* should be added to the bill, to soothe his wounded feelings. Mr Smythe withdrew, suavely pleased, and closed the door quietly behind him.

'Quick—lock the door, Dot! Someone else will waltz in and expect a hearing before breakfast,' cried Phryne, and then added, 'now don't open it for anyone except Room Service! Gosh, what was that quotation—"I never was so bethumped with words since first I called my brother's father Dad". Shakespeare, I think. Sasha! Time to get up!'

The young man, who had evidently fallen asleep again, leapt from the bedclothes and was dressed in a minute. He joined Phryne on the sofa looking irritatingly alert and uncrumpled. Phryne glared at him resentfully.

'How can you possibly look so healthy at this hour? It's unnatural. Ghastly. However. What do you have to do today?'

'I must call at Scott's; my sister and I have a matinee at ten, and another at three, and an evening show tonight at the Tivoli. I think that the Princesse would like to talk to you,' he added.

'And I would like to talk to her. Oh, Lord, now what?'

Dot answered the knock, and came back with the breakfast trolley.

'At last,' said Phryne, and collected a boiled egg.

By nine she was accompanying Sasha down the steps and around the corner to Scott's hotel. Two letters awaited her at the desk on the way out: a thin blue envelope with gold edges and a thick white one with no decoration at all. She put them into her clutch-purse to read later, concealing them from Sasha. Phryne did not intend to share all of her information with anyone. Dot had her orders, and the telephone number of the admirable policeman, if Phryne should not return within three hours. Sasha offered his arm, and Phryne slipped her gloved hand between his elbow and his smooth, muscular side. He really was very attractive.

He seemed to catch her thought, for his mouth curved up at the corners, and he smiled an intimate and self-satisfied smile which, in another man, Phryne would have found very irritating. In Sasha it was endearing. There was no masculine pride of conquest in him, but a childish, actor's pride in the deserved applause of an educated audience. The sun shone thinly, fashioning a cap of red light for Phryne's shiny hair. They approached Scott's, a hotel not of the *dernier cri*, but respectable. The doorman surveyed Sasha's costume with deep disapproval, but allowed him in, pulling the door open grudgingly. Phryne did not tip him, which deepened his depression.

In their room the Princesse and Elli looked up from the counting of a pile of shillings as Sasha swept in, then returned to their task.

'Boy, you must bathe and dress,' snapped the Princesse. 'You have a performance in an hour. Elli, take up all the coins and put them away. Please be seated, Miss Fisher. Tea?'

Phryne assented, removed three laddered pairs of tights from an easy chair and sat down, prepared to be receptive.

The Princesse filled a bone-china cup from her samovar and passed it over, while Elli poured the coins into a soft bag and vanished into another room, presumably to supply Sasha with a clean leotard and tights. Phryne remembered the death-mask, and produced it from her coat pocket. The Princesse snatched it, and pointed a long, gnarled finger at the red smudges along one edge.

'You?' her voice was sharp. Phryne flicked a hand toward the other room.

'Him,' she returned, equally brisk.

The old woman's face seemed to shrink in on itself.

'Ah. He will tell me, then. You were unhurt?'

'Of course,' replied Phryne. 'And he was not too badly injured. Just a scratch along the arm. Not enough to hamper him.'

'Ah,' gloated the Princesse. 'You found him a pleasant diversion? If only someone would marry him. That is almost his only skill—that and dancing. If we do not have some good fortune, he will become a gigolo, and that is no life for a descendant of princes. How useless we are! I was taught nothing, nothing, when I was a child, because it was thought that only peasants worked. But I learned by finding things out for myself. Then the Tsar's daughters became nurses, and so I was allowed to acquire another skill. It was not until I came to Paris, though, that I discovered that my most saleable skill was the same as Sasha's. Ah me...it has all been most amusing, and it may all come to an end very soon. What happened?'

'Someone was chasing him. We escaped by a ruse. Princesse, did you know that the powder which you sold me was salt?'

The lined face showed no change of emotion, but the voice dropped a half-octave, and the old woman replied slowly, 'Salt? That is not what I paid for. What is Gerda playing at?'

'I don't know. Have you bought any of the same product from her before?'

'*En effet...mais pas tout-à-fait,*' explained the Princess. 'She always found some reason not to sell.'

'Reason not to sell?'

'Yes. Sometimes that Madame was watching her, that the stuff had not been delivered, that it had all been sold...*Tiens!* Salt! And we paid cocaine prices for it!'

The old woman began to laugh, and after a moment, it struck Phryne as funny too. Phryne tasted her tea; it was very strong, flavoured with lemon, and she disliked it.

There still remained the matter of the packet of real cocaine that had been found in her pocket, with the cryptic note. And the policeman, Ellis, had gasped, 'just as she said' when the chemist's packet had fallen out of her pocket. That argued that the person who had set Phryne up for a drug-possession charge knew about the Princesse's transaction in Madame Breda's. That limited the persons to the Princesse and her suite, Gerda, and possibly Madame Breda—any one of whom might have slipped Phryne the real cocaine.

The Princesse stopped laughing, mopped her eyes, and poured herself some more tea. She tilted her chin at Phryne. 'Are you further along in this investigation?' demanded the old woman, and Phryne shook her head.

'I have an address; or perhaps, a person,' said the Princesse. 'It may help you.' She extracted a folded slip of paper from the recesses of her costume, which, at this hour, consisted of an old-fashioned corset cover, and a long, sumptuous blue satin robe, partially faded. Phryne unfolded the paper.

'Seventy-nine Little Lon,' she read with difficulty, it being scrawled in villianous ink.

'Who is this Lon?' asked the Princesse. 'That is what I would like to know. Perhaps he is our *succinsin*.'

'*Succinsin*?'

'Scoundrel.'

'I'll find him,' promised Phryne, and took her leave of the de Grasses. The beautiful Sasha kissed her very gently and presented her to his sister to kiss. Phryne found the two of them so similar that she did not object. She knew they had designs on sharing her, and began to think that might prove extremely engrossing—then dragged her salacious mind and body away. She walked loudly down the hall as she left, then crept back to listen at the door. She heard the voice of the old woman speaking their familiar French.

'How was the *milch* cow, eh? Did you please her?'

'Certainly,' said Sasha smugly. 'I stroked her until she purred. She is of a sensuality unusual in English women. I think that I have ensnared her. She will want me again.'

'Did she pay you?' grated the old voice, and Sasha must have shrugged, for Phryne heard the old woman slap him lightly.

'Grandmama, do not be so greedy!' he protested, laughing. 'Next time she will pay. In the end, I think she will marry me.'

Phryne hoped that her grinding teeth could not be heard through the door.

'Perhaps. At least, you shall not waste your strength in vain. She is generous, I think. Yes. And she is clever.'

'Truly, she saved me by a trick—she thinks with remarkable speed. I think she will find the *Roi des Neiges*.'

'Yes, she will find him, and then you will follow her. And then…' she made a choking noise, probably accompanied by a graphic gesture.

'Revenge is sweet, children, and we shall have every *centime* out of him before he dies. With that profit, I believe that you may retire, and your sister may marry for love.'

The old woman cackled gleefully. Elli protested.

'I shall not marry. I do not like men. Take me with you, Sasha, when you go to Miss Fisher again! Please, Sashushka, please!'

'I do not know if she would like that...' said Sasha, considering. 'But I will ask her. I must bathe—we have a performance. Come and wash my back,' said Sasha. Phryne went soundlessly down the hall. She passed the doorman without a word. He awarded a gloomy stare to her retreating back, and sighed. That woman was class, the doorman could see that, and it was wise to be on the side of class. Or so the doorman had been told. It had never done him any good.

Phryne soon realized that first, she was attracting attention by hurrying, and that second, running in a tight skirt, loose coat and high heels required concentration of a high order, which she did not feel that she could spare at the moment. Therefore she walked into a café and ordered a pot of tea, lit a gasper, and fumed. So that was why the Russians had adopted her! As a decoy duck! The perfidy of such creatures!

She drank the tea too quickly and burnt her mouth. There was no point in getting angry with them. The Russians were as amoral and attractive as kittens. One thing, however, she vowed. Not one penny would Sasha extract from her purse, and she was not going to marry him. To be exploited was the fate of many women, but Phryne was not going to be one of them if she could help it.

⁂

Phryne opened the first of her letters and found that the solid white envelope contained an invitation, in impeccable taste, from Mr Sanderson, MP, to dinner that night. She replaced the card in its envelope and tore open the scented one. A large sheet of violently violet paper bore the subscription of Lydia Andrews' house, and a short message asking Miss Fisher to call at her earliest opportunity. Phryne snorted. The woman was a clinger, after all. She crumpled the message and left the café, dropping Lydia's invitation into a rubbish-bin. She would go to dinner with Sanderson, but before then she and Dot had places to go and people to see.

The first thing to do was to hire a car. Phryne was a good driver, and disliked having to constantly call taxis.

There was a garage in this street, she recollected, down at the edge of the city, where the livery stables had been for the city's hansom cabs. Phryne caught a cable-car, holding on tightly as instructed, and breathed in the strange, ozone-flavoured burned dust scent, until she was dropped off at the corner of Spencer Street. The garage was large and newly painted and an attentive, if oil-stained young man stood up suddenly as she entered. The dim interior of the ex-stable was gleaming with brass lamps and lovingly polished paintwork. The young man wiped his hands hastily on a piece of cotton waste and hurried toward her.

'Yes, Ma'am, what can I do for you?'

'I want to hire a car,' said Phryne. 'What have you got?'

The young man gestured toward a sober Duchesse, high-axled, with a closed body built by a coachmaker. Phryne grinned.

'I'm not ready for something as quiet as that. What about this one?' she asked, patting the bright red enamel of a Hispano-Suiza racing car. It was built rakishly low, wide-bodied to hold up an engine of fiendish power. The young man looked Phryne up and down, attempting to gauge her nerve.

'Take it out for a spin, shall we? Then you will see that I can drive her all right. I wouldn't harm a lovely lady like this—but I need a fast car. Come on.'

The young man threw down the cotton rag and followed helplessly.

He watched Phryne narrowly as she choked the engine, swung the starter with a skilled flip, and started the engine. The cylinders cut in with a roar; the muffler was not a standard piece of equipment on this car. Phryne took the wheel, released the brake, and the car rolled out into Spencer Street. She achieved a neat turn to the left.

They were a mile out along past the cricket ground when she opened the throttle and allowed the full power of the engine to surge forward. The mileometer flicked up into the red; the mechanic leaned forward and bellowed, 'That's fast enough, Miss! I'm convinced! You can have her!'

Phryne allowed the car to slacken speed and, for the first time, took her eye off the road. She seemed a little disappointed.

'Oh, very well,' she grumbled, completed a screaming U-turn, and proceeded to whisk the mechanic back to his garage with more expedition and skill than he had before experienced.

They swept into the garage, and Phryne stopped the engine.

'I want it for a week, to begin with,' she said affably. The young man observed that her shining cap of black hair was not even ruffled. 'I don't mind what it costs,' she added. 'And if you really jib at hiring it out, I'll buy it. A lovely vehicle...how much?'

'I don't want to sell it, Miss, I'm going to race it myself...I rebuilt the engine, took me two months...'

'Fifty quid for the week?' offered Phryne, and the mechanic, with a celerity not entirely induced by this monstrous offer, tossed the starting handle into the car and received the bundle of notes.

Phryne restarted the warm engine, set the car at Spencer Street as she would set a hunting hack at a hedge, and roared out, scattering pedestrians. The young man picked up the card, noticed that his client was staying at the Windsor, and closed the shop early. He needed a drink.

Phryne rolled to a halt at the main entrance to the hotel and called to the doorman.

'Where can I leave her?'

The man's jaw dropped. He hurried forward.

'Park her just here, Miss, and I'll keep an eye on her. Beautiful car, Miss. Lagonda, is she?'

'Hispano-Suiza; see the stork on the radiator cap? First one was built for King Alfonso of Spain—this is the 46CV, isn't she splendid?'

Phryne eased the car into the indicated kerb and switched off the engine. She swallowed to regain her hearing. The Hispano-Suiza had been roaring like a lion.

She ran up the steps and ascended the great staircase, reached her own suite, and surprised Dot in the middle of darning a stocking, so that she ran a needle into her finger.

'Leave that, Dot, we're going for a ride.'

'A ride, Miss? In a motor-car?' Dot sucked her finger and draped the stocking over the chair back. 'What shall you wear?'

Phryne was already rummaging in the wardrobe, flinging clothes out by the armload.

'Trousers, perhaps, and a big coat. I know that it's May, but it's freezing out there. Shall we go for a picnic?'

'It might rain,' said Dot doubtfully, rehanging the garments as Phryne tossed them away.

'Never mind. The car's got a hood. Ring down and ask the kitchen for a luncheon basket. And an umbrella.'

Phryne found her greatcoat and donned trousers in dark respectable bank-manager's serge, while Dot obeyed.

'Ten minutes, they say, Miss.'

'Good. And what are you going to wear? Would you like to borrow some trousers?'

Dot shuddered, and Phryne laughed.

'Take your winter coat, the blue cloche, and the carriage rug, then you'll be warm enough. I don't know how far we'll be going.'

'Why, Miss, there's all the parks to have picnics in, we don't have to go out of the city,' protested Dot, who had no love for open, unsafe spaces with no conveniences.

'Now then, off we go!' said Phryne. 'Got everything?'

Dot picked up her handbag and the coat and the carriage-rug, which was of kangaroo-skin, and trailed her excitable employer down the stairs.

The kitchen had provided a hamper, which the doorman had already loaded into the rear of the auto, and Phryne leapt into the driver's seat as Dot ensconced herself, very gingerly, in the passenger's seat.

'Miss, do you mean to drive?' she whispered, and Phryne laughed.

'Miss May Cunliffe, champion of the 1924 Cairo road race, taught me to drive, and said that I had the makings of a racer,' she declared, as the doorman swung the engine over and it caught with a throaty roar. 'You're safe enough with me, Dot. Thanks,' she screamed to the doorman, tossing him a two-bob bit. He bowed.

'All clear, Miss,' he yelled and Phryne steered the car out into the road. Dot shut her eyes and commended her soul to God.

'Eight litre engine, overhead cam, multiple disc clutch, live axle drive,' Phryne was yelling over the noise of the car, which sounded to Dot like a big gun. 'Won the challenge at the Brickyard seventy miles an hour for eighteen hours—oh, it's a spiffing machine! One hundred horse power at 1600 revs per minute—I wonder if he'd change his mind and sell it to me? Dot? Dot, open your eyes!'

Dot obeyed, saw a looming market van skid to a halt, and shut them again.

'It will be better when we're out of the city. I need to pick up a couple of friends of mine. They should be waiting at the corner of Spencer Street…ah, there they are!'

She jammed on the brakes, and waved. Dot, thrown forward, peered apprehensively at a battered taxi-cab, and saw an arm wave, giving some sort of signal; then Phryne pushed the Hispano-Suiza into a higher gear. The railway yards shot past, and Dot, surprised to find herself alive, squinted under her hat-brim, tears filling her eyes as the wind whipped past. Landmarks were flowing away from her. They were on Dynon Road, heading West with tearing speed. The long, grey-green swamps, owned by the railways, were almost gone; the bridge slipped under the fleeting wheels, and the roar of the massive engine, vibrating, seemed to enter Dot's bones. Half an hour passed in this way.

'Where are we going?' yelled Dot, surprising herself with the volume she could produce. Phryne's gaze did not move from the road.

'Just along the river here, and then we'll stop,' she shrieked. 'Look back, Dot, and see if they're following...'

Toiling in their magnificent wake, motor labouring gallantly, the Morris taxi-cab was visible only as a spot in the road. Phryne slowed the Hispano-Suiza and they trundled along the unmade road by the river, where many craft were moored, mostly small yachts and pleasure-boats.

On the other bank, the market gardens stretched as far as Dot could see. She sighted the flat cane hats of the Chinese working among the winter-cabbage and broccoli.

'Oh, we're going to the Tea gardens!' Dot exclaimed, as the Morris jounced and turned the corner, and the two cars proceeded at a more decorous pace.

These gardens had been well-planned, and put to use the excellent soil to be found by the river in planting beds of exotic flowers, augmenting the pleasance created by groves of lemon-scented gum and wattle. It being May, the gardens were silent and a little bedraggled. Even evergreens look depressed in the winter, Phryne thought, as she brought the car to a standstill and told Dot that she was safe. The Morris halted and seemed to sag on its wheels, while the bonnet gave forth a cloud of steam.

A resident peacock surveyed the newcomers, considered displaying his tail, and decided against it. A voice was heard from the other side of the Morris.

'Cec! Give a man a hand, can't ye?'

'Whassamatter?' asked Cec, who sounded sleepy.

'Bloody door's come undone again. Got a bit of wire?'

There was a scuffle as Cec found a piece of wire and secured the door, and they both got out and surveyed their vehicle.

'I reckon she's about had it, mate,' observed Cec, sadly. Bert took off his hat, wiped his forehead, and replaced it.

'No, mate, she'll be apples. She just needs a spell. We can fill her up again before we go—plenty of water in the creek.'

They walked over to where Phryne knelt, offering Dot a sip of brandy.

'Come over all unnecessary, has she?' asked Bert. 'I reckon a drop's the best cure. Always cures me, eh, Cec? That car's a bit of all right, though, goes like a bat out of...I mean, goes well. Lucky there aren't no coppers round.'

Dot sat up, refused the brandy, and declared her complete fitness for anything.

'Well, gentlemen, I've brought a picnic lunch. Where shall we eat it?' asked Phryne, stowing the flask in a side-pocket of the car. Bert looked at Cec.

'There's the thingummy,' he suggested, indicating a gazebo evidently shipped direct from Brighton Pavilion.

'Well, it has a roof, and there's not room for us all and the picnic in the car,' sighed Phryne, who loathed Rococo architecture. 'Come on.'

Bert and Cec picked up the basket and Dot gathered the rug and the handbags. It was not until they were seated in relative comfort, with the plates loaded with pheasant and ham and Russian salad, that she broached her subject.

'I want your help, gentlemen, and you want mine,' she said. 'More salad?'

Bert, to whom *salade russe* was a novelty to which he would like to become accustomed, accepted more and nodded.

'Where did you two meet?' Phryne asked on impulse. Bert swallowed his mouthful and grinned.

'In the army first. Then I was working down the docks, and Cec was too. Me and Cec palled up, because we were on the same gang. The Reds, they called us. The Party ain't too popular with the Bosses, so we found we didn't get picked up at the Wailing Wall any more, the Bucks sorta looked over our heads.'

'Wailing Wall?' asked Phryne, fogged. 'Bucks?'

'The pick-up point, that's the Wailing Wall, and the foremen, they're the Bucks,' explained Bert. 'So me and Cec, we give it up as a bad job, and a mate of ours lent us the cab, and we been making a crust as a taxi. Hard yakka, but,' observed Bert, sadly. 'And all that "yes sir" and "no sir" is against our nature. Still, it's a living,' he concluded. 'Any more of that fowl? And what do you want us to do, Miss? And what's your game? Being polite, you know.'

'Fill up your glasses and I'll tell you some of the story.'

Suppressing the matter of the poisoning of Lydia Andrews, which Phryne now regarded as an excellent idea, she told the cab drivers the tale of the Russian dancers, the Bath House of Madame Breda, the police search, and the packet of real cocaine. She disclosed her only clue: Seventy-nine Little Lon.

'Little Lonsdale Street!' exclaimed Bert. 'And you reckon that these counter-revolutionaries ain't tumbled to it?'

'I don't think so,' temporized Phryne. 'They would not have asked anyone else, and they assumed Little Lon. was a person. It might be a trap, though. I suspect that Gerda is playing the Princesse along for what she can get—I've got no evidence against Madame Breda except Sasha's insistence that he was following her when he was stabbed. That was the night you picked us up in Toorak.'

'Yair, and you stuck a gun in me ear,' chuckled Bert, not at all abashed by the memory. 'Would you recognize the gangsters again, Miss?'

'Yes,' said Phryne. The repulsive faces of Thugs One and Two were imprinted on her memory. 'Did you see them?'

'Nah, but we might a seen 'em earlier. You saw Cokey Billings, eh, Cec?'

'When? and where?' demanded Phryne. Cec rubbed his jaw.

'About half after midnight, in that street, too. With Gentleman Jim and the Bull.'

'Who are they?'

'Bad men, Miss. Cokey Billings never worked with us—he's a tea-leaf—lift your roll out of your kick without a qualm. He'd do anything for coke, since he started on it. Dentist gave it to him to pull a tooth, and he's been mad for the stuff ever since. Gentleman Jim is a con-artist—they called him Gentleman because he keeps saying, "A gentleman should not mix with low company", and things like that. Used to carry a shiv, and could use it—some eytie in the blood, I reckon. And the Bull—he's a big bloke, real big, and dumber than an ox. Strong? He'd pull a door off its hinges rather than work out how to turn a key. No brains at all.'

'Cokey and Gentleman Jim sound like my gangsters,' observed Phryne. 'But they had guns as well. Why, come to think of it, did they stab Sasha instead of shooting him?'

'Quiet, a shiv in the ribs, and he should have been dead as a doornail. Not a sound. When he got away, they had to risk the St Valentine's Day massacre stuff. But if it's them we're up against, then we're in real trouble. Bad men, as I said.'

As Bert only appeared to use the phrase 'bad men' for multiple murders, Phryne was inclined to agree.

'What I want to do is to go to Seventy-nine Little Lon. and see what, and who, is there. Do you know the place?'

'Yair. Behind the Synagogue, it is. Near the corner of Spring Street. Boarding houses, mostly. Do you know Seventy-nine, Cec?' Cec emptied his glass and set it down with great care.

'It's the dark stone place, mate, with the shop in front. Sells all them remedies, Beecham's Pills and them. Next door's old Mother James'.'

'Amazing, Cec is. Got a map in his head, he has. Just have to ask and he knows where any place is. It's a chemist's,' added Bert superfluously. 'As if they needed one in Little Lon.'

'Yair. All-in and any up the last, that's Little Lon. Bricks, shivs, boots, broken bottles—and every gang in Melbourne goes there for settling any little disagreement that they might have. You can't go there, Miss.'

'Oh, can't I?' asked Phryne ominously. 'Are there no women in Little Lon.?'

'Yair, well, there's tarts all right, but they ain't like the sorts in the movies. I don't reckon there's a heart of gold in any moll in the street. And they fight, them sheilas, like bloomin' cats—the hair-pulling and the scratching and the shrieks! Turn a man's stomach to hear 'em.'

'And what does Mother James do?' asked Phryne. 'Is it a brothel?'

'No, Miss, not exactly. She sells coffee and tea and soup and bangers and mash and sly grog on the side. And pies, if you're silly enough to buy 'em.'

'She sounds like a remarkable woman,' said Phryne politely and implacably, and Bert recognized a determined woman when he met one.

'All right, Miss, what do you want me and Cec for?'

'Guides and bodyguards,' said Phryne, as Dot brought out the dessert, a pudding made with raspberries.

'Miss, me and Cec ain't got no quarrel but with the capitalists.'

'Have some pudding. There's tea in this flask. Think. I must go to this place, and I can't ask Dot to accompany me—she's a good girl. It's a dangerous place, as you've just explained. I'll give you enough to buy a new car. I need your help, gentlemen.'

'Thanks, but no deal,' said Bert. Cec said nothing.

'Think of this, then. Cocaine is nasty. You can get addicted in three or four doses, and then must take ever increasing amounts. It rots the brain and damages the eyes and throat if you sniff it. Withdrawal from it is terrible—you yawn and sweat and convulse and cramp and cry with pain, and you start seeing things and then you start to itch, and rip your skin to rags if you're not stopped. It's an evil thing. And somewhere, in a lovely house in a leafy suburb, far away from the noise and the screaming, there's a fat man with a cigar, raking in the profits and laughing at the world. A capitalist, rolling in cocaine money, with a chauffeur and three housemaids and a sable coat.

'Also, you want me to do something for you. One good turn, eh Bert?'

Phryne poured a cup of tea, which she felt she had deserved. Cec looked at Bert. Bert looked at the ground for a long moment. Dot filled his cup. He stared down into the steaming depths and fought a battle between his communist principles and his deep instinct for self-preservation.

'All right,' he muttered. 'Me and Cec is on.'

'Good. I'll meet you at midnight at the same place as today. Now, back to the business at hand. I have decided on the Footscray Post Office because it is an automatic exchange. We don't want to have to explain our business to an operator. How many numbers have you got?'

'Three,' said Bert, producing a matchbox with writing on the back.

'And I've got one,' volunteered Dot. 'Muriel said that it was a nurse, though.'

'Good work. You shall see that I keep my side of the bargain, Bert. We shall find this Butcher George. Anyone got any pennies?'

Cec grinned, reached into his pocket, and poured pennies into Phryne's hand.

⁂

The two cars made short work of the road to the post office. Phryne parked the Hispano-Suiza and disembarked, leaving Dot in charge.

'Hoot the horn if you want help,' she informed her nervous maid, and folded herself, the matchbox and the pennies into the red telephone booth.

The next ten minutes were most trying. The first number rang twelve times before a guarded female voice answered.

'Yes?'

'I'm in trouble,' whispered Phryne in her best Australian accent. There was a silence at the other end.

'I've just moved into this house,' said the woman. 'Are you looking for Mrs Smith?'

'Yes,' said Phryne. 'She had a nursing home.'

'That's right. I'm afraid she's gone. She didn't leave a forwarding address. Sorry.' She hung up. Phryne dialled again.

'Yes?' another woman.

Phryne repeated herself. 'I'm in trouble.'

The voice became sympathetic.

'Are you dear? Well, we shall have to do something about that. How far gone are you?'

'Two months.'

'It will be twenty pounds. Doctor does them here every Tuesday. All nice and clean, dear, ether and all.'

'A doctor?' asked Phryne. The voice became brisk.

'Certainly, dear, we don't want any complications, do we? Nothing to eat for twenty-four hours beforehand. Will you take down the address?'

'No, I'll have to think about it,' faltered Phryne. This was not Butcher George's establishment.

'All right, dear, but don't leave it too long, will you? Doctor won't do them after three months.'

'Thank you,' said Phryne, and hung up.

Somewhat shaken, she tried the last number on the matchbox. A man answered. Phryne repeated her whimper.

'I'm in trouble.'

'And what business is that of mine?' snarled the voice. Phryne had a stab at a password.

'I'm looking for George.'

'Oh, are yer? Should have said so at once. You'll be met under the clocks tomorrow at three. Wear a red flower. Bring ten quid. What's yer name, girl?'

'Joan Barnard,' said Phryne and the voice became unctuous.

'See yer temorrer, Joanie.'

He hung up. Phryne felt sick. She drew in a deep breath, and pushed another penny into the coin receiver.

'This is Phryne Fisher. Can you call Dr MacMillan? Yes, it is important. Yes, I will wait.' She gave a thumbs-up signal through the glass to Bert and Cec. Bert grinned. She returned her attention to the telephone.

'Elizabeth, I've set up a meeting with your abortionist. What was your nice policeman's name again? Robinson, that was it. I'll call him. Of course I'll be careful. Good-bye.' She lit a gasper and used the last of Cec's coins to call Russell Street.

After some argument, she obtained the detective-inspector's ear.

'If a policewoman wearing a red flower waits under the clocks tomorrow at three, she will be picked up by your Butcher George. I have set this up by phone. The name I gave was Joan Barnard. Is that clear?'

She listened impatiently to his expostulation, and cut in crisply, 'I used my common sense. You could have done the same. I can't imagine why you didn't. Except that you do not use the talents God gave to geese. If you want to know more, you can call me at the Windsor. But this is your best chance of catching him. By the way, it costs ten pounds,' she added, and rang off.

She extracted herself from the telephone booth and explained the arrangement to Bert and Cec.

'It was your number, Bert, do you remember where you got it?' asked Phryne. Bert looked at the ground. Phryne sighed.

'Well, tell your source that the number is now U.P.'

Bert laughed.

'When do you want to go to Little Lon, Miss?'

'Why, tomorrow night, of course. I am dining with an MP tonight. I don't want to miss the Melba Gala.'

'Of course,' agreed Bert. 'The Melba Gala.'

⁂

Detective-Inspector Robinson bellowed out of his office, 'Sergeant! Who's on duty tomorrow? Women?'

'Only WPC Jones, Sir.'

'Send her in,' he grunted, and the sergeant called up WPC Jones and wondered what had got his chief into such a snit.

'Jones, I want you to come in tomorrow in plain clothes. You want to look poor and as though you're expecting. We're out to catch that George who murdered them girls.'

'Butcher George, Sir? You've got a lead on him at last?' asked Jones eagerly. Women were just tolerated in the force, made necessary only by the number of abandoned children and prostitutes who came to the attention of the Victoria Police. She knew that she would never become an officer and that her pay remained lower than that of a clerk, but this might be her chance for promotion. They couldn't send a male officer to catch an abortionist. Jones loathed this George. She had dealt with the outraged and mutilated body of Lil Marchent. Prostitute or no prostitute, she haunted Jones, and Butcher George would not find her such easy prey.

Her boss, however, did not seem as happy as she would have thought about the prospect of bringing in a notorious murderer.

'We'll have a car following the van,' said the detective-inspector, 'and a few men on foot. All you have to do is look miserable and pay him the money. Ten quid. Take note of anything he says,' he added, 'and be careful. If it looks dangerous, bail out.'

'I will, Sir. How did you get the lead?'

'Information received,' sighed the detective-inspector resignedly. 'Information received, Jones.'

Chapter Eleven

I do not know which to prefer
The beauty of inflections
Or the beauty of innuendoes.
The blackbird whistling
Or just after.

'Thirteen Ways of Looking at a Blackbird',
Wallace Stevens

Phyrne had many things to do, and sorted her priorities briskly as she slid the big car into top gear along Footscray Road. Dot closed her eyes initially, but allowed herself to peep through her fingers. Eventually, she thought, I may get used to this. In about a hundred years. The wind tore at her hair. The old cab was left far behind, toiling along ant-like in Phyrne's wake.

'I'll have to go shopping first. Dot, where's the cheapest place to buy clothes in the city?'

'Paynes,' yelled Dot. 'Cheap and nasty. Not something you could wear, Miss!'

'We shall see. Then I must dash off to Toorak and visit Lydia, and then I am bidden to dinner and a gala by Mr Sanderson. And after that—home and to sleep.'

She slung the car around the corner of Spring Street and drew up outside the hotel, tossed the keys to the doorman and was halfway up the steps before she noticed that she was talking to herself.

'Dot,' she called, 'you can open your eyes now!'

Dot blushed and clambered out of the Hispano-Suiza with more haste than grace and ran to join Phryne.

'Now for Paynes and a really outrageous dress,' her errant Mistress said. 'Come with me, Dot, I want your opinion.'

So it was that Phryne acquired a skimpy costume of Fugi cotton, with fringes, in a blinding shade of pink known colloquially as 'baby's bottom', a pair of near-kid boots with two-inch heels, an evening bag fringed and beaded to within an inch of complete inutility, stockings in peach, and a dreadful cloche hat with a drunken brim in electric blue plush.

Her method in choosing these garments was simple. Anything at which Dot exclaimed, 'Oh, no, Miss!' she bought. She also purchased a pink wrap with pockets, trimmed with maribou which looked ragged even when new. She dropped in at Woolworth's and collected two rings, a six foot length of beads that could not possibly have come from Venice, and jazz garters. She equipped herself with cheap undergarments from the same shop.

Laden with parcels, she returned to the Windsor and gave Dot the oddest instructions she had yet received.

'Dress up in all that tatty finery, Dot, and wear it in for me. I haven't time.'

'Wear it in, Miss?'

'Yes. Tread over the heels, roll around the floor a bit, spill something down the dress and wash it off, but not too well, rip the hem a little and mend it. This stuff has got to look well-worn. Break some of the feathers too. Bash that appalling hat in and out. You get the idea?'

'Yes, Miss,' sighed Dot, and took all the parcels into her own room.

Phryne reclaimed the car and was soon travelling fast down Punt Road, and recalling to mind the matter on which she had been sent to Australia.

I wonder if Lydia is addicted; I really can't see that oaf John poisoning anyone—he wouldn't have the imagination. Strangling, yes, beating of the head with the nearest blunt instrument, certainly, but poisoning? No. On the other hand, if one wished to be rid of a husband like that—and who wouldn't?—then self-administration of something relatively harmless...oh, wait a minute...what was it that Lydia wrote? *I'm ill, but Johnnie just goes to his club.*

She was so preoccupied with the sudden insight which had flashed over her that she had to brake hard to avoid a tram. Fortunately, racing cars have excellent brakes. She eased off her speed to the legal limit down Toorak Road to give herself time to think.

'If I'm right, it is relatively easy to prove,' she thought. 'I need only suborn a maid...and I don't think she treats her maids well...'

⁂

The Irish maid, nervous and voluble, babbled, 'Oh, Miss Fisher, it's you. Mistress is ill and abed, but she sent word that you was to be let in if you came. This way, Miss.'

Phryne followed the young woman and took her arm.

'Not so fast. Tell me about Mrs Andrews' illness. Does it come on her suddenly?'

'Yes, Miss, she was well enough last night, and then this terrible vomiting—and the Doctor doesn't know what it is. Nothing seems to work.'

'How long do these attacks usually last?'

'One day, or two days, not longer, but she's that weary after them. Takes her a week to recover.'

'And Mr Andrews, is he ill too?'

'No, Miss, that's what's got 'em all puzzled. Otherwise they'd think it was something she ate. But they eat the same, Miss, and we finish it up in the kitchen, and we ain't sick. It's a mystery,' concluded the maid, stopping outside a pink door. 'Here we are.'

'Wait another moment. What's your name?'

'Maureen, Miss.'

'Maureen, I'm trying to find out what causes this illness, and I need some help. I'm sent by Mrs Andrews' family in England. There is some information I need.'

She held out a ten shilling note. Maureen's fingers closed on it, savouring the feel of the paper.

'First, where is Mr Andrews?'

'At his club, Miss. He used to stay home when she was sick but lately he seems to have lost interest.'

'Do you like him?'

'Oh, Miss!' protested the maid, squirming. Phryne waited. Finally the answer came, in a tense whisper.

'No. I dislikes both of 'em. She's soft and cruel, seems all sweet and hard as a rock, and he's all hands. I'm leaving as soon as I can get a job in the factory. Better wages and hours and company, too.'

'Good. I thought as much. How do they get along?'

'Badly, Miss. They quarrel all the time, it used to be about his little bits on the side. Now they fight about money, mostly. She says that he's wasting all his fortune on lunatic schemes thought up by that Hon. Matthews. He says she's got no courage. Then she cries and he storms out.'

'How long has the money argument been going on?'

'Years, Miss—but it's much worse ever since he met up with that Hon.'

'You have been very helpful. There's something more. Do you get on with her personal maid?'

'I ought to, she's me sister Brigit.'

'Good. Here's what I want you to do, and there's ten quid in it for both of you.'

Phryne told Maureen what she wanted. The girl nodded.

'We can manage that,' she agreed. 'But why?'

'Never mind. Deliver the stuff to Dr MacMillan at the Queen Victoria Hospital, and tell her I sent you. And if you get caught and sacked, come and see me at the Windsor. But I'd advise you not to get caught,' she added, suddenly struck with the knowledge that she might be endangering this girl's safety. Maureen smiled.

'Brigit and me have done harder things than that,' she said softly. 'And now I'll announce you, Miss.'

'Very well. If you're questioned, just say I wanted gossip.'

'And so ye did,' agreed Maureen, and opened the pink door.

'Miss Fisher, Mrs Andrews,' she announced in her clear Donegal voice, and Phryne went in.

The room was pinker than anything else Phryne had ever seen. In deference to modern tastes in decorating, it was not frilled and hung with tulle or muslin, and neither was there a four-poster bed. But the walls were papered with pink-and-pink flowers, there was a pink Morris-designed carpet on the floor, and two standard lamps and a bedside light all with pink frames, bases and shades. Phryne, in charcoal and green, felt that she clashed badly.

Lydia was reposing on a chaise-longue covered with pink velvet, and she was herself attired in an expensive silk robe of blinding pinkness. Phryne felt as if she had stepped into a nightmare. Lydia looked just like a doll—the curly blonde hair, the delicate porcelain skin, the soft plump little hands...Phryne sat down on the end of the sofa and asked, she hoped sympathetically, 'How are you, Lydia?'

The little-girl voice whined as high as a gnat.

'I'm not at all well, and no one's come to see me, and I sent for you hours ago, and I've been waiting all this time!'

'I'm sorry, Lydia, but I was not in when your message arrived. I came as soon as I could. Has the doctor been?'

'Yes, and he can't find anything wrong with me. But there is something wrong with me. It's not fair. John eats the same as I do, and he's not ill. And he's not here. He's so cruel!'

'Is there nothing that you eat that he doesn't eat?' asked Phryne. Lydia's smooth forehead wrinkled.

'Only chocolates. He doesn't like chocolates.'

'Poor Lydia. Can I order something for you? A cup of beef tea? Some soup?'

'No, I couldn't eat anything,' declared Lydia, flinging herself back into the embrace of her pillows. Phryne, fighting her instincts, took the small hand in her own. It was hot.

'Lydia, have you ever thought that you might be poisoned?' she asked as gently as she could. There did not seem to be an acceptably euphemistic way of putting the question. Lydia gave a dramatic wail of terror and hid her face.

'Come, you have thought of it, haven't you?' Lydia sobbed aloud, but Phryne, bending close, made out, 'John...so cruel...'

'Well, I suppose that he must be chief suspect. How do you get your chocolates?'

'Why, John buys them...he always has...' The china-blue eyes opened wide. 'The chocolates! I've always been ill after eating chocolates! And he bought them! It must be him!'

'Calm yourself, Lydia. Come now, this isn't the first time the idea had occurred to you, is it?'

From out of the depths of the pillows came a muffled, 'No.'

'Have you never said anything to him about it?'

'No, Phryne, how could I?' The white face emerged, hair tousled attractively.

'Why don't you let me speak to him?' asked Phryne, and was immediately clutched hard by surprisingly strong fingers.

'No!' The voice was a scream. 'No, you mustn't! Phryne you must swear—you must promise not to say anything to him! I couldn't bear it!'

'Why not?' asked Phryne in a reasonable tone. 'If he's trying to kill you, he should be warned that we're onto him. One warning should be enough.'

'No! Promise!' and Phryne relented.

'There, there, I shan't say anything. I promise. I swear. But you see that we can't leave it at that, Lydia.'

'Yes, we can,' announced Lydia with hysterics threatening in her voice. 'I won't eat anything that he doesn't eat, and then I'll be safe.'

'Very well, I must go now, Lydia, I've got to dress, I'm going to the Melba Gala tonight. Shall I call your maid?'

'No. I'm all right,' said Lydia. 'But come and see me again soon?' she pleaded, and Phryne found her own way out, deeply thoughtful and not a little disgusted.

She drove back to the Windsor, finding Dot in her own garments again, placidly mending stockings and listening to the wireless. A sugary arrangement of Strauss waltzes offended Phryne's ears and she hurtled into the bedroom to rummage through the clothes.

'Do turn that off, Dot, I'm oversweetened for one day, and run me a bath. How did you get on with the garments?'

'They're still crumpling nicely, Miss,' said Dot, pointing out a bundle of pink cloth which had been damped and screwed into a ball. 'By tomorrow midnight they'll be dry and such as no good girl would think of wearing. I've scuffed the shoes and the hat will never be the same again,' she added.

'Good girl. Now what am I to wear to the Gala? The gold? No, too obvious. Perhaps the peacock-blue...yes. Dot! Find my sapphire earrings and black underthings. The black shoes and sables.'

Phryne stripped off her charcoal and green costume and rang for Turkish coffee. She wanted, if possible, to remain alert.

Chapter Twelve

I was the world in which I walked, and what I saw
Or heard or felt came not but from myself
And there I found myself more truly and more strange.

'Tea in the Palaz of Hoon',
Wallace Stevens

The Sanderson home was imposing, but understated; more like the houses of the wealthy in Europe than the flashy Cryer establishment. A butler showed her in to a drawing room decorated with restrained elegance and the company rose to meet her.

Here, to her surprise, was Bobby, *soi-disant* Hon. Matthews of cricket ball fame, John Andrews, without his wife, and several politicians, who were so close to identical that Phryne could not recall if she was speaking to Mr Turner (Independent) or Mr Jackson (Labor) or Mr Berry (Conservative). Their wives obviously patronized the same milliner and the same couturier and were also hard to distinguish from each other. Phryne greeted Mr Sanderson with affection and met his wife, a rounded, shrewd woman with a twinkling eye. The rest of the guests seemed uncertain as to how to take Miss Fisher. Bobby Matthews, at least, showed an unequivocal reaction. When he saw that he was unobserved, he scowled blackly. Phryne smiled.

Sherry was brought, and conversation became general. Phryne slipped through the crowd and bobbed up at the Hon. Bobby's elbow, causing him to start and almost spill his drink.

'Well, well, Bobby, how very unpleasant to see you again! Sent you out to the colonies, did they? I wonder what the colonies did to deserve you. What have you been doing in Melbourne? Floated a few companies? Sold a few shares in Argentinian gold mines?'

'I'm involved in several business ventures,' replied Matthews stiffly. 'And I don't like your tone, Miss Fisher. What were you doing in Paris all that time, eh? Would you like me to tell this company about the *Rue du Chat-qui-Pêche?*'

'Certainly, and I'll extol your prowess at cricket.' Phryne smiled dazzlingly and held out her cigarette for a light. Bobby lit it with the look of a man who wished that it was Phryne that he was igniting, and said in a conspiratorial tone, 'Look, you don't have to ruin me, Miss Fisher. I've got a good thing going here. These colonials are a lay-down misère for a county accent and a title. I'll split the proceeds, if you like.'

'Sit down, Bobby, and stop looking so scared. I am not intending to expose you...but you can rely on me doing so if you damage anyone I'm fond of.'

'How will I know who to steer clear of?'

'Put it this way—you can make hay of all of the present company, except for Dr MacMillan.'

'That leaves me enough scope.'

'Do you know anything about the coke trade here?'

'Cocaine? I don't get entangled in that sort of thing.'

'Too virtuous?' asked Phryne, blowing a smoke ring.

'Too careful of my own skin. They are not nice people to know. But I've heard a few things. The main man is called the King of Snow, but no one seems to have any idea who he is. I believe that the stuff is being imported in sackfuls but it's not my business.'

'And how long has this King been reigning?'

'Three years, I think—I gather that he has taken over all the little operators, and some of them have been found in the Yarra encased in concrete. His methods are rather crude. A friend of mine is in the trade—he says that the only way to survive is to pay the King whatever price he demands. You'll be fished up in a cement waistcoat if you don't watch your step.'

'I have every intention of watching my step. Don't rejoice too soon, my Bobby. Now, tell me all you know about the Andrews family.'

'So far,' smiled Bobby, 'it has been small pickings. The man is an idiot. Unfortunately, his wife doesn't like me. She has quite a bit on her own account but she has resisted me fiercely…she's the brains of that outfit.'

'Is she, indeed? And she hasn't fallen into your most attractive arms, Bobby? Strange.'

'That's what I thought,' agreed Bobby without modesty. 'Most of these *hoi-polloi* have been positively predatory. She's got a whopping big share in several very good companies. No Argentinian gold mines for Mrs Andrews. Luckily her husband has bought a controlling interest in more than a few of the useful stocks which I had the forethought to bring with me when I was banished. I have a big deal coming off soon, with Andrews. If it works, we'll be rich.'

'And if it doesn't work?'

'Then *I'll* be rich.'

'Good luck with it, Bobby. Your secret is fairly safe with me—but let me know if you get a line on the King of Snow. I'm interested in him.'

'And I'll send lilies for your funeral,' promised Bobby.

Phryne floated away to engage herself in an interesting discussion on water supplies with all four politicians.

She was agreeably surprised by dinner, which was well-served and beautifully prepared, and she complimented her hostess. Mrs Sanderson smiled.

'My dear, when you've done as many dinners as I have, you are prepared for anything. Politicians seem to spend half their lives talking, and the other half eating. Tonight's company is rather select—some of those parliamentarians eat like pigs. Are you looking forward to the concert, Miss Fisher?'

'Indeed. It is in honour of the hospital, is it not?'

'Yes, Madame Melba arranged the concert herself, in order to help her less fortunate sisters. All proceeds are going to the Queen Victoria Hospital—and they could do with the money. Madame Melba is not accepting a fee. She is a most charitable woman.'

'Have you met her, Mrs Sanderson?'

'Once—yesterday. Small, plump and imperious, but with a lovely speaking voice and a charming manner. The concert should be most interesting. I hope to meet Dr MacMillan there—I sent her a voucher for our box, for she could not come to dinner.'

'Dr MacMillan? My Dr MacMillan?' asked Phryne.

'I didn't know that she was yours, my dear, but if you mean the Scotch lady doctor, then that is she.'

'How do you know her, Mrs Sanderson?'

'I'm on the board of the Queen Victoria Hospital. I do hope that she does find a skirt to wear, I fear that Melbourne is not ready for her trousers.'

'Had I known that she was coming, I would have gone and dressed her with my own hands,' said Phryne. 'She is a most amazing woman.'

'My dear, I know! She had to go to Edinburgh for her degree, and all those men wouldn't let her practice, they even tried to ban women students from learning anatomy, God forgive them, and now I see in the newspaper that they are trying to keep them out of the wards again, saying that now there is a hospital for women they can go there, and not interrupt the men's reign in the others. Really, the folly of men makes me seriously angry. Dr MacMillan must have been very dedicated in order to ever become a doctor.'

The gala was everything that Melbourne had hoped. The Town Hall was crowded, all seats had been sold, and to Phryne's delight,

Dr MacMillan was there, dressed in a respectable dark velvet gown and hat, though she was scented with iodine, as always.

'Well, are you here, Phryne? You see that I am in all my glad rags. They dressed me like a child and forbade me my trousers. I've told all my patients not to dare to give birth until I come back so all should be well. Is this Melba woman in good voice?'

'I believe so, hush. Here she comes.'

A storm of applause greeted the singer as she was welcomed by the conductor. Madame Melba wore flowing, dark red silks, heavily beaded on hem and shoulder, and Phryne reflected that she must be a strong woman to stand up under the weight of her garments. The orchestra began the 'Addio' from *La Bohême*, and Melba began to sing.

It was an authoritative voice, pure and pearly without being in the least thin, every word meticulously pronounced and carefully pitched. But what endeared her to Phryne was the amount of emotion with which she loaded every note. Here was a dying courtesan bidding farewell to life and to love, and tears pricked Phryne's eyes. The short stout woman had gone; here was languour and white draperies and fainting suitors. She finished the song and allowed the orchestra to display its talents in several rondos; then she was back with the 'Willow Song' from *Otello* and the 'Ave Maria' and she had most of her audience in tears.

Finally, garlanded and knee deep in flowers, she came back to sing 'Voi che Sapete' with such clarity and mastery that the audience were dragged to their feet, to cheer, throw flowers and applaud until they split their gloves.

'Fine voice,' said Dr MacMillan. 'She could sing seals out of the sea.'

'I want a word,' said Phryne, recovering from a dream of music. 'I may send you some stuff to be analysed for mineral poisons—can you do that for me?'

'Aye, or at least, the laboratory can—what about the cocaine, Phryne? Are you not getting yourself into deep waters?'

'Yes, and there are sharks. Here, take this, and give twenty quid of it to the girl who brings you the samples—her name's Maureen or Brigit—and I'll come and see you tomorrow.'

Phryne kissed Dr MacMillan goodbye, thanked her hostess heartily for the excellent entertainment, and swept out in the milling crowds to walk back to the Windsor.

'I hope,' she added to herself as she stalked up the hill toward Parliament House, 'I do hope that I know what I am doing.'

She found Dot drinking tea and reading the newspaper.

'Did you have a nice time, Miss?' she asked, putting down her cup.

'Delightful,' Phryne called over her shoulder as she sailed into her bedchamber to remove her clothes. 'Did anyone call?'

'Yes, Miss, Mrs Andrews telephoned and asked you to remember that you promised to see her soon.'

'Anyone else?' came Phryne's voice, muffled in cloth.

'No, Miss, except for that cop. He was most upset that you were out, Miss. Asked you to ring him as soon as you come in.'

'I'll call him tomorrow—it's after midnight. Throw me a dressing-gown, Dot, please.'

Dot passed her the gown and Phryne came out of the bathroom. 'There's a letter for you, Miss.'

Phryne took the envelope. It was marked with the Scott's Hotel emblem at the top left hand corner. She tore it open.

'Dearest Phryne,' it began in a flowing and extravagant script. 'Please allow me once more to worship at the temple of your beauty. I will call at your hotel at eleven.' It was signed, 'Your devoted Sasha.' Phryne snorted, crumpled the letter, and flung it into the waste paper basket. Sasha's mercenary nature was fully revealed. However, Phryne thought as she tucked herself into bed, he had his charms.

Smiling a little, she fell asleep, and her treacherous body recalled Sasha very well. Two hours later she awoke, flushed and wet, and took her second bath of the evening entirely on his account.

Chapter Thirteen

Poison grows in this dark
It is in the water of tears
Its black blooms rise

'Another Weeping Woman',
Wallace Stevens

Woman Police-Officer Jones pinned a red geranium to the shoulder of her thin, cheap suit, and walked the steps of the station. She had arrived at ten minutes before three and it was now five minutes past. She feared that Butcher George had smelt a rat and was not going to show. She was excited rather than afraid, and she clasped hands that were innocent of a wedding ring across her artfully padded middle. She eyed the traffic, always heavy around Flinders Street Station, and noticed a battered cab, which she was sure she had seen pass only five minutes ago. It slid past again. She paced the pavement and looked into the hatter's window, trying to control her breathing.

When she turned again there was the van as promised, and a tall man with short hair was beckoning.

'You Joan Barnard?' asked the man. Jones nodded. 'You got the money?' She held up her purse. 'Come on, then, in the back,' and she climbed into a musty-smelling interior, and sat down on the floor. She could not see out of the windows. They seemed to turn a corner, then another and down a long street with a few lurching stops. The gears were faulty, and grated. She could not see the driver.

The van stopped in a noisy street with a smell of cooking. The door opened, and she was grabbed roughly by the arm and dragged so swiftly that she only had time to notice that she was in Little Bourke Street, and the taxi she had noticed before had stopped nearby.

She was ushered through a blistered door and into a parlour. It was very old-fashioned, with a piano and easy chairs and a table with a wax bouquet under glass. Incongruously, there were two camp beds with old blankets on them in the corner away from the window.

'Got the money?' demanded the tall man with the cropped hair, putting out a dirty hand. Jones gave him the ten-pound note and he grinned unpleasantly.

'Take off your underwear and lie down on the table and we'll soon have you fixed,' he said as he removed the wax flowers and the tablecloth off the dining table.

'Lie down and I'll take all your troubles away. Then you can go back to being a virgin again.'

He advanced on her, unbuckling his belt, and Jones backed until she came up against the table, fumbling for her purse as she went.

'If you want to be relieved of your burden, girlie, I'm the one to do it. I'll even give you a discount—if you please me. Ten per cent eh?'

Jones found her whistle, and blew hard. The whistle shrilled in the small room and Butcher George jumped, still clutching the glass dome and the tablecloth, then ran for the inner door. Jones, shaking with outrage, dived after him, tripped him, and sat down hard on his back, dragging his hands back and twisting his arms viciously. All the fight went out of him and he whimpered.

Three policemen broke down the door a minute later, and relieved Jones of her prisoner. They handcuffed his hands behind his back and led him out into the street.

The old cab was still there, and two men were standing by it. One was tall and blond and one was short and dark.

'That's him,' remarked one to the other.

Cec approached Jones.

'Is that George Fletcher?' he inquired politely. Jones nodded. Cec took two paces, turned the head of the tall man toward him, and hit Butcher George with the best left hook seen in Little Lon. since the police strike. His heels lifted, his chin snapped back, and he fell poleaxed into the startled Jones' arms. Bert and Cec got back into their cab and drove away. Jones and her colleagues loaded Butcher George into a police car and headed for Russell Street.

'Who was that bloke with the hook?' asked Constable Ellis.

'I don't know, but we are not going to mention it,' replied Jones, settling her hair. 'Are we?'

'Is he really Butcher George?'

'He is,' replied Jones.

'Then we ain't going to mention it,' agreed Ellis.

As she had promised, Phryne slept until noon, requiring Dot to turn the lovelorn Sasha away. Once she awoke, Phryne breakfasted lightly, then set off for the Melbourne baths. She obtained temporary possession of a towel, a locker, and use of the large swimming bath for a few pennies. She donned her brief black costume, without skirt or back, and pulled a rubber cap down over her hair, flung herself in, and began to swim up and down. She always found that swimming assisted her thought processes.

Her problems were twofold, she reasoned. First, there was Lydia, who did seem to be the subject of poisoning.

Dr MacMillan's tests on the hair and fingernails obtained by the Irish maids would probably confirm that. Arsenic was the most likely drug—it had been fashionable for centuries in such matters, and was still, it seemed, in style. Andrews stood to inherit a fortune if Lydia died without issue, which made him the most obvious suspect. His dealings with Bobby were not going to yield him a profit—Lydia was right there. One could not trust Bobby Matthews. But then, could one trust Lydia? She was a clinging vine of the most insidious kind, but she had a financial mind that would be envied by most actuaries, and was shrewd in her assessment of people. And there was the other problem. What of the Bath House of Madame Breda?

Phryne reached the end of the pool, turned, and swam back. The water sluiced over her shoulders and swirled around her neck. There was no other lady in the swimming baths. Every splash she made seemed to echo.

Madame Breda. Impossible that she should be selling drugs. She was too honest and healthy. However, it was a big building, and it backed onto Little Lonsdale Street, that den of thieves. Phryne vaguely recalled a brass plate on the door as the maid had let her and the Princesse in…what had it been? She turned on her back and floated, closing her eyes. Aha. *Chasseur et Cie*, cosmetics. But none of the powders and products shown by Gerda had been of that brand. They had all been marked with Madame Breda's Egyptian bird. If drugs were coming through Madame's establishment there was a fair chance that *Chasseur et Cie* might be the dealers. And the indispensable Gerda must be the courier. Gerda was the only person who could have put that packet of real coke into Phryne's pocket. Gerda had, therefore, left her the message to beware of the rose.

Madame Breda went to visit her patrons and Gerda went with her—that had been the case when Sasha had been caught in Toorak. Simplicity itself for Gerda to contact the person in the house who was addicted to *Chasseur et Cie*'s products and to arrange the sale. Gerda had a grudge against Madame, and what better way to be avenged than to use her Temple of Health for drug-running?

Temples brought Sasha, and sex, to mind. Hmmm. The bath-maiden at Madame Breda's had caressed her in an intimate and sapphic manner and seemed to be very practised at it. Was that why Lydia had not escaped elimination by becoming pregnant? Was she a lesbian? Andrews had, come to think of it, a frustrated manner, and his cruelty might be the result of being constantly rejected by his wife. Lydia might have been a sapphic since her schooldays, and her father had said that she lived with a rackety crowd in Paris. In that city, Phryne knew, there was a whole lesbian subculture, wearing men's clothes, riding in the Bois, frequenting certain bars. Her old friend and gigolo Georges Santin had accompanied her to several such establishments. The women did not seem to resent Georges. Unlike most gigolos, he really liked women. Phryne had little leaning towards homosexuality, but she had liked the lesbian bars. They were free of the domination of men, creating their own society.

'I wonder where I can find someone who knew Lydia in Paris?' she said aloud, and the words came echoing back to her. No time.

'I shall go exploring tonight, and see what I can find,' decided Phryne, duck-diving to the end of the pool. But who was the rose? A person? A place? Presumably she was not being warned about an exploding bouquet. What were the common characteristics of roses? Scent? They came in all colours. Phryne gave it up, hauled herself out of the water, and went to the hot water baths for a soak.

She was back to the hotel at five, in time to receive a delighted phone call from Dr MacMillan.

'My dear, they've caught that George the Butcher! The nice policeman just rang to tell me. He's had to call in the police-surgeon. Your Cec broke the bastard's jaw.'

'Was there a fight?' asked Phryne.

'No, I gather not. Cec just hit him. Well, that will be a load off my mind. And he's confessing as fast as his wired-up jaw will allow, so there will be no need for Alice to give evidence. And what have you to say about these grisly relics ye've sent me?'

'Hair and fingernails? Any arsenic?'

'Chock-full, m'girl. From the examination of the hair shaft I'd say the person has been absorbing arsenic for about six months. Should you not call the police, Phryne? Are they from a cadaver?'

'No, the lady's alive. I shall notify the police, Elizabeth, but in my own time. You keep those samples safely and I'll get back to you. Have you time for dinner tonight?'

'I have not. I've a miscarriage in casualty at this moment. Goodbye, Phryne, take care!'

Dr MacMillan had sounded worried, Phryne thought. People were always worrying about her. It gives them something to do, Phryne thought, and dressed for dinner.

She came back to her room at about eleven to find Dot surveying the sorry wreckage of the Paynes' clothes. The dress had crumpled and spotted as it dried, and the tear Dot had made in the hem had been clumsily mended. It went to Dot's heart to cobble the material together, but Phryne smiled and said, 'Splendid.' She looked out of the window, but there was nothing interesting there.

'Tell me, Dot, what comes into your head when I say the word "rose"?'

Dot looked up from her sad contemplation of the mend.

'Why, the colour, Miss. Pink, you know.'

'Yes,' said Phryne with a flood of realization, and a momentary dizziness. 'Of course.'

'I don't know how long I'll be, but don't wait up. Until I get back, Dot, please stay here and keep the door locked. Don't let anyone in who isn't me. Got all that? Oh, and here's your wages in advance—and a reference—just in case.'

'Yes, Miss. Can I help you dress?'

'Yes, bolt the door and bring the disguise.'

Dot did as she was bid and arrayed Phryne in the damaged dress, the carefully holed stockings, the scuffed shoes and the battered hat. Dot had broken three feathers over one shoulder and they dangled sadly. Phryne removed all her own jewellery and looped the glass beads twice around her neck. They hung down to the jazz garters.

'Shoe polish, Dot, I'm too clean,' she declared, and gave herself a watermark around the neck, and grey fingernails. She took the clean shine off her black hair with powder and painted her cheeks thickly with Dot's Coles rouge.

'Revolting,' she declared, surveying herself in the mirror. 'What's the time?'

'Half past eleven. You can't go out of the Windsor looking like that, Miss! And what shall I do if anyone calls?'

'Tell them I'm asleep and have given orders not to be woken; it's more than your place is worth to try. I won't send anyone, Dot, so bolt the door and stand siege until I come back. If I don't come back tonight, wait until midday, then take that package to the policeman. Understood?'

'Yes, Miss.'

'And I'm not going out like this. Give me the big black cloak, I can carry the hat. Now have I got everything…money, gun, cigarettes, lighter…yes. Goodbye, Dot. See you tomorrow—or sometime.'

She was gone, swathed in the big cloak. Dot bolted the door as she had been ordered and sat down to worry.

Chapter Fourteen

'Do you approve of clubs for women, Uncle?'
'Yes, but only after every other method of
quieting them has failed.'
Punch cartoon, 1928

There was a keyed-up aimlessness in the fuggy air of Little Lonsdale Street which affected Phryne like a drug. Several women
were within her view as she perched on a grimy stool outside
Mother James' drinking her revolting tea as though she enjoyed it.

The street was quiet, but sordid during the day, and really
only came into its own towards midnight. The small, squalid
shops were lit up, the street was filled with a crowd, and voices
and music bounced off the canyon-like walls of the few taller
buildings which backed onto that mangy thoroughfare. It smelt
strongly of fish and chips, dust, burning rubbish, and unwashed
humans, with an overlay of Californian Poppy, of which the
coiffures of the young men seemed to be chiefly composed.

Phryne had been watching trade in the pharmacy for an hour,
and was fairly sure that this was, indeed, the drug distribution
centre she had been seeking.

The shop was an open front with a counter, on which were
perched the two great glass jars of green and red liquid which

marked it in the popular mind as a chemist's. Behind the counter stood a small, fat man, and an assistant with bottle-blonde hair in a fringed dress of viridian green, who handed out plasters and powders to the passing trade. Some clients, quite well-dressed, and one a real gentleman in evening dress, came to the counter and asked for their needs in a whisper. For them the small man dispensed a pink packet of powder, and accepted five pounds for it. Lesser clientele for the same powders bought a leaf that might hold a saltspoon for ten shillings. Strain her ears as she might, Phryne could not hear what it was these customers were saying.

'Time for a saunter, chaps,' she murmured to Bert, who gulped down his tea and stood up. Cec remained where he was. Phryne teetered a little in the abominable shoes, took Bert's arm, and tiptoed to the door of the pharmacy. She patted Bert and spoke in a slurred Australian accent.

'You wait here, love, and I'll get us something,' she promised and approached the counter, taking a little time.

The small fat man turned his attention to this half-cut floozy. He hadn't seen her before, but as he often said, 'You couldn't know every tart on Little Lon.'. Phryne beckoned him.

'Some of them pink powders,' she slurred. The chemist hesitated, as if waiting for her to complete a slogan. Phryne's mind, working overtime, provided her with an idea. Seen on every railway siding was the legend '*Dr Parkinson's pink pills for pale people*'.

'Those pink powders for pale people,' she finished, and held out her ten shilling note. The man nodded, and exchanged her note for a slip of pink paper, embossed with the title 'Peterson's pink powders for pale people' and containing a small quantity of the requisite stuff. Phryne nodded woozily at him and found her way back to Bert.

'Come on, sailor,' she said, leaning on him heavily. 'Let's go back to my place.'

Bert put an arm around her and led her away, back to where the Morris squatted in the gutter, sagging a little as was its wont. Cec had followed them, soft footed.

'Cec, you take this to Dr MacMillan at the Royal Women's Hospital and come back. Bert and I will continue our carouse,' ordered Phryne, putting the paper into Cec's pocket. 'Back to Mother James, my old darling.'

'Ain't you got what you want?' hissed Bert. He was finding the proceedings nerve-wracking, though holding Phryne close was some compensation.

'Not yet. I want to see who else visits here,' answered Phryne, and conducted Bert back down the street again.

They found other seats at Mother James'. The hostelry was unique in Phryne's experience. It was the front of an old house, the verandah open to the street. Mother James herself, a monstrous Irishwoman around three hundred years old, with a face that would curdle milk and an arm of iron, served her noxious beverages to customers sitting on the pavement or on the verandah. The house was noisome, stinking of old excrement and new frying, and Phryne reflected that nothing, not even advanced starvation, would induce her to eat anything out of a kitchen into whose depths no health inspector would dare to step.

There were three or four ladies of the night supping gin or beer on the verandah, under the curling galvanized iron, and they surveyed Phryne closely. She reflected that she was surrounded with dangers. Not only was she investigating a cocaine ring, but one of these girls might take exception to her presence on their beat and cause a scene, or call their pimp. A nasty thought. She said loudly to Bert, 'I reckon that we ought be going home, love. I got to get back to the factory termorra.'

The women's gaze wavered and turned away. An amateur, they thought, out for a good time and a little extra in the pay packet. No threat. Phryne breathed easy.

'This is like waiting to go over the top,' commented Bert.

'I thought you said war was a capitalist plot,' murmured Phryne.

'Yair, it is. But we was in it, me and Cec. I first met Cec on a rock face at Gallipoli,' continued Bert. 'He saved me life by shoving me head down behind a trench wall when a Turk had drawn a bead on me bonce. We got out of it alive, and many didn't. We was lucky,' he concluded. 'And waiting is always like this.'

More customers for the coke merchant. Phryne calculated that, in three hours, he had taken close on a hundred pounds. She congratulated herself on her clothes. The garish dress and the holed stockings matched the milieu perfectly. Nothing interesting seemed to be happening, and she was about to nudge Bert and suggest that they call it a night when a cloaked figure paused for a moment under a street light and she caught her breath.

'Oh, Gawd!' she whispered and cocked her head. Bert saw a tall, theatrical figure who stalked into the chemist's and demanded:

'Cocaine.'

'It's Sasha,' whispered Phryne, aghast. 'That's torn it!'

'That the bloke we picked up with a shiv in his side?' Bert whispered, putting his mouth to Phryne's ear. She nodded.

'Do we have to rescue him?' asked Bert, wearily. He did not like foreigners, except comrades. And this was a counter-revolutionary.

Phryne produced a high-pitched giggle and slapped his hand, which she had placed on her knee.

The chemist had paled to an interesting shade of tallow, and his assistant had prudently vanished. Mother James' regulars had all sat up and were taking notice. Three men, with unusual precision for Little Lon., had begun to move toward Sasha. Phryne ground her teeth. Only an artist or an idiot could behave like this!

'Cec should be back by now,' worried Bert. 'Not like him to be late for a stoush.'

'Do you know them?' asked Phryne. Bert nodded, and Phryne belatedly recognized Thugs One and Two.

'Cokey, the Gentleman, and the one at the back is the Bull,' he commented.

Phryne stared, awed, at the Bull. He must have been six-and-a-half feet high, with shoulders three axehandles across and hands like shovels. While they homed in on Sasha, the Bull took his cigarette out of the corner of his mouth and ground it out in the palm of his hand.

'Did you see that?' asked Phryne.

'Yair. Used to be a bricklayer,' said Bert, unimpressed.

'There doesn't seem any help for it. We'll have to rescue Sasha,' sighed Phryne. Bert held her back as she began to rise.

'You want to find out who's behind all this? They'll take him to the boss, and we'll follow.'

'What if they just kill him here?'

'Nah, they'll want to know what he knows,' said Bert out of the corner of his mouth, and began to roll a smoke.

'Won't the cops come?'

'In Little Lon.? They only come here in force. You just watch the fight and then we'll see. There'll be hundreds of blokes here in a jiff, a fight attracts 'em like flies to a honeypot—you watch!'

The first attacker had reached Sasha, and thrown a punch. Sasha ducked, and the Bull's fist hit the wall, slogged through the flimsy plaster and lath, and stuck. Gentleman Jim slid under his companion's arm and feinted with his right, and as Sasha swayed away connected with a wicked left to the chest. Sasha staggered, recovered, kicked hard for the knee, missed, and got the Gentleman in the shins. His language was most ungentlemanly as Cokey Billings, obviously well-primed, seized Sasha from behind and threw a weighted scarf around his neck.

'Fight, fight!' chanted the regulars at Mother James', several of them stumbling out into the street to join in. Punches were thrown indiscriminately, one landing with some force on Phryne's shoulder. She kicked her attacker in the shins and followed Bert into the street. Shrieks and groans abounded, together with the monotonous thud of fist hitting flesh and body hitting road. Bert ducked and weaved through the mill, tripping over feet and the occasional body until he had fought his way to the chemist's doorway.

They were just in time to see the Bull, bellowing like his namesake, extract his hand from the wall with a rending of timbers and stumble after the Gentleman and Cokey, who had Sasha slung over one shoulder. The small fat chemist was attempting to pull down his shutters, but there were too many people in the way. A door opened at the end of the counter, and shut behind the procession.

'Out, Bert!' shrieked Phryne, and they pummelled their way out of the mob into the comparative quietness of the side street.

'Where are we?'

'This is the Synagogue. The alley leads into the grounds. I wonder where Cec is? Spare me days, a man can't rely on anyone!'

Phryne pulled down her dress and ran her hands through her hair. Then she suddenly seized Bert in a close embrace.

Bert's mouth came down upon hers, and she kissed him hungrily. His mouth was soft and strong and her arms, tightening around his waist, felt his muscular body. He pulled her close against him and she tottered on the broken heels.

A light flashed on them. Bert raised his head, continuing his embrace.

'Can't you see a man's busy?' he snarled, and the bearer of the light apologized and walked away. It was Cokey Billings.

'They ain't onto us yet,' he whispered.

'No, not yet. Where does this house finish? And you needn't hold me quite so close.'

Bert released her at once.

'I reckon it butts onto that Bath House,' he said slowly.

'Madame Breda?' asked Phryne. She lit a cigarette, a cheap local brand which fitted her part, and leaned back against the alley wall. 'Fight seems to be dying down.'

Bert peeped around the corner.

'Yair, they don't last long. There's Cec. Hey, mate! I got just the tart for us!' he yelled, and Cec approached, unperturbed. He rounded the corner without attracting attention.

'She says its kosher,' commented Cec. 'Now what?'

'Problems,' said Phryne, outlining the position briefly.

'Here we are, with this wall between us and Sasha. I reckon that the chemist is the back of Madame Breda's. What shall we do?'

'You're the boss,' said Cec, unhelpfully. Phryne concentrated. At that moment came a loud scream of outrage and pain, and a stream of Russian oaths.

'Well, he ain't dead,' said Bert. They both looked at her. Phryne was galvanized by that scream. Sasha was undoubtedly an idiot and one who would take the prize at any competition of morons of the Western World, but Phryne had lain next to him and had conceived a deep affection for that flesh now being maltreated behind the high brick wall.

'I'm going to climb,' she decided. 'Can you give me a boost?' Cec looked at Bert, who shrugged. The wall was only eight feet high. Bert went to cup his hands.

'Stay around,' whispered Phryne, flashing them a smile through her over-rouged face. 'Things might get interesting.'

'Is that all?' demanded Bert.

'Get the cops,' she added, inserting one foot in Bert's hands, and springing lightly up. She straddled the wall in a flash of stockings, and let herself down on the other side, hanging to the full stretch of her arms and dropping as silently as possible.

The yard behind the chemist's shop was dank, slimy, and very dark. Phryne had to feel her way along the wall until she found the further house, stopping only to disentangle herself from yards and yards of what felt like wet washing-line. She could not imagine anyone in that house doing any washing. The yard was full of old tins and bottles and she finally dropped to her hands and feet and crawled through the rubbish. She thus made closer acquaintance than she would have liked with the disgusting ground, and she was delighted when she found the house wall and, feeling along it, located the door.

There was a line of light under it, and she pressed her ear against the wood. The murmur of voices was impossible to distinguish. She felt further along and found a window, high up and dirty, but a better conductor of sound than the door.

Her heart was beating appreciably faster, and she took more rapid breaths, but she was enjoying herself. Adventuresses are born, not made.

'Take me to your King, then,' Sasha was yelling hoarsely. 'I want to meet him before I die!'

'Oh, you'll meet him, dago, he's dying to meet you! You and your family have been a considerable nuisance to him,' said the Gentleman. 'Where are those meddlesome women? We should present His Highness with a complete bag.'

'I don't know,' said Sasha, sullenly. There was a silent interval, during which someone struck a match. Then there was that scream again. The noise was fraying at Phryne's nerves. She could not try the door while someone might be looking at it; so she felt along the house again, around the corner and out of ear-shot. On one side, the house shared a wall with another house; that was no good. Slowly, and without noise, she moved back to the right-hand side and found that a narrow alley, two feet wide, had been left between the house and the brick wall. Along this she slid, hoping for an unguarded window.

The back door was flung open with a crash, and Phryne froze with her mouth against the stone. A light from an electric torch illuminated the area, blinding her. Then the door slammed.

'Nah, no one,' she heard the Bull say as the door closed. 'You're getting the jumps, Cokey.'

'He's getting the jumps,' thought Phryne, crooking cold fingers over a likely sill and removing a knife from her jazz garter. She found the latch by touch and forced it easily, raising the window with only a few heart-stopping creaks and drawing herself up. She stepped into a dark room, closed the window behind her, and sat down on the sill, listening.

She had not replaced her knife, and when attack came upon her without warning, she stabbed upwards with all her force, and caught the sagging body. Although trained in street fighting by apache masters, she had never stabbed anyone and she fought back nausea as she rolled out from under her attacker and allowed the body to slump to the floor. A little street lighting seeped through the window, and as she turned the body over she saw that her assailant had been Madame Breda's maid, Gerda. This was evidently her bedroom. Gerda's limp hand released the cook's chopper which she had been holding. Phryne listened at her breast. She was not dead. The knife had caught her under the collarbone and delivered a nasty but non-lethal wound, and Phryne's teachers would have been disgusted by their pupil's relief.

Phryne lit a match, located Gerda's candle, and stripped a pillowcase off her bed to bind the wound. Because Phryne had let go of the knife once it struck, as she had been expressly told not to do, not much blood had been spilled. She ascertained that Gerda had merely fainted, bound her up like a mummy, and used the rest of the woman's garments to tie her to the bed and gag her. Phryne had the notion that Gerda would not wake up in a pleasant mood. Meanwhile, there was Sasha downstairs, still screaming, and the King of Snow to interview.

Phryne crept to the door and listened, knife in hand. She hefted Gerda's chopper experimentally and decided that it really was too heavy for agile use, and laid it under Gerda's bed. No sound from the kitchen, now, but there were footsteps pacing up and down the hall. She caught a puff of the delicious scent of the bath which was the specialty of Madame Breda, and longed to go to the front of the house for a quick wash. Gerda had a water-jug and wash-stand, and Phryne removed the filth of the yard with good soap as she listened to the feet in the hall, passing, and re-passing.

Opening the door a crack after she had extinguished her candle, Phryne saw Cokey Billings. Gnawing his nails, he approached the front door, opened it, looked out, sighed, and closed it. Apparently it had been some time since his last dose. It would be impossible to slip past him. Sasha was silent—what were they doing to him? Had they killed him? Phryne rummaged through Gerda's clothes and found a bathrobe. She stripped off her holed stockings, put her gun in the pocket, and peeped out again. Cokey had been joined by Gentleman Jim.

'Stop pacing about like a caged animal,' snapped the Gentleman. 'His Majesty said you were to have four doses a day, and you've had them. It's three hours until tomorrow.'

'It doesn't last like it used to,' whined Cokey. 'Just a sniff...
just a whiff...me nerves is bad...'

'No, I told you the King said four doses,' he retorted.

'Just...a pinch...it'll never be missed...' begged Cokey, and
the Gentleman relented, taking a paper from his pocket.

'Just this once, mind,' said the Gentleman, stalking away
to the kitchen. Phryne waited until Cokey was sitting on the
stairs with his eyes closed, then flitted past into the front of the
house. Cokey was off in his own world and did not see her go.

Chapter Fifteen

Of langours rekindled and rallied
Of barren delights and unclean
Things monstrous and fruitless, a pallid
And poisonous Queen
'Dolores', Algernon Swinburne

Dr MacMillan, roused from her bed, accepted yet another mysterious parcel from a laconic messenger, and padded downstairs to the laboratory in her slippers to apply the usual tests. She ascertained that it was common salt, cochineal and about five per cent cocaine, then wrote a brief analysis, wrapped sample and script up in a bundle and placed it in the laboratory safe.

'I hope that she's nearing the end of this adventure,' muttered Dr MacMillan, making herself tea on the gas-ring in the night nurses' kitchen. 'I worry about the child.'

She had nearly finished the cup, when an excited probationary nurse came calling for her. Still worrying, she gulped down the rest of the tea and lumbered away to attend to the breech delivery in Ward Four.

⁂

Dot, asleep in her bed with the door bolted, heard a brief tapping, then a click as the door was unlocked. She froze, trying not to breathe, as the door was gently pushed twice, against the restraining bolt. There was an exasperated sigh, and the lock was turned into place. Nothing else happened for the rest of the night, but Dot did not sleep. She pulled the blankets over her head and wished she had never left Collingwood.

Phryne found herself in Madame Breda's office, out of Cokey's line of sight, and continued as far as the steam rooms, just to assure herself that it was the same place. The delicate scent was all about her. She returned to the office, leaving the door just ajar, and began to search by the light coming in through the hall. She found a locked drawer, forced it, and brought a wad of documents to the light. Bills of lading for bath salts and cosmetic preparations from France. *Chasseur et Cie.* Packets of pink powder. She returned the papers to the drawer, and backed away as Cokey Billings threw the door open with a crash.

'Who are you?' he demanded. Phryne adopted an accent.

'I am the cousin of Gerda. I got lost, looking for the convenience.' She looked down, so as not to catch his eye, and drew her bathrobe closer across her bosom. She would have succeeded if Cokey had not had his intelligence restored by his recent dose.

'You're that tart I saw in Toorak!' he exclaimed, and lunged for her.

His yell attracted the Bull and the Gentleman and all three pounced together. She eluded the Bull with ease but just as she was reaching for the knife in her garter, Gentleman Jim threw a towel over her head and struck her sharply with a blunt instrument. The world receded, but she did not lose consciousness. She sagged in her captor's arms, listening hard.

'I tell you she's the tart I met in Toorak Road, the night we stabbed that dago!' she heard Cokey explain.

'Well, we shall put both the birds into one cage, and His Majesty shall deal with both of them. Come on, Bull; stop slavering. She's only a little tart. No lady would wear those undergarments,' Gentleman Jim replied.

The Bull's hands roamed over Phryne's flesh, and she had to remind herself not to shudder.

'Throw her in with the other; we may get something if they talk—hurry up, Bull, the King's due in an hour!'

Phryne was aware that she had been dropped on a cold oil-cloth covered floor, and that a light was shone on her face at some stage in the next few hours.

It was not until dawn had brought an end to the most fright-ful night of her experience that she returned to consciousness. She was lying in Sasha's arms, and she had a terrible headache.

'I must give up mixed cocktails,' she said muzzily, turning her face against his chest. 'My head hurts.'

Realization had flooded in on her as soon as she had woken. Sasha opened his mouth to speak and she covered it with a firm hand. She moved up in his embrace and put her mouth to his ear.

'We don't know each other,' she mouthed, then groaned and dropped into her Australian accent.

'Who are you?' she demanded, sitting up cautiously. Sasha had taken the hint.

He replied stiffly, 'I am Sasha, Mademoiselle. Who are you?'

'Janey Theodore,' answered Phryne, grasping at the first name that entered her head, and thus libelling a prominent politician. 'My head hurts. Where are we?'

She looked around. It was a small room with a high, leadlight window in blue and red. The room was relatively clean and was furnished with two couches and a cabinet. It appeared, from the smell of liniment, to have been used as a massage room. Phryne examined herself. They had found her gun and the knife in her garter, and her bathrobe was gone. She was clad in French cami-knickers and the rags of her dress, which left her with less clothes than are generally considered sufficient to go bathing in. Sasha was sitting on the floor, where he had been cradling Phryne all night. He was dressed in flannels and a dark shirt, much cut about and torn, and his eyes were hollow with shock.

'They left us some water; have a drink,' he suggested. Phryne washed out her mouth with the liquid and then spat it out.

'Never know what might be in it,' she said. 'What happened during the night?'

'After they locked me in here, they brought you, as well. I feared that you were dead, Mademoiselle, but you were not. Two hours or so later someone looked in; I could not see who they were, but they flashed a torch on your face, seemed to recognize you and shut off the light. Since then, nothing.'

'What did they do to you?' asked Phryne in her own voice. Subterfuge was not going to be of any more assistance. Sasha opened his shirt, and Phryne saw deep blisters on the smooth skin.

'Cigarette end?' she guessed. Sasha nodded.

'They wanted to know where Gran'mere and Elli are. I did not tell them. But I expect that they will be back.' His voice was heavy with Slavic fatalism. Phryne felt the stirrings of anger, and wavered to her feet.

'It's morning; they could at least give us some breakfast. Hello!' she yelled, kicking the door and instantly regretting it—she had bare feet. 'Hello, yoo-hoo! How about some breakfast!'

The door was wrenched open. The Bull seized Phryne in one giant paw and Sasha in the other. He bore them, unresisting, out of the massage room, through the hall, and into the room with the pool, where he thrust them into cane chairs.

'Wait,' mumbled the Bull, and slammed the door behind him. Phryne at once got out of her chair and began inspecting the exits. The windows were barred, the door locked, and the furnishings were rudimentary. Phryne discovered her feathered mantle flung over a chair. The gun was gone, but her cigarettes were still in the pocket. She lit one for Sasha and they smoked in silence.

'What are they going to do with us?' asked Sasha.

'Probably something pointlessly hideous to make us realize the depths of our stupidity in attempting to dethrone the King of Snow, and then the good old river with the dear old brick, I suspect. Dear me, I wonder who inherits my money? I haven't made a will. I should have liked to have left it to the Cats' Home.'

'No time,' grinned Cokey Billings from the doorway. 'But it ain't the river—too many bodies turn up that way. We've got what the King calls "a nice scandalous demise" planned for you, Miss Fisher, and this gigolo.'

'Do you mean that I've waited all this time and I'm not going to meet his Majesty?' demanded Phryne, outraged.

At that moment, Cokey was pushed aside and the King of Snow came into the room, taking a cane chair with the suggestion of royalty. Sasha gaped. Phryne lit another cigarette.

'Hello, Lydia,' she said indifferently. 'Recovered from your little bout of arsenic overdose?'

Lydia Andrews stared with fevered eyes at Phryne, insulted by her lack of surprise. Sasha grasped Phryne by the arm.

'The King of Snow—she is him?' he asked, bewildered.

'Oh, yes. And she was setting up ever such a neat murder of her husband. Admittedly he is a lout and is wasting the family fortune, but arsenic is such a foul way to die. I would not be astonished if dear old Beatrice and Ariadne weren't planning a similar demise for their unsatisfactory spouses. These things do tend to run in threes—like indecent exposure and plane crashes. You could at least offer me a cup of tea, Lydia, before you kill me!'

'What do you mean about my husband? He's trying to poison me—you suggested it yourself.'

'Lydia, I may have been caught by your thugs by an elementary mistake—I should never have tried to break in without help, but Sasha is my lover and your friends were torturing him... you must allow for the natural feelings of a woman. But I'm not stupid. When your maid reported that you had a packet of arsenic in your dressing case, and your hair and fingernails are chock-full of the stuff, any idiot would have seen what you were doing. Little doses, carefully graded, just enough to make you sick, building up your resistance, and then—demise of prominent businessman, arsenic found, wife suspected, then arsenic found in wife, evidence to show that she switched cups on him while taking the evening cocoa, and *voilà*! Businessman was trying to murder wife, death by misadventure, lots of sympathy and all of the estate. Quite neat, Lydia, quite neat. Now can I have a cup of tea?'

'Fetch tea, Cokey,' ordered Lydia. 'Bull, stand there and break Miss Fisher's arm if she makes a move toward me.'

Sasha had caught sight of the bird brooch which adorned Lydia's overdressed person. He leaned closer to stare at it. When he had seen it last, it had been holding an orchid on his mother's shoulder.

'But why the murder, when you must be making a mint out of the coke trade?' asked Phryne, to keep the conversation going. Lydia shuddered.

'He was making…demands upon me. He called it his marital rights. He is…disgusting. He must go,' concluded Lydia.

Phryne stared at her. She still looked like a porcelain doll: curly blonde hair, pink cheeks, baby-face. There was something indescribably horrible about the dainty way she ordered her men about. Phryne leaned against Sasha, who put an arm around her.

'You know, I could have sworn that you had designs upon me yourself,' she commented softly. 'Do your tastes lie in my direction, Lydia?'

The tea trolley arrived, pushed by a sour-faced Cokey.

'Shall I be mother?' smiled Lydia, and poured out.

'Sugar and milk?' Sasha and Phryne looked at each other in bewilderment.

'Milk, but no sugar,' said Phryne. 'Strong, if you please, I think I've had rather a shock.'

She drank the tea thirstily and ate two cucumber sandwiches. She wondered if the Bull had cut them and muffled a laugh. Sasha drank his tea in complete astonishment.

'Now, you have a choice, Miss Fisher,' said Lydia formally. 'Come in with me, or…er…die.'

'Come in with you? Does that include going to bed with you?' asked Phryne coarsely. 'If so, no thank you.'

Lydia blushed. 'Not at all. It is an excellent business. Overheads are low, shipping charges moderate, and the personnel trustworthy.'

'How did you get to be the King of Snow?' demanded Phryne. Lydia fingered the Fabergé brooch.

'I was looking for a good investment, when I was in Paris in the first year of my marriage. I made an acquaintance, a woman, who was thinking of retiring from the Kingship. She had all her markets in Europe, and had never thought of Australia. I had some money from Auntie to invest, and I had to make myself independent of my husband. So I bought the business, out-right. The stockists deliver to Paris—I have nothing to do with that—and the merchandise enters as *Chasseur et Cie* bath salts. We have a very exclusive clientele, all wealthy ladies, and Gerda delivers the beauty powders when she is taken with Madame to do massages.'

'Is Madame Breda in on this?' asked Phryne.

'No. She allows us to use her rooms to store the cosmetics of *Chasseur et Cie*, for a consideration. She would never be a party to anything so unhealthy as drugs. Gerda, her maid, is our main sales agent, as I said.'

'And the chemist's shop in Little Lon.?' prompted Phryne, accepting her second cup of tea.

'Yes, that is our street outlet,' agreed Lydia, sipping delicately. It was an excellent tea. 'Come, Miss Fisher, with your connec-tions, we could have a world-wide trade, not just Paris and Melbourne. Millions of pounds are spent on drugs every day. It seems a pity that we cannot...I believe the term is "corner the market".'

'An interesting proposition. What is the alternative?'

'We will strip you both and put you in the Turkish bath together,' said Lydia, biting a precise semicircle out of her sand-wich. 'You should suffocate in about three hours.'

'Won't that be a little difficult to explain to Madame Breda?' asked Phryne. Lydia considered.

'No. We will tell her that you particularly wanted to enjoy your new diversion—I mean him,' she pointed to Sasha with a pearly forefinger, 'in a jungle atmosphere. You were so exhausted by transports of lust that you fell asleep—and a terrible accident happened. They may close the Turkish bath, but they will never suspect the truth.'

'Good. Now I feel it only fair to tell you that I have left a full statement of your part in this ring: your attempt to murder your husband, plus samples of your wares; to be delivered to that nice policeman, whose name escapes me, if I don't return to the Windsor at noon. Put that in your pipe and smoke it. More tea, please,' requested Phryne. Lydia refilled her cup and sat staring at her.

'Now where would you have left it? With that disagreeable suffragette doctor? Or in your room with your maid? I can't get in to your room, the girl has bolted the door—no doubt on your orders. But I think that's a blind. I think that the doctor is the one.'

'Oh, do you? And where do you suppose I dined last night?' misdirected Phryne.

Lydia paled. 'Mr Sanderson's?'

'What do you think? Where would such a commission be safest? In the hands of a silly girl or an old woman, or with a parliamentarian and statesman, who moreover has a safe? Your goose is cooked, Lydia. Better give it up.'

Lydia stood up, rigid with fury. 'Come,' she snapped at the hovering men, and led the way out of the room.

Phryne waited until the door was shut and locked before she took the last sandwich and pulled it apart.

'Plaster your burns with this, Sasha, and listen. I think I've got our Mrs Andrews' weak spot.'

Sasha obediently smeared his burns with butter and listened.

'It will not work,' he said at length.

'It had better,' replied Phryne. 'Or do you fancy being pressure-cooked into Sasha Surprise? She'll send one to each: Sanderson, and Dot, and Elizabeth. They can all look after themselves, I hope. That leaves her to us. Will you co-operate or not?'

'I am not at my best,' admitted Sasha, smoothing down his hair. 'But I shall try.'

Phryne began to listen at the door.

'You go to the Windsor, Bull, and obtain the letter which Miss Fisher told us of. She is in suite thirty-three. Don't draw attention to yourself and don't come back without it, or I shall be very cross. Mr Billings: you will break into the Queen Victoria Hospital, threaten the disagreeable woman with whatever occurs to you and get the samples and the script, if there is one. Then you may kill her, if you like. And then you shall have a whole ounce to yourself when you come back. James, you will tackle Mr Sanderson. I imagine that the letter is in his safe. Be careful, all of you. And if you fail…' she giggled, 'I shall be very cross indeed. You all remember what happened to Thomas, when he flouted me? I still have the very gun with which I shot him, and no one has missed him yet. Off you go,' concluded Lydia.

'I wonder,' Phryne murmured in Sasha's ear, 'I wonder if she truly is a sapphic, or whether she just loathes the flesh? What do you think, moon of my delight?'

'I do not think that she has any pleasures of the flesh,' commented Sasha, his mouth against Phryne's neck. 'Is that shoe-polish which I can smell?'

'Yes, I wanted to look unwashed. Not a sapphic, then?'

'I do not think so. Her manner towards you is not…not confiding enough. She is more like a child, with a child's will and the single mind. She does not touch you, or me—*quant à ça*, that would be a trial. She finds sex loathsome, that is plain. Dirty. Disgusting. Her husband has mistreated her; no woman is born icy…what is the word?'

'Frigid. Then all this is a substitute?' .

'No,' whispered Sasha. 'It is power that she loves. Did you see her eyes when she spoke of murdering us? They glistened like those of a woman in love. It is power she loves.'

'And sex she hates.'

'And on her hatred and loathing of sex our only chance depends, *hein*?'

'*Oui*,' agreed Phryne.

Dr MacMillan had had a hard struggle with the breech baby, and when that was safe, with the mother, who seemed obstinately set upon dying. It was nine o'clock before she was satisfied that they both intended to stay, and she could go upstairs for a bath, a cup of strong coffee and an hour's sleep before the day's work began. She had arisen from her bed and was dressed, combing her pepper-and-salt hair before the mirror, when a noise at the window attracted her attention. Someone was climbing the drainpipe. It was a lithe man, with a black silk scarf around his neck.

The doctor was used to the fact that any all-woman establishment attracts peeping Toms and perverts of all descriptions. She called to mind the hand-to-hand struggle she had once had with a drunken carter in Glasgow, and chuckled. Waiting until Cokey Billings' head was crowning through the open window, she struck him forcibly on the occiput with the washstand basin—which was of thick, white hospital china—and followed his downward course with a practised eye. She reckoned that a fall of two storeys would probably not kill him, and walked down to provide life-saving measures if necessary.

'Waste of a good basin,' muttered Dr MacMillan, regretfully.

The Bull found the Windsor without getting lost more than three or four times and eyed the doorman sourly. He had been denied admittance with a fluency of language which he found wounding, and was now at a loss. If he couldn't get in, how could he search suite thirty-three for this letter the boss wanted? Thinking always gave the Bull a headache. While waiting, he decided to have a drink at the nearby hostelry, where he could keep an eye on the door.

Gentleman Jim, stepping through the window of Mr Sanderson's library, located the safe and rolled the tumblers between his fingers. His ears, trained to such work, found the first faint click that would begin to release the combination. He was only two numbers away from it when he was grabbed roughly by two policemen and handcuffed. Mr Sanderson had fitted his library window with the new telephone burglar alarm, which rang at Russell Street. As befitted a gentleman, he went quietly.

⌘

Dot became more and more alarmed as the clock ticked on. There had been no message from Phryne, but someone had inquired for her at the desk.

She had mended all the stockings, and was not comfortable waiting with nothing to do. She was also very hungry, being unused to going without her breakfast since she had come into Phryne's service.

It was ten o'clock in the morning.

⌘

Phryne laid herself out across Sasha's knees as she heard the brisk clack of Lydia's heels on the uncarpeted floor of the hall.

The door was unlocked, and Lydia, returning without companions, found a shocking spectacle to offend her eye. Phryne's damaged dress was discarded and Sasha's cut and bloodstained shirt lay on the floor. Phryne had ripped her camiknickers down to the crotch to allow free play for Sasha's hands and was lying back, eyes glazed with desire.

Lydia stopped short and shrieked, 'Stop that!'

The lovers paid her no heed. She flourished the gun, took another step, and shrieked again, spattering Sasha with spittle.

'Let her alone!' Her face distorted into a grimace. Teeth bared, she struck at Sasha with the gun, and at that moment Phryne flung the shirt over her head and seized the gun hand.

They rolled about the floor, Lydia grunting and attempting to bite while Phryne knelt astride her, bashing her hand hard down on the tiles at the edge of the swimming bath.

'Help me, Sasha, she's as strong as a horse!' gasped Phryne, and the young man added his weight to Phryne's.

Lydia released the gun, her hand being broken. Phryne rolled her over and tied her wrists with the remains of the mistreated dress. Lydia struggled silently and furiously until Sasha caught her ankles to tie her feet together, when she went as lax as a rag doll and whimpered.

'What's taken all the fight out of her?' wondered Phryne, sucking a bitten finger. Sasha shuddered.

'She thought that I meant to rape her,' he answered, his complexion greening.

'You sit and watch her, Sasha, and don't go any closer than that. Just watch—you don't have to talk to her. I want a look around. I hope that the house is empty, but I don't know. And you really have no talent for intrigue.'

Phryne opened the door carefully and listened. There was no one stirring. Overhead, she heard a slow thumping that indicated that Gerda was alive; she owed Gerda a favour. It had been she who had warned her of the Rose.

Phryne found some rope in the kitchen and looked out into the little yard. Seeing it in daylight, she shuddered to think that she had ever been near it.

'A couple of cans of paraffin and a match would do that place a world of good,' she muttered. She bolted the door, not wishing for any surprises from behind, and rejoined Sasha. Together they trussed Lydia Andrews as close as a Christmas turkey. Phryne recovered her tattered mantle and pulled it on.

'I don't understand it,' murmured Lydia's pale lips. 'It was all going so well until you came along...'

'And you know the cream of the jest, don't you?' chuckled Phryne. 'Your father sent me, to find out if your husband was poisoning you. I only got into this snow business because it killed Sasha's mother. Well, now you've found your King of Snow, Sasha, the man you swore to kill—do you still want to?'

Sasha flinched. 'She is a monstrous woman,' he said slowly. 'A daughter of a dog, a servant of the anti-Christ, but I do not want to kill her.'

'We've got company,' said Phryne, repossessing herself of the gun as the front window shattered, and Bert leapt in, followed by Cec and several policemen.

'We should have known, Cec,' he exclaimed, disgusted, as he came to a full stop out of Phryne's line of fire. 'Rescuing? She don't want rescuing. Not though it don't look like she's had a time of it,' he added, observing Phryne's elegant figure, most of which was evident through the rents in her garments. 'I've brung a few coppers along, Miss, and I've been delayed because the lame-brains wouldn't believe me. They had to gather in your little chemist and his girl and comb the stock before they were convinced. Cops? Don't talk to me about cops.'

An embarrassed policeman came forward to handcuff Lydia. She moved passively, but turned in their grip to spit full in Sasha's face.

'Manners,' said the policeman reprovingly. 'I've got a message for you from the detective-inspector, Miss Fisher. He's got all the samples and he'd like to see you as soon as may be. Perhaps when you're dressed,' he added, averting his eyes.

'How did Dot get her message through?' asked Phryne. The policeman grinned.

'She rang the inspector and asked him to fetch it. Simple, eh? And we picked up a bloke as he tried to waylay your maid when she came out with the inspector. The hotel clerk pointed her out to him. Huge big bloke. Took four of us to bring him down. I'll be taking this one in, Miss.'

'Show me your warrant card, please,' asked Phryne, who had never put down her pistol. The policeman obligingly exhibited a card that identified him as Detective-Constable Malleson, and Phryne lowered the gun.

'I have a suspicious mind,' she confessed. 'There is also Gerda. She put me on to Mrs Andrews. Unfortunately I had to stab her and I've tied her to her bed. You'll need a stretcher.'

Detective-Constable Malleson nodded, gave some orders, and accompanied by three constables, carried Lydia out, loaded her into a van, and watched it drive away. Phryne flung her arms around Bert's neck and kissed him on the mouth.

'We did it!' she cried. 'Quick, let's find a pub and celebrate. No, better still, you shall all come to lunch with me.'

'Er…you goin' to travel like that, Miss?' asked Bert, smirking. Phryne pulled Sasha's shirt on over her ruined undergarments and re-donned her mantle. She looked quite indescribable.

There was a burst of astounded German at the door, as Madame Breda, entering, encountered Gerda on her stretcher, leaving. Madame Breda's healthy cheeks took on a cyclamen colour when she heard what Gerda called her.

'No time to explain, Madame. Your establishment has been used for drug-dealing. Come to lunch and I'll explain it all—or most of it. One o'clock, at the Windsor!'

Phryne spat out a stray feather and, embracing Sasha and Bert, danced down into the disreputable taxi, en route for the most exclusive hotel in Melbourne, dressed only in a shirt and a smile.

Chapter Sixteen

As his pure intellect applies its laws
He moves not on his coppery keen claws
'The Bird with the Coppery Keen Claws',
Wallace Stevens

The apparition of Miss Fisher, clad in rags, escorted up to the front door by a shirtless dancer and two grinning cab-drivers made a lasting impression on the doorman, who had previously been willing to bet that he had seen everything.

Dot was standing on the steps, weeping like a funeral, but the ebullient Miss Fisher kicked her bare legs in the air as she passed the doorman, and continued through the lobby and into the lift as though she did not present an appalling spectacle. The doorman's world wavered on its axis.

Phryne embraced Dot in a close hug.

'You did splendidly, Dot, splendidly—I'm proud of you. Now, order coffee for four, and find Sasha a shirt, for he must go home and fetch la Princesse and Elli. Yes, you must,' she reproved, silencing Sasha with a kiss full on the mouth. 'And I must have a bath, I'm putrid. At one o'clock, Sasha, in the luncheon room. Ring down and order a table for ten, Dot. Come in Bert, Cec—and excuse me.'

Phryne flew into the bathroom and planted herself under the showerbath. A puff of steam emerged and snatches of song could be heard. Dot handed Sasha a gentleman's butcher-blue shirt which Phryne sometimes wore with a black skirt, and he left. Bert and Cec sat down gingerly in the midst of all this luxury and accepted coffee in small cups.

'Is it all over?' asked Dot in a small voice. Bert reached over and patted her soothingly.

'Yair, the cocaine ring's all smashed, and the leader's in jail, as well as all the bad men. You can sleep safe in your bed tonight.'

Dot mopped her face and smiled for the first time in days.

'Oh, the lunch table!' she exclaimed, and rang up the *maître d'* with great aplomb. Bert was impressed.

'I reckon,' he said, taking another cup of coffee, 'that she wasn't scared at all. She must have been in deep trouble in that bath house but she was cool as a cucumber. What a girl!'

Cec nodded agreement. Dot considered that their language was rather free, but was too tired to resent it. She poured herself some coffee, drank it with a grimace, and went to find Phryne a robe, lest she forget her company and burst naked out of the bathroom.

Phryne, meanwhile, was revelling in the heat of the water and the speed at which eau-de-Little Lon. was being replaced with 'Le Fruit Deféndu'. She towelled her hair roughly and sat down in the bath to soak her hands and feet clean and remove the mud and dung from her numerous grazes. She hoped that she would not contract tetanus. She anointed them all with iodine, refusing to wince, and creamed her face with 'Facial Youth', a steal at a shilling a tube.

Dot entered with a robe as Phryne was examining her knees.

'No Charleston for me for at least three weeks,' she mourned. 'But no worse than that. Thanks, Dot. Now, go put on your best dress. You're coming to lunch, too. Yes, you are! And give Dr MacMillan, the nice Detective-Inspector Robinson and WPC Jones a ring and ask them, too. Are Bert and Cec still here?'

'Yes, Miss.'

'Good. I owe them fifty quid.'

Phryne put on the robe, a sober one in dark shades of gold, went out, and sat down on the couch next to Bert.

'I haven't thanked you for rescuing me,' she observed, lighting one of her own cigarettes with great delight. 'How did you get there so promptly?'

'It would have been sooner, and maybe have saved that friend of yours a few burns on his chest, but I couldn't get the thick-headed coppers to listen to me. I had to near drag one out to the chemist's in Little Lon. and buy him one of the powders. It numbed his tongue, all right, so he sent for the others, and they raided the chemist's first, despite us saying that you were in the front building. It wasn't until morning that we got it through their heads that we were serious. Still, we got there at last.'

'So you did, and I am very grateful. Here's the price we agreed on. We might work together again,' said Phryne, and to her astonishment, Cec replied.

'Too right.' It was the first opinion she had heard him express, unprompted. Bert looked at his mate in surprise.

'You reckon?'

'Too right,' said Cec again, just to show that it wasn't a fluke. 'Me and Bert have to go and check out some other business, but we'll be in on the lunch. Wouldn't miss it for quids.'

Phryne and Bert stared at Cec, then at each other. Never had they seen him so animated. Something was up, but neither knew what.

Bert and Cec took their leave and Phryne and Dot prepared for lunch.

Phryne donned the undergarments and dress handed to her by Dot, who was arrayed in her embroidered linen. She brushed her hair vigorously and put on a small, blue hat with a pert brim. Dot was wearing a close-fitting cloche.

They surveyed themselves in the big mirror, slim young women in stylish clothes.

'Are you giving your notice, Dot?' asked Phryne of Dot's reflection. 'This has been a bit above and beyond the call of, you know.'

'No, Miss!' Dot's reflection looked dismayed. 'What, give this up when I'm just getting good at it?'

'Alice, the lady doctor says that you can go home next week.' Cec was sitting by Alice's bed and holding her hand. She had small plump hands that were chillblained and red with washing. But almost all of the blemishes were gone. Enforced rest had given Alice the hands of a lady for the first time in her life. They were getting stronger, Cec thought, as he squeezed the hand, and Alice returned the squeeze. 'What I mean to say is...Will you marry me? I've got a half-share in a taxi and a place to live and...I don't mind about the hound who got you into trouble, though I'd break his neck if I knew him and...I think it would be a good idea...' faltered Cec, blushing painfully.

Propped up, Alice looked at him. He was tall and lanky and devoted, and she loved him dearly. But Alice was not going to make a mistake this time around.

'You're sorry for me,' she said. 'I don't want you to marry me just because you're sorry for me.'

'That's not the reason I want to marry you,' said Cec. Alice felt the strength of the grip on the white hospital coverlet and looked into his deep, brown eyes.

'Give it six months,' suggested Alice. 'Till I'm better and in my own world again. Back with mum and dad. Ask me again in six months, Cec,' said Alice, 'and we'll see.'

Cec smiled his peculiarly beautiful smile and patted her shoulder. 'It'll be apples,' he said.

'So, what did she say?' asked Bert, who'd been waiting outside. Cec grinned.

'Six months, she said to ask again in six months.'

'That ain't so good,' commented Bert.

'It's good enough for me!' exulted Cec.

'Aar, you're stuck on that girl,' snarled Bert, not at all pleased by this new turn of events. 'Carm on, lover boy, this might be our only chance to have lunch at the Windsor.'

The Windsor's dining room was crowded, and a table for ten had only been obtained by the *maître d'hotel* rushing one party through their meal with amazing haste, seeing them off with a glittering, breathless smile, whipping off the cloth with his own hands and summoning five menials to re-lay the table in record time.

Miss Fisher's guests were arriving. Dr MacMillan was refusing Veuve Clicquot and demanding a little whisky. Detective-Inspector Robinson, leaving three sergeants in charge of counting and weighing *Chasseur et Cie* cocaine from Madame Breda's Bath House, had brought Woman Police-Officer Jones with him as ordered. He did not really know what to say to her, out of uniform. She solved his problem by talking to Sasha, who had swept in with his sister and the old woman, and was starting hungrily on the hors d'oeuvres as though he had not eaten for a week. A loose artistic shirt covered his burns, and he was as attractive as ever. WPC Jones thought that he looked like a sheik, and hung on his every word.

Detective-Inspector Robinson engaged Dr MacMillan in conversation.

'How is that girl, the last victim of Butcher George?'

'Oh, she will be fine. I believe that she will suffer no lasting ill-effects. A strong young woman. How is the monster taking his imprisonment?'

'Not too well, I am glad to say. It seems that he can't stand confined spaces. He confessed it all, you know, including the rapes and the murders, but said that they were all little tarts who deserved all that he did to them. But he isn't mad,' said Robinson, taking a cheesy thing from the tray of entrées. 'Not legally mad. He'll hang before spring, thank the Lord. And the world will be a safer place without him. And we've broken the coke ring. Even my chief has noticed.'

'You mean Phryne broke the ring, and captured the criminals.'

'That's true.'

'And without her you would not have got your Butcher George, either, would you?'

'No. A wonderful girl. Pity we can't have her in the detective force.'

'A few years ago they were saying that women could not become doctors,' retorted Dr MacMillan crushingly. Robinson called for more whisky.

Phryne, Dot, Bert and Cec came into the luncheon room together. Their table began to applaud. Bert and Cec stood aghast. Phryne swept a full court curtsey, and Sasha led her to the head of the table, beating Cec by a short half-head to the seat on her right. The dancer possessed himself of her hand, and kissed it to general approbation.

She leant across the table to kiss his cheek and whispered, 'I still won't marry you, and I definitely won't pay you!'

'I am in your debt, for you have avenged me,' Sasha said seriously. 'Now there can be no repayment of what I owe you. And I never thought that you would marry me, which is sad. But do not tell the Princesse, or she will sell me elsewhere.' Phryne kissed his other cheek, and then his mouth.

'What has happened to Cec?' asked Dr MacMillan. 'He looks like he has won a lottery!'

'Aah, makes a man sick,' complained Bert. 'That sheila we took to your place. Doctor, Cec has fallen for her like a ton of bricks. And just today it looks like she's fallen for him, too. Turns a man's stomach.' Bert downed a glass of champagne, a drink which was new to him. He did not like the taste, but it clothed the world in a rosier glow and he was disposed to think more kindly, even of Alice, who was going to steal his mate away.

Phryne completed the confounding of Cec by giving him a congratulatory kiss as well. She was in a demonstrative mood.

'I've seen your King, Miss Fisher,' said Dectective-Inspector Robinson. 'She don't look up to much.'

'That's not how she looked when she was going to cook me and Sasha into a casserole in the Turkish bath.'

'My Turkish bath!' moaned Madame Breda, and was plied with champagne by Bert, though she protested that she never took wine.

'Begin at the beginning, girl!' admonished Dr MacMillan. 'We want to hear the whole tale.'

The Detective-Inspector, knowing that this was most irregular, was about to protest and withdraw when he caught the doctor's eye, and decided not to. Soup was served, and Phryne began to talk.

As veal followed the soup and chicken ragoût the veal, and then cheeses and ices and coffee made their appearance, she ploughed through the story, omitting the delicate parts. Even the outline gave her hearers enough trouble. Fabergé brooches and the Russian Revolution, the Cryers and the chemist in Little Lon., the planted packets of powder turning up all through the story, sapphism and crime...

'It's an unbelievable tale,' summed up Dr MacMillan. 'The scheming bitch is in jail now, and all her associates captured. Cokey Billings is in hospital with a broken ankle and a dent in his head. What happened to the others?'

'The Bull and Gentleman Jim are both lodged with me,' said Robinson, with quiet satisfaction. 'And the chemist, and the chemist's girl, and Gerda. That was a nicely judged blow, Miss Fisher, another inch to the right and you'd have killed her.'

Phryne, sipping coffee, suppressed the intelligence that it had not been nice judgment, but blind luck, which had preserved Gerda's life.

'To Phryne Fisher.' Dr MacMillan raised her glass. 'May she continue to be an example to us all!'

All drank. Cec murmured, 'Too right.'

Phryne drained her glass.

'I seem to be established as an investigator,' she mused, considering the thought gravely. 'It could be most diverting. In the meantime, there's champagne and Sasha. Cheers!' she cried, holding up a refilled glass. Life was very good.

Flying Too High

Chapter One

A sad tale's best for Winter
The Winter's Tale, Shakespeare

Candida Alice Maldon was being a bad girl. Firstly, she had not told anyone that she had found a threepence on the street. Secondly, she had not mentioned to anyone in the house that she was going out, because she knew that she would not be allowed. Thirdly, since she had lost one of her teeth, she was not supposed to be eating sweets, anyway.

The consciousness of wrongdoing had never stopped Candida from doing anything she wanted. She was prepared to be punished, and even prepared to feel sorry. Later. She approached the sweet-shop counter, clutching her threepence in her hand, and stared at the treasures within. Laid out, like those Egyptian treasures her father had shown her photos of in the paper, were sweets enough to give the whole world toothache.

There were red and green toffee umbrellas and toffee horses on a stick. There were jelly-beans and jelly-babies and snakes in lots of colours, and lolly bananas and snow-balls and acid drops. These had the advantage that they were twenty-four a penny, but they were too sour for Candida's taste. She dismissed wine-gums as too gluey and musk sticks as too crumbly, and humbugs as too peppery. She considered boiled lollies in all the colours of the millefiore brooch which her grandmother wore, and barley-sugar in long, glassy canes. There were ring sticks with real rings around them, and rainbow balls and honeybears and chocolate toffs. Candida breathed heavily on the glass and wiped it with her sleeve.

'What would you like, dear?' asked the shopkeeper.

'My name is Candida,' the child informed her, 'and I have threepence. I would like a ha'porth of honeybears, a ha'porth of coffee buds, a ha'porth of mint-leaves, a ha'porth of silver sticks…a ha'porth of umbrellas and a ha'porth of bananas.'

'There you are, Miss Candida,' said the shopkeeper, accepting the sweaty, warm coin. 'Here are your lollies. Don't eat them all at once!'

Candida walked out of the shop, and began to trail her way home. She was not in a hurry because no one knew she was gone.

She was hopping in and out of the gutter, as she had been expressly forbidden to do, when a car drew up beside her. It was a black car shaped like a beetle. Nothing like her father's little Austin. Candida looked up with a start.

'Candida! There you are! Your daddy sent me to look for you. Where have you been?' A woman opened the car door and extended a hand.

Candida stepped closer to look. The woman had yellow hair and Candida did not like her smile.

'Come along now, dear. We'll take you home.'

'I don't believe you,' Candida said clearly. 'I don't believe my daddy sent you. I shall tell him you're a liar,' and she jumped back onto the pavement to run home. But someone in the back of the car was too quick. She was seized by strong hands and an odd-smelling handkerchief was clamped over her face. Then the world went dark green.

*

Phryne Fisher was enduring afternoon tea at the Traveller's Club with Mrs William McNaughton for a special reason. This did not make the ordeal any more pleasant, but it gave her the necessary spinal fortitude. Not that there was anything wrong with the tea. There were scones and strawberry jam with cream obviously obtained from contented cows. There were *petit fours* in delightful colours and brandy snaps. There was Ceylon tea in the big silver teapot, and fine Chinese cups from which to drink it.

The only fly in the afternoon's ointment was Mrs William McNaughton. She was a pale, drooping woman, dressed in an unbecoming grey. Her sheaf of pale hair was coming adrift from its pins. These disadvantages could have been overcome with the correct choice of hairdresser and *couturière*, but the essential soppiness of her character was irreparable. Mrs William McNaughton reminded Phryne of jelly-cake and aspens and other quivering things, but there was steel under her flinching. This was a woman who had all the marks of extensive abuse: the hollow eyes, the nervous movements, the habit of starting at a sudden sound. But she had survived in her own way. She might cower, but she would not release hold of an idea once she had grasped it, and she could keep a secret or embark on a clandestine path. Her concealment of her character and her desires would be close to absolute, and torture would not break her now if her past had not killed her. However, despite the reasons, Phryne could not like her. Phryne herself met all challenges head-on, and the Devil take the hindmost.

'It's my son, Miss Fisher,' said Mrs McNaughton, handing Phryne a cup of tea. 'I'm worried about him.'

'Well, what worries you?' asked Phryne, pouring her cup of anaemic tea into the slop-bowl and filling it with a stronger brew. 'Have you spoken to him about it?'

'Oh, no!' Mrs McNaughton recoiled. Phryne added milk and sugar to her tea and stirred thoughtfully. The process of finding out what was bothering McNaughton was like extracting teeth from an uncooperative ox.

'Tell me, then, and perhaps I may be able to help,' she suggested.

'I have heard of your talents, Miss Fisher,' observed Mrs McNaughton artlessly. 'I hoped that you might be able to help me without causing a scandal. Lady Rose speaks very highly of you. She's a connection of my mother's, you know.'

'Indeed,' agreed Phryne, taking a brandy snap and smiling. Lady Rose had mislaid her emerald earrings, and was positive that her maid of long standing had not stolen them, thus contradicting her greedy nephew and heir, as well as the local policeman. She had hired Phryne to find the earrings, and this Phryne had done in one afternoon's inquiry amongst the local *Montes de Piété*, where the nephew had pawned them. He had made an unwise investment in the fourth at Flemington, putting the proceeds on a horse which was possessed of insufficient zeal and had not been able to redeem them. Lady Rose had been less than generous with the fee, but more than generous with her recommendations. Since Phryne did not need the money, she was pleased with the bargain. Lady Rose had told her immediate acquaintance that 'She may look like a flapper—she smokes cigarettes and drinks cocktails and I believe that she can fly an aeroplane—but she has brains and bottom and I thoroughly approve of her.'

Since she had made the decision to become an investigator, Phryne had not been out of work. She had found the Persian kitten for which the little son of the Spanish ambassador was pining. It had been seduced by the delights of the nearby fish-shop's storehouse, and had been shut in. Phryne had released it, and (after it had suffered three baths) it was restored to its doting admirer. She had worked three weeks in an office, watching a costing clerk skimming the warehouse and blaming the shortfall on the inefficiency of a female stores clerk. Phryne had taken a certain delight in catching that one. She had watched a brutal and violent husband for long enough to obtain sufficient evidence for his battered wife to divorce him. For, in addition to her bruises and broken fingers, she needed to prove adultery. Phryne, who never shrank from a little bending of the rules, had provided the adulterer with a suitable partner from among the working girls of her acquaintance, and had paid the photographer's fee out of her own bounty. The husband was informed that the negatives would be handed over after the delivery of the decree absolute, and everyone wondered that such a determined and hard man went through his divorce like a lamb. His divorced wife was in possession of a comfortable competence and was reported to be very happy.

The result of all this work was that Phryne, to her surprise, was busy and occupied and had not been bored for months. She considered that she had found her *métier*. Physically, Phryne had been described by the redoubtable Lady Rose as 'small, thin, with black hair cut in what I am told is a bob, disconcerting grey-green eyes and porcelain skin. Looks like a Dutch doll'. Phryne admitted this was a fair depiction.

For the interview with Mrs McNaughton, she had selected a beige dress of mannish cut, which she felt made her look like the directress of a women's prison, and matching taupe shoes and stockings. Her cloche hat was of a quiet dusty pink felt.

She was not getting anywhere with Mrs McNaughton, who had sounded frantic on the phone, but who now seemed unable to get to the point.

Phryne bit into the brandy snap and waited. Mrs McNaughton (who had not asked Phryne to call her Frieda) took a gulp of her watery tea and finally blurted out what was on her mind.

'I'm afraid my son is going to kill my husband!'

Phryne swallowed her brandy snap with some difficulty. This was not what she had been expecting.

'Why do you think that?' asked Phryne, calmly.

Mrs McNaughton felt inside her large knitting bag, which had reposed on the sofa beside her, and handed Phryne a crumpled letter. It looked like it had been retrieved from the fire, for it was singed at one edge.

Phryne unfolded it carefully, as the paper was brittle.

'If the pater doesn't come to the party, it will be all up,' she read aloud. 'Might have to remove him. Anyway, I am going to talk to him about it tonight, so wish me luck, kid.' It was signed, 'Yours as ever, Bill.'

'You see?' whispered Mrs McNaughton. 'He means to kill William. What am I to do?'

'Where did you find this?' asked Phryne. 'In the grate, was it?'

'Yes, how clever of you, Miss Fisher. My maid found it this morning when she was doing the rooms, it's a carbon copy. Bill always keeps carbons of his letters. He's so business like. He made a special arrangement to talk to William in the study tonight about this new venture, and I,' Mrs McNaughton's voice wavered, 'don't know what to do.'

'Remove could have other meanings than murder, Mrs McNaughton. What sort of venture?'

'Something to do with aeroplanes. Bill is a pilot, you know, and has won all sorts of races and things. It's so worrying for a mother, Miss Fisher, having him flying. Those planes don't look strong enough to stay up in the sky, and I don't really believe they can, you know, being heavier than the air. He conducts a school at Essendon, Miss Fisher, teaching people to fly. But he wants capital from William for a new venture.'

'And what is that?' asked Phryne, interested. She loved planes.

'They want to fly over the South Pole—apparently the North Pole is old hat. "No one has tried planes down here," he said to me. "It's no use staying on the ground. It's all ice and desert, but in the air we can cover miles in minutes." And he wants William to put money into it.'

'And your husband does not agree?'

'He won't do it. They've had some terrible fights about money. William put up the capital to start the flying school, and it hasn't been going well. He insisted that he be Chairman of Directors of the company, and he has all the books brought to him every month, then he calls Bill in and they have an awful argument about how the business is going. He was furious about the purchase of the new plane.'

'Why?'

'He says that a company with such a cash problem can't extend on capital—at least I think that's what he said. I don't know any of these business terms, I'm afraid. They are both big, hot tempered men with strong opinions—they are very like each other—and they have been fighting since Bill was born, it seems,' said Mrs McNaughton with suprising shrewdness. 'Amelia escaped a lot of it because she's a girl, and William does not expect anything of girls. Anyway she's dabbling in art at the moment, and she's hardly ever here. She wanted an allowance to go and live in a studio, but William put his foot down about that. "No daughter of mine is going to live like a Bohemian," he said, and wouldn't give her any money, but she enrolled in the gallery school against his wishes and she only comes home to sleep. She's no trouble,' said Mrs McNaughton, dismissing her daughter with a wave of her tea-cup. 'But Bill clashes. He disagrees with William to his face. I don't think they'll ever get on, and they behave as though they hate one another. Nothing but noise and shouting and my nerves can't bear much more. I've already had to go to Daylesford for the waters. I'm afraid that Bill will lose his temper and…and…do what he threatened, Miss Fisher. Can't you do something?'

'What would you like me to do?'

'I don't know,' wailed Mrs McNaughton. 'Something!' It appeared that she had relied on Phryne to wave a magic wand. As her hostess appeared to be on the verge of the vapours, Phryne made haste to assent.

'Well, I'll try. Where is Bill now?'

'He'll be at the airfield, Miss Fisher. The Sky-High Flying School. It's the red hangar at Essendon. You can't miss it.'

'I'll go there now,' said Phryne, putting down her cup. 'And I don't think you have any reason to be really upset, Mrs McNaughton. I think "remove" means "remove him from the board of directors" not "remove him from this world". But I'll talk to Bill, anyway.'

'Oh, thank you, Miss Fisher,' said Mrs McNaughton, fumbling for her smelling salts.

Phryne started the Hispano-Suiza which was her pride and dearest possession and sped back to the Windsor Hotel. She had found a house and was moving out, and hoped that her new home would be as comfortable as the hotel. The Windsor had everything Phryne needed: style, comfort, and room service. She parked her car and ran up the stairs.

'Dot, do you want to come for a ride in a plane?' called Phryne from the bathroom to her invaluable and devoted maid. Dot, who had come by way of attempted manslaughter into Phryne's service, was a conservative young woman who had so far resisted the temptation to bob her long brown hair. She was a slim plain girl and was wearing her favourite brown overall. Dot did not like the idea of the Hispano-Suiza and the thought of being bodily hauled through the firmament, which should contain only birds and angels, did not appeal to her. She went to the bathroom door with a leather flying jacket over her arm.

'No, Miss. I don't want a ride in a plane.'

'All right, 'fraidy cat, what are you doing this afternoon? Want to come and watch, or have you something interesting to do?'

'I'll come and watch, Miss, but just don't ask me to go up in one of them things. Here's your breeches, and the leather coat. What about a hat, Miss?'

'There should be a flying helmet in the big chest.' Phryne pulled on breeches, a warm jersey and boots, then rummaged in the trunk, finally finding what looked like a battered leather bucket.

'Here we are. Take a coat, Dot, and come on. We have to go to Essendon to talk to Bill McNaughton. He's got a flying school. His mother thinks he's going to kill his father.'

Dot, inured to the shocking things that Phryne was prone to say, gathered up her blue winter coat and followed her employer down the stairs.

'And is he, Miss?'

'I don't know. The mother is the most nervous woman God ever put breath into. Both father and son sound like bruisers. However, we shall see. It's been too long since I was in a plane.'

The Hispano-Suiza roared into life. Phryne swung the big car out into traffic with efficient ease, and Dot closed her eyes, as she always did at the beginning of a journey in this car. It was so big, and so red and so noticeable, and Phryne's style of driving was so insolent and fast, that Dot found the whole equipage unladylike.

They covered the road to Essendon in little over half an hour and pulled to a stop near a red hangar. A neatly painted sign informed them that this was the 'Sky-High Flying School Pty Ltd, Prop: W. McNaughton'.

'Here we are, Dot, and off we go. This may be a stormy interview, so stay on the edges of the crowd and be ready for a quick retreat.'

'Why difficult, Miss?'

'Well, you think of a delicate way to ask someone if they are going to kill their father.'

'Oh,' said Dot. She clutched her blue coat closer. It was a cold, clear afternoon, with little wind. Perfect, as Phryne saw, for flying. Three small planes were up, more or less, being flown by nervous, amateur hands. A bigger, faster two seater did a quick wing-wobble and dropped neatly, landing and running along the grassy strip with the minimum of bounce. The pilot taxied the machine to its resting place and climbed out, shouting at the top of his voice.

'A sweet little goer!' he enthused. 'Light on the controls, and just a bit nose heavy, but you warned me about that, Bill. Hello hello hello! Who's the lady?'

Phryne walked close enough to put out a hand, and shook the airman's gauntlet.

'I'm Phryne Fisher. I've done a little flying, but I haven't seen that 'bus before. What is it?'

'Fokker, a German company, made it. One of theirs flew the North Pole, mounted on skis. Jack Leonard, Miss Fisher. Glad to meet you. This is Bill McNaughton. It's his plane.'

Phryne put out her hand and had it engulfed to the wrist by a large paw. Mrs McNaughton had not told her that Bill stood six feet high and was built like a brick wall. Phryne's eyes ran up the scaffolding of leather flying suit to reach a large and ugly face. He was blond, with curls like a Hereford bull and intense blue eyes. The face was redeemed by a friendly grin.

'Pleased to meet you, Miss Fisher. Done some flying?' The sceptical tone offended Phryne. She had two hundred solo hours and a taste for stunt flying. She was no amateur. Bill might need some convincing.

'Yes, just a little,' she said sweetly. 'Perhaps I can take one of the Moths?'

'I'll come up too, Miss Fisher,' he said condescendingly. 'Just to keep you company.'

Phryne smiled again and climbed into the Moth. It was a sturdy biplane, perfect for beginners. It could land and take off on a handkerchief and had a stalling speed of forty miles per hour. She pulled on her helmet, breathing in the bracing scent of aviation fuel and grease.

'Let her go, Jack,' she yelled over the fracturing roar of the engine. Jack Leonard swung the propellor. The Gypsy Moth trundled on her bicycle wheels along the grassy paddock and lifted intoxicatingly into the air. Take-off was Phryne's favourite moment: the heart-lifting jolt as gravity gave way under pressure and the earth let go of the plane.

She steered the Moth into a loose circle above the landing-field. She could see the Hispano-Suiza below, gleaming like a Christmas beetle, and the matchstick figures of Dot and Jack Leonard. Behind her Bill McNaughton yelled, 'Not a bad take-off, Miss Fisher, what else can you do?'

Phryne pulled back on the joystick and the little machine gained height. She scanned the sky carefully. No one around. The last nervous would-be flier had landed. The air was empty, cloudless and still. She glanced over her shoulder long enough to see Bill's smug grin. Phryne decided the time had come to wipe the smile off his face and stabbed down hand on the ailerons.

With an agonized whine, the Moth began to spin. Phryne blinked under the goggles as the air tore past her face. Down came her heel on the cable, paralysing the nursemaid controls which Bill was attempting to operate.

Falling like a leaf, spilling the wind from her wings, the Moth pancaked down. To all observers she appeared out of control. Phryne, her heart in her mouth, waited until she could see the look of horror on Dot's face quite clearly before she threw the little plane into a forward roll, turning with the spin, and spiralled it back up into the sky. Bill swore breathlessly. She let the Moth find her controls again and turned back to smile her sweetest.

'Do you think that I can fly, Mr McNaughton?' she shouted against the wind. She saw him nod. Then she released the cable and said, 'If you can keep this steady at fifty miles an hour, I'll show you an interesting trick.'

Phryne was completely above herself with reckless delight.

'All right, fifty she is,' agreed Bill, taking control.

'Keep her wings quite flat,' yelled Phryne. The plane levelled out and was flying quite smoothly. Phryne seized a scrut, hung on tight, and got one knee up onto the top wing. Before the astounded Bill could cry out, she had gained the upper surface and was walking calmly along the wing, while he delicately rolled the plane a little to compensate for her weight. Sweat ran down his forehead and into his eyes. She had reached the end of the wing. She turned to come back.

Phryne faced into the gale with delight. The wind was no worse than in a racing car and the wing of the Moth was laced with struts of a suitable size into which to wedge a toe. She waved at the group on the ground and walked slowly back, noting that the tilt was being beautifully handled by her pilot.

He may not be a nice man but he flies like an angel, she thought, hanging briefly by her hands six hundred feet above an unforgiving earth before she dropped into her cockpit again.

'Good flying,' she yelled at Bill, but he did not answer.

Phryne took the Moth down to a near-textbook landing and hopped out of the pilot's seat into an admiring crowd.

'By Jove, Miss Fisher, haven't you any nerves at all?' asked Jack Leonard, pumping her hand up and down. 'We must have a drink on this. Come into the mess, we shall make you a member.'

Dot, who had ceased to watch when Phryne had climbed out onto the wing, was being escorted into the hangar by an attentive young man who was promising her tea. Bill followed slowly, shaking his head.

Jack showed Phryne into a small room at the back of the hangar, which had a bar and a lot of bentwood chairs. The metal walls were hung with trophies and photographs of grinning airmen with terrific moustaches, as well as a grim picture of a biplane breaking up in the course of a loop-the-loop.

He procured her a whisky and soda and sat down to admire.

'Where did you learn to fly?' he asked, as Bill joined him with a large glass of neat brandy, which he swallowed in one gulp.

'In England,' said Phryne. 'I learned to fly in a Moth. Beautiful little planes. You can make them do anything.'

'So I saw. That spin didn't look very controlled from down here but I expect you knew exactly what you were doing, eh, Miss Fisher?' Jack enthused. Bill grunted.

'You are a born flier, Miss Fisher. If you got the impression I thought otherwise, I apologize. I had my insides in a twist the whole time you were aloft on the wing. What a stunt! Why haven't I heard of you before? Would you like to do some exhibition flying for us?'

'Who is "us"?' asked Phryne, sipping her drink, and wondering when her hands and shins were going to thaw.

'The Sky-High Flying School. It's my company.'

'I see. Well, perhaps it could be arranged. Mr Leonard, could I trouble you to look after my maid? I think she's had a shock.'

She gave Jack Leonard a forty-watt smile and he moved over to speak to Dot, who looked pale and weak. Phryne seized her moment and stared Bill in the eye.

'I had tea with your mother this morning. She wants me to ask you not to kill your father,' she whispered, and the big face flamed crimson.

'What? You insolent bitch, what has my family to do with you?'

'Keep your hair on and your voice down. I don't think you are going to kill your father, and if you call me an insolent bitch again I'll break your arm.' She put a delicate hand on his right wrist. 'That arm. If you can't control that temper of yours you will get into trouble. Now listen. You are having some sort of meeting with your father tonight, are you not?'

The huge man nodded dumbly.

'All right, then. Your mother is so frightened by the loud and angry way you and your father conduct your affairs that she truly thinks you might kill the old man. Why not try peaceful means? Is all that sound and fury essential?'

'It isn't me,' protested Bill. 'It's him. He knows a lot about business but nothing about flying—he's scared to death in the air, he's only been up once—and he tries to lay down the law to me about flying and I get angry, then he gets angry and then...'

'And then your poor mother has to put up with a scene that shatters her nerves again.'

'Well, what business is it of yours, Miss Fisher?'

'I told you. Your mother called me in to stop you from killing your father. I'm an investigator. I don't think you are really meaning to assassinate the man, but I have to do something to earn my retainer. Perhaps you could conduct your arguments somewhere else, if that is how you have to carry on,' she suggested. 'Here, for instance. No neighbours near, and your mother need never know.'

'That might be an idea. Of course, the mater has never been strong, but I didn't know it was upsetting her all that much. Amelia was always saying that the mater flinched at every sound, but you can't believe Amelia.'

'Why not?'

Bill snorted and leaned forward to whisper.

'The girl's potty. Gone off to be an artist, joined the gallery school and talks of nothing but light and colour. I never pay any attention to her. She's not interested in flying. But you, Miss Fisher, you're different. I'll do what I can,' conceded Bill. 'I don't want the mater to worry.'

'That's handsome of you,' said Phryne ironically, and began to talk aeroplane shop.

An hour later she extracted Dot from the friendly attentions of Jack Leonard and drove back to the city, exhilarated by her adventure and satisfied that Bill would curb his anger when he met with his father that night.

⚭

'Have you seen Candida?' asked Molly Maldon, perplexed. There were times when the strain of coping with Candida and her father told on Molly. She was a small woman, fiery and logical, with a wild Celtic streak. Henry Maldon always said that her temper had come with her red hair.

Molly could cope with the baby Alexander, because he was not subtle and because he was very young, but Candida frequently reduced her to pulp. She was an honest child who did not scruple to lie like a trooper if it suited her. She was a delicate asthmatic with the strength of ten and the willpower of Attila the Hun. She was a sweet, affectionate angel who had nearly bitten her baby brother's ear off. Candida was very intelligent, and had taught herself to read, but occasionally did things that were so stupid that Molly wondered if the child was touched. Candida's natural mother had died in an asylum and Molly had been known to comment, in moments of complete exasperation, that it was Candida who had driven her there.

Henry Maldon looked up from his navigation tables. He was a tall vague man, with blue eyes and weathered skin. He always seemed to be looking into far horizons. This meant that he had scattered Melbourne with his keys, wallets, hats, cigarette lighters and on one inexplicable occasion, both socks.

'Oh, Henry, do buck up. Where is Candida?'

'She was right there,' said Henry, dragging his mind away from the South Pole. 'Sitting on the floor reading the newspaper. She liked the treasures from Luxor, and I promised to help her make a pyramid out of blocks if she let me alone to finish my sums. Then she was quiet for…good God, a whole hour…and I never heard her go out.'

'She knows that she is not allowed to leave the garden,' said Molly. 'The first thing to do is to search the house. Wake up, Henry, do! I have a nasty feeling about this.' Henry, alert at last, rummaged his way through the ground floor of the small house which he had recently bought. It had been so complete a windfall that he was still not altogether sure that it had happened. Most of the belongings were still in boxes, and it was not difficult to scour the places where even a cunning and vindictive six year old might secrete herself.

'Try the roof,' suggested Molly.

There was a ring at the doorbell. Molly ran down the passage and snatched the door open.

'You bad, bad girl,' she said, and realized that the caller was looking rather puzzled. It was her husband's old crony, Jack Leonard.

'I say, Molly, what's afoot? Been through the wars?'

'Candida's missing!' exclaimed Molly, bursting into tears. 'The spanking I shall give the little madam when I find her, she won't sit down for a week. Oh, Jack did you come in a car?'

'Yes, got the old motor outside. Do you want me to look for her?'

'Oh, Jack, please. She's only a little girl and I'm worried. She could have been gone for an hour.'

'Cheer up, old thing, that kid is as tough as...I mean,' amended Jack Leonard, seeing a furious light in Molly's eyes, 'she's clever, Candida is. She won't come to any harm. I'll have a scout about. I'll find her, never fret. I say, Henry, this is a nice house. Bought with the...er...proceeds, I expect?'

'Yes, with the new plane and the money in the trust fund for the kids, I'm nearly as broke as when it happened. Molly hasn't even had time to unpack all the new furniture and things yet, and the garden's not even planted. All right, Molly,' said Henry Maldon hastily, detecting signs of combustion in his red-headed spouse. 'We'll go out directly. Come on, Jack.'

'Saw the most amazing thing this morning,' commented Jack Leonard as he piloted the car out from the curb. 'This spiffing young woman turned up at Bill McNaughton's school and spun a Moth.'

'They will spin, if you mistreat 'em bad enough,' agreed Henry Maldon absently. He was beginning to wonder about Candida. Usually she was reliable, but she had a strange, wilful streak and might wander anywhere, if it struck her as a compellingly good idea. 'Amateur, was she?'

'No, old boy, an expert. It was a controlled spin down to three hundred feet, then she zoomed out of it, and all with good old Bill in the dickey. Then she upped and waltzed out onto the top wing and walked from one end to another. I tell you one thing, Henry, if I could find a woman like that, damned if I wouldn't marry her. But she wouldn't have me. Poor Bill, he was as white as a sheet when Miss Fisher finally let him take the crate down. Nearly kissed the runway. You aren't listening, are you, Henry?'

'No,' agreed Henry. 'I can't see her anywhere.'

'Miss Fisher?'

'Candida!' he snapped. 'Drive round again, Jack, and do stop talking. I want to think.' Jack Leonard, although childless, did not take offence, and turned the car yet again.

Chapter Two

To be poor and independent
is very nearly an impossibility
Advice to Young Men,
William Cobbett

Phryne whisked Dot into town, taking St Kilda Road at a sedate twenty miles an hour.

'Are you all right, old thing?' she called. Dot, huddled into her blue coat, did not answer. Phryne pulled up outside a small house on The Esplanade, which was her newest acquisition, and turned off the engine.

'Dot?' she asked, shaking her maid by the shoulder.

Dot turned on Phryne, her face still blanched with shock.

'You nearly scared me to death, Miss. When I saw you climb out of that machine I thought...I thought...' Phryne enveloped Dot in a warm hug.

'Oh, dear Dot, you mustn't start worrying about me. I'm sorry I scared you, my dear old bean...there, dry your eyes, now, and don't concern yourself. I've done that trick thousands of times, it's easy. Anyway, next time I do something like that, don't watch. All right? Now, have you got the keys? All the inside work should be finished, and the housekeeper should be here.'

Dot sniffed, pocketed her handkerchief and found the keys. She smiled shakily at Phryne who had leapt lightly out of the car and was waiting at the front gate.

It was a neat, bijou townhouse, faced with shining white stucco so that it looked like an iced cake. It had two storeys and a delightful attic room with a gable-window which Dot had claimed. She had never had a bedroom of her own until she had come to work for Phryne, and she still found the idea tantalizing. A room with a door which you could lock, a place to be completely alone until you wanted to let the world in.

Phryne stood aside in the little porch to allow Dot to open the front door, which was solid mahogany. The hall was dark, and Phryne had lightened it with white paint, upon which the stained glass fanlight cast beautiful colours. The ground level rooms, which as yet were sparsely furnished, were floored with bare polished boards and overlaid with fine Turkish rugs. In front of the large fireplace was a rug made of sheepskin, on which Phryne intended to recline. The decor was cool greens and gold, reflecting the timber floor, and there was only one painting; a full-length nude holding a jar out of which water was spilling, to fall in a cascade at her feet. It was called 'La Source' and it bore a striking resemblance to Phryne herself. Dot disliked this painting intensely.

Phryne called into the silent house 'Hello? Anyone here?' and in answer a stout women in a wrapper fought her way through the bead curtain and said, 'Well, Miss Fisher, is it? I'm Mrs Butler. The agency sent me. Mr Butler is outside, dealing with the plumber.'

'Phryne Fisher, and this is Miss Dorothy Williams, my personal maid and secretary. What's wrong with the plumbing?' asked Phryne, wearily, for she had spent weeks on the design of a luxurious bathroom and indoor WC and she was going to have them no matter what the plumber said. So far he had charged her twice his quoted price and she was minded to become quite harsh with him if the house was not entirely ready, with everything that was supposed to flush, flushing.

'Mr Butler is dealing with him, Miss. You'll find that it will all be ready tomorrow when you move in, just as you wish,' soothed Mrs Butler, with a hint of steel in her voice. If she cooked as well as he managed plumbers, Mr and Mrs Butler were going to be a find.

'Now, what about a cup of tea, Miss? I've got the kettle on, and perhaps you'd like to see the kitchen, now that it is all finished?'

'Yes, I would, thank you, we've had a tiring day, eh, Dot? And more shocks than are good for us, perhaps.'

Dot followed Phryne through the bead curtain into the kitchen. It was a big room, with a red brick floor and new green gas stove on legs. There were two sinks, newly installed, and a hot-water heater with a permanent flame. Phryne's new dishes had all been washed and stacked in an old pine dresser, and the window was open onto her neat backyard, with garden furniture and a fernery. The despised outdoor lavatory was newly scrubbed and painted for the use of the domestics.

Mrs Butler tipped boiling water into the teapot and set it down. Phryne took a chair.

'Well, it all looks nice. How do you think you'll like it here, Mrs Butler? Is there anything you need?'

'Not so far, Miss. The tradesmen call every morning, and all the appliances work. Nice to have a gas stove. An Aga stove is warm in the winter, and there's nothing better for bread, but it's a trial in the summer, to be sure. And the electrical fires are lit, and the real ones, Miss. The house will warm up in a few hours. It will be ready for you tomorrow, with luncheon on the table. Will you be dining in?'

'Yes. I haven't much on hand at the moment. How about your room, Mrs Butler? I thought that you would rather bring your own things.'

'Yes, Miss, it's fine. Nice view over the yard, and my suite fits in perfect. I'm sure we'll be very happy here. Your tea, Miss.'

Phryne drank her tea, and paid attention to the raised voices in the yard. Mr Butler and the plumber appeared to be exchanging hearty curses. Phryne noticed that Dot still looked rather pinched and suggested, 'Come up and have a look at your room, Dot. You'll want to see how the furniture fits in. Thanks for the tea, Mrs B. I hope we'll be here about eleven tomorrow.'

Dot raced up the stairs to the first floor, where Phryne had a bedroom in moss green and a sitting-room in marine tones. She opened the door to her own little stair. It was carpeted with brown felt, had an enchanting twist in the middle and led into the attic room.

Because it was at the top of the house it was always warm, and Dot, who had been chilled to the bone since early childhood, luxuriated in heat. She had chosen the furniture herself: a plain bed, wardrobe and dressing-table, a wash-stand and jug, and a table and padded chair by the window. It was all painted in Dot's favourite collection of colours; oranges and beiges and browns. Covering her bed was a bedspread made of thousands of velvet autumn leaves. Dot sank down on it with delight.

'I saw it in the market, and thought that you'd like it,' said Phryne's voice behind her. 'Here are your keys, Dot. This is the room and this is the door at the bottom of your stair. I've got a spare pair and Mrs Butler has them in her bunch so she can clean, but otherwise you are on your own. I'll just go and look at my bed-hangings.' Phryne went out, closing the door behind her.

Dot rubbed her face on the velvet, then smoothed it into place again. Of all presents she had been given in her short life, and they had not been many, this was the best. This space was hers alone. No one else had any rights in it. She could put something down and it would remain there. She could lock her door and no one had a right to make her unlock it. Her mistress might be vain, promiscuous, and vague, not to mention prone to frightening Dot to death, but she had given Dot a great gift and had sufficient tact to go away and let her enjoy it. Dot sat in her padded chair, stared out to sea and loved Phryne from her heart.

Phryne inspected her bed-hangings, which were black silk embroidered with green leaves, and her mossy sheets, which were dark to show off her white body. Her carpet was green and soft as new grass, and her mirrors appropriately pink, and framed in ceramic vine leaves. All she needed now was a bacchanalian lover to match the room.

She smiled as she surveyed her male acquaintance. No one leapt to mind. However, something would come along. She might leave it for awhile until she found out how her staff would react. She had yet to meet the plumber-conquering Mr Butler. Phryne calculated that she had given Dot enough time to enjoy her room and called softly, 'Dot? Let's go and have dinner, or would you like to stay? You can come along in the morning, and help me pack.'

Phryne did not hear the feet on the stairs, but Dot's voice was close. 'Oh, can I stay, Miss?'

'Certainly. Come to the hotel at about eight, though. We've got a lot to do.'

'Oh, yes, Miss,' breathed Dot.

Phryne collected her coat and drove back to the city. She telephoned a flying friend she knew from her schooldays, and asked her to dinner, to re-acquaint herself with the aeroplane world.

'Bunji' Ross was a bracing young woman with an Eton crop and shoulders like a wrestler. She had begun life as a track rider, but had been discovered to be female and thrown out of the stables. She had no chance of becoming a jockey as she was too tall and heavy but found that the same qualifications that had made her a good rider made her a good flier. She had sharp reflexes, strong hands and most importantly, she never panicked.

'Of course, Phryne, you never met Ruth Law, did you?' asked Bunji, as she sat down in the Windsor's plush dining-room and stared hopelessly at the menu. 'I say, old girl, I don't really go for all this stuff, you know. I suppose steak and chips is out of the question?'

'Steak and chips you shall have, Bunji, old bean,' agreed Phryne, turning to the waiter. '*Filet mignon* and *pommes frites* for Madame, and bring me lobster mayonnaise. Champagne,' she added to the hovering wine waiter. 'The Widow '23. No, I didn't meet Ruth Law, what was she like?'

'A charming woman, and a simply ripping flier. But she was involved in a bad crash and her husband had a *crise de nerfs* and begged her not to fly again. As far as I know she hasn't. Terrible waste. I hear you did a Perils of Pauline on a Moth, Phryne.'

'News travels fast out here.'

'Well, everyone knows everyone in the flying fraternity. Mostly it is a fraternity, too, only a few other females in Melbourne. But there's more coming up, you know. I've got six in my class at the moment; good girls, too. Like I always say, all you need for flying is good reflexes and light hands. You don't need brute force. In fact brute force will crash you nine times out of ten. Trouble is the cost of a 'bus. Look at Bill McNaughton, he's just spent a small fortune on a new Fokker, and what is he going to do with it? Fly over the South Pole, by all that's crazy.'

'I met him,' said Phryne, as the waiter filled her glass.

'Did you?'

'Yes, he was flying the Moth while I did my stunt.'

'You're a braver woman than me, then.'

'Why, what's wrong with him?'

'Brute force, like I say. Wrenches his machine around as if there were no such things as metal fatigue and tensile strengths. Saw him rip the wings off a Moth once, and that takes doing. You know how forgiving they are, nicest little things, apart from a tendency to buck—a child could fly them. But Bill has never learned that muscle ain't the solution to every problem. That's what's wrong with him.'

'I told him to keep her to a steady path and compensate for the tilt, and he did.'

'Well, that's more than I would have thought of him. I wouldn't try it. He'd be just as likely to loop the loop with you aloft. I'd say you had a lucky escape, old girl. Let me fill up your glass. You look pale.'

'I feel pale,' agreed Phryne. 'What do you know about him, then?'

'Bill? His father stumped up manfully for him to start his flying school. It ain't going well. He's a lousy teacher. Yells at his pupils and frightens them into fits, then won't let them try on their own. They either give up flying or come to me. I've had three of his ex-pupils. He'd reduced all of them to pulp, especially the men. He doesn't really think that women can fly, so he's not so hard on 'em. It don't do a young man any harm to be pulped occasionally. Stop 'em from getting above 'emselves. However, you can't expect them to pay for it. He's a bruising flier—brave but brash, and he breaks his machines. Luckily, he's a good mechanic so he can repair his own. Word is that he gets on very badly with his dad, which is not surprising, because they are much alike. Both big, loud, self-opinionated bastards. This steak is jolly good,' added Bunji, and tucked in joyfully. Phryne picked at her lobster mayonnaise and sipped champagne. She was obscurely worried about Bill McNaughton. Having intruded into his life, she now felt responsible for him.

'Why not fly over the South Pole?' she asked, idly.

'Too big,' said Bunji with her mouth full. 'The North Pole is big, but most of it is ice, and so when some of the ice melts there's a lot less land to cross. The South Pole, I believe is mostly land overlaid with ice and when the ice melts it ain't going to get any smaller. And ice does funny things to planes. Look at poor old Nobile, the Italian, who took the airship over the North Pole. The planes sent out to rescue him all crashed, either on landing or on taking off again. That Fokker of McNaughton's was one of the planes they sent out after him, and it only managed one journey before it crashed, nose heavy in icy air. Nothing can carry enough fuel to stay up all the way over, that's the problem. If we could refuel in mid-air it would be different. Without a working radio and a few new inventions, it ain't possible, Phryne. And I'm the woman who flew the Pyrenees in January. I know about snow. What shall we have for dessert? And can you lend me a gown, Phryne? I've got to go to a ball, to get a prize for that speed event, and they won't let me wear my flying togs.'

Phryne sighed, as every dress she had ever lent Bunji had come back ruined; but she smiled, suggested trifle for dessert, and agreed. After all, considering her childhood of miserable poverty, it was nice to have so many dresses that it did not matter that one of them was ruined. She ate her trifle, reflecting that grinding poverty, though loathsome while one is in it, has the advantage of making one enjoy money in a way denied to the rich-from-birth.

It also enabled one to fulfil one's sillier impulses. She reached into her bag and gave Bunji her newly printed card.

'Miss Phryne Fisher. Investigations. 221B, The Esplanade, St Kilda,' read Bunji. 'You becoming a private Dick, eh? What larks! And what luck about the address.'

'It wasn't luck, I just added a B to 221. I bought the house for the number. You must drop in and see me, Bunji. Now come upstairs and we'll find you a gown.'

Luckily, none of Phryne's favourite gowns would fit the chunky Bunji, who was satisfied with a plain, loose artist's smock in dark velvet which Phryne had bought on a whim and had never worn.

'No, I don't want it back. I never liked it, and it suits you beautifully. How about a hat?'

Bunji chose an extravagent felt with a bunch of violets over one ear in which she looked indescribable. Phryne did not shudder but packed it up in a box and rang for tea.

'By the way, there's a daughter in that family—Amelia, I think that's her name. She came to watch Bill fly once. Arty type. Grubby but pretty, slender and pale. I asked her if she wanted to go up with me and she came over all faint, had to be helped to a chair,' Bunji snorted, not unkindly.

'Poor kid, living with them two, she's had all the spirit crushed out of her. But she did a fine watercolour of the flight. Don't know anything about art but I thought she was rather good. She gave it to me, and I put it on the wall at once. Bill saw it and said, "It's very nice of you to encourage my sister, Bunji," as if the stuff was rubbish, and I came right back at him and said that I thought it was a jolly good painting and that he was a Philistine, but by then the girl had crept away. He's a brute, Bill is. I don't like him. Anyway, dear, ta for the tea and the dinner, and thanks for the gown. I'll come and see you when you're settled, Sherlock, and if you want a bit of a fly, just look me up.'

Bunji breezed off, and Phryne, rather depressed, put herself to bed.

Chapter Three

'Qu'ils mangent de la brioche'
('Let them eat cake')
Marie Antoinette (attributed)

Dot sat down to an early tea with Mr and Mrs Butler. There was thick vegetable soup, an egg-and-bacon pie, and apple crumble, with many cups of strong kitchen tea.

'Well, Else, I reckon it's a nice little house and she's a nice girl, eh?' beamed Mr Butler, who had won his duel with the plumber. Everything that Miss Fisher had decreed should flush, now flushed enthusiastically, and the electric fires about which Mr Butler had had doubts, were working perfectly. Dot frowned. She did not know if this was a correct way to speak about Phryne.

'She's a lady,' reproved Mrs Butler. 'And don't you forget it, Ted. She's got grand relations at Home and her dad is related to the King.'

'She's still a nice girl. Knows what she wants and gets it. And pays for it. Us, for instance.'

'You see, my dear,' Mrs B. said to Dot, 'we weren't going to take another place when our old gentleman died. Such a nice man. He had good connections, too. He left us enough money to retire—a little house in Richmond and a bit of garden, just what we've always wanted. But Ted and me, we ain't old yet and somehow we didn't really want to retire, not if we could find a good place. A smaller establishment, with no children and other help coming in for the laundry and the rough work. We put ourselves on the books of the most exclusive agency, and doubled our wages. Miss Fisher sent the solicitor to interview us and we told the lawyer what we wanted. All Miss Fisher required was that we swore not to disclose any of her personal affairs to anyone, and naturally we'd never do that. Then the solicitor upped and asked us when we could move in to supervise the alterations, and so we agreed to try out for six months and see if we suited one another. So far it's going well. What about you, dear?'

'I've been with her for three months,' replied Dot. 'She helped me out of a scrape. I was out of place because the son of the house was chasing me, and she took me on. Since we started this private investigator stuff it's been all go. The only thing that might annoy you is tea at all hours if she's working on a problem, otherwise she's lovely,' said Dot, taking another mouthful of apple crumble. 'This is delicious,' she added. Mrs Butler smiled. Like all good cooks, she loved feeding people.

'Do you like cars, Mr Butler?' Dot asked.

'Call me Ted. I love cars. Always wanted to handle a machine like Miss Fisher's. Lagonda, is it?'

'Hispano-Suiza,' corrected Dot. 'She drives like a demon.'

Ted's eyes lit up. 'I expect she'll let me drive her to parties and balls and so on. I shall have to get a chauffeur's cap.'

Dot wondered how she was to mention Phryne's habit of strewing her boudoir with beautiful naked young men. She could not think of a method of introducing the subject and decided to leave it to Phryne to cope with.

'Well, Miss Williams, the bath water's hot if you want it,' said Mr Butler. 'And the whatsername works, at last. I'm going to polish the silver,' he said, and took himself off into the back of the house.

'Call me Dot. I've got to be at the hotel by eight, Mrs Butler, so can you manage some breakfast at seven? Just tea and toast. Good night.'

Dot climbed the stairs to her own room, washed her face and hands, and fell into a dreamless sleep in her own bed, in her own room. Outside the sea roared in the first of the winter's storms, but in 221B The Esplanade Dot was as snug as a bug in a rug.

Breakfast the next morning was bacon and eggs. Mrs Butler exclaimed at the idea of sending such a thin young woman out for a long day's work on tea and toast. Unusually full, Dot caught the tram and arrived at the Windsor in a lowering chill. The wind had dropped but the sky was full of rain. Dot clutched her coat close and ran up the steps, greeting the doorman as she passed.

'You must be freezing!' she exclaimed, as he fumbled with the big door.

'Not as bad yet as it's going to be,' he opined, cocking a knowing eye at the sky. 'Miss Fisher ain't going to walk any aeroplanes today.'

Dot found Phryne dropping her third armload of dresses onto her bed and staring at them.

'I had no idea that I had this many clothes, Dot. I should give them away, what a collection.'

'No, you need them all, Miss. You sit down and I'll start packing. You make out a cheque for the bill, and I'll have this all put away in a jiffy. By the way, the doorman knew about your stunt in the plane. You must be in the paper.'

'Oh, good. I'll go down and buy one. Can you cope?'

Dot nodded. She would cope much better if Phryne was not there. Phryne took her cheque book and bag and went out to drink coffee in the morning room and check each item in a voluminous bill. She was sorry to leave the Windsor. In it she had found great joy with her lover, Sasha of the *Compagnie des Ballets Masques*, now returned to France. While staying here she had broken a cocaine ring and had been instrumental in catching a notorious abortionist. It had been a fascinating three months but one could not live in a hotel all one's life. She sighed and poured more coffee. A bottle of Benedictine? When had she ordered that?

Left alone, Dot packed away all of the clothes, the shoes and hats and multitudinous undergarments and cosmetics and books and papers. She counted the jewellery into its casket, locked it and pocketed the key. Then she rang the bell for the minions and went downstairs to see if Bert and Cec had arrived to carry the luggage.

Offending the Windsor's sacred precincts stood Bert, in deep conversation with the doorman. Bert was short and stout. He had curly brown hair and a hand-rolled cigarette firmly glued to his lower lip. His mate Cec, lanky and blonde, stood guarding a dreadful van at the foot of the steps. Traffic edged around it, hooting bitterly.

Phryne made three corrections in the bill, added it up anew, wrote out a cheque for a truly staggering amount and summoned the manager. He came with a long tail of staff members behind him, each wishing to be remembered by Miss Fisher.

Her pile of luggage was being carried out by Bert, Cec and several boys who wished to acquire merit. Phryne rewarded them all, beginning with the smallest boy, and working her way up to the august Manager himself, to whom she handed a sizeable *douceur*, which he took without a flicker.

'Goodbye,' said Phryne, giving him her hand. 'I really hate to leave you, but there it is. Thank you so much.' she smiled upon the enriched and grateful, and walked out of the Windsor, trailing her clouds of glory.

She took her seat in the Hispano-Suiza, making the journey quickly, for it was freezing in the open car, despite her furs. She pulled up in style to meet Mr Butler at the gate. Dot preferred to travel with Bert and Cec.

'Just bring her in here, Miss, and mind the paintwork. Nicely she goes,' he instructed, and Phryne took the car in without mishap.

Mr Butler grinned and passed a doting hand over the red bonnet.

'Mr Butler, I presume? Do you like the car?'

'That I do, Miss. She's a beauty.'

'Good. See if you can get the hood up, I'm frozen. Winter seems to have come, eh? I'm expecting you to drive this car for me, so you can take her out for a little practice later, if you like. But be careful of her, she's the only one in Australia, and where we shall get parts for her I do not know. I must go in, my toes have gone numb,' were Phryne's parting words before she ran up the garden path to the back door.

She walked into a wave of warmth and the scent of cooking and dropped into a chair in the sitting-room, where there was a small bright fire. Mrs Butler bustled in.

'Tea, Miss? Are you cold?'

'Frozen, but rapidly thawing. Coffee might be better, but you'll need to make tea for Bert and Cec and Dot, who are coming with the luggage.'

'Very good, Miss. Cutlets for lunch, with creamed potatoes? Apple pie for dessert?'

Phryne nodded, and took off one shoe. Her toes really had gone numb. She rubbed them briskly, reflecting that the Melbourne winter looked like being long and trying. She was grateful for the fire and all her other blessings for a quiet five minutes, before there was a thump at the door and she knew that the luggage had arrived.

Bert and Cec were a team. They had worked together for so long, in the army and on the wharf, that each seemed to sense where the other was. Consequently they were very efficient.

Apart from a few loud comments on her decor, Phryne did not hear a word or a bump as her possessions were carried up the stairs with ease and despatch.

'Come and have tea,' Phryne shouted as the last chest was carried in and Dot shut the doors of the sagging van.

Mrs Butler brought in a trolley laden with cakes and sandwiches, and the big kitchen teapot. Bert and Cec clumped down the stairs to accept cups and perch themselves on the over-stuffed chairs.

'How have things been going?' she asked, and Bert grinned.

'We bought a bonzer new taxi,' he took a sandwich, 'and we sold the old grid. It's been going good, Miss. And you're in the paper, did you see?' he added, flourishing the early *Herald*. Phryne looked at the front page. Bert's stubby finger pointed out a picture of a young woman poised on the upper wing of a biplane, with the legend 'The Hon. Phryne Fisher in Flight' then her eyes dropped to a stop press underneath.

'Mr William McNaughton was found dead on his tennis court today from head injuries. Police inquiries are continuing.'

'Oh, Bert, look at that,' she whispered.

Bert read the paragraph and said, 'Yair? Another capitalist bites the dust. So what?'

'His wife is a client of mine. Are you on, if I need you?' Bert handed Cec a cake and took one himself.

'Yair, Cec and me is on,' he agreed. 'Good cakes these.'

Dot finished her tea and ran lightly up the stairs to begin unpacking. Mr Butler accompanied her, more ponderously, with a pinch bar to open the tea-chests. Phryne wondered whether she should ring Mrs McNaughton, while Bert read another part of the paper aloud.

'Irish Lottery won by Melbourne Flyer,' he said. 'Blimey! What a bloke could do with ten thousand quid.'

'Really?' asked Phryne. 'What bloke is that?'

'It's here, in yesterday's *Herald*. Henry Maldon, famous flyer, who last year won the air race from Sydney to Brisbane, has been confirmed as the winner of the Irish Christmas Lottery, a sum exceeding ten thousand pounds sterling. Mr Maldon today refused to either confirm or deny that he was the winner, but his housemaid Elsie Skinner agreed the letter bearing the superscription "Irish Lottery" had arrived on that Monday in January, and that both Mr and Mrs Maldon seemed very happy. Mr Maldon has been married for three years to the former Miss Molly Hunter, the daughter of a prominent grazier family. They have one child, Alexander. The six-year-old child of Mr Maldon's former marriage, Candida, lives with the family. When asked what he would do with the money, Mr Maldon closed the door and refused to talk to our reporter.'

'I don't blame him,' commented Phryne.

'Yair, and I can think of one housemaid who is now out of a job,' said Bert.

'Yes. Will you stay for lunch?' asked Phryne, and Bert shook his head.

'We got a living to make,' he said gloomily, then spoiled the effect by grinning. 'So give us a shout if we can help with any of the...er...rough work, Miss.'

He collected Cec and departed. Phryne took up the newspaper and began to read. She was restless and could not concentrate. How had Mr McNaughton died? Had Bill been arrested? Should she call Mrs McNaughton, who would be a bundle of hysterics by now?

Phryne was summoned by Dot, who wanted her to make the final decision on which of her clothes were to be given away, and the subject proved so absorbing that lunch was announced before the two of them had finished more than half of the garments.

The cutlets, creamed potato and peas and the apple pie were excellent, and Phryne said so, treating herself to two cups of coffee before she allowed Dot to drag her back to her room. After another hour, Dot had stored all the good clothes and had a heap of rejects in the middle of the floor.

Phryne stood up and said decisively, 'You can have whatever you like, Dot, and then you have my full permission to dispose of the rest. I am going to ring Mrs McNaughton. I should have done so before, but she is going to be in such a state...'

At that moment, the doorbell rang, and Phryne heard Mr Butler's firm tread in the hall. There was the sound of the door opening, then a faint shriek and a thud. Phryne ran down the stairs and encountered Mr B. carrying a limp bundle with some difficulty.

'Mrs McNaughton, Miss,' he observed gravely.

'Lay her on the couch, please, and ask Mrs B. for some tea.' Phryne removed the woman's hat and elevated her feet. Dot produced smelling salts.

'They've arrested Bill,' whispered Mrs McNaughton, and lapsed back into unconsciousness.

Mrs McNaughton had not been treated well by the stresses inherent in having a murdered husband and a murderous son. Her face was puffy with long crying and her fair hair straggled all down her unmatching dress and coat. As Phryne eased her into a more comfortable position, three soaked handkerchiefs fell out of her sleeve.

'Poor woman,' observed Phryne. 'I think we need a doctor, Dot. See if there's a local one. Mrs B. might know. Tell him we can pick him up if he hasn't got any transport. Ask Mr B. to ring the lady's house and tell her staff that she is here, in case they are worried about her. And I shall fetch a blanket,' she added to the empty room. She found a soft grey blanket in the linen closet and wrapped Mrs McNaughton carefully, as she was now shivering. She sat down on her new easy chair and began to search her patient's handbag.

There were keys, more wet hankies, salts, powder compact, a search warrant for the house, telephone number of Russell Street's Police Station, one fountain pen (leaking), Phryne's card, a card-case (mother-of-pearl), two letters tied with ribbon, a purse with seven pound three and eightpence, and some powders in paper, marked 'Mrs McNaughton. One powder as required'.

Phryne replaced all the chattels except the letters and opened them carefully, sliding off the elaborate bow of ribbon. She read rapidly, with one eye on her inert client, who moaned occasionally. As she read, her eyebrows rose until they disappeared under her bangs.

'A fine robust turn of phrase the gentleman has,' she commented aloud. 'Who is he?' She leafed through the pages of passionate prose and found the signature. 'Your devoted Gerald'. Gerald had not carried his frankness as far as putting his full name or address on the letters. Phryne folded them carefully in their original creases and slipped them back into the envelopes and the ribbon. Mrs McNaughton had hidden depths. Her husband's name was—or had been—William and she had been married for many years. The letters were recent, the paper and ink were fresh. The incriminating correspondence was back in the bag and Phryne was staring idly into the fire by the time Dot and Mr B. re-entered, escorting a very young doctor.

He was tall and slim, with curly hair and dark brown eyes. Phryne felt an immediate interest and stood up to greet him. He took a stride forward, caught his foot in the hearthrug, and almost fell into Phryne's arms. She embraced him heartily, feeling the strong flat muscles in his back before she replaced him on his feet and smiled at him.

'I'm Phryne Fisher,' she said warmly. 'Are you the local doctor?'

'Yes,' stammered the enchanting young man, blushing with embarrassment. 'Sorry. I still haven't got used to the length of my legs. Hope I didn't hurt you. I'm Dr Fielding. I've just started with old Dr Dorset, I've only been here a few months.'

'I've just moved in,' said Phryne. 'I hope we shall be friends. Meanwhile, this is Mrs McNaughton.' She indicated the supine woman, and Dr Fielding lost his clumsiness. He took a chair and sat down beside the patient, gestured to Mr B. to bring his bag, then gently pulled back the ragged hair from her face. He unhooked his watch and took her pulse, put away the watch, and laid the limp hot hand down carefully.

'She's collapsed from some terrible shock,' he said sternly. 'What has happened?'

'Her son has just been arrested for murdering her husband,' said Phryne. 'I think that you would call that a terrible shock. She arrived at the door in a state and fainted into Mr B.'s arms. Did she say anything, Mr Butler?'

'No, Miss Fisher. Just her name. Then she keeled over. Shall I fetch anything, Doctor?' His voice was quietly respectful.

'Yes, can you go down to the chemist and fill this prescription.' Dr Fielding scribbled busily. 'I can give her an injection which will help for the moment, and then she should be put to bed.'

'Doctor, she doesn't live here,' protested Phryne. 'She should be taken to her own home. And if I am to investigate the matter, I need her awake, at least for a short time, to tell me what happened when her husband was murdered.'

Dr Fielding looked Phryne in the eye.

'I will not give the patient anything that will act to her detriment, Miss Fisher.'

'I am not asking you to, Dr Fielding. All I want is a safe stimulant so that she can tell me what she wants me to do. I can't act without instructions, and only she can give them to me. If she's going to be laid up with an attack of brain fever or something she might be *non compos* for weeks.' Dr Fielding compressed his lips, shook his head, counted the pulse again, then filled a syringe with a clear liquid. He gave the injection, then sat down again, watching his patient's face attentively.

Mrs McNaughton stirred and tried to sit up. Phryne brought a glass of water, and she sipped.

'Oh, Miss Fisher, you must help me. They've arrested Bill.'

'Delighted to help, but you must calm down, take a deep breath, and tell me what happened.'

'I went out to call in Danny the dog. It was getting dark and I heard him howling, on the tennis-court. I went out and there was William lying on the court with his head…horrible, all that blood…and I screamed, and the police came, and took Bill away and now they'll hang him.'

Her voice was rising into hysteria. Dr Fielding put a large soothing hand on her wrist. Phryne smiled as confidently as she could.

'Calm yourself, my dear. I will investigate the matter. Today I'll go and see Bill and I'll do my best to get him out. All you have to do is close your eyes and rest. You won't be useful to Bill in your present state. Now Dr Fielding will give you an injection and when you wake up you'll be in your own house.'

Dr Fielding was prompt upon his cue and the tortured eyes lost their rigid gaze.

'Right, now we shall see what we shall see. Mr B., what about the medicine?'

'I've sent the boy next door for it, Miss. I thought that I should call Mrs McNaughton's home.'

'Quite right. Was anyone home?'

'Yes, Miss, the lady's daughter. She is on her way to fetch her mother and asks that we wait for her. She has also given me the name and telephone number of the lady's own medical practitioner. I've telephoned him and he would like a word with Dr Fielding.'

Dr Fielding paled, tripped over a small table, and took the receiver. There was a short converation which Phryne did not catch, then he hung up. A relieved smile illuminated his pleasant face.

'I appear to have adopted the right course of treatment. Her doctor says that she is a nervous subject. Well, you don't need me any more, Miss Fisher.'

'Oh yes I do,' said Phryne hurriedly, unwilling to let the first pretty young man she had seen for weeks out of her sight. 'Please stay until the daughter comes and oversee the start of the journey, at least. Sit down, Doctor. We shall have tea.'

Dr Fielding was a skilled medical practitioner, but his social encounters had been limited. Against Phryne he did not stand a chance.

He sat down and accepted a cup of tea.

Molly Maldon received the return of Jack Leonard and her husband with barely-concealed anxiety.

'Nothing?' she whispered. Henry shook his head.

'She was angry with me for not taking her to the lolly shop.' Mrs Maldon sat down suddenly. 'She stopped asking me, after a while, and that isn't like Candida. The lolly shop. Of course!' Without taking off her apron or putting on her hat, Molly Maldon ran down the hall and out through the door, into the street like a steeplechaser. Jack and Henry looked at each other, and shook their heads. There was no accounting for women. It was well-known.

Molly tore round the corner and struggled through the bamboo curtain. The window was packed with gingerbread men in golden coats. How Candida had coveted those sixpenny gingerbread soldiers. After her spanking she should have a whole one to herself, thought Molly. The shop bell jangled wildly.

'Have you seen a small girl in a blue dress, fair hair, and an Alice band?'

'Why yes,' said the shopkeeper. 'She told me her name—Candida, she said. Spent threepence on lollies. I told her not to eat them all at once. Why? Ain't her dad brought her home yet? He left a good two hours ago.'

'Her dad?' gasped Molly, wondering for a distracted moment if Henry were playing a joke on her. If so, he would know how she felt about it seconds after he gave Candida back.

'Yes, in a big black car, a woman and a man.'

'What kind of car?'

'Like I said, a big black one. My Jimmy might have noticed more, clean mad about motors, he is.'

'Where is Jimmy, then?'

'He's gone to school, Missus, he was only here for lunch, but he'll be home at half-past three, if you want to come back. What's the trouble? Has something happened to the little girl?'

'Yes,' said Molly, and ran out of the shop.

There, lying in the gutter, was a bag of sweets. Mint leaves and silver sticks spilled onto the ground. Molly gathered them up tenderly and ran back to her husband.

'Hello, old girl, did you find her?' asked Henry, looking up from the depths of a comfortable armchair. Molly flung the bag of lollies into his lap and screamed.

'I think she's been kidnapped. The sweet-shop woman saw her taken away in a big black car. Call the police!'

Henry brushed off the cascade of honeybears and bananas and stood up to take his wife in a close embrace. She was weeping bitterly.

'Call the police,' she whispered into his chest. 'Call the police.'

He shook her gently. 'Hang on, dear girl, let's not go off half-cocked. If she's been kidnapped for money then we must wait for a ransom note. If we bring the police into it they might hurt her...they might...' He could not go on.

Jack Leonard handed him a whisky and soda which was mostly whisky.

They settled down to wait. Henry Maldon would have preferred flying over Antarctica in a blizzard.

Chapter Four

All Art is quite useless
Picture of Dorian Gray, Oscar Wilde

'Miss Amelia McNaughton, Miss Fisher,' announced Mr Butler.

Phryne and the young doctor had been getting on famously when a faltering ring of the doorbell had interrupted their flirtation. Phryne pulled her mind back to the task at hand and took a good look at the daughter of the McNaughton house. It was not encouraging. Amelia was tall and thin, with ruthlessly cropped, mousy hair and blotchy skin. She had beautifully shaped hands, long and white, but they were stained with paint and the nails had been gnawed down to the quick. She had obviously dressed in a hurry or in the dark, for she was wearing a shapeless knitted skirt, darned black lisle stockings, and an over-large shirt and jacket. Her pale blue eyes flicked from Phryne to Dr Fielding and she was biting her lower lip.

Dr Fielding stood up and offered her his chair.

'Please sit down, Miss McNaughton, and have some tea,' invited Phryne. 'Your mother is quite all right for the moment. Dr Fielding has given her a sedative. You must be cold. Mr B., could you get more tea? No, on second thoughts, a cocktail would be more suitable,' she went on, observing the blue lips and the features pinched, as if with cold.

Miss McNaughton sank down into the chair and held out her gnawed fingers to the bright fire.

'Thank you, Miss Fisher. I don't know what to do. Father is dead, and Bill arrested, and mother in a state, and I've no one to turn to...'

'Have you no relatives in Melbourne who might help?'

'God, no. There's my father's brothers; Uncle Ted and Uncle Bob. Both of them worse than useless. We have never been a close family. Uncle Ted telephoned but all he wanted to say was that Father had left him some shares in his will and that now was the time to transfer them, because the market was turning down and they should be sold.'

'Charming,' commented Phryne. Dr Fielding got to his feet and kicked the fire-irons over.

'Lord, man, can't you keep your seat?' snapped Phryne. 'We have enough to worry about without you doing three rounds with the furniture. I want you here to take Mrs McNaughton home and I'd be obliged if you would stay put.'

Dr Fielding stiffened.

'I would not be remiss in my duty to the patient, but I did not wish to be third-party to a conference,' he announced. 'I shall sit in the kitchen until you are ready, Miss Fisher.'

He stalked out to be comforted by Mrs Butler with tea-cake.

'"It is offended: see, it stalks away,"' quoted Phryne and chuckled. 'What a strong sense of propriety, to be sure. Miss McNaughton, I am reluctant to leave you in that house with no one to look after you.'

'Oh, that's all right,' muttered Miss McNaughton gracelessly. 'Mama's maid was my nurse. We shall do well together. And now that Father is...is dead, Mama's nerves will be better.'

'If your father was anything like your brother Bill, then he must have been rather...er...robust in his private life.'

'He was a loud, crass, overbearing selfish brute,' said Miss McNaughton flatly. 'He nearly drove Mother mad and he always treated me like a chattel.' She gulped her cocktail thirstily. 'Do you know what he wanted to do, Miss Fisher? In this year of 1928? He wanted to marry me off.'

'How medieval,' said Phryne. 'How did you feel about that? I should have dug in my heels.'

'So I did,' agreed the young woman rather muzzily. Mr Butler's cocktails had some authority. 'I told him I'd see him damned first. I have my own man.'

She cast Phryne a glance both proud and oddly ashamed.

'Oh, good. An artist, is he?'

Miss McNaughton's pale eyes glowed.

'He's a sculptor. He is in the forefront of modern art. Father would not have spat on him, because he is a foreigner.'

'I have always been interested in art,' agreed Phryne. 'What sort of foreigner?'

'An Italian. Paolo Raguzzi. You will have heard of him, if you are interested in art.'

'I haven't investigated the Melbourne art world at all, Miss McNaughton, I have only been here for three months. However, are you now intending to marry?'

'Of course.'

'You must invite me to the wedding. Now, perhaps we had better get your mother home. I'll come too, and have a squiz at the scene of the crime. What is the name of the investigating policeman?'

'I can't remember...Barton, was it? No, Benton. Detective-inspector Benton.'

'Right. How did you get here? Do you have a car?'

'Yes, I took Father's Bentley. He didn't know that I could drive. We'd better call back that doctor.'

Phryne rang the electric bell. When Mr Butler appeared, she asked for Dr Fielding. He came, in offended silence, certified Mrs McNaughton safe to drive, and carried her out to the car. Phryne saw that although he was tall and clumsy, he carried the not inconsiderable burden of the unconscious woman without apparent effort.

Phryne took hat, gloves and coat from Dot and dismissed her at the door.

'You stay here and mind the phone, Dot. Call me at McNaughton's if anything interesting happens. Stay home, I might need you. Do you have Bert's number?'

'Yes, Miss. Be careful, Miss.'

'I'm not going flying again today, Dot, I promise. Have a nice cosy evening, and tell Mrs B. that I shall be dining out.' Phryne sailed down the steps in a red cloth coat with an astrakhan collar which made her look as though she was wearing a sheep around her neck. Her hat was black felt and her boots Russian leather. Dr Fielding straightened up from depositing Mrs McNaughton in the car and came face-to-face with her. She smelt bewitchingly of 'Jicky'.

'Do not be offended, Doctor. One is prone to be sharp when one is upset. I beg your pardon, and I hope to see you again in a less clinical circumstance. Come to dinner on Thursday at seven.'

She gave him a dazzling smile and her strong, scented hand. He floated off down the street to his Austin in a strange state between insult and adoration. Phryne smiled after him, satisfied with the impression she had created, and hopped into the Bentley next to the sleeping woman.

Miss McNaughton was a good, if reckless driver, and Phryne had nothing to do during the drive but to cushion Mrs McNaughton against the bumps. Amelia McNaughton took corners as though they were a personal affront.

After about half-an-hour, during which Phryne sustained a number of bruises, the car turned and swept up the paved drive of a big, modern house. Miss Amelia leapt out of the car and ran into the house to find aid in carrying her mother. Phryne eased herself out of her position between Mrs McNaughton and the door and got out.

It was three o'clock on a fine, breezy winter's day. The beech and elm trees that lined the drive had lost all of their foliage, but the house evidently kept a gardener, for there was not a leaf to be seen lying on the smooth lawns. The house was of a modern shape; cubist, with a mural consisting of slabs of rainbow colours over the front door. The mural was reminiscent of art deco jewellery, and Phryne liked it, especially against the smooth, flat planes of the building. Without the decoration the house would have been just a collection of different sized boxes in a cool grey brick.

The designer of this residence had decided that privacy was the keynote; and had placed the house in the very centre of the available space and surrounded it with a formal garden on one side, a kitchen garden at the back, and rolling park-like garden with tennis-court on the sides facing the road. No other houses could be seen. The house appeared as a little island of habitation in a wild and possibly dangerous wood. Even the traffic could not be heard, and at the bottom of the garden was the Studley Park rift. This was a deep valley with the river at the bottom and untouched forest occupying the slopes. It would be a very lonely place for the nervous. Phryne wondered how Mrs McNaughton liked living there and whether she had been consulted at all in the building of it.

Amelia returned with a gardener and a stout woman in an apron. Together they lifted Mrs McNaughton and bore her into the hall and up the stairs to a small room with a narrow bed.

'Surely this isn't her room?' asked Phryne in surprise.

'Yes, since she stopped sleeping with Father. He wouldn't let her have another room. He said that she could stay with him in the big room or have this, so she chose this. She says it makes her feel safe; there are no windows, just the light from the stairwell. But she doesn't have to lock herself in any more,' said Miss McNaughton as she straightened her mother's limbs and composed them for further slumber. 'And here's one door he won't batter against again.'

She stepped out of the room, leaving the stout woman to sit by the bed, and pointed to dents and cracks in the wood. The door had done nobly in fending off the master of the house. The timbers had cracked a little, but they had not broken.

'Ah,' said Phryne, deeply disgusted and wondering whether she wanted to find out who killed Mr McNaughton.

'He used to hit her—and me, too,' said Miss McNaughton matter-of-factly. 'But he stopped hitting me because I said I'd leave and that I'd take Mother with me. That frightened him, he was terrified of scandal, and I could have made a very impressive one. He didn't beat Mother while I was here, but I wasn't here very often. I am at the Gallery School, you know.'

'Yes, your brother told me you were an artist. And Bunji still has your watercolour of a plane on her wall.' Phryne was fishing. In all this time Miss McNaughton had not mentioned her brother.

'Bill didn't think that I could paint. He has the artistic sensibilities of an ox. And he called Paolo a greasy little dago. But he didn't kill my father,' stated Miss McNaughton, stopping on the stairs with one hand on the bannister. 'If Bill had killed Father he would have announced it to the world. He would not have run away. He takes after Father—everything he does has to be right. He and Father never made a mistake or offered an apology in their lives. Bill would have stood over the body and announced that he had a perfect right to kill his own father if he liked, and would anyone care to argue about it? I don't know who killed Father, but it was not Bill. I don't care if you don't find who killed him. In fact I'd rather you did not. Father had thousands of people who rightly hated him and any one of them is more valuable than Father. I loathed him and I hated what he did to me and my mother; do you know, after he had pounded on Mother's door and been refused, he used to come and make an attempt on me?'

'Did he succeed?' asked Phryne gently. Miss McNaughton stared through Phryne with her pale blue eyes.

'When I was younger,' she said quietly. 'He managed to catch me in the bathroom. Twice. After that I put a chair under the handle. He used to stand outside and bellow at me to let him in. I considered it, because it might have calmed him down, but I couldn't, I really couldn't. That's why Paolo is the only man I have ever loved—could ever love. He took such pains with me, he was so patient when I flinched and cried, and…and…'

'I know,' observed Phryne quietly. 'But it happens to a lot of women. You and I are fortunate in that we have found lovers who could coax us out of our shells. Come down, Miss McNaughton, and let's get warm. Then you can show me your work.'

'Please call me Amelia,' said Miss McNaughton suddenly. 'You are the only person apart from Paolo that I have told…come and sit by the fire in the drawing room, and I'll bring the stuff down. You might not like it,' she warned, and ran upstairs again.

Phryne was shown into a fine big drawing room with Chinese furnishings. The ceiling was lacquered red and the walls were hung with scroll painting and embroideries. Several brocade garments decorated the chimney piece, and the chairs were pierced and decorated blackwood, with silk cushions and legs carved with lions and clouds.

On the mantleshelf stood one free-standing jade sculpture of a rather self-satisfied dragon devouring a deer. The deer's eyes reminded Phryne uncomfortably of Mrs McNaughton's and Phryne turned away from it to study the silk painting by the square, latticed window. She recognized it as a copy of a famous artist. It was 'Two Gentlemen Discoursing Upon Fish'. 'Look how the fish disport themselves in the clear water,' enthused one gentleman. 'That is how the Almighty gives pleasure to fish'. 'You are not a fish,' objected the other. 'How do you know what gives pleasure to fish?' 'You are not I,' replied the first. 'How do you know that I do not know what gives pleasure to fish?' And that, of course, was unanswerable.

What did any of us know about the other, mused Phryne. If she had met the late and entirely unlamented Mr McNaughton, would she have known that he was a domestic tyrant, who when refused by his wife had sexually assaulted his daughter?

Amelia came in with a rush, and shoved a portfolio of impressive proportions into Phryne's arms.

'I'll see about the tea,' she muttered, and rushed out again. Phryne diagnosed artistic modesty. She emptied the folio onto the blackwood table and spread out the contents. There were watercolours, a few oil sketches, and charcoal and red chalk drawings. They were good, Phryne found with pleasure. It was always easier to genuinely praise than to try and find something nice to say about rubbish.

There were three watercolours of aeroplanes, with a pale wash of sky behind them. There were sharp, clear pencil drawings of flowers and birds, exhibiting signs of a Chinese phase. There were several rather muddy landscapes and a clever cubist house; but Miss McNaughton's real skill was in portraiture. With chalk or charcoal she could catch a likeness more clearly than a photograph. Here was Bill in flying togs, hulking and self-confident, but with a hint of reckless good-humour which Phryne had also seen. Here was her mother, in pastels, worn and lined, with the fluffy, harried look so familiar to Phryne. It was evident that Amelia's skills were not yet perfect, she was prone to a certain lack of confidence in her lines and some of her colours might have been bolder. Phryne searched through the portraits with delight. Here was a group of children, somewhat after Murillo but none-the-less charming. Here were eleven studies of a cat; she had caught the creature's elusive muscularity under the fur. Here was a swarthy man, thin and intense, with deep eyes and charming faun-like face; he had pointed ears, and the whole gave an impression of power and patience. Phryne was reminded of a Medici, and wondered if it was a copy of a Renaissance work. She turned the oil over. 'Paolo'. Aha. Good looking, but not beautiful. Deep, and a strong personality. Such a man must have made a potent impression on Amelia, who was not familiar with any powerful man who did not brawl and rape. She looked forward to meeting him.

There was a portrait of a woman. Phryne recognized her friend Isola di Fraoli, the ballad singer. She had caught her perfectly; the mass of black hair, the glint of earrings, the deep bosom and rounded arms and the wicked, penetrating half-smile. The last oil was a portrait of a man. Broad and tall but running to fat, he stood with legs straddled, dominating the artist with his presence. He had a jowled, big-boned face, mottled with red across the cheeks and nose. One hand was clenched and the mouth was open, as if in command. It was just a shade this side of caricature, and so carefully delineated that it was obvious that the artist hated every line in him. Being an artist, however, she had dealt honestly with him. Phryne did not need to turn it over. The resemblance to Bill was marked. This was Amelia's father. Phryne regretted that she might have to discover who murdered him. He was the essence of everything she did not like about the male sex.

Amelia and the tea entered simultaneously. Phryne took a cup and commented, 'You have a great deal of skill, Amelia. Would you sell me some of these? I've just moved into a new house and I'm decorating.'

'I can't sell them—they are only sketches. Take what you want, Miss Fisher. I would like to have some of my work in your house.'

'Call me Phryne, and I insist on paying. I wouldn't have someone say that I exploited you, especially since I shall make a packet on them when you are famous.'

'Take whichever you like,' blushed Amelia. 'Five pounds each—that's what students usually charge. Do you really like them?'

'Yes,' said Phryne, sorting rapidly. 'Your professors must have told you that you have an uncommon gift for portraiture. These sketches of the cat are good, too. Have you seen that page of drawings by Leonardo of the cats, turning into dragons? Very hard to draw, cats. There's a bony shape under the skin and you have caught the furriness very well. I'll have the cats, they can go along the stairs, and these chalks, one of the Gipsy Moth, I learned to fly in one of them—lovely little 'bus. Also the children, though they are derivative, don't you think? Do you like children?'

'I love children. I want lots of them. Now Father is...now Father is dead, I shall have my own money and Paolo and I can get married. We shall have a house in Carlton near the galleries with a studio for him and a studio for me and lots of nurseries.'

'Why haven't you married before?' asked Phryne, adding Paolo, Bill, and Isola to her pile. Amelia wriggled with embarrassment.

'Paolo wanted to. He's quite well-off, he's the son of an industrialist. His father disowned him but he has an income from his mother. But I wasn't sure, and I wanted to…'

'To be sure. How long have you known him?'

'Two years. I am sure, now. It is just that Father said such awful things about him, and even hired a private detective to follow him around and to see if he was sleeping with his models.'

'And was he?'

'Oh, yes, but that doesn't matter to me. I know that he loves me. He has put such a lot of work into me that he values me. One always prizes the object on which one has lavished the greatest amount of effort. Take that portrait of Father. I hated him. But to paint him, I had to look at him quite otherwise than usual: I had to examine him as an object, not as a loathsome man who tormented me. I stopped being afraid of him after that. Somehow the process of painting him had disinfected him.'

'I know exactly what you mean,' said Phryne. 'May I have the portrait? Perhaps you would like to keep it. Apart from the Paolo, I think it is your best work.'

'Take it. I was going to burn it.'

'That would be a pity,' said Phryne. She bound up the rejects in the portfolio and wrote out a cheque.

'Perhaps you would consider a commission,' she added. 'I have a full length female nude—you may have seen it…'

'Yes. 'La Source'. It's you, isn't it. A bit Pre-Raphaelite, but skilful. Do you want something to match?'

'Yes, a male nude in the same pose. Do you draw from the figure? Or haven't you got up to that yet?'

'Yes, but it's difficult. In oil? And the same size? Let me have the dimensions, and I'll see what I can do. I haven't done a big oil. Father would never give me the money for enough paint, and students aren't supposed to sell their work. There's an acrobat who does some modelling—lovely body, all muscle, but light. My friend Sally did an Eros of him which was super. I'll try it, now I can afford the materials.'

'Good. Now, give me another cup of tea and let's get down to business. Have you a family lawyer? We ought to get Bill out of the cooler if we can.'

'Get him out? But he's been arrested.'

'Yes, but we might be able to bail him.'

'Oh. No, we haven't a lawyer who does criminal matters.'

'Leave it to me, I know just the person. Where does Paolo live? I'd like to see his work.'

Amelia wrote down the address. She was uneasy. She was about to speak when a scruffy maid ran in and announced shrilly: 'That cop's here again, Miss.'

'Put your cap straight,' ordered Phryne. 'Wipe your face on that apron and stand up. A tragedy in the family is no excuse for panic. There. Now, be a good girl. We all need your help, you know. Where would the house be without you?' Phryne smiled into wide brown eyes and tucked a whisp of hair back under the cap.

'There. Now, who is at the door?'

'Detective-inspector Benton, Miss Amelia,' announced the maid and walked proudly out.

'Phryne,' cried Amelia, 'you are wonderful. Please don't leave me.'

'I shall be here. Sit down again.'

Amelia obeyed. The maid returned and announced sedately, 'Detective-inspector Benton, Miss Amelia.'

She cast Phryne a dignified glance and escorted a tubby man into the room. He was red-faced and almost comic, but his dark-brown eyes were sharp and shrewd.

At half-past three Molly Maldon and her husband walked to the lolly shop to cross-examine the shopkeeper's son Jimmy. The child was an unpleasant, sharp stripling, with a spotty face and oily fingernails. Molly, however, was prepared to love anyone who might lead her to Candida, and she asked as gently as any woman seducing an uncertain lover.

'Did you notice a big black car here at lunch-time, Jimmy?'

'Yeah,' drawled the youth. 'Bentley, 1926, black, in a terrible state of polish.'

'Did you see a little girl get into the car?' asked Henry. Jimmy smothered a yawn and Molly bit her lip. Boxing the little thug's ears would probably prove counter-productive.

'Yes, I saw her, they kind of dragged her into the back seat. Leather upholstery,' he added unhelpfully. 'Red leather.'

'Did you notice the number?'

'Some of it. There was mud on the number plate. I reckon it was KG 12 something. Couldn't read the last digit. Sorry. Mum, when's dinner? I'm starving.'

Henry Maldon took Molly's arm before she could do something hasty and dropped a shilling into the boy's ready palm.

'Thanks, son,' he said heavily. Jimmy yawned again.

Chapter Five

She speaks poniards and every word stabs
Much Ado About Nothing,
Shakespeare

'How do you do. My name is Phryne Fisher. I undertake investigations and I have been retained by the McNaughton family to act for them in this matter.'

The policeman took up a commanding position at the mantlepiece and glanced quizzically at Phryne.

'There is no room for amateurs in murder, Miss Fisher,' said the policeman condescendingly. 'But I am sure that you will be a comfort to the ladies.'

'I hope that I shall,' replied Phryne with all the sweetness of a chocolate-coated razor-blade. 'And I hope that you will allow a mere amateur to observe your methods. I am certain that I will learn a lot from your procedures. After all, it is seldom that I have the chance of getting so close to a famous detective like yourself.' Amelia looked up. Surely the man was not going to be taken in by this load of old cobblers? It seemed that Phryne had not under-estimated the receptiveness of the detective to a bit of the old oil. He softened and became positively polite.

'Of course, I shall be delighted to instruct you, Miss Fisher,' he purred. 'But I came to tell Miss Amelia that she should get a lawyer for her brother. He's coming up before the Magistrates tomorrow morning, and he should be represented.'

'Thank you, I shall do that,' said Amelia. 'Are you certain that my brother killed my father, Detective-inspector?'

'Well, Miss, he hasn't admitted it. He says that he came home last night and intended to have a discussion with Mr McNaughton. He admits that he had continual arguments with his father, and that they became violent at times.'

'Yes, that is true,' sighed Amelia.

'He wanted to drive his father to a meeting at the aerodrome so that the mother would not be upset by their argument,' said the detective-inspector. 'He says you suggested it, Miss Fisher. He waited for his father until four o'clock then gave up on him and went for a walk in the park. He says he met no one except an old man with a sack over his shoulder and a young woman, who ran past in a bathing suit.'

'So have you found the girl or the old man?' asked Phryne respectfully. 'I'm sure that you are looking for them.'

'Well, yes.' The policeman paused. 'Yes, so to speak, but we haven't found them. And we won't. I don't for a moment believe that there was a man or a girl, or that he went for a walk in the valley. I am sure that he killed your father, Miss McNaughton.'

'Why?' asked Phryne artlessly.

'Why? Well, such things are not nice for a young woman, Miss Fisher.'

'Ah. Suppose you take me out to look at where it happened. I have always wanted to see the scene of the crime.' Phryne wondered if she was laying it on too thick but it seemed that for this obtuse man no flattery could be too gross.

'Very well, Miss,' agreed the detective-inspector. 'Come along with me.'

'You stay here, Amelia,' instructed Phryne. 'Have some more tea. I shall be quite safe with Detective-inspector Benton.'

Amelia, open mouthed, smothered a giggle in her tea-cup.

Benton led Phryne out of the house and along a fine mossy path to the tennis-court. It was beautifully kept, with a grass surface as smooth as a bowling green. The lines were freshly painted and the net was not in evidence.

'This grass will not hold footprints,' commented Benton. 'But here are the holes caused by Mrs McNaughton's high-heels. She ran off the path here, you see, stood for a moment where the heels have sunk in deep, then ran back to the house. The dog's footprints aren't heavy enough to make a mark except on the flowerbeds. The body lay here.'

Phryne could see that it had. There was a sanded puddle of blood and grey matter, indicating that a very heavy blow had killed Mr McNaughton.

Benton hovered at Phryne's elbow, ready to catch her if she should faint. She did not, however, even pale.

'A head wound,' she said. 'How bad? How heavy a blow?'

'A very heavy blow, Miss. He was hit with a stone, a big rock.'

'Were there any fingerprints on the rock?'

'No, Miss, the surface was too rough to take prints.'

'How do you know it was the murder weapon?'

'Blood and brains all over it,' said the policeman, aiming to shock this young woman out of her unnatural composure.

'And why should Bill McNaughton have delivered it?'

'It was a good, solid skull-cracking blow, Miss. Split the head almost in two. No woman could have delivered it.'

'I see.' Phryne scanned the garden. There was not a gap in the flowerbeds, which were in any case edged with wood.

'Where did the rock come from?' she asked. Benton spluttered.

'Where did the...'

'Yes, where did it come from? Look around. There's not a stone in sight. In the opportunistic crime which you describe, the murderer would have snatched up anything to hit his father with and left him lying. You are assuming that Mr McNaughton followed his father out here to continue the argument and it developed into a fight? And that under the influence of fury, Bill McNaughton went beserk and just donged his father with whatever was to hand? Is that not the idea?'

'Yes. I take your point, Miss. This must have been premeditated. He must have had the rock all ready, then lured his father out here and killed him.'

Phryne briefly wondered how anyone could cling to a theory with this intransigence, in the face of all the evidence.

Phryne had moved away to lean against the old oak which had one branch overhanging the lawn. She patted it idly—she loved trees—and looked up into the branches.

'There's a scar on that branch,' she observed. 'Something hung here.'

'Quite the little detective, aren't you, Miss? That was a swing—a tyre. Miss McNaughton put it there for the neighbouring children. Very fond of children, Miss McNaughton,' said the detective-inspector, evidently approving of this womanly passion. 'The cook tells me she was always inviting them in for tea on Sundays, and playing games with them. We took the tyre away to be tested but there are no bloodstains on it. Miss McNaughton will be able to put the swing back, if she wants to. After the place has been cleaned up, of course. Nice young woman, pity she is so plain. Should have children of her own.'

Phryne agreed. Miss McNaughton would enjoy having children of her own. She withdrew her gaze from the tree.

'So Mrs McNaughton came out here—why was Mr McNaughton here?'

'He must have come out here to continue his argument with his son, of course. Then it developed into a fight, no, hang on, there's the point about the stone. Bill McNaughton brought his father out here, and had the rock ready, and asked his father to look at something, perhaps, and then...bang, then he panics, leaves the stone, and runs off down the valley to recover himself.'

'Would he have had blood on him?'

'I asked the police surgeon that, Miss. He says that if he hit him from behind, which is what he thinks happened, then he wouldn't have to have any blood on him. I thought like you, Miss,' continued Benton, honouring Phryne by implying that they shared the same reasoning, 'I thought that he was going down to the river to wash. But he still had the same clothes on when we apprehended him last night, and there ain't no mark on them.'

'I see. Well, watching your methods has been most illuminating, Detective-inspector. Thank you so much.' Phryne took her leave and went back to the house. Danny the dog cried after her from where he was tied in the kitchen garden.

'Amelia, I have to go and find a lawyer for Bill,' she called into the Chinese room. 'Give me my paintings and see what you can do about getting me a taxi.'

'I'll drive you,' offered Amelia. Phryne shook her head.

'I need you here, and so does your mother.'

The maid went off to telephone for a cab, and Amelia seized Phryne by the sleeve.

'Do you think Bill did it?' she breathed.

'I don't know. Tell me, the children who play in the garden, did your father know about them?'

'Not until recently—he was always out during Sunday. He came home early last week and caught me with them, and threw them out, the brute. The poor little things haven't anywhere else to play, and their mothers know that they are safe with me. I used to give them tea. And cakes. Bill likes children, too. He rigged up that swing with the tyre for them.' Amelia shuddered suddenly, and all the colour drained out of her face.

'The police took the tyre away, but they said I can have it back. I'll have to find somewhere else to put it.'

'Have you seen the children since your father died?'

'No, they have stayed away, poor things, I suppose that they are frightened.'

'Why don't you invite them again?' suggested Phryne. 'They will make you feel better, and you can have them in the house, now.'

'What a good idea. I can have a party! Oh, but not with Bill—'

'Nonsense. Have your party. Let me know when it is. I like children, too,' lied Phryne. 'Your brother will come up at the

Melbourne Magistrates' Court tomorrow at ten. Perhaps you should be there, and bring some money.'

'Where shall I get money?'

'Oh, dear, have you not got your father's bankbooks? Did he have a safe in the house?'

'Of course. The detective-inspector brought the keys back. The police have already searched it. Come on, let's have a look.'

She led the way upstairs to a huge bedroom, decorated in the extreme of modernity. The walls were jazz-coloured and the stark gigantic bed looked like it was made of industrial piping.

'Did your father really like all this stuff?' asked Phryne, as Amelia swung a picture aside and unlocked the safe.

'Father? I don't know,' admitted Amelia, her brow furrowing as she spun the combination wheel. 'He had the house built in the most modern style and then said that the inside had to match the outside. The designer did all the rest. It was very expensive. Ah. There's the click. I remembered the combination correctly after all.' The safe door swung open and Phryne received an armload of paper, jewel cases and a document case.

'There are mother's sapphires—he told her he had sold them,' observed Amelia, opening the blue-velvet boxes. 'And Granny's pearls, and Great-Granny's emerald set. Oh, and here is the enamel from that German exhibition.'

Amelia put into Phryne's hand one of the most beautiful pieces of jewellery she had ever seen. It was a mermaid in enamel, seated on a baroque pearl. Her delicately modelled body was of ivory; her hair was malachite, and tiny emeralds sparkled as her eyes. Bronze threads shone in her seaweed-green hair.

'Isn't she pretty? Even Father appreciated her. Is there any money?'

'Yes, here's two thou in notes, that should be enough to spring Bill and pay the wages until the estate is settled. Hang on while I just have a bit of a look through these papers.'

The document case contained several reports from the 'Discretion Private Investigations Agency' which listed Mrs McNaughton's movements through a whole week. They concluded that there was nothing suspicious in her actions. Did Mr McNaughton know about Gerald? Phryne wondered. Amelia pinned the mermaid brooch to the bosom of her drab dress and contemplated herself artlessly in the mirror which covered one whole wall of the room. It was all lights and surfaces and Phryne felt it to be intensely uncomfortable. The agency reported that Paolo Raguzzi was known to be sleeping with two of his models, and included names and dates. As a strategy designed to detach Amelia, it had not been any more successful than it deserved. Phryne leafed through several bank statements and cheque books and a pile of share certificates. The deeds to the house were there, as was the will.

She glanced through it. The bulk of the estate went to the wife, as long as she should not remarry. Ten thousand pounds was left to 'my daughter, Amelia, as long as she shall not marry'. The old bastard, thought Phryne, trying to hang on to his control of his family even after he was dead.

A firm of solicitors were the executors. The estate seemed to be worth about fifty thousand. This did not include the house which was freehold. Phryne reflected that Mrs McNaughton could live very comfortably on the interest.

'Here's the will, do you know what's in it?'

'Oh, yes. He's left me some money provided I don't marry. But he can't stop me from having Granny's money. It was left to me but he took it and invested it and wouldn't give me an allowance. The papers should be there...yes.' She plucked an old parchment and probate out of the pile. "To my grand-daughter Amelia the sum of five thousand pounds". That will keep me for life. I don't want any of my father's money.'

Fine words, thought Phryne. I wonder if Paolo thinks the same.

'Did you tell Paolo about the will?'

'Oh, yes,' said Amelia indifferently. 'He just said that he would expect such a thing from Father. Well, if that is all, Phryne, your taxi should be waiting, and I'll put all this stuff back in the safe. I will see you tomorrow?'

'Yes, I shall be there. Take heart, my dear. I shall get your brother out of prison.'

'Thanks,' murmured Amelia. Phryne took her leave and ordered the taxi to take her to Carlton.

At the door of a rather dingy office building she asked her cab to wait and leapt up the stairs, taking the route indicated by the brass plate 'Henderson, Jones, and Mayhew'. Luckily, the light was still on, although the secretary had gone home.

'Hello, Jilly, old bean, are you home?'

'Certainly, come through, Phryne. What brings you to this haunt of probate and miscellaneous offences?'

Jillian Henderson was a short, stout woman of about forty, who had taken her father's place in his firm. She was still a junior partner and prone to collect more than her share of divorces and family problems. None the less she had built up a flourishing little practice in crime and was always on the lookout for a murder, where she thought she would make her reputation.

'Got a murder for you, Jilly, and you'll have to apply for bail for him tomorrow morning, can you manage?'

'Oh, Phryne, how super! A murder of my very own. What's his name?'

'Bill McNaughton. You might have read about it in the newspaper. Have you no fire in these rooms? I'm perishing.'

Phryne went into Jillian's office, and ensconced herself in front of a meagre kerosene heater.

'Tell me all about it.'

Phryne recounted the history and proceedings of the investigation, and Jillian pursed her lips.

'And you are going to find the real murderer for him, are you?'

'I'm going to try.'

'Well, think carefully before you tell me what you find. They have a very slim case against your Bill. His finger-prints are not on the stone, and he says he was in the river valley. Two people are supposed to have seen him.'

'Yes. And he is definitely not my Bill.'

'Now what if you find these two people and they can't remember seeing Bill? People are very unobservant. I would not trust any eyewitness evidence if it was served up to me on a plate. It is most unreliable. If you don't find them, I can suggest that they exist but just haven't been found. If you find 'em and they can be discounted as evidence, the prosecution has a weapon. See?'

'I'm shocked,' declared Phryne. 'Have you no regard for truth?'

'If you had entered the law, you will know that truth is a very dicey quality. "What is truth?" said Pilate, and I have always thought he must have been a solicitor. However, I'll apply for bail tomorrow, and see if the police have any objections. It depends on who the prosecutor is, and the informant.'

'I think the informant must be Detective-inspector Benton.' Jillian groaned, and made a note. 'I ought to charge double for dealing with him. He has a theory, I gather?'

'Yes, that Bill lured his father out onto the tennis-court and hit him with a rock imported for the purpose.'

'Then he'll stick to it through thick, thin, and soupy. I've had some struggles with him. I've never met such a stubborn man in my entire life,' said Jillian, rubbing her hands, and seeming to relish a new conflict. 'Well, well, good old Benton. This may be fun. Am I definitely retained? You have the family's authority?'

'Yes, I do, and you are retained like billy-o. Go to it and the Lord speed your footsteps. Now I've got to go and see a sculptor. Miss McNaughton has two thou in cash—will that cover the surety?'

'I think so. We may have to go to the Supreme Court tomorrow, if the Magistrate won't cooperate. Will the old bank account stand that?'

'It will. Got to go, Jilly. See you tomorrow at ten.'

'I shall be there,' said Jillian smugly. 'And you shall have Bill shortly after.'

Phryne retrieved her taxi and set off for the studio of Paolo Ragazzi.

Chapter Six

I can resist anything except temptation
Lady Windermere's Fan, Oscar Wilde

The studio of Paolo Raguzzi was on the third floor of a rundown boarding house at the depressed end of Princes Street. Phryne trod slowly up the stairs, the lift being out of order, and knocked on a flimsy wooden door. Something loud and vaguely operatic was playing on a gramophone inside. Phryne knocked again.

The door was flung open by a girl in a coat and hat.

'Oh, good, dearie, you're just in time. He's doing his block in there. I told him that I'd have to leave early but he just keeps going on about his nymph. Good luck, and don't take no notice. He ain't bad; just loud.' So saying, she tripped lightly down the stairs and Phryne was confronted with a burst of what she assumed were swear words in Italian. They proceeded from behind a beaded curtain, and a voice yelled, '*Avanti! Vieni, vieni qua, signorina.* I haven't got all night and you're letting the cold in. Come along! I won't bite, whatever Mary told you at the door.'

This sounded promising and the voice was light and pleasant, so Phryne brushed the beads aside and went in.

The studio was a large, light room, with the winter sun fading through the skylight. At one end was the artist's living quarters,

which were in neat array; at the other a bed, and a model's throne
covered by a worn velvet cloth in Phryne's favourite shade of
green. There was a delightful scent of buttered toast. The artist,
attired in a very old shirt and flannel bags, was crunching the last
crumb. He was not much taller than Phryne and had fine brown
eyes, which smiled. Otherwise he looked just like his portrait.

'I'm…' began Phryne, and the artist waved his tea-cup.

'I'm delighted to meet you, *signorina*. You have just the limbs
that I require. You can put your clothes over there, and call me
when you are ready.'

This was interesting. She had been mistaken for a model.
Paolo had already retreated behind the screen and Phryne had
often modelled for artists in her days in the apache quarter of
Paris. She shrugged out of her coat and boots and hung the rest
of her clothes on the hook which seemed to have been placed
there on purpose. She took her seat on the model's throne and
called, 'Ready.'

Paolo, having finished his tea, appeared and flicked the
cloth off a small clay model. It was a nymph, hair in disarray,
accepting the embraces of a satyr with evident pleasure. The
delicate limbs wrapped the hairy goatskin haunches, and she
leaned back in delight against the embracing arms. Although
the detail of the genitalia was decorously covered by thigh and
hand, it was evident that both bodies had just joined. The satyr
was crouched, and the whole structure depended upon his
cloven feet and the long legs of the nymph, whose toes were
just touching the ground.

Technically, it was a difficult piece, presenting intriguing
problems of mass and balance. Of itself, it glowed with an
innocent eroticism and good humour.

'It is lovely,' commented Phryne. The sculptor looked as
surprised as if his anatomy textbook had just spoken.

'Thank you, but the curve of this arm is not right. Will you
lean back a little more, *signorina*, and bend your wrist down…
no, it does not work. You need something to embrace.' Paolo left
the clay and dived for Phryne, arranging her limbs around him.

'You see, she is joined to him, thus…move that leg a little… and his arms are holding her weight…thus.'

Phryne's mouth was near the artist's, and his arms were very strong. She relaxed a little, and he shook her.

'*No, no, no!* She is not languid, she is afire with passion. The body is thrust against him, with force, to engulf him. So.' He leaned forward without warning and kissed one breast, then the other. Her nipples hardened. The Renaissance head bent to suckle. Phryne gasped. Her hands tightened on his back. She arched. For a moment, he held her strongly, and he felt her tremble.

'Later. Do not move,' he said, stuffing a big cushion into her arms.

Stunned, Phryne clutched the pillow, frozen with tension into the position she had been placed. Clay flew. She heard it fall with sad little sounds to the floor. She could not see the progress of the figure, but Paolo was pleased.

'Oh, excellent, excellent…now the shoulder…do not move.' Phryne was torn between rage and laughter. The studio was getting very cold. She fell into her model's dreaming trance and recalled the Paris studios where her dearest friends had been surrealists. She had once been offered a Dada dinner, which consisted of boiled string. She heard the sculptor calling her as if from a long way away.

'*Vieni, carissima.* See what you have done. It is finished.'

She untangled herself from the cushion and bent her stiff limbs. Paolo seized her and rubbed her into mobility with his large, strong hands, then led her to the covered model.

'See, *bella*, what you have wrought. For weeks I have been trying to capture that curve, that intense clutch—and there it is. It is complete.'

'What shall you cast it in?'

'Silver-gilt, nothing else. Nothing else is good enough for such a work. I thank you from the bottom of my heart.'

He kissed Phryne enthusiastically and she discovered that her aroused passion had been frozen, not absent. It was now thawing.

She beat the sculptor to the warm blankets of his bed by a short half-head, and wrapped them both. The blankets were clean, as was the sculptor. He smelt delightfully of clay and leather and tobacco and something vaguely herbal. She continued to kiss him, caressing the pointed ears, the mobile mouth and the long, beautiful line of muscle from back to buttock. He laid his head upon her breast and sighed with pleasure.

'Ah, *bella,* how fortunate I am to find you. Sure a pure line; so delicate, so true.' He rubbed his face across her breasts, catching at the nipples as his mouth passed. 'And now, do you want me?'

Phryne, who had always been a woman of strong passions, was decided.

'I do,' she answered, then clutched him close.

Paolo was a good lover; deft, sensitive and passionate. What woman could ask more? As he lay with her he breathed praises into her ear; *bella, bella, bellissima.*

Satisfied, Phryne kissed her lover firmly, got up, and donned her clothes.

'You must go? But I do not even know your name,' he cried.

'You are coming too. I'm taking you to dinner. Is there anything good around here? My name is Phryne Fisher. I'm investigating McNaughton's murder.'

'Then you are not a professional model,' concluded the artist in triumph. 'I knew it. No model could have made me finish my nymph. Only a new young lady could be a sufficient inspiration. Have you seen my fiancée? Is she well? She told me not to come to her, or I should not be here.'

'Amelia is fine. I have just come from there. I wanted to ask you some questions about the matter. But I was…diverted.'

'Ah, *signorina,* do not think that I am insensible of the honour. I, too, have been much diverted. But now I shall dress and we shall go to dinner. I thank you for your care of Amelia. As it is not possible for even the most foolish of policemen to think that I had anything to do with the murder of that swine, I shall go to Amelia tomorrow, and I shall not leave her. Especially since I have finished the nymph,' added Paolo artlessly.

'Why Amelia, above all the others?' asked Phryne suddenly. Paolo had found trousers and boots but could not locate his shirt. He searched hopelessly, then found it on the model's throne, where he had flung it.

'Why Amelia?' repeated Phryne. 'It is not her money; she gets none under her father's will.'

'That I know. It is nothing. She has a little money, but it is not that. I could have had princesses—and have, in my time,' he added complacently through the folds of the shirt. 'Look at that shelf, over there, *bella*.'

Phryne surveyed the shelf. There were five nude statues, each beautifully modelled, and each was of the same woman. Paolo breathed in Phryne's ear.

'Look at her. She is perfect. The length of limb, the straight back; for a sculptor she is perfect in every way. You should see her as I do, *bella*—without her clothes. You, now, are pretty—in fact I would say that you are striking. You would never be mistaken for anyone but yourself. If you were modelled as Venus or Diana or St Joan everyone would say, "Ah! Miss Fisher," because you have the distinctive face. But the body—pure of line, yes, delicate of bone, assuredly. But only that. As you age—I beg your pardon, *bella*—you will sag like every other woman. You will still be beautiful and distinctive. But my Amelia will be a sculptor's dream; old, sagging, pregnant. She is the universal woman. When I met her she was ashamed—her father was a brute, a swine, a beast. But I coaxed her, I flattered her, I taught her to pose nude and enjoy her body, and now she is complete. I could never find another like her. Money, pah! A body like that you could search a century for and never find. It is undoubtedly due to the special intervention of St Anthony, who has guarded me all my life, that I have found her, and I would not risk losing her for the undoubted pleasure of wiping her detestable father off the face of the earth.'

'Ah,' agreed Phryne. 'Dinner?'

'We shall go to the Café Royale,' announced Paolo. 'If you are paying. You can ask me whatever you like, and I shall answer, *bellissima*.'

He had found all his clothes. He took his hat, keys and cigarettes and led the bemused Phryne out of the studio.

The Café Royale was the haunt of bohemians and artists. Phryne had always meant to go there. One entered through a small, iron-studded door which led into a cobwebby cellar with many barrels, and then into a large, smoky room with lanterns hanging from the beams. It was a little like the Hall of the Mountain King and a little like the hold of a ship. It smelt delightfully of garlic, roasting meat, Turkish cigarettes and coffee. The log fire had been burning all day and the smoke added to the aromatic, raffish air.

Phryne was escorted to a table with ceremony by three waiters, who took her coat and supplied her with a bottle and a glass. The wine was Lambrusco, a strong sweet red wine of the Po Valley. It was just what was needed on a frosty night.

Paolo was known in the Café Royale and the proprietor himself came out of the kitchen to welcome him and his guest.

Paolo leaned back in the wooden chair and raised his glass.

'I have completed my nymph, with the admirable assistance of this young lady. It has been a severe labour. Therefore, Guiseppe, we require food. What is good tonight?'

Guiseppe smiled a huge smile which revealed a treasury of gold teeth, and began to speak expansively in Italian.

'Will you allow me to order?' asked Paolo. Phryne nodded, impressed with his manners.

Guiseppe concluded his address with a wide gesture, and bellowed an order into the kitchen. Paolo poured Phryne another glass of wine.

'Why did you come to Australia, Paolo?'

'Ah. I come from *Firenze*—Florence. You have been there?' Phryne nodded again. The faun's countenance was fascinating in the flickering light, and she privately congratulated Amelia on her luck, or judgement.

'Then you know that it is a city filled with art. If one is in the least susceptible, then one must appreciate it. My father makes cement. I believe that it is good cement, and he has made a fortune out of it. I do not like cement, and I have no head for business. When he sent me out on errands, I was to be found gazing with awe at the great gates, or the Roman marbles, or the bronzes in the public squares. This did not please my father. He sent me to oversee the cement works. I could not command the workers, and in any case I discovered Carrara marble was also mined there. When he told me I would never see his face again until I stopped being an artist, ah, *bella*. I thought of all the faces I would create and all the beauty I would have to surrender. My father has not such a compelling countenance to enable me to renounce all the world's beauties. So he cut me out of his will. He is, in any case, a peasant, and peasants do not appreciate art. My mother was from a minor aristocratic house. She gave me all her money and said, "Go forth, my son, and create beautiful things. Come and see me when your father is dead. But you must leave Italy." I took half of the money and I was free in the world. Ah. Here is the good Guiseppe with the pasta. This you will enjoy, *bella*. It is as I ate it in the old country, but better. Here the ingredients are of the quality which one cannot afford in Italy.'

Guiseppe set down a dish of strange green noodles, mixed through with oil, olives, chicken livers, onions and mushrooms. It smelt delicious. Paolo ladled out a plateful then continued.

'I then asked myself, where should I go? America? I did not like the Americans I had met. I wandered down to the docks in Marseille, and sat down in a tavern to think. There I met some of the crew of an Australian ship. They were stokers and boiler-minders, and such faces! Such bodies! I speak from an artistic point of view, you understand, I have no sexual interest in men.' He took several huge mouthfuls of the succulent pasta, and waved his fork for emphasis.

'They asked me to sit down, and I shared several bottles with them. It enabled me to try out my English on a native speaker, but I could not understand them at first. The accent is very marked, you understand. The ship was leaving that night. They took me on as the keeper of a racehorse, whose stableman had been arrested by the police for an affray in a brothel. Marseilles is a very rough place. I have always been fond of horses, so I agreed to take care of "Dark Day" until we reached Australia. He was going on to New Zealand. A stallion. The struggles I had with him! A beast of great pride; but the spirit of a demon. Later his owner paid me three hundred pounds for the bronze I made of him. I found his cure, though.'

'What was that?'

'When he would rear and scream—so that I feared for his knees and even more for my life—I fed him honey-soaked oatmeal and brandy. He did not relish the taste at first, but after a while he would sidle over and try to seize the bottle from my hand. It would make him calm and happy again and lie down in his stall. Fortunately horses do not suffer from the hangover. I got to Melbourne and left "Dark Day" with regret. He was sorry to part with me, too, but I instructed his new keeper about the brandy. He arrived safe in New Zealand and sired many children. I wandered around Melbourne until I found this place, and Guiseppe took me to his chest. He found me a studio and introduced me to many artists, and I have not had to touch my mother's money. I am a good sculptor. And I like it here. The food is good and the climate is like Florence and the women are beautiful and complaisant. A reasonable man cannot ask for more. Then, more was given to me. Amelia was at a party given for the gallery students, and when I saw her I realized that here was the body I had been looking for all my life. She was a crushed little thing, and I could hardly get a word out of her. Even the brandy did not make her effusive, just sleepy and sad. It was not until I had laid siege to her for many months that she let me get closer. It was a heart-breaking thing when I finally discovered why she was not the virgin which her bearing and manner led me to expect.' Paolo finished his pasta and gulped more wine.

'Imagine forcing a child! Her father was a monster and I am profoundly glad that someone has seen fit to remove him from this world. It was not, however, me. I am going to marry Amelia and remove her from that house of sorrow and she will grow fatter and happier and have many children. She loves children. I, also. I must show you the figures I did of her protegés. *Scugnizzi,* street-children, one and all, but the vitality of those undernourished bodies! And another thing. Have you seen her portraits?'

'Yes,' said Phryne, laying down her fork. 'I just bought an armload of them.'

'Then you must have seen, *bella.* You are a lady of taste and refinement. She has a great gift. She needs to do more work, her lines are still uncertain and her colour needs developing, but she can catch a likeness. Only one in three hundred students has that skill. She will be very good, when she gets away and comes to live with me.'

'What about your family? You are a Roman Catholic, aren't you?'

'This is not an impediment. I have spoken to Father John. She will become a Catholic, and thus avoid eternal damnation which she would not like. Then we shall be married in the Church. I, in turn, will renounce the delights of my models, once we are married. Thus it is fortunate for me that you came to me when you did, for I shall always remember you, *bella.*'

'I will also remember you, Paolo, *carissime.* Have you any idea who could have killed McNaughton?'

Paolo shrugged eloquently.

'It could have been anyone. But I think that it is Bill the brother. Him I do not admire. He is too much like his godforsaken father. I can see him hitting his father over the head with a rock; yes, certainly.

'Otherwise, *bella,* the possibilities are endless. He tortured his wife, and she has a secret lover. I do not know anything about him, but I assure you that there is one. I overheard her speaking to him on the telephone. "No, dearest," she said. "It is too dangerous. He will kill you. There is no hope for us," she sighed, and hung up the receiver. Her sigh would have broken your heart, *bella.* It seemed to contain all the sorrow of the world. Then she turned and saw me and begged me to say nothing. Naturally, I agreed.'

'Did you tell Amelia?'

'Of course not. She had enough to bear. But what a man, this McNaughton! Everyone hated him. His servants loathed him. He dismissed his driver recently, and beat him and kicked him into the road. He might have crept back and laid an ambush. In any case, *carissima*, it was a good deed and I hope that you do not find who did it.'

'I have to get Bill out of trouble, Paolo. Therefore I must find out who did it.'

'It is a sad world,' said Paolo portentously, 'when one who does Australia a signal service must suffer for it. Here is Guiseppe with the fish. You will like this, *bella*, it is a Neapolitan recipe. Did you say that you hope to get the brother Bill out of jail? Then perhaps I should take Amelia to my studio. He does not like me.'

'You shall go and comfort Amelia. She needs you badly,' stated Phryne, taking another glass of wine. 'I shall deal with Bill. I promise that he will not say a word.'

Paolo took up her hand and kissed it.

The fish was highly spiced, and Phryne was feeling more than a little tipsy. She ordered strong black coffee and it came with a glass of cold water. She nibbled small almond biscuits and surveyed the room.

There was a shriek of recognition before Isola hurled herself across the café and threw herself into Phryne's arms.

'*Carissima*! It has been centuries. And Paolo, my dearest. How do you come to be here together? Aha! Paolo, you wicked goat, you have been seducing my friends again.'

Paolo grinned. 'How could I resist, when all your friends are so like you?'

Isola slapped playfully at his cheek, and missed. Phryne, finding Isola something of an armful, deposited her on a chair brought by a waiter, who winked. Phryne should have guessed that Isola had captured Paolo. She had a supernatural talent for finding skilful lovers. Sometimes they came in odd shapes, but if they had been Isola's choice they could be relied on to be worth the trouble. She had been honing her instincts on Melbourne men for some years.

'How is the poor Amelia?' demanded Isola, tossing back her thick tangled hair. 'I heard of the death of her disgusting father. I suppose that it was not you, Paolo?'

'No, I regret.'

'Pity. I was intending to kiss the murderer soundly.'

'It is a sad loss to me,' murmured Paolo. 'But I did not do it, Isola. Amelia, it appears, is fairly well. Tomorrow I go to her. Phryne has taken over the investigation.'

'Phryne, if you find him I shall be seriously displeased,' announced Isola in her deepest, throatiest voice.

'I shall be desolated,' said Phryne politely. 'What is that dress, Isola? You must be freezing.'

'It is the mode *Égyptienne*. Is it not seductive?' Isola stood up. She was clothed in a long, white, closely pleated gown. A collar of bright turquoise beads covered her shoulders, and her magnificent breasts lifted the fabric so that it fell uninterrupted to the floor. She looked like a lewd Corinthian column. She certainly looked seductive, but Isola would have looked seductive in gunny sacks tied with old rope.

'Is this new?'

'But certainly. Have you not seen the illustrated papers? There have been great discoveries at Luxor. They have found the tombs of many kings, and in them linen and jewellery and many fine objects. Everyone knows about Luxor! Even the children are playing pyramids. Madame *la Modiste* in the building where I live made this for me, provided that I wore it into society. I am the first, but there will be many others. Do you like it, Paolo?'

'Magnificent. I would like to sculpt you. To capture the smoothness and lightness of the fabric, while suggesting the body underneath, presents a fascinating problem. Come and model for me and I shall essay, Isola. If your current lover does not object.'

'Him? Pah! I have discarded him. He demanded that I leave the stage and go and become a good wife. Me, I have sung for princes. But I have no time to sit for you, *carissime,* at the moment.'

Glancing hungrily at one of the waiters, she floated away. Paolo shrugged again.

'Ah, that Isola! The only woman I have ever met who looks on love in the same way as a man.'

'Still, her judgement is to be trusted,' observed Phryne. 'And you have to admit that she is magnificent.'

'Assuredly. She has always been so. The gown, that *Égyptienne* gown, I shall obtain one from the modiste and sculpt Amelia. I shall call on the woman tomorrow and have the gown and some clay sent to the house. Amelia likes sitting for me, it calms her. My mind is clear, now that I have completed the nymph.'

'Are you selling it?' asked Phryne. Paolo shook his head. 'I am collecting sufficient pieces for an exhibition. There, *bella,* you may buy if you wish.'

'I will look forward to it,' said Phryne. 'And now I must go. I have to be at court tomorrow. I shall see you again, Paolo.'

'At the house of McNaughton,' agreed Paolo, standing up. Phryne paid Guiseppe the surprisingly small total and took herself wearily home.

⟨⟩

There had been no word about Candida. Jack Leonard was running out of what he had previously thought was an endless fund of aeroplane talk. Molly had gone upstairs to feed baby Alexander, and now sat rocking him and dropping tears on the upturned face. The baby resented this and did not suckle freely. Henry Maldon started when the telephone rang and snatched it from the receiver.

'Yes?'

'Henry Maldon?' whispered an androgynous voice.

'Yes.'

'We've got your little girl. She'll be fine if you sit tight and don't call in the police. A letter will arrive tomorrow. Carry out the instructions and you will have her back unhurt. Call the cops or try anything, and you'll have her back in little pieces.'

'I won't call the police,' gasped Henry. 'Is she all right? Let me speak to her.'

'Tomorrow,' promised the voice, and there was the final click of a breaking contact. Henry threw down the phone and swore.

'Was that them?'

'Yes, Jack. They say that we have to wait for a letter. Oh, Jack, how am I going to tell Molly? And how are we going to bear it?'

'You can bear most things,' said Jack. 'You're a brave man. What about the time you walked out of the Sahara?'

'That's different,' snapped Henry. 'That was only me. This time, it's Candida.'

Haggard with exhaustion and strain, he poured another whisky. It was going to be a long night.

Chapter Seven

Wrest once the law to your authority:
To do a great right, do a little wrong
The Merchant of Venice, Shakespeare

The Melbourne Magistrates' Court was cold and stony, and Phryne was not feeling very well. The crowd of solicitors did not elevate her mood. All men, it appeared. She caught sight of Jillian across the depressing courtyard and struggled through the press of suits to catch her by the arm.

'Ah, Phryne, I have spoken to the prosecutor and he has no objection to bail with reporting conditions. The informant is our old friend and he hasn't any objection either. I just have to go in and get the matter on and we should have Bill out in two ticks.'

Phryne caught sight of Detective-inspector Benton, and called to him. He ploughed through the crowd toward them.

'Miss Fisher! How is the detecting?'

'I still have much to learn. Thank you for not objecting to bail. Tell me, can I see the body? And can I have a look at the murder weapon?'

'What will young ladies take up next? Very well, Miss Fisher. Come over to my office once you have regained possession of your client and I will show you the weapon. You can't see the body, I'm afraid, but you can read the Coroner's Report if that will do.'

'It will indeed,' said Phryne, pleased. She really did not like corpses much. She pushed her way into Court One and saw that Jillian Henderson was on her feet. She looked as plump and self-confident as the city pigeons outside, and as sure of her place.

'If I might draw the Court's attention to the matter of McNaughton, your Worship?'

A very old magistrate found his glasses, focused them on Jillian and smiled thinly.

'Yes, Miss Henderson?'

'A bail application, your Worship. I have spoken to the informant and the learned prosecutor and I believe that they have no objection.'

'Is that the case, Senior-sergeant?'

A huge policeman scrambled to his feet.

'Yes, your Worship. The informant agrees that there is no reason why the accused should not be bailed.'

'Very well, Miss Henderson; now all you have to do is convince me.' The magistrate leaned back in his chair and shut his eyes.

Phryne was close enough to hear the prosecutor mutter: 'Damn the old cuss! This'll take all day.' He sorted his notes, looking for the details of the crime.

'This is an alleged murder, your Worship. The victim was my client's father. The evidence against him can be summarized in three points: Firstly, he had a violent argument with his father. Secondly, he cannot be proven not to have been at the scene of the crime when his father died. Thirdly, he is very strong, and the crime required strength. For want of better evidence, your Worship, I shall be moving that the matter be struck out at Committal. For the moment, your Worship, even supposing that my client did kill his father, which is strenuously denied, there is no point in keeping him in custody. In your Worship's vast experience, your Worship must have seen a lot of domestic murderers. They do not repeat their crime. I may add to this that my client is a man of unblemished reputation with no criminal record. He has never come to the attention of the courts before. He is willing to surrender his passport and offer a surety and agree to whatever reporting conditions your Worship considers proper. As your Worship pleases...' Jillian sat down. Phryne was impressed. So, evidently, was the magistrate.

'Yes, well, I see no reason not to accede to your request, Miss Henderson. Stand up, accused. You are bailed on your own recognizance to appear at this Court on the 17th of August 1928, at ten of the forenoon, and not then to leave the precincts of the Court until the matter has been dealt with according to law. You are required to report to Carlton Police Station between the hours of nine in the morning and nine at night every Friday until the date of your hearing. Should you fail to report or appear or otherwise breach the conditions of your bail a warrant will be issued for your immediate arrest and you will have a further charge to answer in addition to those already preferred against you. Is that clear?'

'Yes, sir,' muttered Bill.

'Does your client agree to the terms of his release, Miss Henderson?'

Jillian leapt to her feet.

'He does, your Worship.'

'Take him down, usher. Accused, you will be detained until you sign your bail notice, and then you are free to go.'

Jillian and Phryne left the court.

'This way, and we'll collect Bill. Golly, Phryne, that was easier than I expected. Old Jenkins must be tired. Usually it takes a good hour of solid argument to persuade him to let anyone out of police clutches.'

She led Phryne out of the court building and along the street to the watch-house. It was a grimy building that smelt of despair and carbolic in roughly equal proportions. Phryne hated it instantly.

'Yes, it does pong,' agreed Jillian, having noticed Phryne's grimace. 'And you never get used to it, somehow. Good morning, Sergeant. How are you this bleak and miserable Wednesday?'

'I've been better, Miss Henderson. Have you come for McNaughton?'

'I have, so hand him over—surely you don't want to keep him?'

'Not particularly,' replied the desk-sergeant, a gloomy individual with a long, drooping face. 'I'll see if they've finished with him.'

He was gone for ten minutes. He returned with Bill and the bail notice.

'Please check your belongings, sir, and sign this if they are all correct.'

Bill, who was shaky and subdued, checked his hat, keys, wallet, cigarette case, lighter, miscellaneous coins, and spark-plug.

He signed. The copy of the bail bond was ceremonially folded and placed in an envelope. Phryne was close enough to Bill to feel him quivering with impatience.

'Steady,' she murmured. 'We shall be out of here soon.' She laid a hand on his arm as though he might bolt. Jillian, on the other side, did the same. Bill contained himself until they were out in the street again. Once there, he drew in long breaths of comparatively clean, cold air.

'My God! I need a drink. Come on ladies—the Courthouse Hotel.'

Although the Courthouse was not an ideal hotel for ladies, neither Phryne nor Jillian demurred. Bill offered both of them an arm and almost ran across the street into the comfortable beery snug, where he ordered a jug of beer. Phryne had gin and Jillian tonic water, as she had a conference in the afternoon and did not want to breathe all over the client.

'They lose confidence,' she explained, 'if you stink of alcohol. It's a dry profession,' she added. Bill had not spoken since the beer had arrived. He had been supplied with a glass but he disdained it. Lifting the jug effortlessly he engulfed the drink in a seemingly endless gulp. When he lowered it, the jug was half empty.

'Miss Fisher, I didn't kill my father.'

'I know. This is Jillian Henderson, a dear friend of mine, who has undertaken your defence.'

'Pleased to meet you, Miss Henderson. You certainly did a job on that old magistrate. He was giving the other applications a very nasty time indeed. I was surprised to see you, but I'll be delighted if you'll manage my defence.'

Here was an alteration. Three days in jail had humbled Bill McNaughton most impressively. Phryne called the barman and ordered another jug.

He brought it, and set it down in front of Bill.

'This one's on the house, mate. Boss says you're a great advertisement for his brew.'

Bill laughed, finished the first jug, and then grew solemn again.

'If I didn't kill him—and I didn't—then who did?'

'That's what I'm trying to find out. All I need from you is an exact description of the two people you saw on your walk.'

'I think you'll do this better on your own. Let me know, Phryne. Don't forget to report, Mr McNaughton, or we may not be so lucky next time. Bye,' said Jillian and zoomed off to free more birds from the constabulary cage. Bill looked after her.

'Miss Fisher, I feel like the prodigal son. I would have been better off with the swine and the husks. Do you have any idea of what a place like that is like?'

'I once spent a night in a Turkish prison. It sounded and felt like the depths of hell and there were bedbugs.'

'Yes, that is it. The depths of hell with bedbugs. I'll do anything to avoid going back there. I say, that woman is hot stuff in court, isn't she? You could see that the magistrate was pleased. She didn't waste a word. Would it be all right if I sent her some flowers? I could have kissed her, but I didn't think that she'd like that.'

'Here is her card. I'm sure that she would love some flowers. Now drink up. Before you go back to your mother's house for a long bath, a bed with sheets and a proper shave, there are a few things I need to tell you.

'Amelia is a very good artist. She will be great. Therefore, I would have you pay her the proper respect. There is an uncertainty in her work which I attribute entirely to you. Yes?'

'She really is good? I never really looked at her stuff. Father scoffed at it so I didn't bother. Very well. I'll not tease poor Amelia. An artist, eh?'

'Here. This is a portrait of your father.'

'It's caught the pater perfectly. Who did it?'

'Amelia. I bought it from her.'

'Lord, really? Amelia?' He took a gulp of beer.

'And another thing. When you get home you will probably find Paolo Raguzzi there. You will not call him a greasy little dago. You will be nice to him. He is not only a good sculptor but he loves your sister truly and…er…fairly faithfully and she needs his support. He will probably want to model you; if so, you will agree. In return I will get you out of trouble.'

'You'll find the murderer if I do my Angel of the House and don't upset the mater?'

'Yes.'

'Deal,' said Bill promptly.

'The people who passed you on the path. What did they look like?'

'The first was an old man, a tramp, with a battered old felt hat and a sugar sack over his shoulder. I didn't see his face. The girl was a pretty young slip, in a red bathing-costume and cap. I couldn't see her hair but she was tanned and small—maybe five feet tall. I seem to have seen the girl before, but not the old man.'

'Any smell?'

'Smell? What do you think I am, a bloodhound? None in particular.'

Phryne wondered again at the noselessness of man.

'Had the girl been in the water?'

Bill absorbed more beer and thought deeply.

'Yes, her costume was sticking to her body, and her arms and shoulders were shiny.'

'Did you get the impression that the old man and the girl were connected?'

Bill thought some more and finished the beer.

'I didn't notice, really. I was in a rage. I often run down to the river and go for a quick swim when things get too personal at home.'

'I thought you were going to the aerodrome for your arguments in future.'

'Yes, I was to take the old man out there.'

'Did you kill him?'

Bill looked Phryne in the eye and said solemnly, 'No, I wish I had. Then I wouldn't mind being charged.'

'All right. Now, I shall see you into a taxi.'

'No fear! I'm going to walk. I need to stretch my legs. I will behave, Miss Fisher. I just hope you can get me out of trouble.'

She watched him stride off down the street in the direction of Kew. She crossed to the police station to find Benton and the murder weapon.

She was directed to his office and sat down while he fetched the rock from the safe.

'Can't have important clues lying about. See,' he said, opening the grey cardboard box and exhibiting a squarish block of bluestone. 'It was brought down with great force. Much more than any woman could muster. There's blood and matter on the obverse, but none on the back, indicating the blood did not spurt. The murderer might not have had a spot on him. Seen enough?'

Phryne looked very carefully at the sides of the stone, and especially the blotch of blood on the striking face.

'Doesn't that bloodstain fade toward the middle? Have a look. There seems to be less blood in the centre than you would find at the sides. What could cause that, do you think?'

Benton came to look.

'No, I can't see that, Miss Fisher. Is that all?'

'Was there anything on the stone apart from blood and brain?'

'Hair, Miss, a clover burr, a few hemp strands, a few leaves, a bit of bubblegum. Nothing important.'

'No. Thank you, that was most interesting.'

'Here's the Coroner's Report. Cause of death: massive head injuries.'

Phryne skimmed through the report. 'Body of well-nourished middle aged man...cleft cranium...'

'It seems to have fallen on the top of his head rather than the back,' she observed.

'Depends on how you look at it. Now I think he was donged from behind. The fact that the rock is a flat surface makes it difficult to say. The cranium is quite cloven through the middle.'

'Hmm. Well, thanks a lot. Have you found those witnesses yet?'

'No,' muttered the detective-inspector, straight-faced.

'Thank you so much for your time,' said Phryne politely, and left.

She sat in the car and wrote a hasty note to Bert and Cec, then drove to Carlton to drop it into their boarding-house. She wondered what Bert would do when Cec got married at the end of the year, and decided that he would manage. Cec's intended was a sensible young woman who understood the bond between the two men. There would be no separating Bert and Cec this side of the death which they had so often faced together. They were skilled, if rather direct, investigators and Phryne left her problem in their hands with a certain relief.

She arrived home very tired and ate the lunch served to her by Mrs Butler with an easy mind. A telephone message in Dot's neat schoolgirl hand informed her that Paolo was with Amelia, that Mrs McNaughton was as well as could be expected and that Bill had arrived and was behaving like an angel. Phryne decided that she had done enough detecting for one day, and went to take a long hot bath with her *Nuit de Paris* bathsalts. After that she took what she considered to be a richly-deserved rest.

Jack Leonard rolled off the couch in the Maldons' living room and strove to unkink his muscles. It had been the most uncomfortable night of his life, equalling in discomfort the Turkish brothel with the bedbugs, but without the compensating atmosphere.

Molly and the baby had retired fairly early. Molly had slept because her husband had poured a sizeable slug of chloral into her chocolate. Jack and Henry had sat up until three, when Henry had been persuaded to go to bed by Jack, who felt unequal to the strain of any more speech.

It was late in the morning; soon even Molly would be up, and no message had yet been delivered.

The Maldons trailed down to face with disgust an unwanted breakfast, and it was while looking a good nourishing fried egg in the yolk that Jack Leonard had an idea. He pushed away the plate and grabbed Henry by the arm. He had just remembered something which his fellow fliers had told him.

'What you need, old man, is Miss Fisher. Top hole detective, so Bunji Ross says—brave as a lion.'

'Miss Fisher?' asked Molly, dropping her cup of tea so that it glugged down onto the breakfast-room rug.

'Certainly. High class inquiries, that sort of thing. She's been retained to get our mutual friend Bill out of trouble. I'm sure that she will be able to help. I've put good money on her getting Bill off. Amazin' record. Never fails.'

Henry seemed uncertain. His wife spoke decidedly.

'Ring her, Jack. Ring her right away.'

Phryne woke at three o'clock feeling like she had the black death. She dragged her weary body out of bed, ran another bath, and reflected that if she kept using this restorative she had better have her skin waterproofed. She felt better after her bath and decided that coffee would complete the cure.

'Oh, Miss Fisher, there is a message for you,' said Mr Butler as she sat down in the parlour. 'A child has been kidnapped and they want you to investigate. I said that I should not dare to wake you, and that you would call when you arose.'

'If it is anything like that again, Mr Butler, please wake me. Particularly if it is anything to do with a child. There are some strange people around and the first five hours are crucial. Ask Mrs B. for some coffee and get me the number, will you. Where is Dot?'

'I believe that she is in the kitchen with Mrs Butler, Miss Fisher. I shall fetch coffee at once.'

Mr B., rather abashed, gave the order for coffee and the summons to Dot, then rang the number and escorted Miss Fisher to the phone.

'Hello, Miss Fisher. Jack Leonard here. You remember me?'

'The airman, of course. What's this about a child?'

'I'm at the home of my old friend Henry Maldon. He won all that money in the Irish Lottery at Christmas, you recall. His little daughter Candida has gone missing, and we have a witness who saw her taken away in a big black car.'

'Have you a note?'

'Not yet.'

'Sit tight, Mr Leonard, and I'll be with you soon. What's the address?' Phryne scribbled busily. 'Good. Stay by the phone but don't tie it up. They might ring. Tell the parents that the child will be perfectly safe until the note arrives—then we might have to move fast. Make sure that they eat some dinner. If someone calls, try to keep them talking. Ask to speak to the child, and say that you need proof that she is alive before you give them anything. And whatever they want, agree. I'll be with you by four. Bye.'

'Dot, did you hear any of that?'

'Yes, Miss. Little girl gone missing. Terrible. Are you taking the case?'

'Of course.'

'But, Miss, what about Mr McNaughton?'

'Oh, I think I know how that happened. I just can't prove it yet. Bert and Cec will complete it. This is urgent, Dot. Get your coat and hat and come on. I might need you.'

Dot ran upstairs for her outdoor garments. Phryne drank two cups of black coffee and assembled her thoughts. The police couldn't be brought into the case officially, however there was a certain policeman who owed her a favour. She checked that she had her address book and her keys and enough cigarettes to sustain a long wait and joined Dot at the door.

'Mr B. I'm going out on a case. I don't know when I shall be back. Ask Mrs B. to leave me some soup, and just have your dinner as usual. I can be reached at this number, but only if it is really urgent.'

She was gone before he could say, 'Certainly, Miss Fisher.' He heard the roar of the great car reverberate through the house.

'She's a live wire, our Miss Fisher,' he chuckled, and went back to the kitchen.

Phryne arrived outside the new house just before four o'clock, to be met by Jack Leonard. He was not smiling.

'She really has gone,' he confided. 'We had a phone call. Not a bad little kid, Candida. And her father is an old friend of mine. I hope that you can find her, Miss Fisher.'

'So do I. This is Dot—you remember her, no doubt. All right, Jack, lead me to it.'

Molly Maldon was sitting, white as milk, in a deep armchair, staring into space. Henry Maldon was pacing up and down and seemed to have been doing so for some time. They both looked up in sudden hope as Phryne came in.

'I'm Phryne Fisher, and this is my assistant, Miss Williams. Tell me all about it.'

Hesitantly, they told her the whole story. Molly grabbed Phryne's hand.

'She's only six,' she whispered. 'Just a little girl, and she didn't even get her sweets!' She exhibited the broken bag and burst into tears again.

⚬⚬⚬

Candida swam muzzily back into consciousness and was immediately sick all over the car-seat and the man who was holding her. He shoved her roughly aside. She had never been cruelly handled before and she was highly intelligent. She kept her mouth shut and listened intently, although she had realized that she had been stolen and all her instincts were urging her to scream and cry and kick.

'The little brute spewed all over me,' complained the man, in a high, unpleasant voice. The woman in the front seat turned around, sneering.

'You wanted to snatch her, Sidney. You put up with it. You were the one who wanted to lay hands on all that young flesh.'

Candida did not know what this meant, but she sensed that vomiting over Sidney had removed some threat. She had done something clever. Her spirits rose a little.

Sidney was wiping at his lap with an inadequate handkerchief. It made little difference. His suit was ruined. The car stank. The driver, a big man with a bald head and a blue singlet, said, 'We're almost there. Then you can hang your suit out to dry and have a bath. How about that?'

Candida liked this man. He had a deep and soothing voice. She wondered how long they had been driving. She thought that it was no use asking and that the pose of unconsciousness might be useful. She was feeling better, but she had lost her sweets, and her daddy did not know where she was. She racked her brains. What had she read about these situations? The Grimms fairy-tale method would not work. She had nothing to drop, and she could not reach the window. It began to look, she thought dismally, as though she might die like the babes in the wood, when the birds came and covered them with leaves.

The car turned off the main road. There were bumps, and the driver cursed. Then the car stopped and Candida was carried into the fresh air. Sidney was still swearing behind her.

'Did you have the note delivered?' asked the woman in her thin, whining voice.

'Yair, I sent it by reliable hands with her hair-ribbon. We'll get the dough, all right. Now carry the poor little thing inside and give her a drink and a bit of a clean-up, Ann. We're home.'

⁂

Bert collected Phryne's note and read it aloud to Cec.

'She says, "Dear Bert and Cec, I have several things which I would like you to do, for the usual rates. Find the old man and the young woman who were climbing the cliff path in Studley Park at about four o'clock on the Friday of the murder. Try the local police station—the old man is probably well known in the district. The girl is a local who was swimming in the river. When you have found them, see if they remember Bill, and then take them around and see if they know him. If they do, we are more-or-less home and dried.

"Then I want you to search the bush and ground just outside the McNaughton home for a worn hemp rope. It will probably be about five or six feet long, and I'm hoping that it has blood on it.

"Next, ask around for the local head kid. Find out what their favourite game was the week before the McNaughton murder. Please also collect for me all the illustrated papers for the last three weeks. Don't forget the *Illustrated London News*.

"Last of all, scour the area for a place where they are replacing the gutter. McNaughton was killed with a large bluestone pitcher, and I want to know where it came from. It looked like a gutter stone to me. I rely on your intelligence and discretion. Don't tell anyone what you are up to if you can avoid it by any means short of prison. Best regards and get your finger out. I need this stuff as soon as I can get it. Phryne Fisher. PS. A description of the girl and the old man is attached, and here is a few quid for expenses. PF." '

Bert shook his head.

'Where do we start, Cec?'

'At the beginning, mate,' replied Cec easily. 'At the beginning.'

The doorbell rang in the Maldon house, and Henry raced for the door. He returned with an envelope in his hand.

'No one there,' he said. 'But this letter.'

'Handle it by the edges,' said Phryne. 'Slit the top. We don't want to spoil any fingerprints, do we? Good. One sheet of cheap Coles' paper enscribed by someone who is not used to writing.

'"Dere Mr Maldon,"' she read, '"we have yore dorter. Here is her ribon. We want five thou. Leave it in the holow tree stump in the Geelong Gardens tonite. You shal have her bak tomorrow. The tree stump is on the left of the path, next to the band rotunda. A frend."'

She shook the envelope and a blue Alice band fluttered out. Henry Maldon took it into both hands as if it was the Host and kissed it gently.

'Right, produce the money and let's get cracking.'

'I can't,' said Henry simply. 'I don't have any money. I've spent it all. I bought two houses and a plane and an annuity. I can sell them but it will take time. And meanwhile…'

'Candida will be fine,' announced Molly, refreshed by an hour in the uncomplicated company of baby Alexander. 'About now, I bet they are wishing they hadn't taken her.'

Henry forced a small and rusty laugh.

Candida had been washed and clothed in an old white nightgown, and had accepted some bread and milk. She was as wary as a small animal and kept as far as possible from Sidney, who now regarded her with loathing. The big man, Mike, was nicer. He had a large and commanding presence. The woman, Ann, she hated. After a small altercation about the nightgown, which was much too big for her, Ann had slapped Candida across the face. It was the insult rather than the pain which caused the child's eyes to follow Ann round the room with a black, implacable gaze. At last, as always, the glare made itself felt.

'Stop looking at me like that, you little toad!' shrieked Ann. Candida regarded her coolly.

'How do you want me to look at you?' she asked, imitating her mother's most infuriatingly logical voice. 'I shall not look at you at all, if you like,' she went on generously. Ann went to Mike and leaned on his shoulder.

'Make her stop looking at me, Mike,' she fawned. The child gave her a disapproving glare. Mike smiled.

'If you don't stop glaring at me, I'll tell Mike's spider to crawl right off his chest and come and bite you in your sleep,' threatened Ann. Candida was interested. Her fascination with insect life had often got her into trouble. No one had let her forget about her snail collection, which she had put down by the kitchen stove so that they could be cosy in the night. The snails had had a different idea of comfort and had glided away, some of them getting as far as the baby's room. Alexander had eaten one and Mummy had been very angry.

She got up from her seat on the hearth and disposed her nightgown around her feet. She looked up at Mike with a charming smile.

'May I see the spider on your chest?' she asked politely. Mike laughed.

'She's got guts, anyway,' he commented. 'Do you like spiders?'

'Yes. I have thirty-seven at home. Black ones,' elaborated the child calmly.

Mike stripped off his singlet and Candida edged closer, fascinated. The spider would have covered the span of both her hands. It was impressively hairy with little red eyes. Mike took a breath and flexed his pectoral muscles, and the spider wriggled.

Candida clapped her hands.

'Do it again,' she chuckled. 'Make the spider dance again!'

'It's time for you to go to bed,' snapped Ann, and grabbed the child's wrist in a grip like a handcuff. Candida resisted.

'I have to take my asthma medicine,' she stated. 'And then say my prayers, and I cannot go to sleep without Bear. Where is he?'

She scanned the blank faces before her and her temper, never under the best of control, broke. She had lost her lollies and Daddy and Mummy and it was too much that she should have lost Bear, as well.

Mike saw her face empurple, and her body swell.

'I want Mummy and Daddy and I want my lollies and I want Bear!' she shrieked in a full-throated operatic soprano. She continued to scream until she began to cough, and then to choke. She doubled over, gasping, and a dreadful wheeze was forced from her lungs as she hauled in each breath.

'She's having an asthma attack—my sister gets them,' said Ann. 'If we don't get her medicine, she could die.'

'So what. We don't need her alive any more,' snarled Sidney. Mike felled him with a weighty cuff around the right ear.

'Say something like that again and I'll take the girl and go straight to the cops. Now shut up and let me think. We can't call in a doctor. Where's the nearest chemist?'

'Geelong. I'll find one,' offered Ann. 'I can be back in an hour.'

'Go,' agreed Mike. Candida heard the car start. She had learned two interesting things. One was that Mike did not really have his heart in this kidnapping and the other was that they were half-an-hour from Geelong. Candida's mind was clear—she was used to asthma attacks. She was in pain but she could still hear. The other two obviously thought she could not.

'Why did you choose this place, Sid?' asked Mike.

'It's nice and quiet. No one comes to Queenscliff in the winter. It's near Geelong for the pick-up and once we have the dough all we need to do is continue along the road to Adelaide.'

Candida wheezed loudly and both men looked at her. She grimaced with pain and turned away from them.

'I wish Ann would get a move on. The poor little thing will be turning up her toes and then bang goes our chance of five thousand quid. And it's murder, too. We'll swing for it.'

'You take your chances in this game,' sneered Sid. Mike made a move towards him, then froze. Sid produced a pistol.

'I didn't know you had a gun,' muttered Mike. 'I thought we said no guns. They only get used. Put it away. I'm not going to hurt you. So what's the plan for the pick-up?'

'I'll take the car and pick up the money. If we decide to loose the kid we just set her down in the main street. She can find plenty of help. We take off to Adelaide, then you give your share to your wife, and I take a boat. There's still three warrants out for me in Victoria, and the cops would love to get their claws into me.'

'Yair, I know. I never thought I'd have sunk so low as to work with a child-molester.'

'You shouldn't have married a moll who gets you into debt then. And who is dumb enough to borrow from Red Jack. He'll break her arms and legs if she don't get him the money.'

'I know,' said Mike gloomily. 'But she likes pretty things, clothes and shoes and I can't afford to buy 'em for her.'

'And you're afraid that she'll go off with someone who can if you don't come up with the mazuma?'

Mike made the same angry, arrested movement. Candida coughed.

'Here, you sit up, little girl,' said Mike, shifting her clumsily to lean against his arm. 'Would you like a drink?'

Candida shook her head. She did not have enough breath to drink. She tugged at the tight strings of the nightgown. Mike loosened them and fetched an old pillowcase to wipe her face. Candida hooked one arm around his neck and laid her hot cheek against the spider tattoo. Mike held her very carefully, as though she might break. He could feel the massive effort which each breath cost the child and the strain and trembling in all her muscles.

'Sid, go and get us a blanket,' he ordered, disregarding the gun in Sid's hand. Such was the power of Mike's personality that Sid obeyed. Mike unlatched Candida long enough to wrap her closely and then resumed his place. She cried after him like a puppy if he moved. He had not known that children were like this; intense in their loves and hates, and very brave. Mike admired courage. He sat like that for a long time.

At last there was the sound of the car, and Ann slammed back into the house. She put a bottle of foul, red medicine on the table and rummaged for a glass in the unfamiliar kitchen.

'I had to wake the chemist up,' she said. 'And he charged me three-and-six for the stuff. I hope it works. Here, girlie, drink this.'

She shoved the glass at Candida and the child turned her face to one side. Mike pushed Ann away.

'Let me do it. Here you are, Candida. Here is the medicine, and soon you will have Mummy and Daddy and Bear and the lollies...'

Candida drank the mixture. She was sure that they had given her double the usual dose. It tasted just as disgusting as usual. She leaned back on Mike as though he was a chair, and began to control her breathing. The adrenalin and ephedrine in the elixir had their effect. She paled to the whiteness of marble, and her lips and fingernails took on a bluish tinge. Mike thought that she looked like a tombstone angel. The wheeze faded and she accepted a drink of hot milk grudgingly prepared by Ann. At last she could speak again. She snuggled against the big man and looked up at him accusingly.

'You didn't plan this very well, did you?'

Chapter Eight

Sister Anne, Sister Anne,
do you see the horsemen coming?

Bluebeard, Charles Perrault

It was time for Phryne to call in the debts that were owed her after the affair of the Cocaine Blues. Thus she found herself in an office the size of a cupboard sitting opposite Detective-inspector Robinson. He looked quite pleased to see her—'Call me Jack, Miss Fisher, everyone does'—and offered her a cup of tea. Phryne had tasted police-station tea before, but accepted it anyway.

'Well, Miss Fisher, what have you been up to? My colleague, Benton, has been quite terse about you.'

'Oh, has he? Is the man stupid, or just very, very stubborn?'

'I wouldn't call him stupid. He's a good detective. He just has theories, that's all. And when he has a theory nothing will turn him off it. They even call him "Theory" around here. He's not a bad chap, though we don't see eye-to-eye about a lot of things, one of them being you. I told him to take you seriously or risk public embarrassment, but he wouldn't listen. If you want a really biased opinion of old Theory, ask WPC Jones. He told her he didn't approve of women in the police force when she went to get her Gallantry Medal from the Chief Commissioner.'

'Gallantry Medal? I must congratulate her. What for?'

'She was acting as bait for a rapist. We didn't know that he had a knife—dirty, great cane-cutter. He got Jones down and was about to cut her throat when she rolled out from under him, stepped on his wrist and threw the weapon away; then she dropped on his chest, handcuffed his hands and feet together, and told him what she thought of him. Poor bloke. He was begging us to take him to a nice safe cell by the time the patrol caught up. A lovely job and he was lucky that she is a restrained lady, or she might have cut his balls off which was what she was threatening to do. Jones has not liked Theory Benton since. You can't blame her. He's an irritating man. Still if you come up with overwhelming evidence I'm sure that you'll give him a chance to make a manly confession, before you drop him into the soup.'

'Of course, but I don't think it will do the slightest good.'

Phryne sipped her tea, and placed the cup back on the desk. She produced the kidnap note in a larger envelope.

'Is this what you want me to do?' asked the detective-inspector resignedly. 'I didn't really think you had come just to see me and to drink police-station tea.'

'Good, because I haven't. When we were mutually involved in that cocaine affair, you were telling me that you could sometimes get fingerprints off paper. Could you have a go with this? And tell me whether they are on record?'

'I expect that I could. What's the paper?'

'A ransom note. Another thing. A big black car, probably a Bentley, and I have most of the licence number. Can you tell me who owns it?'

'How much of the number?'

'The first two digits and the two letters.'

'Yes, I can do that. But will I?'

'If I ask you very nicely and throw in a solution to the McNaughton murder?'

'We already have a solution to the McNaughton murder.'

'The real solution—and a gang of kidnappers,' offered Phryne. Robinson leaned forward.

'Kidnapping is dangerous to investigate and usually ends in the victim getting killed. If you allow that to happen my name will be mud and I will personally prosecute you for interfering with the course of a police inquiry. You know that, eh?'

'Yes, Jack, I know that.'

'Has this incident been reported to the police?'

'No.'

'So it is between you and me.'

'Yes.'

'And you are confident that you can find the gang and wrap the whole thing up neatly?'

'They shall be delivered to your door in a plain brown wrapper.'

'And you need my help, eh?'

'Yes. If you would be so kind.'

'Right, then, we know where we stand. All right. I trust you, Miss Fisher. Is there anything else that you need?'

'Not at the moment.'

'Good. Perhaps you'd like to have a word with Jones. You'll find her in Prisoner Reception this week. Give me an hour. If the stuff is on file, I'll find it,' Jack said. Phryne shook his hand and went to look for Jones.

She found the short and muscular policewoman engaged in an argument with a prisoner.

'I tell you I had ten quid on me when they picked me up. Them thieving jacks have robbed me!' a cross-eyed gentleman was roaring. Jones had been roared at by experts and did not turn a hair.

'That's all that was in your pockets, Mr Murphy.'

'It's here,' said Phryne, tweaking the ten-pound note out of an unsavoury watch pocket. 'Be more careful in future.'

Mr Murphy thanked her in an alcoholic mumble and took his leave. Jones smiled.

'Hello, Miss Fisher, you haven't half put it across old Theory. If only you can show up the old cuss! Do you know what he said to me?'

'Yes, Jack Robinson just told me. Outrageous. Can you come out for a cuppa?'

'My shift finishes in ten minutes, if you can wait.'

'I'll just find the Ladies. I don't think that the tea here agrees with me.'

'It don't agree with anyone. Even the drunks are complaining.'

Phryne rejoined WPC Jones, who was rather pretty when out of a uniform designed to remove all dangerous allure from the female form. She had curly hair which Phryne had only seen severely repressed under her cap. Jones led the way to a coffee shop and ordered a black coffee.

'It's hard to sleep in the daytime, and I'm so tired I can hardly keep my eyes propped open. Thank the Lord that I change shifts tomorrow.'

'I heard about your medal—congratulations,' said Phryne, gulping down a mouthful of coffee to wash the taste of the tea away.

'Thanks, but I really didn't deserve it. It wasn't cold courage. I lost my temper with the bastard. It was lucky that I threw that knife out of reach or I might have done him an injury. That wouldn't have done my career much good. Now, tell me about Theory. I know what he thinks happened. Do you think you can bring him undone?'

'Oh, yes. I can't prove it yet. But the safe money is definitely on Bill McNaughton's innocence.'

'You made an impression on Benton—even though he is sure that no woman could outsmart him, he's uneasy. He's asked two DI's to look at the murder weapon. I do hope you can prove him wrong.'

'There is no doubt.'

'Well, I've got to go. Thanks for the coffee, and if you need anything, just give me a call. Delighted to help,' said WPC Jones, and Phryne took herself for a walk in the Art Gallery.

She returned and found a note from Jack pinned to his desk.

'Dear Miss Fisher, there are three sets of unknown prints on the letter. The only one on record is that of Sidney Brayshaw, a child-molester whom we have been very anxious to interview. If you catch him it will warm the cockles of my Chief Super's heart (assuming he has one). The only black Bentley with those prefixes in its number plate belongs to one Anthony Michael Herbert, of 342 Bell Street, Preston. He hasn't any form. Hope this is of use. Watch your step. Jack.'

Phryne folded the note, placed it in her bag and went to reclaim her car from the urchin who was minding it. She gave him a shilling and he sped off before she could change her mind.

The address in Preston was that of a rundown boarding-house. Phryne rang at the bell and it fell into her hand. The door was open in any case. She walked in.

'Yes, dear? Who do you want to see?' demanded the raucous voice. The speaker surveyed Phryne's black suit, silk shirt, English felt hat and handmade shoes. A toff. The woman moderated her tone from that which she reserved for the local tarts seeking custom, to that used to address her bank manager.

'Give me that bell, dear. It always does that. I'm Mrs O'Brien. What can I do for you?'

'I'm looking for Mr Herbert.'

'Mike? Him and his missus have been gone two days, Miss.'

'Gone? What—gone forever?' Phryne felt a chill at her heart. She was relying on this clue.

'No. Just gone for a holiday. Somewhere down the coast. He's a nice bloke, Mike, but his missus is a trial.'

'Do you have an address?' asked Phryne, allowing a five pound note to appear in the woman's peripheral vision. The red eyes lit up, but the puffy face sagged with disappointment, and the cigarette in the corner of the painted mouth drooped.

'No, dear, I don't know where they are. I'm expecting them back soon. They were going to stay with their mate Sid, that's all I know. They did mention Queenscliff. Beautiful place it is. She always had to have new things—kept him skint for years, and then he lost his job when the factory closed down. He inherited that big car from his uncle but he usually can't afford the petrol. I'll keep my ear out, dear.'

'Could I have a look at their room?' asked Phryne, idly waving the banknote. The landlady scraped a hennaed curl out of her eyes and temporized, 'Well, I don't know…' Phryne produced a ten pound note. Mrs O'Brien led the way up the stairs.

At the door, her remaining scruples came to the fore.

'You won't take anything away, will you, dear? They might be back, you know.'

'I promise. You can stand and watch me.'

Phryne began a systematic search of the freshly painted room. The lino was new and the curtains crisp. A wardrobe, stuffed full of new clothes in the worst taste, occupied one corner. Phryne looked in all the pockets and handbags, stripped and searched the mattress, turned it over and searched all the crannies of the iron bedstead. She went through a pile of magazines and all the male clothes, and sounded the floorboards for a loose one. In all this she found no sign of the destination of Anthony Michael Herbert and his wife Ann. Then a piece of newspaper caught her eye. It had been carefully trimmed out and laid among the illustrated papers. It was the cutting from the *Herald* which announced the Maldon Lottery win.

Phryne handed over the money and asked, 'How long have they been with you?'

'Three years, dear.'

'No children?'

'No, he often said that he'd like children but she refused to have any until they could rent a house of their own. And I don't allow them here. Dirty little pests. Anything else?'

'If you remember their address, telephone me at this number. It will be worth twenty quid to you, but not after Friday. Good morning,' and Phryne left.

Sidney Brayshaw's fingerprints on the note, thought Phryne. Gone to Queenscliff with their mate Sid. This was only twenty miles from Geelong. There must be a connection. Phryne drove herself home to lunch.

⁂

Bert and Cec parked their new cab in the 'Inspector only' section of the yard and marched into the Kew Police Station with determination. Neither of them liked police. While they had escaped legal notice in the past, they both had far too many dealings in dubious property to be entirely comfortable under the gaze of constabulary eyes.

'Gidday,' Bert greeted the desk-sergeant. 'We come to make some inquiries.'

'Oh, yair?' asked the desk-sergeant with irony. 'You know, I thought that we did the asking.'

'You always that funny? You should be at the Tivoli, you're wasted in a police station. Just have a look at your daybook for Friday and give a man a go.'

'I'm not even going to ask why you want me to look at my daybook for Friday. In fact, I'm such a nice policeman that I'm going to do it. What time?'

'After four in the afternoon,' growled Bert.

'Hmm. Friday was a quiet day. Nothing much happened around that time. Except that a fetching young woman in a bathing costume came in and made a complaint.'

'The tarts often wear bathing togs in the street in this part of Kew, do they? Cec, we're living on the wrong side of town.'

'She had a good reason for her lack of attire. The old Undertaker had nicked her clothes.'

'Well, well, the things that people do. It's a criminal world.'

'Yair, luckily you haven't been caught yet. Undertaker is wellknown in these parts. He was in that line of business before the grog got him. Anyway, we got her clothes back. Another case solved. That enough for yer?'

'Where can we find this Undertaker?'

'Heaven. At least I hope so. Of course, it depends on the kind of life he led.'

The desk-sergeant folded his hands piously. Bert snorted.

'If you mean that he's dead, why not say so? What about the tart?'

'She, as far as I know, is still with us.'

'You got her name and address there, ain't you?'

'Wild horses would not drag it from me.'

'How about ten quid?'

'Ten quid, on the other hand, might.'

He wrote out the name and address on a piece of paper and handed it to Bert. Bert gave him the money.

'Anything else I can do for you?'

'Take a long walk off a short pier,' requested Bert and he and Cec found themselves in the yard. As they started off again, he growled.

'Only one thing worse than a clean cop, and that's a funny cop.'

'Too right,' said Cec.

The young lady's name, it appeared, was Wilson. Her address was close to the river, but she was not at home. Bert consulted the list.

'Perhaps we should do the searching while the weather's still clear. It looks like it might rain, eh, Cec?'

Cec considered the sky.

'Too right.'

They split up, working in opposite directions. Cec found the rope. It was, as Phryne had foretold, of worn hemp, and there were dark stains at regular intervals.

'Where did you find it, mate?'

Cec indicated a pile of bluestone pitchers. They had been piled carelessly, but under them Bert found a collection of small objects—a whistle, three chewing-gum cards in the Famous Kings and Queens in British History Series, the carriage of a toy train and three rings with bright glass stones. There was a licorice block and eleven lead soldiers, overpainted with what looked like white kilts.

'What do you reckon this means, mate?'

Cec shook his head. 'Maybe some kids were building a cubby house,' he suggested. 'Do we leave 'em here?'

'Yair. Now to find where they are digging up the street. I reckon they are kerbstones, Cec. Back to the cab, mate. I reckon we have earned a drink. That's two on the list. Then we look for the kids and go back for this Wilson sheila. I hope she ain't dead, too.'

'Too right,' said Cec.

Having been placated with Mike's blue singlet tied up to make a doll which substituted for Bear, Candida had fallen asleep. Mike had lain down beside her, to protect the child from any attack, and was snoring gently. Ann looked bitterly at the smooth face of the child and Mike's peaceful countenance.

'How can he sleep at a time like this!' she snarled. Sidney was loading the gun.

'He don't have to wake up ever again,' Sidney suggested. 'All I got to do is have a little accident with this gun. Then there's only two ways to split the money and no need to release the child. She's bright. She'd be able to identify us. And I got nothing to lose. If the jacks catch me they'll hang me high.'

Ann surveyed Sidney. He was a snivelling little monster, devoid of any attraction, but he could be used. Once he had the money, what was to stop her having the same accident? Then she wouldn't have to split the money at all. The world owed her some favours. All her life she had longed for money; for furs and jewellery and luxury. Five thousand pounds could buy quite a lot of pleasure. She smiled on the detestable Sidney, who had clearly seen too many gangster films.

'All right. But first we get the money. Then we deal.'

'Think about it, honey,' said Sidney. 'It ain't an offer I'll make twice.'

You horrible little worm, thought Ann. She laid a hand on his, over the revolver.

'It's a deal.'

Candida was awake and listening. This rag thing was not Bear. She could not sleep without Bear. She kept her eyes closed.

'What's the time?' asked Ann.

'Ten...and it's a forty-mile drive. Better go. I'll be back as soon as I can.'

'Oh, Sidney,' crooned Ann, both hands on his shoulders, 'if you don't come back, I'll find you, and when I find you, I'll kill you. Do you understand?'

Sidney's eyes dropped. 'I'll come back, baby,' he quoted, from the last gangster movie he'd seen.

Ann grabbed her coat. 'And I'll make sure of it,' she agreed. 'Mike can take care of the kid. You ain't going nowhere without me, Sid.'

Sullenly, Sid led the way to the car. Candida closed her eyes. It was about time, she decided, that someone came to rescue her.

Chapter Nine

The truth is rarely pure and never simple.
The Importance of Being Earnest,
Oscar Wilde

Phryne got dressed for the long night ahead. She chose black trousers, boots, a tight-fitting cloche hat and a large, loose black wool jacket with several big pockets. As she dressed she gave Dot details of the coming adventure, and received the latest news.

'Mr Leonard rang twice. Nothing new. Miss McNaughton says that she is having her children's party on Friday. Miss, how are we going to rescue that little girl?'

'This one, Dot, we shall have to fly entirely by the seat of our pants.'

'What does that mean?'

'That I really haven't the faintest idea. Get me Detective-inspector Robinson on the phone. Here's his number. I've got another favour to ask him.'

When she had the policeman's ear Phryne said, 'If you alert the Queenscliff police to the fact that an arrest may be made in their area of a notorious criminal, and that I have your personal authority to direct it, then tomorrow might bring you good news.'

'I'll attend to it. I get so little good news in this job.'

Phryne rang off and sat down to think with the aid of a tantalus, a bottle of Napoleon brandy, and a map of Victoria. Dot, tiptoeing, withdrew.

By three in the afternoon she had come to the conclusion that her first theory had been correct. There was only one way to find out where Candida was, and that was to go home with the pick-up man. She put her small pearl-handled revolver in her pocket along with other essential supplies. A box of ammunition went into the pocket on the other side. She also carried a wad of money and a driving licence, a large bag of barley sugar, and a long light rope which she wound around her waist. She included her flying goggles and went to the kitchen to canvass Mr Butler's opinion on a matter involving paint.

She set out for the Maldon household half-an-hour later, driving the red car, and Dot failed to get a word out of her. After ten minutes, she stopped trying.

'How are they, Jack?' asked Phryne, as she stepped through the door. Jack looked at her. She was a slight figure when dressed all in black, even to the cloche which hid her hair. The only colour in the whole ensemble was the bright pink of her cheeks and the grey-green of her eyes.

'Not too good. They have been arguing about going to the police for hours now. Molly is all for it and Henry's all against it.'

'It may not be necessary,' commented Phryne. 'I have a plan. But if it doesn't work we can still call the cops. I have spoken informally to my old friend Detective-inspector Robinson. Jack, can you lay your hands on a 'bus. We need a strong, fairly light plane.'

'Well, I don't own a plane and neither does Henry. He has an order in for the new Avro, but it hasn't arrived yet. I could ask Bill.'

'Of course. Tell Bill that I need to borrow the Fokker. Tell him that I will personally guarantee that I'll buy him another if we break it…call him now, Jack, we need the plane for tonight.'

Jack went off to telephone and Phryne opened the door into the parlour.

It bore all the signs of a day of unbearable strain. The ashtray was piled high with butts. The air was foul with smoke and fear. Molly was drinking her thirtieth cup of tea for the day and Jack was lighting yet another cigarette. A scratch meal of bacon and eggs had congealed on its plates and had not been cleared away.

'Right, everyone pull themselves together. Buck up! You shall have Candida back by tomorrow or my name isn't Phryne Fisher—which of course, it is. Open the window, Molly. Start a nice little fire in that grate, Henry, it's cold. Is your cook here? I'll go and see her. Put all that depressing food in the chook pail. Come on, up and at 'em!'

She galvanized the couple, who had not spoken since Molly had accused Henry of failing to discipline Candida and Henry had accused Molly of crushing the child's spirit. Their voices were creaky with disuse. They stood up, flinching as muscles creaked and tendons twanged. Jack came back.

'I can go and get the Fokker any time. Where are we taking it?'

'Don't know. About forty miles to Geelong and twenty more beyond that. Take a full load of fuel because I don't know where we are going to land. Dot, can you ring Bunji Ross for me and ask her if she is free to take a little fly? Now I'm going to the kitchen. Both of you, out for a brisk walk around the block. On the double!' Molly and Henry, dazed, obeyed. Jack Leonard smiled.

'You are a wonderful girl, Miss Fisher.'

'Call me Phryne, I've been calling you Jack for days. Don't be insulted that I'm asking Bunji to fly the Fokker. I'm entrusting you with a much greater honour.'

'What's that?'

'You are going to drive my car,' said Phryne. 'Help me clean up. Nothing is more depressing than a room in which three people have spent all day worrying. Get some more wood and re-light that fire, if you please. I'll tidy…no, Dot will tidy, she's better at it than me.'

Dot returned and reported that Bunji had professed herself delighted to assist and free for the next two days. Phryne waved a hand at the mess and Dot took off her coat and hung it on the door.

Phryne found the kitchen. The cook and the maid were sitting at the table. They had evidently been weeping for hours. The maid in particular could hardly see out of her eyes. The table was littered with the remains of lunch, or possibly breakfast, and no washing up had been done.

Phryne blew into the room like a cold South wind.

'Come on ladies, buck up. We are going to find the child and bring her back by tomorrow. Up we get, Mabel.' She hoisted the maid under the arms. 'Go and wash your face in cold water and comb your hair. What would your young man think of you if he saw you like that? Come on Cook, let's get all this cleared away and I'll help you with the washing-up. The master and mistress will be back from their walk and then you and Mabel are going out, too. Is the stove still hot? Good. I suggest something soothing for a late lunch. What about a cheese omelette and a nice solid sweet?'

'Apple and coconut crumble,' said the cook, drying her eyes and stowing her handkerchief about her person. 'We can manage that, Miss. We *have* been giving way. It's because she's such a lovely little girl. Not an angel, she's a strong-minded little creature but very clever and very good hearted. When I had a headache she brought me two of her mother's aspirin and her bear to hold.' Cook managed not to burst into tears again. She relieved her feelings by stroking the stove until it ignited with a great roar of wind in the chimney. The kettle sang and the iron skillet, uncleaned after bacon and eggs had been cooked, sizzled. Cook carried it into the scullery. She scraped the plates which Dot had brought in. Mabel returned, mopped-up and collected, drew a bucket of hot water from the stove and began to wash up.

Jack Leonard and Dot had straightened the disordered room and the fire was burning brightly. A cold and refreshing breeze blew through the open front door.

'That looks better,' commented Phryne. 'You have a natural talent for order, Dot. Ah. They are back. Go and tell Cook and the maid to take their walk. A fast walk. I want them back in ten minutes. Now, when you spoke to Bill, Jack, how did he sound?'

'Quite chirpy, really. He has faith in your star, Phryne, as do we all. Are you really going to allow me to drive the Hispano-Suiza?'

'Yes. If you damage it I'll have your guts for garters. Do not let that bother you, though, just don't drive like a demon. It won't be too difficult. At least I hope not. Now, out you go, Jack. I want you and Bill to modify a big motorcar foglight to run off the engine of the Fokker. I want it to shine straight down.'

'No car headlight will be strong enough to reveal much on the ground, Miss Fisher, unless you are intending to fly at twenty feet.'

'It doesn't have to reveal anything. It only has to be strong enough to hit the road. Off you go. Here is some money. I don't mind how much it costs, but I must have it finished before dark. You'll have to take the 'bus down to Geelong before anything interesting happens. Clear?'

'Clear,' agreed Jack. 'I say, do you really know Bunji Ross?'

'Yes, she's going to fly the plane, and I want Henry to go as her observer. We are going to track the kidnappers to their lair, and we will only have one chance, so we can't afford to mess it up. Call Bunji and ask her from me to help and advise; you'll like her, Jack, but see if you can prevent her from fighting with Bill. Tell him that on Friday I anticipate solving the murder, and he must continue to be the Angel of the House.'

Jack left. Molly and Henry returned from their walk, feeling better, and Phryne asked them to show her around their house. It was new, and some of the chests had not been unpacked. Phryne decided that this would be a splendid occupation for a worried woman.

'Molly, you should unpack all these boxes. I'll send Dot to help you, she's great at putting things away. I tend to just stuff the clothes into a wardrobe. If the door shuts, I think it's all right, but Dot is neat. You stay up here and I'll send her to you. It will be all right, I promise. You have my word. We shall have her back by tomorrow. It's just a matter of getting through the time, and we can't move until tonight. Cook will bring you a light meal and I want you to eat all of it even if you are convinced that it will choke you. I need you in good shape for tonight and you will find that you are hungry after the first three mouthfuls. What a charming room. Did you choose the wallpaper?'

Molly nodded. She had been very proud of that wallpaper. It seemed like such a long time ago now that she had moved into this house in which she had hoped to be very happy. Phryne interpreted the look.

'You'll be happy here again if you can regain your sense of proportion,' she said over her shoulder. 'When I see Candida tonight I'll need some token that I am trust-worthy. What would convince her?'

'Bear,' said Molly with conviction. 'She will be leading those kidnappers a hell of a dance because she hasn't got him. Come this way,' she said, and led Phryne upstairs to the nurseries. Baby Alexander had been sent on a visit to his doting grandmother. His room, decorated with bunnies all round the walls, was empty, but had a feeling of recent occupation. Candida's room was hollow. It was clear that the child who had slept in this little blue bed and worn these pyjamas and played with these toys was missing, not just gone for the day. Molly controlled herself with a great effort and snatched Bear off the bed.

Phryne retreated from the room and shut the door. There was a limit to what a stepmother could stand. She held up Bear and looked at him. He had been a proper golden plush Pooh-bear at one stage in his life, but he had been extravagently loved for some years since then, and he was a little battered. One of his ears had been carefully re-stitched, and his joints were loose. His squeaker no longer worked and the repairs to his face after some childish accident had given him a lop-sided grin. He was a Bear of great, if raffish, charm and Phryne could understand why Candida relied on his company and counsel. This might be a Bear of very little brain, but even his furry body had been moulded, by the hugs of years, to fit Candida's embrace. Phryne gave Bear a brief squeeze and tucked him under her arm.

'To your boxes, woman,' she ordered Molly. 'Bear will be safe with me.'

She marched back into the parlour, where Henry had started pacing again.

'Dot, can you go and help Mrs Maldon? She's upstairs, unpacking. Talk to her about her new house, baby Alexander, and anything else that occurs to you. Don't go into Candida's room if you can help it.'

Dot obeyed. From the kitchen came the appetizing scent of an omelette cooking, and bread toasting. Henry took Bear out of Phryne's arms and hugged him. Phryne glanced at his face and went out. She decided that Bear should be left alone to work his magic.

She dialled her own house. Mrs Butler answered the phone.

'Mr Butler has got the paint you ordered, Miss, and says that what you need to deliver it is the bladder from a football. He's just gone out to buy one.'

'Good. He is a jewel among men and I hope that you are very happy with him.'

'And your two cabbies are here with a load of papers which they say you asked them to buy.'

'Good again. Tell them to wait until Mr B. comes back and to bring the doings over to the Maldons'. Did they say if they found the rope?'

'Mr Bert is here, Miss, I'll put him on.'

Bert, who was unused to telephones, roared in Phryne's ear.

'Bert here, Miss. We got the rope.'

'Good, but keep your voice down. Was it where I said it would be?'

'Yair. Cec found it, and a pile of pitchers. We reckon they are kerbstones. We'll go out looking for the street repairs later. The rope had blood on it all right. Reckon it was used to tie someone up. The stains are all spaced out, like. And there were all these little things under the stones.'

'What sort of little things?'

'Lollies, and toys, and gum cards, and lead soldiers. Someone had painted over their uniforms and given them white skirts.'

'Ah,' said Phryne with deep satisfaction. 'Had they. Have I told you lately how invaluable you are, Bert?'

'Not lately,' said Bert, 'but I'll pass your recommendation on to Cec. Now about the old bloke and the girl—no wonder the poor sheila was chasing him up the path. He'd pinched her clothes. This smarmy cop thought it was real funny. Cost me ten squid to square him. Is that all right?'

'Cheap at the price,' said Phryne. 'Come over here with the paint and the footy, as soon as you can. The game's afoot, Bert, and I'm hoping to have Candida back before tomorrow night. After that we shall see. You keep looking for the local top cocky, and the street repairs, and I'll see you soon. Bye.'

Phryne could hear Bert ask, 'What do I do with this thing now?' as she rang off.

Bert and Cec arrived an hour later in their new taxi. Omelettes and jam roll had been consumed, the household having run out of coconut, and Molly Maldon was so absorbed in telling Dot all about what a bargain her new carpet had been that she did not flinch when the doorbell rang. The two cabbies came in with the bladder and the paint, and an armload of illustrated papers. Phryne waved her scissors at them.

'Come in! I'm just cutting up five thousand pounds worth of valuable newspaper. Put them down there on the sofa,' she directed, and Bert laid down his burden. 'This is Henry Maldon, the flier. Tell me about the funny cop.'

'Pleased to meetcher,' growled Bert, who did not approve of capitalists. He took a tense hand and shook it. Henry Maldon looked much better than he had two hours ago, but there was enough residual agony in his face to make Bert revise his opinion. 'He couldn't help winning the money,' he told Cec later. 'And the poor coot looked like he'd been strained through a sieve backwards. Sitting there clutching that teddy bear. Must'a belonged to the kid.'

Bert abated his gruffness instantly and strove to amuse.

He made a good story out of the cop, and coaxed a smile out of the distracted flier. Phryne bound her newspaper bundles with a real note on the top and bottom, and placed a bundle of real fivers on the top. The notes were packed into a cloth bag. There was a strained silence.

'Come down to the pub, mate,' offered Bert to his own astonishment. 'Man needs a beer. Still an hour before time.'

The ormolu clock on the mantelpiece said five. Phryne refrained from hugging Bert and observed, 'We can't do anything until it's dark. You go with Bert and Cec. I'll come and get you if something happens. Which pub are you going to?'

'The Railway,' said Henry, and the two cabbies took him away. This was a relief to Phryne, who had not been able to find Henry an occupation. There was still a couple of hours to go before there was any point in setting out for Geelong.

Phryne heard the voice of the cook raised in comfortable converse with the butter-cream-and-egg man, who was late.

'What are you coming here at this time of night for?' she demanded, and Phryne heard the reply from the back yard.

'Couldn't go any faster, Missus, not even to woo me old sweetheart. The bleedin' Council have dug up the bleedin' road and I had to wheel me trike all the way from the shop. My boss is creatin'. So don't you start on me, there's a love.'

'Language,' cautioned the cook. 'And don't come smoogin' up to me. Them eggs you brought yesterday was mostly rotten.'

'What? My eggs?' exclaimed the delivery boy, as outraged as if he had laid them personally. 'My eggs, rotten? You show me a rotten egg I've delivered. You must have got 'em mixed up with them tichy little ones from your own chooks.'

'The chooks ain't laying,' returned the cook, 'or I wouldn't have to buy your rotten ones.'

'Give a man a break,' complained the boy, who sounded about fifteen. 'The boss says, "Take them eggs", so I take 'em. I ain't got no choice. How many of 'em were off, anyway?'

'Three out of the dozen, and I had to throw away a whole cake batter with a pound of butter in it. I wouldn't have offered it to a pig. I ought to get onto your boss, however,' admitted the cook handsomely. 'I suppose that it ain't your fault. Give me a dozen more, and two pounds of butter, no cream today.'

There was a thud as the parcel was placed on the kitchen table. 'See you temorrer, my old darling,' cried the boy, and took off quickly, in time to avoid a slap.

'Not so much of the "old",' snarled the cook, and slammed the kitchen door, much invigorated.

Phryne took up the illustrated papers and leafed through them. A characteristic passage met her eye.

'The recent discoveries at Luxor have sent the whole Empire mad about Egypt,' it said smugly. 'Lord Avon, who has been largely responsible for financing the expedition, said that the public interest was most gratifying. "There is a whole civilization under the sand here," he said to our special correspondent. "And one of very high standards. The decorative patterns, the linen, the beading and the magnificent tomb painting of the Pharoah are unforgettable and as fresh as the day they were painted. I expect to find many more tombs in this area. It seems to have been a flourishing city. I also hope to find the chamber which I am convinced lies under the great Pyramid, the resting place of Cheops himself. Further interesting discoveries are expected daily."'

She laid the magazines open at the pictures of the objects discovered in the rock chambers. A dagger inland with hunting cats. A diadem for a queen, with lotus flowers in lapis lazuli. A bracelet for an archer inlaid with the Eye of Horus to safeguard his aim. Tomb paintings of the Pharoah hunting lions, and mixing wine, and embracing his wife. Small figurines of gods and slaves and workmen: little women kneading dough, herding cattle, shearing sheep and reaping wheat. They were enchanting. Phryne stared longest at the gold statue of the Goddess Pasht, a graceful cat with an earring in one of her upstanding ears and kittens at her delicate feet.

That is beautiful beyond belief, thought Phryne. I wonder if I could steal it?

Chapter Ten

Night makes no difference 'twixt Priest and Clerk
Joan as my Lady's as good i' the dark
No Difference in the Dark, Herrick

At last it was getting dark. Phryne packed Dot, Molly, Jack Leonard and herself into the Hispano-Suiza. She checked that she had all the impedimenta that had been improvised and collected during the day. Though she and her hosts had eaten an early dinner they added a picnic basket to the load, as well as a brandy flask, and of course, Bear.

'It's not all that far to Geelong but I don't want to hurry,' she said as Jack Leonard swung the starting handle. 'Are we clear as to what we are going to do?'

Everyone nodded.

'Right,' said Phryne, taking a deep breath. 'Off we go, then.'

She located the Geelong Road without difficulty and soon they were bowling along in the darkness. There would be a moon but it had not yet risen. It was clear and frosty and the stars were very bright. Phryne hoped that she wouldn't freeze to death on the escapade which she had in mind. She had already fought a fierce action with Jack Leonard, once he heard what she intended to do.

'Don't be silly, Jack. Look at the size of you. I'm five feet three and I weigh eight stone with all these clothes and goods. How much do you weigh?'

'Twelve stone. I suppose that you are right. But what if you fall off?'

'Then you shall pick me up,' said Phryne, and the conversation was at an end.

Dot was talking to Molly Maldon to distract herself from how cold she was, how worried about Phryne, and how fast the car was going. Molly was keyed-up. After what seemed like years of hanging about and worrying, there was now a chance of some action and she was all for it. The afternoon among her possessions had soothed her spirit and she had great faith in Phryne. She was beginning to believe that she would recover Candida. She had the bag of lollies in the picnic basket, though she had an instinctive and superstitious dread of picturing how glad Candida would be to see them, and paid as much attention as she could to Dot's account of one of Phryne's previous cases.

'And this abortionist was her capture, was he?'

'No, that was a police-lady called…Miss, what was the police-lady's name, that caught that…er…you know, the chap that operated on women.'

Dot would not say the word 'abortionist', any more than she would swear in church.

'WPC Jones. I saw her today. She got a medal for seizing the Brunswick rapist.'

Dot could feel her cheeks burning. Everything she said seemed to have a sexual meaning.

Phryne, perceiving her embarrassment, launched into flying-shop talk with Jack Leonard.

'Did you like Bunji, Jack?'

'She's a ball of lightning, isn't she? Bustled in and spent twenty minutes with her head in the engine, and then she and Bill worked out how to mount the light. It's a drain on the power supply but I don't think it's enough to significantly affect the performance.'

'Did she argue with Bill?'

'All day. You could tell that they were both having a lovely time. And she's a sporting flier. Took the Alps and even flew over the Himalayas. Said that all you had to do to thoroughly depress the spirits was to look down. Nowhere at all to land—just rocks.'

Phryne laughed, and shifted into top gear.

The Geelong Road was visible only as a tarmac trail that gleamed faintly in the lights of the powerful car. There was no sound but the roar of the engine and the swish of the slipstream. Luckily Mr Butler had managed to put the hood into place or the passengers would have been even colder than they were. The stars shone down like lanterns—no, they were on the road—two swaying lights. An odd noise began to make itself heard. Phryne listened attentively. It was halfway between a clatter and a clop like hooves. She racked her memory, and concluded that she really was hearing a new sound.

'Can you hear that?' she asked.

Dot cried out, 'Slow down!'

Phryne applied the brakes and the car lost momentum. She had almost stopped when the explanation was vouch-safed to her.

A wave of advancing sheep circled the car, their fleeces oddly grey in the starlight. The moon was rising. The lanterns gleamed. A ghostly stockman, looking like a revenant from the past, raised a casual hand. Two jinkers clattered past, with bags slung underneath for the dogs to rest in. A dog barked. The sheep trotted down the road.

'Thank you, Dot, I might have ploughed right into them. I didn't know they took sheep along this road. And in the dark. How dangerous! They must be going to Borthwicks—and there's the cemetery. How convenient. Well, tally-ho, and if anyone sights a flock of flamingoes or a herd of elephants, just let me know.'

'Where are we?' asked Molly.

'About halfway I should think. We have to look out for Bunji and Henry in the Fokker outside Geelong. They should be over on the left side of the road, near the railway bridge. Give me a shout if you see them. Then we have to test the plan. I would feel very silly if I went ahead with it and it turned out not to function. I'd be left on my own with the kidnappers and they are probably armed.'

'Are you?' asked Jack. Phryne nodded.

'Certainly. But I hope not to have to use it. I do not approve of guns.'

'Good shot, are you?'

'Not particularly. At the distance one has the most use for a pistol, however, it makes no difference. A man is too big a target to miss at a range of five feet.'

'Why five feet?'

'Any closer and he can grab,' explained Phryne. 'Let's talk about something else.'

Jack Leonard obliged with a dissertation on the merits of Rolls Royce engines which lasted until they were nearing Geelong.

'They bore their engine blocks, put them out to weather in a field for two years, and then re-bore them. I have never come across a Rolls with cylinder trouble. Marvellous machines... Hello! There's the Fokker.'

Phryne swung the car off the road and drew to a halt on a flat paddock. The flying machine was stopped and had been turned on the grass so it could be got back into the air with the greatest dispatch. Bunji Ross, short and plump in her flying suit and boots, strolled over and grinned at Phryne.

'Hello, Phryne. You'll be pleased to hear that the gown was a great success. I only spilt a little tomato soup on it, which is good, for me. I've mounted the light, m'dear and I can cast a fairish light on the road, but only at very low altitude. I can't make much impression on it over fifty to seventy feet. What's the landscape from here to where you are going? Any mountains?'

'Not as long as you follow the road. Leave the road and the ground gets very lumpy away to the left. If you can keep the plane to the right of the road, you'll be fine.'

'Good, will do. I've got Henry with me. He has a good pair of Zeiss-Ikon binoculars and seems competent in the air. Come and let's give this idea a try. Run her back toward Melbourne, pet, we don't want to muddy our trail.'

Phryne dabbed a small drop of paint on the road, then took the car slowly along, dripping a little paint out of the driver's side. She continued for a quarter of a mile, then took the car off the road and waited.

Overhead, but only just overhead, the Fokker engine roared. The plane circled once above the car. She dipped her wings, and flew off towards Geelong.

'Good. It works. Bunji really is a brick. We are almost there. Jack, you take the wheel and remember what I said about garters.'

Geelong was a sizeable town, encircled by grain silos and storehouses, with a respectable townhall and wide streets. It did not keep late hours. The only person Phryne saw who seemed to be awake was a strolling policeman. Phryne took note of the moon. It was now bright and full.

'There's the park, Jack, stop for a while at that corner near those big elms. Light a cigarette and look bored. Stand there until you finish the smoke, then you can go into the park and stop short of the band rotunda. According to the map, it must be about three hundred yards over that way. Molly takes the money and puts it into the hollow stump. Don't stop and stare, just drop the bag in and walk away. Then you start the car and give her a lot of high revs in case they are already here. Then get back on the road and wait. We could be here all night, but don't go to sleep. You wait for the plane, and keep a good way behind it. You'll be able to see the light for quite long way. In any case I think that we are going to Queenscliff. Break a leg,' said Phryne, and slipped into the darkness. In her black garb she was hard to see, and she stopped at a convenient mud-puddle and smeared her face.

The band rotunda was white wrought-iron, and it stood out under the moon like the bare ribcage and spine of a fabulous monster. Phryne waited until her eyes had got used to the light, then began to creep, sloshing slightly with her bladder of fluo-rescent paint, across the invisible grass.

Luckily it was not yet frosty, although it would certainly be so before dawn. She told herself that she was as good and ruthless a hunter as the Egyptian cats, and paused with one hand on a tree. She stepped into shadow, rolling her foot carefully forward from the heel: not a twig cracked under her feet. She had reached the rotunda and was about to cross the path when she saw a point of light, and heard someone whistling softly. There was a man, sitting at ease on the rotunda steps and smoking. Phryne's spirits rose. This did not look like a professional kidnapping. Of course he might not be the one—but what sane man would have been found sitting in a rotunda at midnight in the middle of winter?

She was confirmed in this opinion by his behaviour when the noise of the Hispano-Suiza was heard. He threw his cigarette away and crouched down below the railings.

Phryne also crouched. She heard the crunch of Molly's feet on the gravel and the thud as the bag dropped into the hollow stump. Molly's feet moved away again and there was the revving of a big engine.

Don't get too carried away with my car, Jack Leonard, thought Phryne. Is this my man or not? Damn him, won't he move? I'm freezing to the spot.

Sid moved at last. He sauntered over to the stump, extracted the bag, and ripped open the top. He stuffed a handful of fivers into his pocket and tucked the bag under his arm. He walked jauntily down the path toward the other side of the park and did not give the slightest thought to the shadow that moved when he did.

He was planning to go back to Queenscliff to eliminate the witnesses, not share the money. He still had five shots in his revolver. That would finish Mike, the woman sitting silently in the car, and the kid. He would leave the pistol in Mike's hand then catch a boat from Adelaide bound to anywhere, with five thousand quid in his kick. He licked his lips at the thought of the ten-year-old child slaves he could buy in Turkey, with that amount of money.

The Bentley was warm and he only needed to swing the starting handle before the engine caught. Sidney did not so much as glance at Ann as he got in and drove away.

Phryne had not had any difficulty in ensconcing her slight frame behind the rumble seat. She unwound the line from her waist and lashed herself to the back of the car, using the convenient lugs placed there for tying up luggage. Tonight, thought Phryne, he hasn't got luggage, he's got baggage. This feeble witticism amused her as she hung on when the Bentley rounded a corner. She had the bladder of paint in a sling contrived by Dot, placed on her right hip. All she needed to do to drop some paint was to give the bladder a soft thump. The excreted paint would shine on the black surface of the road as soon as the light from the plane touched it.

Phryne had not gone fifty yards before she began to curse her own cleverness. This was ingenious, but couldn't much the same effect have been obtained by tying the bladder to the car? She supposed not. She had no way of timing because she could not spare a hand to hold her watch. Bear was safe and snug against her chest. Phryne banged the bladder and a drop of paint squeezed out. She began to sing under her breath as the car whizzed along and the cold wind slashed at her hands.

She thumped the bladder at the end of each line. Observing angels would have heard had they been hovering over her in the dark:

John Brown's body lies a-mouldering in the (thump)
John Brown's body lies a-mouldering in the (thud)
John Brown's body lies a-mouldering in the (thump)
But his soul goes marching (thud)!

Phryne hoped that by this novel method she could space out the drops of paint so that the plane could follow them. Geelong was fleeting past. Soon they were out into the open paddocks again. The moon was high and the light bright enough for Phryne to read the engine specifications embossed on the Bentley's rear.

She was exquisitely uncomfortable. She had bound herself as tightly as Andromeda to the rock, as she did not relish being flung off into the night. Struck at thirty miles an hour, the road was sure to be very hard indeed. Her fingers, in their leather gloves, were beginning to cramp. She eased the pressure by leaning into her line, and though it took her weight, it creaked rather alarmingly. Her feet were wedged above the bumper bar, where the maker of the car had decided to make a definite little shelf about ten inches long.

The car surged up and over a hump in the road, and Phryne lost her grip. Her clawing hand met the tail light and she hung on to it as though she had been glued while she scrabbled with her feet for the step. She found it and gave the bladder a hearty thump. Geelong was now not even a glow on the skyline, and the moon was westering. Where was the plane? Had the paint failed to work? That would be disastrous.

Phryne freed a hand to scratch her itching nose and reminded herself that poor little Candida was at the end of this wild ride. If she was still alive. Phryne banged the bladder again.

> The grand old Duke of (thump)
> He had ten thousand (thud)
> He marched them up to the (thud) of the hill and
>   he marched them (thump) again.
> And when they were up they were (bang)
> And when they were down they were (slosh)
> And when they were only halfway (thud)
> They were neither up nor (bump)
> Oh, the Grand old Duke of (thump)

Phryne began again, when she heard the buzz of a plane engine. She strained her ears, and risked a brief glance over her shoulder.

Riding up, circling majestically, the Fokker came into sight in the moon-glow, gleaming as silver as a trey bit. A faint stream of light radiated from her belly. It had worked. Phryne cheered silently, and barked her knuckles as the driver turned off the main road.

The plane was being flown by an expert—Bunji was to be congratulated. Phryne saw that the slow, sweeping circles, the most dangerous and difficult of all manouevres to attempt at night, covered the road with light while not making it obvious to the drivers underneath. They had not, as it happened, seen any other motors, as the winter attracted few people to the coastal resorts, and the locals knew better than to be out at this hour in this weather.

The road surface had worsened. Phryne kept her face pressed against the car, as the big machine spurned the stones and flung them high. One sneaked through her guard and cut her over the eyebrow. She wondered how Candida, a well-brought up little girl, would react if she had to catch her before Phryne had a chance to wash her face. Probably scream and run.

She wiped some of the blood off to clear her eyes, and then remembered that she had goggles. The struggle to extract them from her pocket, keep thumping, and not fall off in the process took her mind off the pain for five miles of gravel and a mile-and-a-half of mud.

Relieved of the fear of road gravel in the eyes, she donned the goggles and looked for the plane. It was about a quarter of a mile behind, flying as evenly as an eagle. Bunji was credited with the ability to smell the ground. The sweeping swing would have taken a less brilliant pilot straight into the deck, and it was very hard to judge how much height had been lost at the edge of each circle. The mud road was more comfortable, and Phryne prayed that they did not get bogged.

She listened for the familiar sound of the Hispano-Suiza but could hear nothing above the roar of Sid's car.

In the cockpit of the Fokker, Bunji Ross was examining her instruments by the light of a torch. Flying speed was satisfactory, they had plenty of fuel, and the moon was giving almost enough light to fly by. At the bottom of each swoop she dropped the plane to within fifty feet of the road, and waited for Henry to call, 'Got it!' before she took to the air again. The engine was running sweetly. Bunji took a swig of black coffee from her thermos and offered it to Henry.

Henry gulped the bitter brew and returned the flask. He was lying on his face with the binoculars out of the hole which Jack and Bill had cut in the superstructure. Bill had not turned a hair when Bunji had announced that this was the only way she could devise of seeing out of the bottom of a plane. Hard struts dug into all the sensitive portions of his anatomy, including some which he had not known were sensitive before, but he did not care. He was on his way to retrieve the infuriating but beloved Candida.

⁂

Jack Leonard was controlling the big car with a minimum of effort. She was fleeing as softly along this dirt road as a spectre. Dot was handing out cups of thermos tea, and ham sandwiches. Jack bit into one absently. He kept the plane in the right-hand corner of the windscreen. He could not see the car which it was following, but that was according to Phryne's orders. They would not just chase along behind and be seen, or seize the pick-up man and beat him to a jelly, because of Candida. Nervous kidnappers kill their charges. Molly drank her tea and ate two sandwiches without prompting. She was half-tranced by this midnight ride on the empty road, and was possessed by the odd illusion that all the outside world was flying past, and the car was still, at the heart of the darkness.

Chapter Eleven

When in doubt, win the trick
Hoyle's Games:
Whist 24 Short Rules for Beginners

Bert and Cec had discovered the street repairs. Bluestones were stacked into a rough wall all along Paris St, where the workmen were replacing them with cement gutters. Several local households had helped themselves to a wheelbarrow load to construct their own rockery or a garden wall.

'This is the place, Cec. They've been here a few days, too, see, the grass is starting to grow over them. What's the last item on our list, eh? Oh, yair, the kids. This looks like a good street for kids. There's a gang of 'em now...what have they got? A cat, is it?'

Cec was already running towards the group of five children who appeared to be tormenting a cat. Cec plucked the half-grown kitten out of their grasp and caught it under his arm so that he could examine it. It seemed to have sustained only a wounded front paw. One of the claws had been unskilfully cut.

'Give me a bit of that rag,' ordered Cec, pointing with his free hand to a pile of bandages on the ground. One of the children, a grubby girl, burst into tears and another bit the end of her plait. The smallest urchin began to howl.

'It's all right, kids, don't go crook. We ain't going to hurt you, nor take you home to your mothers neither. We just want some information.'

Cec had bandaged the cat's front paw.

'We weren't going to hurt it, Mister, but it wouldn't keep still, and kept on scratching, so we thought we'd cut its claws. We didn't know that they'd bleed,' said a wiry little kid with a collarless shirt and knotted braces. Bert had caught up by now and was getting his breath back. The children stared at him righteously.

'We didn't know it was going to bleed, did we?' repeated the kid. Heads all nodded in chorus. The grubby girl wiped her face on a far-from-clean calico petticoat. The plait-sucking child said nothing.

'Are you the kids who play in McNaughton's?'

They nodded again. The smallest one howled and one of the others stopped his mouth with a pre-loved rainbow ball.

'That's Mickey. He howls,' said the wiry kid. 'I'm Jim, this is Elsie.' The plait-chewer nodded. 'And Janey.' The grubby girl made a bob. 'And Lucy, she's Mickey's sister and she has to take him with her.' Lucy grinned, showing that she had not received two front teeth for Christmas. Mickey was silenced by the gobstopper.

'Listen, kids, I want some information and I'm willing to pay for it. What will it be? A deener's worth of lollies?'

Mouths watered all around the circle. Jim considered.

'That's old Mother Ellis's cat,' he said. 'We sort of borrowed it and if she finds out that we hurt its paw, she'll tell all of our mums and we'll all get a hiding. If you can fix it with Mother Ellis, and give us the lollies, it's a deal.'

Bert looked at Cec, who was cradling the cat. The cat, which was a fine midnight-black pedigreed short-hair and no doubt very valuable, had placed one paw on either side of Cec's chin and was gazing lovingly up into his eyes.

'Can you do it, mate?'

Cec nodded. Jim escorted him to the house and watched with admiration as Cec walked straight up to the front door and banged the knocker, loud. The door opened and Jim ran for his life.

Mrs Ellis was a vicious old bitch, who punctured footballs kicked over her fence and shot at trespassing dogs with an air rifle.

She had never given back a tennis ball, either, or a kite, and the children believed that she sold them. Mr Ellis had thankfully given up the ghost twenty years before and no man who was not a relative had crossed her threshold since. The house was offensively clean and stank of carbolic. There was a trail of newspapers laid down the hall over the polished floor. The children called her a witch and her letterbox never missed its cracker on Bonfire night.

Although the house was cold as a grave, no smoke ever trailed from its chimneys. The kids believed she had the fires of Hell to warm her. She wore her thin web of hair scraped over her scalp and knotted at the back of her head, and was always dressed in black. Her face reminded Cec of a boarding-house pudding with currants for eyes.

'Mrs Ellis?' he asked in his soft warm voice. 'I've brought you back your cat.'

The black cat turned in his embrace and stared the old woman straight in the eye, as if daring her to start something. She saw the bandage on the paw.

'What's happened to him? Have those little devils hurt him? I'll have all of their bottoms tanned if they've touched a whisker.'

Her voice rose to an eldritch screech.

'The kids might have had nothing to do with it,' said Cec reasonably. 'It's only his front claw that's broken. He might have caught it in something. Does he like climbing trees?'

'Yes, he does, the varmint,' she said, patting her cat.

'And it was the street kids who put the bandage on his paw and told me where he belongs,' continued Cec, as if there was nothing in the world such as perjury. 'He'll be as good as gold after dinner and a sleep. The claw will grow again in about a month.'

'You know a lot about cats?'

'A bit,' said Cec, who had inflicted six of them on his long-suffering landlady.

'Come in,' she invited, and Cec stepped inside. The watching children gasped in chorus.

Mrs Ellis took Cec into her kitchen, where an electric heater warmed the room. The four cats who had draped themselves over the dresser and chairs lifted their heads and pricked their ears. They were all beautiful. Apart from the midnight-black in Cec's arms, there was a tortoiseshell, a silver tabby, a mackerel tabby, and a ginger Tom. They were all well fed and groomed. The old woman went to the ice-chest and took out two jointed rabbits.

'Dinner, my dears,' called Mrs Ellis. The cats rose, stretched, and approached their food with royal leisure. Cec set the black cat down by his plate and he began to eat hungrily. Mrs Ellis stroked it with her gnarled hands, and Cec found himself close to tears. He swallowed.

'Well, Mrs Ellis, I must go. Hope that the little fellow recovers well. I'm sure he'll be bonzer in a couple of days. Your cats are beauties,' commented Cec. Mrs Ellis accompanied him to the door and thrust a penny in his hand.

'Tell them kids not to make so much noise outside my house,' she snapped, and slammed the door with less than her usual force.

Cec was met at the gate by Jim.

'She gave me a penny for you.' He handed it over. 'She's not such a bad old chook if you leave her cats alone.'

Jim stood open-mouthed. A man invited into old Mother Ellis' house who emerges not only with his life but with a reward!

'All right,' said Jim, gathering his clan around the cabbies. 'What do you want to know?'

Bert told them the story of poor Bill McNaughton, unjustly accused of killing his father. He reminded them that on that very Friday they were going to a party with Miss McNaughton, where they would be entertained and fed. Could they take the lady's jelly and buns and ginger-beer and refuse to help her brother? Jim thought about it, and they drew off to confer. Elsie uncorked her mouth and said her first words. 'Tell them, Jim. I trust them.'

This seemed to be some sort of talisman. Bert had the whole story in ten minutes. He marvelled at the perspicacity of Miss Fisher once again, and handed over the shilling. He had just got some new change from the bank, so it was a bright and shiny shilling. The children gazed at it as it lay in Jim's hand. Unnoticed, little Mickey edged close to him and made a sudden grab.

'Quick, he'll swallow it!' screamed Lucy. Bert, the eldest of six children, acted with dispatch. He seized Mickey and turned him upside down like a chicken to be slaughtered, then gave him a hard thump in the middle of the back. Out shot the shilling. Elsie dived on it and tied it into her handkerchief. She stowed the hankie in the leg of her bloomers. Bert put Mickey down on his feet. He howled. It seemed to be his forte.

'Lost my rainbow ball!' he screamed. Lucy found it on the pavement and stuffed it back into the gaping mouth. Bert shuddered, but then reflected that children, like ostriches, seemed to be able to digest anything.

'All right, kids, we'll see you at Miss McNaughton's party on Friday. Not a word until then, eh?'

The heads nodded in a row. Bert and Cec went to reclaim their cab. A sudden thought struck Bert. He came back.

'What did you want to do to that cat?' he asked. Jim looked up from the old envelope on which he was taking orders for lollies.

He told Bert what they wanted with the cat. Bert roared with laughter.

'You're supposed to wait until they're dead!' The children blushed.

⁙

Seconds before the last of Phryne's sinews gave out, the car arrived at its destination. It stopped in a dark spot under the gumtrees. Phryne untied herself and fell backwards onto the road, before the roar of the engine died. Ann and Sidney got out of the car without noticing her, and walked into the house.

Phryne was bruised all over and her hands and feet were cramped and pinched. For a minute she lay still, unable to move, then gently she flexed and stretched until she was able to get to her feet.

There was still plenty of paint in the bladder. Lavishly, she traced a big cross on the road. A plane flew over and dipped both wings in salute.

Success. Phryne shook her shoulders and the folds of her jacket fell into place, loaded with equipment. She drew a line to the front gate of the house, and crept around it like a Red Indian tracking a particular scalp. The only light she could see came from the back of the house. She guessed it was the kitchen.

Sidney opened the front door with his key and took the gun out of his pocket. Ann was behind him, soft-footed. The house was silent. Just three shots, thought Sidney, and I'm home and dried.

The kitchen door creaked and woke Mike. It also woke Candida, who was lying curled up against his back, her thumb in her mouth and the singlet doll clutched to her chest.

As Sid crept in, Mike said contemptuously, 'I thought you'd try that. Put it down, you murdering swine.'

'You were right,' agreed Sidney. 'In a few moments the whole five thou will be mine.'

'You double-crossing bastard,' spat Ann, standing in the doorway. 'You promised you'd take me, too.'

Mike shifted his concentration from Sidney, to his wife, then lunged at her. But he was too late. Sidney had turned as she spoke and fired at point-blank range into her heart. She fell, and instead of strangling his wife Mike was now cradling her lifeless body in his arms. Sid swung round to take wavering aim at Candida. She shrieked, and Mike dropped his wife and dived across the kitchen, shattering the back door with his shoulder. He pushed Candida out into the night. 'Run!' he yelled. 'I'll deal with this bastard.'

Sid fired. The bullet scraped along Mike's arm and buried itself into the mistreated door. Then Mike had hold of the gun hand. Sidney was the smaller and weaker, but he was a tough street fighter. Mike could not get him down.

'Excuse me,' came a clipped voice from the back doorstep. 'Could you possibly hold up the gun hand?'

It was an indescribably dirty young woman. Her face was streaked with blood and mud and her features could not be told, but she had a steady hand and held a pearl-handled revolver with it. Mike gaped briefly, then hauled the gun wrist up until Sid was nearly clear of the ground.

'Thanks,' said Phryne coolly, and placed a neat hole in Sid's wrist. He dropped the gun. Mike knelt on him and tied him up with the length of rope that the surprising young woman produced.

'I really should tie you up, too,' she commented. 'Except that I saw you rescue Candida. We'd better go and find her.'

'I told her to run,' frowned Mike, kicking Sidney in the ribs as an aid to meditation. 'She might not have stopped yet.'

'I've got a lure that will bring her back,' smiled Phryne, and produced the teddybear from the sling.

'Is that Bear?' asked Mike. 'That's good.' He was contemplating his wife's body.

'I gather she gave you a hard time,' said Phryne.

'It was my own fault,' said Mike ruefully. 'Candida!' he called. 'The lady has brought Bear.'

A small voice spoke from somewhere close. 'I don't believe you. Put him on the step.'

Phryne placed Bear reverently on the step and a rustling was heard in the bushes. A small dirty hand shot out, seized Bear by the leg and dragged him off the step. There was silence. Phryne began to be rather worried.

'Candida? Daddy and Mummy are on their way. They will be here soon. Come inside and er, no, don't come inside. Go out to the car and I'll meet you there.' Phryne heard a faint, relieved sobbing, muffled in teddybear fur.

'Oh, Bear, I knew you'd come. And now Daddy is coming and Mummy is coming and my lollies are coming and the nasty man is caught and the nasty lady is dead.'

Phryne went back into the kitchen. Candida was fine where she was.

'Who are you?' she asked the big man.

'Mike. Mike Herbert. I didn't want to be in this, but I had to support my wife.'

'Did you? Why?'

'She liked pretty things and I couldn't afford to buy them—I lost my job, the factory closed down. I'm a carpenter. She borrowed some money off...a certain person...and then she couldn't pay it back, and I couldn't either, so...the certain person was going to send the boys around, and...'

'Break both her legs, eh? Let's have a look at her. Where did she fall?'

'In the bathroom. I think that she's dead. Poor Ann. She should have been born rich.'

Phryne bent over the body, supine on the oilcloth. She felt for a heartbeat in the cooling breast, and found none. The flesh was clammy and limp against her palm. She stood up and wiped her hands on her trousers.

'I'm sorry,' she said to Mike. 'She can't have felt anything, you know, the bullet drilled her heart.'

Mike knelt, drew his wife's skirt down until it covered her knees, and kissed her gently on the cheek.

'Goodbye, Annie,' Phryne heard him say as she tactfully withdrew. 'I would have done anything to make you happy, but it never worked. You shouldn't have got involved with me. I can't even bury you properly.'

After about ten minutes, Mike came back to the kitchen, where Phryne was bandaging Sid's wrist lest he bleed to an untimely death. He whimpered as she handled him and she observed with pleasure that her aim had been perfect. The hole was in the exact middle of the wrist and had not even chipped a bone. The tendons were, as she had purposed, cut neatly though. He would not use that hand to molest any more children.

Mike came into the kitchen and took Phryne by the shoulder, turning her carefully toward him.

'I never meant to hurt the little girl,' he pleaded.

'Well, she doesn't need you any longer,' commented Phryne. 'So now we must decide what to do. I think that I shall cast you as heroic rescuer. I think I'd better bind up your arm and give you some money. Then you can have a wash and a shave, go home to your dear landlady, Mrs O'Brien, and report your car stolen. You thought your wife had it, but she's not come back, and you're afraid that something has happened to her. Did you write the note?'

'No,' said Mike through lips numb with astonishment.

'Good. Now let's wash this wound. It's little more than a scratch, just keep it dry. I'll take off this disgusting hat and find my face.'

Phryne put her head under the cold-water tap and scrubbed vigorously. She emerged as a young woman of some distinction with a bleeding cut over one eye. Phryne dabbed at it with her handkerchief.

'You need a bit of sticky plaster,' offered Mike. He found some in the cupboard and applied it neatly. Phryne washed her face again. She was aching all over.

'Henry, I'll try to give you as much altitude as I can, but I think this is a silly idea,' yelled Bunji as she hauled the plane into another turn. 'You can't even see the ground. The moon's down.'

'I can see that dirty great cross that Phryne's drawn on that road and I'm going to come down right in the middle of it,' said Henry confidently. 'There's no wind. If I haul in the slacks I should drop right on their heads.'

'Oh, all right, old chum, far be it from me to stop a friend anxious to break his neck. Careful as you go over, don't catch anything on the wing. *Merde!*' yelled Bunji. 'Now!'

She had judged it nicely. The man's body fell out of vision. A pale flower blossomed, cutting off her sight of the luminous cross. Right on target. Bunji drank another mouthful of the luke-warm coffee and looked for a place to set down.

Candida, who occasionally did as she was told, had taken Bear out to the road and was sitting quietly on the running board of the Bentley. She looked at the road. It was glowing.

'They must have awful big snails here, Bear, to leave a trail like that. Big enough to ride on. Perhaps we can catch one and ride home.' She yawned. It had been an exciting evening.

Dropping out of the sky into the centre of the snail tracks came a man clad all in leather. Candida froze. He cursed a bit as he loosened the parachute cords and Candida and Bear edged closer. The voice was familiar. Then the man tore off his flying helmet and she saw his face in the lights that were now streaming from the house.

'Daddy!' shrieked Candida, and flew to him, scaling his body and settling back into his embrace. She held him as tight as a limpet for five minutes as he stroked her hair, then she looked up.

'Where have you been?' she asked severely. 'Why did you let those people steal me?'

Chapter Twelve

I met murder on the way
The Mask of Anarchy, P.B. Shelley

Phryne found a bottle of rum and two glasses, and lit her first gasper in hours. She leaned back on the draining board and smoked luxuriously.

'You'd better hit the road, Mike. Don't forget to report the car stolen.'

Mike, dressed in a clean shirt and combed and shaved, looked like a respectable working man. Phryne peeled off a hundred pounds from her wad of notes.

'This should take care of you for a while. I'll look after Candida. Her family will be arriving soon.'

Mike knocked back the rum and pointed at the bundle, which was Sid, on the floor.

'What about him? He'll sing like a canary.'

'I'll take care of him,' said Phryne quietly. Sidney, hearing her, winced.

'Don't look back,' she advised Mike. 'Keep going. There's the right woman, and children, waiting for you yet. If you need any help with a job, come to me.' She tucked her card into his pocket with the money, and let him out the front door.

They were both arrested by the sight of what appeared to be an angel, fallen from the sky. He stood tall and shapely, draped in his billowing wings. Candida and Bear were in his arms.

'Mike,' squealed Candida. 'Daddy's come.'

Mike walked over to her and took her hand.

'Well, everything's worked out then. I've got to go, Candida. I've come to say goodbye.'

Candida, who always associated goodbyes with kisses, turned her cheek. Mike bent and kissed her. Then he took Henry Maldon's hand and shook it firmly. He turned away and walked into the night.

'Mike!' cried Candida, 'you'll get lost in the dark.' But his step did not falter.

Phryne walked over to Henry. 'I think you'd better get off the highway, dear man, or you'll be run over by the rescuers. Excuse me for a moment.' Phryne went back into the kitchen and propped Sid up against a cabinet.

'I want to talk to you,' said Phryne. 'What will you take for keeping your mouth shut?'

'Why should I? I'll swing as soon as the cops lay their hands on me.'

'Yes, you will. But I might be able to gratify any last wish.'

Her voice contained a hint of perversion. Sidney licked his lips.

'Can you smuggle me a girl before I go to the gallows?'

'I think so,' said Phryne.

Sid wriggled. 'I mean my sort of girl. A child.'

'Perhaps. How old?'

'Twelve at the most.'

Phryne thought of her friend Klara, a lesbian who got a great kick from getting money out of men. Especially men like Sid. She dressed in a gym slip and looked almost prepubescent. The child-molesters who constituted most of her clientele fuelled her loathing and it would not be the first time her little-girl's body had been purchased by one who was about to die.

From her extensive knowledge of the Underworld Phryne knew that it was no great matter to smuggle anything into a prison. All that was needed were a few timely words and more than a few coins of the realm. She recalled that the orgy which preceded the death of the Carlton murderer Jackson had been described to her in great detail by the prison guard who let the three girls in, disguised as prisoners. He said he had stayed to 'supervise' and fend off any inquiries. What had been his name? Briggs, that was it, a Northern Irishman of flexible morality and an ever-open palm. He volunteered for the duty which the other warders avoided; sitting up with the man to be hanged on the morrow. Stranger things than Klara had been taken into Pentridge for the comfort of those about to die, though the strangest was probably a bushranger's horse. He had wanted to say farewell to it in person.

'I think I can manage that, yes,' she agreed.

'In the death cell?' bargained Sidney. Phryne wondered how long he had been in love with death. Perhaps the desired culmination of his whole career would be his judicial execution at the hands of stronger men. She poured out some rum and helped him drink it. Sidney, dispossessed of his gun, was a pathetic creature.

Ann was less pathetic because she was so very dead. Phryne stood over the corpse and looked down on her. The expression of surprise had faded. She looked now as if she was asleep. The thirsty spirit had gone, presumably back to its maker. Phryne collected up the few personal belongings that pointed to a second man having been present and stuffed them in her pockets. Then she went to sit on the front step and wait for the car. She was aching and bruised and tired out but pleased with the night's work.

Phryne offered Henry a cigarette and lit her own. Candida and Bear were wrapped up in the parachute. They were awake, but warm. The lights of the big car approached. Tree trunks sprang into visibility.

'Here they are at last,' said Phryne. 'I'd kill for a cup of tea. Look, Henry, it's picaninny daylight. The sun will be up in an hour.'

The car drew up and disgorged Dot, Molly, Jack Leonard and Bunji. They saw two bedraggled figures sitting on the front step of the small house. They were smoking. Next to them was a bundle of white silk, in which one could see a straggling head of pale hair and a Bear.

'Is it all right, Miss?' asked Dot, breaking the silence. Molly flew to Candida, who embraced her frantically.

'Daddy came down out of the sky and the lady brought Bear so I knew that it was all right,' she informed Molly. Then she wriggled down and laid herself out across Molly's knees.

'What are you doing, Candida Alice?' asked Molly fondly.

'I want my spanking, and then I want my lollies!' said Candida.

Molly laughed, sobbed, and delivered five moderate slaps. Candida sat up and Dot put her bag of lollies into her hands. The child checked through them carefully. The whole threepence work was there, even if somewhat muddy. Candida filled her mouth with mint leaves and began to cry.

They all piled into the car as the sun was rising and took the road for the town. Phryne laughed aloud at the sight of them, all dusty and streaked, and reflected she must be the most bedraggled of them all.

'What's the best hotel in Queenscliff?' she called to Molly.

Molly could not reply because she had unwisely accepted Candida's offer of a toffee and her teeth were glued together.

Henry said, 'The Queenscliff Hotel is the best, but we can't go there looking like this.'

'Yes we can,' said Phryne flatly. 'You should have seen the state in which we once entered the Windsor. I'm positively overdressed by comparison.'

Dot remembered it well. Phryne looked a lot more respectable in her present attire.

They drew up outside the Queenscliff Hotel and climbed the stone steps wearily. There, Phryne's money, charm, and air of authority obtained three rooms, one with a bath, and breakfast as soon as it should be laid. Phryne saw that her guests were settled in front of a hastily-lit fire in the drawing-room then sent a boy out for a roll of brown paper and some string. She wrapped Sid in the paper, using knots taught to her by a young sailor she had loved briefly during World War One. By the time she had finished, only Sid's head was free. With the help of the hotel porter, she then carried Sid to the police station and deposited him on the counter.

The desk-sergeant looked up, blinked, and dropped his pen. 'What's all this about, Miss?'

Phryne sank wearily into a chair and pointed at the uncomfortable felon.

'Read the label,' she said.

The desk-sergeant called for a constable and walked around into the room. He surveyed Sid carefully and read the label aloud.

'"For Detective-inspector Jack Robinson, Russell Street, Melbourne. A present from Phryne Fisher." Aha, we had a message about you, Miss Fisher. They telephoned from Geelong. Every cooperation, they said. You are a respected person, evidently.'

Phryne smiled faintly.

'His name is Sidney Brayshaw, and you've been looking for him for some time, I believe. You'd better get a doctor fairly soon, because I had a little trouble picking him up and he got damaged. Detective-inspector Robinson is going to be furious if you let him bleed to death.'

The sergeant ripped off the paper and led Sidney away. As Sidney was leaving the room, he broke the silence he had maintained throughout his humiliation and called to Phryne, 'You better not forget, lady. Remember—I'm not dead yet.'

'You look like you could do with a doctor, too,' suggested the young constable. 'You seem to have taken a bit of a battering. I'll just give the local man a call, shall I?'

'Yes indeed, if you want Sidney to live to hang. He is undoubtedly the most unpleasant person I have ever met in my whole life. How I would love to squeeze the life out of the little rat. Have you heard of him, Constable...'

'Constable Smith, Miss Fisher. I am astounded that you have come in with Sidney Brayshaw. Why, there's his portrait on the wall,' commented the young man, pointing out a 'Most Wanted' poster. He took it down.

'He ain't wanted any more,' he said. Phryne laughed. The constable did not think he had ever seen a face so drawn. The black hat and the black collar enclosed a countenance as white as marble.

'Where are you staying, Miss? If you don't mind my saying, you look all in.'

'The Queenscliff Hotel. Can you drive my car there? And make me a present of that poster? It will make a perfect souvenir.' Constable Smith, who had a sense of occasion, rolled up the poster and presented it with a bow. Then he vanished behind the desk, presumably to ask permission to leave and to summon the doctor to Sid.

Phryne was almost asleep on her feet when the constable came back. She gave him the keys, suffered herself to be helped into a seat beside him, and by the time Constable Smith had proudly steered the big red car around the corner she was fast asleep.

Thus Phryne made her most impressive entrance, though she missed it at the time; lolling gracefully with her head on a policeman's shoulder. He stalked up the steps in correct uniform, helmet on and every button gleaming.

He stopped at reception and asked the manager, 'Where shall I put her?'

The manager did not flick so much as an eyebrow. 'Ah, yes, that is Miss Fisher. Room Six. Her maid has just gone out to purchase some necessaries. Follow me, Constable.' Phryne was carried up the carpeted stairs and laid gently on the bed. Constable Smith took off Phryne's boots and flung the quilt over her.

'Thank you, Constable, I think that will be all,' observed the manager. 'I shall inform her maid that Miss Fisher has returned. I believe that a Mr Jack Leonard was expressing a wish to speak to you.'

The Queenscliff Hotel had been built in those spacious days when an Empire was an Empire, and the rooms were lavishly appointed. Constable Smith brushed past a bowl of winter leaves and berries which took up three square feet and saw the strangest assortment of people he had ever set eyes on, gathered around the largest fireplace he had ever seen. You could have roasted an ox in it, as he told his mates later. There was the chink of dishes in the back parlour as breakfast was laid.

The room contained numerous soft couches and two easy chairs. On one of the couches sat a man in flying gear, playing 'scissors, paper, stone' with a very grubby child in a stained white nightgown. Next to him sat a well-dressed and well-groomed young woman with fiery hair who kept patting the child, as if she was not sure that she was real. Between the child and the sofa back reclined a battered teddybear with a handkerchief around its neck.

In one easy chair sat a plump young woman in leather gear, who had taken a cup of coffee into both hands as though to absorb the heat. She was staring into the fire. In the other easy chair sat a very dapper young man with a thin moustache, who stood up.

'Hello, old chap. That was Miss Fisher I saw you carrying up the stairs just now, wasn't it?'

'Yes,' agreed the constable.

'Is she all right?'

'She fell asleep and I couldn't wake her so I put her to bed. I don't think there is anything wrong with her.'

'Good. She told me that if she didn't succeed in telling you the story I was to inform you that we'll be down to the station after lunch to tell all. By the way, there's a dead woman in a house up the hill.' He gave the address. 'Sidney killed her. I'm sure that he will explain.'

'Thank you, sir,' said the dumbfounded constable. 'I'll see about it right away, sir.'

He left the hotel to go and find his sergeant. What a young constable needs when given this sort of information is a sergeant. However, he had a strong suspicion as to what the sergeant would say.

He was right. He was immediately sent to see if there was a dead woman in the house. There was.

Dot had found that the lady who kept the drapers shop lived over her premises, and Dot knocked until a sleepy voice replied that she was coming. At last the door opened.

'Well?' asked Mrs Draper.

'I need a lot of things for three ladies who are benighted in the area,' said Dot. Mrs Draper opened the shop door and switched on the light.

'You look for what you want, dear,' she said kindly. 'I'll just go and make me tea.'

She tottered off. Dot selected a light travelling bag and found a nightgown and a pair of soft, black velvet slippers. Phryne's trousers were all very well but one could not dine in them. Dot took a black skirt in a size W for Bunji and in SSW for Phryne; bought a loose white blouse with dolman sleeves and a bright red jersey top, three gentlemen's shirts and socks and undergarments and three sets of stockings and undies for the ladies. Then she remembered herself and added one more of each. At the back of the shop she spied a quaint, beaded cap, with a long scarf hanging from it. She bought a feather cockade for the black cloche and remembered Bunji's flying boots at the last moment and bought her a pair of slippers, too. She wrestled this mountain of purchases onto the counter and went in search of the draper.

Placidly, the old woman added up the astronomical total, checked it, and gave Dot change. She agreed that the things would be sent instantly to the Queenscliff Hotel and saw her customer to the door, which she locked behind her. Then she chose a comfortable bit of floor and fainted.

Dot hurried back to the hotel. She had the nightgown and slippers in the light bag, and the thought of a cup of tea spurred her on. An aeroplane was attracting a crowd down on the foreshore, and a stern lifeboat man was warning the children away.

Dot ran up the steps and was just in time for breakfast.

'Oh, I say, pity that Phryne is missing this,' opined Jack Leonard. Dot thought so, too. She went up to Room Six and opened the door. Phryne was half-awake.

'What's that delicious smell, Dot? I've had the most amazing dream. I was clinging on to the back of a car…hang on. That wasn't a dream. Dot, where are we?'

'Queenscliff Hotel, Miss, and breakfast is waiting. Why not wash your face and brush your hair and come down? I've never seen a breakfast like it.'

The Queenscliff Hotel was famed for its breakfasts. Phryne put on the black slippers and brushed her hair as ordered. She and Dot descended into a cloud of steam savoury enough to make a glutton swoon. Phryne's stomach growled reproachfully. Dot felt almost faint with hunger. They passed the formal dining-room and the cocktail bar and burst into the back parlour at something not too short of a run. Jack Leonard gave a cheer as Phryne came in and supplied her with a big plate.

'Now, Phryne, you must keep up your strength. There won't always be policemen to carry you around.'

'So I didn't dream the policeman either. How odd.'

'What would you like?' asked Jack, leading her to a long row of silver chafing dishes. 'There are kidneys and devilled ham in this one, scrambled eggs in this one, mushrooms in this one, sausages, rissoles, fried eggs and they can make you an omelette in a moment.'

'This is too much. Get me a bit of everything, Jack, and bless you.'

Phryne sat down at a small table. A waiter took her order for tea and offered her a newspaper, which she waved away. When furnishing the hotel someone had bought a job lot of life-size negro figures made of wood or papier mâché. At the feet of the one with the gold turban sat Candida, eating fruit compote with perfect equanimity. Phryne raised an eyebrow at Molly.

'She says that the poor man must be lonely, so she's gone to keep him company,' Molly explained. 'Have some of this compote, it's marvellous. Essence of summer. I wonder where they found melons, pineapple and strawberries at this time of the year?'

Jack placed Phryne's plate before her and she had demolished it, with three slices of toast and two cups of tea, before he had time to complete one across in the *Times* crossword. Phryne went back to the buffet and gave herself more bacon, scrambled eggs, mushrooms and kedgeree. This she ate with two slices of toast. Dot had found the diversity of things to eat miraculous. All that food! She picked at everything.

Phryne tried the fruit and found it delightful, then stood up and stretched.

'I bags first bath,' she said, and Dot raced after her as she fled up the stairs.

Ten minutes later she was lying in a hot bath and Dot was soaping her feet. She was so stiff that she could not possibly have reached them.

'Oh, your poor toes, Miss!'

'I suppose it isn't any use asking you to call me Phryne, is it, Dot?'

'No. It ain't right. And you are changing the subject. You've bruised them toes so that you won't be able to put a shoe on your feet for a week. You've cut your hands and there's a little cut on your brow. It won't cause a scar, Miss,' commented Dot. 'Let me have your foot again. I've sent your clothes to be cleaned, and they say they'll be back this afternoon. Miss Candida's as well. Mrs Maldon wants to get rid of that nightgown. I didn't think of buying a new one for her. That's better, Miss. Hang on to my hand and...up we go!'

Dot dried Phryne, clad her in the nightgown, and put her to bed between clean sheets.

Dot took a bath, replaced her chemise, and lay down in her own bed for some sleep. She was rather worn out from worrying about Phryne and Candida and Henry and Bunji.

The Maldons had been given a room with a bath, and the hotel had provided a cot draped with white muslin. Candida was impressed with it. It resembled the cradle of the Princess' baby in the *Blue Fairy Book*. She was a cleanly little girl and was delighted to see how much dirt coloured the water. When she was finally ready and wrapped up in several towels, her father claimed the bath and firmly shut the door.

Candida surveyed the room. It was lovely. She admired the gold chandelier, and the swags of ivy picked out in gold leaf on the high ceilings. The French windows opened onto the balcony and through them she could see the sea. The heavy curtains of oyster-grey silk had been elaborately draped in order to frame the view. In front of the window was a carved blackwood loveseat, a round low table with a bowl of roses and three delicate-legged chairs. There was an escritoire and matching chair on one side of the fire and a washstand on the other.

The great bed was of brass and stood at least two feet off the floor. It was heaped with pillows. Candida climbed up and bounced experimentally.

Molly darkened the windows and took off most of her clothes. She got into the bed and found that Bear and Candida were already there.

'Bear wants to know when we are going home.'

'Tomorrow morning. We are just going to have a little sleep. Daddy will be here in a moment. Do you want to sleep in the cot?'

'Me?' asked Candida indignantly. 'It's for a baby.'

Molly smiled and closed her eyes. When Henry came out of the bathroom, he found both of his women fast asleep.

Phryne woke refreshed and stiff at two o'clock. Dot was still sleeping. The blind let through a little cool winter light, and she could hear the sea. She inspected the clothes that Dot had bought, especially the odd little hat. She put it on and peeped into the mirror. It was striking. The beads added weight, so that it sat down well upon her head. She looped the scarf around her throat.

'O woman of mystery,' she said, blowing a kiss to her reflection. She put on the black skirt and the red jersey top, then went downstairs to see if any of the rest of her party were awake.

The desk clerk smiled at her.

'The rest of them have gone for a walk on the shore, Miss Fisher,' he said respectfully. 'The little girl insisted.'

Phryne smiled. Candida was prone to insist. She gathered up her skirt and went down the steps and across the road, following the path to the pier.

It was a cold day, and few people were on the foreshore. Phryne found Candida, her parents, Bunji and Jack sitting on the sand and making rather ineffectual castles.

'That's not right,' said Candida as her castle dissolved before a strong lee wind. 'Make me an aeroplane, Uncle Jack.'

Jack Leonard moved down the beach a little and found that the damper sand held its shape better. Bunji came with him to advise.

'Make a Fokker,' she suggested. 'Did you see her, Phryne? I had to put her down on the sand. Had a bit of a struggle persuading the old girl to stop, seemed to want to go on into the waves, and that wouldn't have done, you know. The lifeguard was delighted to watch it for me. He was in the Royal Flying Corps. Fascinating old bird. I think the nose ought to be a bit longer, Jack.'

Jack obediently lengthened the nose. Candida found suitable pebbles for the finer details. Molly and Henry were sitting on a cold stone step. Molly was leaning back into Henry's embrace. He had his head on her shoulder. Phryne was about to withdraw when Molly held out a hand.

'We owe it all to you, Phryne. We don't know how to repay you.'

'There's no need to repay me. I wouldn't have missed it for worlds. The really brave person in this was Bunji. Henry must have told you what a good flier she is.'

'Great skill,' agreed Henry. 'She can scent the air currents, I reckon. Who is this Mike that Candida keeps talking about?'

'Did you read the Sherlock Holmes stories?' asked Phryne, seating herself at Henry's feet.

'Yes, of course.'

'"I think we must have an amnesty in that direction,"' quoted Phryne. 'He was dragged into the plot by his revolting wife. The monster I delivered to the cops this morning was the prime mover. When Sidney shot the wife and was trying to shoot Candida, Mike realized that he couldn't go along with it, shoved Candida out into the garden and told her to run. Then he attacked Sid. That's where I came in. I shot Sid in the wrist and had a conference with Mike. He saved Candida's life. Even if we all gave character evidence for him he'd be looking at ten years in the pen. So I gave him a hundred quid and told him to go home and report his car stolen. They will suspect him, but they won't be able to prove anything. He is a good chap, Henry met him.'

'So it was Mike who kissed Candida goodbye? I'm glad that I met him. I owe him a great deal.'

'I told him to get in touch with me if he couldn't get a job. If he does, I'll turn him over to you.'

'You did well, Phryne. It would have been awful to have to give evidence against him.'

Molly's eyes strayed to Candida, engaged in making wheels for the plane. The child was dressed in her blue frock, and had Bear secured to her back with a handkerchief.

'I don't think she's suffered too much,' said Phryne, 'though she'll probably have nightmares. She didn't see the woman fall when she was shot and she escaped Siddy's attentions.'

'I was wondering about that. He's a child-molester, isn't he?' asked Henry. 'I...didn't know how to ask her.'

'No need. He may have had designs on her originally, but when she came out from under the ether Sid told me that she was sick all over him.'

Henry laughed aloud. 'That's my girl!'

◦ఌఌ◦

Dinner in the formal dining-room was hilarious. Phryne purchased good champagne and after a while everyone was happy. The food was excellent, from the entrée of cream of pumpkin soup, through an exquisite cheese souffle, a *filet mignon à chasseur*, and sherberts made of peach, nectarine, pomegranate, lemon, orange and grapefruit. The coffee was fragrant and the handmade chocolates remarkable.

Phryne, who had bagged the quaint hat, ate as though she had been fasting for some months. Dot was freshly surprised at each course. Candida, who had been allowed to stay up by special permission, had presided over the ceremonial burning of the nightgown, the last trace of her captivity. She was engaged in assisting Bear to eat his chocolates. Golden candlelight from the tall sconces glittered off the massive silver epergnes and dishes; the log fire burned brightly. Tall vases of lilies and gum tips lent the air a delicate scent. Of all endings to adventure, this was the best possible.

'To Candida!' cried Phryne, and raised her glass. Uncle Jack allowed the child to take a sip from his glass. The bubbles tickled her nose. She chuckled. She knew that it was the custom to respond to a toast. She clutched Bear close to give him confidence, and stood up on her chair.

'Uncle Jack, Aunty Bunji, Mummy, Daddy, Dot and Phryne,' she began. The table was silent. Candida was overcome with sudden affection.

'Thank you for finding me and bringing me Bear,' she said, then launched herself into Phryne's arms, and kissed her moistly on the cheek.

Chapter Thirteen

He that dies pays all debts
The Tempest, Shakespeare

Returned in good order to Melbourne, Phryne spent Thursday afternoon cleaning the car with Mr Butler's assistance. She gave her household an edited account of her adventures, and did not go out until Thursday afternoon to St Kilda. She wanted to find Klara. As Klara was locally notorious, this did not prove difficult.

A thin little gutter sparrow sat in a café, staring into an empty cup of tea. She looked up as Phryne walked in and smiled with genuine tenderness.

'Phryne! Come and buy me some tea. I'm parched. Got a job for me?'

Phryne bought the tea, which she would not have touched for quids, and explained. Ancient eyes started out of a childish face.

'And they'll kill him the next day?'

'Yes.'

'I'll do it for ten quid. If I didn't have to make a living I'd do it for nothing. Sidney Brayshaw, eh? Bonzer. Will you make the arrangements?'

'Can you? I don't know if Briggs is still at Pentridge.'

'Sure. Give me another twenty to square them.'

Phryne produced the money.

'You won't fail me, Klara? I gave my word.'

'No. I'll not fail,' promised Klara, tracing a cross with a grubby forefinger on the flat breast of her gym tunic. Phryne left quickly. She found Klara unsettling.

⌘

Thursday night was appointed for Phryne's seduction of the delightful Dr Fielding. It was not until Mrs Butler was asking her what she fancied for dinner that she remembered.

'Oh, hell, I forgot. Mrs B., I asked that nice young doctor to dinner.'

'You have been busy lately, Miss,' agreed Mrs Butler. 'So we won't quarrel about it this time.'

Phryne took the hint and smiled. 'I hope that there won't be a next time,' she said pleasantly. 'Can you manage a simple, light dinner?'

'Vegetable soup, lamb chops, green beans, *pommes de terre Anna*? Apple pie and cream?' suggested Mrs Butler.

'Good. Very nice. Then coffee and liqueurs in my sitting-room upstairs. Can Mr B. take care of the fire? And leave the woodbox full. After he's brought the coffee, Mrs B., I don't want to be disturbed.'

Mrs Butler pursed her lips and nodded. Phryne wondered if the two of them were going to give notice in the morning. Assuming, of course, that the doctor was amenable to seduction.

Phryne bathed luxuriously and dressed carefully in a loose, warm velvet from Erté. It was black, with deep lapin cuffs and collar and a six-inch band of fur around the hem. She brushed her hair vigorously and applied just a little rouge.

Dot assisted her into the gown and knelt to adjust the soft Russian boots around Phryne's slim ankles.

'You fancy your chances, Miss?'

'Yes, I do. He's clumsy, but rather endearing, don't you think?'

'You be careful,' warned Dot. 'This one's an Aussie. They got different ideas about their girls, not like them Russians.'

'And Italians,' agreed Phryne. 'I'll be careful, Dot. Are you going out or staying in?'

'I'm staying in,' said Dot, giving the bootlace a final tug. 'I've been to the library and I'm going to read and listen to the wireless. I won't disturb you, Miss. I can come and go by my own stair.'

'I hope that this doesn't upset you,' said Phryne. 'Or the Butlers.'

'They'll be sweet,' said Dot. 'Just like I was. It's a bit of a shock at first, but you get used to it. Have a nice time, Miss,' and Dot, innocent of any envy, went down to take her own dinner with the Butlers. Phryne smoked one gasper after another, worrying. Dot was right. Australian men were different. She did not want to get involved in an emotional relationship. She had no patience with dependence and no understanding of jealousy.

She heard the doorbell ring, and sailed downstairs to meet her guest, with outward poise and inward qualms.

He really was beautiful, she reflected as he escorted her into the dining-room. He had pale skin, curly brown hair, was well-built and tall. Phryne took her seat and accepted a glass of white wine from Mr Butler. The young man contrived by a miracle not to knock over the vase of ferns in the centre of the table and smiled ruefully.

'I'm afraid I'm still clumsy, Miss Fisher.'

'Really, you must call me Phryne. I'm not your patient, Dr Fielding.'

'Then you must call me Mark.'

'You haven't been a doctor long, I gather. Why did you choose medicine?'

This was always a safe question to ask any professional. Soup was served. It was good—perhaps a little too much celery. Mark Fielding ate fast, as though he was about to be called away at any moment.

'I want to be useful,' said Mark Fielding. 'I want to heal the hurts of the world.' He laid down his spoon. 'That sounds silly, doesn't it? But there is such a lot of pain and suffering, and I want to ease it. I work with old Dr Dorset, he has great experience, but he's a cynical old man. He says that everyone in the world has ulterior motives. What do you think?'

Phryne took in a sharp breath as the unreadable brown eyes flicked sidelong to look at her. Yes, she could believe it. Her own motives were nothing to boast of.

The excellent dinner concluded, Phryne lured Mark upstairs with a promise of coffee and kirsch. She accepted the tray from Mr Butler, observed that the woodbox next to the fire had been replenished, and gave him a conspiratorial smile.

'I shan't want you again tonight, Mr B.,' she said. 'Sleep well.'

'You too, Miss Fisher,' he replied with perfect gravity, and chuckled all the way down the stairs.

'I know what she is, Mrs B.,' he said at the kitchen door. 'She's a vamp.'

'Ah, well,' sighed his wife. 'At least it ain't like the last place. Young men are clean about the house. It's better than the old gentleman's greyhounds.'

Thereafter Phryne's household always referred to her lovers as 'the pets'.

Mark Fielding leaned back into the feathery embrace of a low, comfortable sofa in front of a bright fire.

'Oh, this is nice,' he sighed. 'Listen to that wind outside. It's beginning to rain, too. I wish I didn't have to go home…I mean,' he corrected himself hurriedly, 'I mean…'

'You don't have to go home,' said Phryne calmly. 'I wouldn't turn a dog out on a night like this. Stay with me, Mark. It's warm in here.'

She was lying at full length on the hearth rug, prone, with her chin cupped in her hands, the short cap of black hair swung forward to hide her face. She had not looked away from the fire as she spoke. The young doctor was astonished. He had never been propositioned by a woman before.

He glanced around the room. Every surface was velvety, textured, soft. The pinkish mirror wreathed in vine leaves reflected his face crowned with a garland. He tried to sit up but the sofa was unwilling to release him. He sipped the remains of his kirsch and yielded up his body to fate.

'It's kismet,' he said softly, as Phryne gathered her gown about her and pulled him down into her arms.

Phryne closed her eyes as the red mouth came down onto hers, the lips parted, then the mouth moved down her throat to the open collar of the velvet gown. For such a clumsy young man, Mark Fielding removed a lady's clothes with startling skill.

Phryne, naked, and stretched out in a pool of velvet and fur, drowsed up out of a fiery trance to glimpse the flash of thigh and buttock and he slid down to lie beside her.

She reached up to catch her fingers in the curly hair, as silky as embroidery floss, and bring the face down for her kiss. As he slid his strong hands between fur and skin to gather her close, he whispered. 'Phryne, are you sure?'

Phryne had seized him, locking his waist with her thighs. She was sure.

Mark abandoned himself to unimagined delights. The heat of the fire caressed his skin. The scent of Phryne's breasts and her hair, musky and amorous, almost drowned him in sweetness.

When Phryne awoke, the fire was out, and someone seemed to have amputated her legs at the hips. She groaned and tried to sit up. The numbness was explained by the weight of the beautiful young man asleep on top of her. Phryne shook him, laughing and shivering. 'Mark, wake up, you're crushing me.'

Mark Fielding was dragged up out of a deep dream by the hand on his shoulder.

'It must be Mrs Murphy's baby,' he murmured. 'All right, I'll be down in a min…no wait, what…oh, Phryne,' he remembered suddenly, shifted his weight, and hauled her into his arms. 'Oh, my dear girl, how cold you are, and how cold I am, too.'

'We fell asleep, and I think we ought to go to bed before we catch our death. You'll have to carry me,' said Phryne smugly. 'I'm numb.'

Mark staggered up, stamped a few times to recover the use of his feet, then lifted Phryne without effort and bore her into the bedroom. He flung her into the huge bed then dived in after her. The invaluable Mrs B. had left a hot waterbottle and they snuggled close together, limbs entwined, and began to thaw into life. Oddly enough, when Mark Fielding was to think of the amazing Phryne Fisher, that was the moment he remembered as being the most intensely erotic.

The morning of Miss McNaughton's party dawned, cold and bright. Phryne did not see it. She breakfasted in bed with Dr Fielding, sharing toast and buttery kisses. He left at nine, begging to be allowed to return that night.

Phryne had obtained Detective-inspector Benton's solemn promise that he would attend Miss McNaughton's party and Jillian Henderson had rather warily agreed to come. Bert and Cec reported that they had completed their investigations and there was only Miss Wilson left to interview.

Phryne decided to ring her. She found the number, and a light, feminine voice identified herself as Margaret Wilson.

'Miss Wilson, this relates to the complaint you made to the police last week.'

'That horrid old man stole my clothes when I was swimming!' exclaimed Miss Wilson. 'I was so mad that I went straight to the police, even though I only had my bathing costume on. But that is all fixed. They lent me a coat to go home in, and the next day I got my clothes back.'

'Think carefully. Did you pass anyone on that path?'

'Yes, Bill McNaughton. I was going to ask him to help me but he was in one of his rages, and there is not a lot of percentage to be got out of Bill when he's like that.'

'Miss Wilson, where have you been all week?'

'In retreat, at Daylesford. I go every year. Why?'

'Bill's father was murdered. You are the only person who can say that Bill was on that path.'

'Lord! Poor Bill. I must go and make a statement, then. Should I go now?'

'No. The slops had their chance. Can you come to Miss McNaughton's children's party tomorrow?'

'Yes, of course. Will that help?'

'About twelve. Do you know Miss McNaughton?'

'Oh, yes, we went to school together. Why didn't Bill say that he saw me?'

'He didn't remember your name.'

'Isn't that just like Bill. He never even *looked* at his sister's friends. All right, Miss Fisher, I shall be there tomorrow. Thank you,' said Miss Wilson, and hung up.

Phryne and Dot drove along the gravelled drive and left the car in the carriage yard. The front door was open and there was the sound of someone playing the piano with more exuberance than skill. The sound of running feet echoed down the hall.

Mabel showed Phryne in and took her coat. The house was clean and decorated with balloons and streamers.

'We've put the table in the conservatory, Miss Fisher. It's out the back. The room with the stone floor. That policeman has arrived. So has Miss Wilson from around the corner, two of your agents, and a lady lawyer called Miss Henderson.'

'How are things now, Mabel?'

'Ever so much better, Miss,' said Mabel, lowering her voice. 'Mr Bill hasn't had a single rage, and Mr Paolo is charming. Such a nice man, for a foreigner. He's playing the piano at the moment so the children can play musical chairs. Come out, Miss, it's such a pretty sight.'

It was. The conservatory was a big block added on to the back of the house. It was floored with black slate and masses of plants were suspended from the beams. Paolo was thumping wildly on a baby grand piano looking like a fatherly faun. A scatter of children were running around a diminishing number of chairs. Presiding over the gingerbeer, orange-pop, lemonade and a quiet tray of cocktails was Mrs McNaughton. Phryne hardly knew her. Her cheeks were flushed and she was wearing a paper hat. With her was a tall man in a Harris tweed coat. He had a moustache of impressive proportions and held a whisky and soda in his left hand. His right hand was missing and the tweed sleeve was neatly pinned up. This was Gerald. He smiled dotingly at Mrs McNaughton and raised his glass to Phryne.

Jillian Henderson was deep in converse with Amelia over the properties of begonias and tuberoses, for which she had a passion. Detective-inspector Benton sat on the edge of the chair looking exquisitely uncomfortable. The children gave him uneasy glances. They knew a cop when they saw one.

Bert and Cec, having been provided with beer, were seated at a cast-iron table, watching the game with approval.

After a final burst of Chopin, Jim was left in regal possession of the last chair. He accepted the prize penny, and gave it to Elsie to store in her drawers.

Phryne stepped into the middle of the floor and clapped her hands.

'Before we have lunch, we are going to play a new game,' she told the children and watching adults. 'The game is called, "Murder".'

There was a buzz of excitement. Bill came in from the garden, saw Margaret Wilson, and roared, 'Margaret Wilson! I knew I'd seen that red bathing costume before.'

'Bill, join in the procession,' ordered Phryne. 'Bert and Cec, you bring the kids. It will be all right. I promise. Come along.'

'Where are we going?' asked Dot.

'To the tennis-court,' said Phryne. She led her congregation across the manicured grass until they all stood under the tree.

'When I spoke to you on this spot last week, Benton, I asked you two good questions, and you didn't listen to them. Do you remember what they were?'

'Where did the rock come from, and why was the deceased on the tennis-court in his street shoes. Yes, I remember. I said that the fact that the stone was imported showed that the crime was premeditated, and that the place was chosen to be out of sight of the road.'

'Yes. You were bending the facts to fit your theory. This is almost always fatal. Now I did not have a theory so I approached the matter with an open mind. Where did the rock come from? Bert?'

'It's the same as the ones in Paris St, Miss. They are taking up the old kerb-stones and replacing them with cement. They've been there a while, and there's clover growing over them.'

'Good. What did you find on the murder weapon, Benton?'

'A clover burr, hemp, chewy, and some grass,' said Benton.

'Good. Now it struck me that whoever imported the stone might have been playing a game. What game have all the children been playing since Luxor was found?'

She pointed at Jim. He faltered. 'Pyramids, Miss.'

'Cec will now take us to where he found the rope.'

Cec led the way, and revealed the pile of bluestone pitchers. They had been tumbled over the fence, and under them was revealed the cache of Pharoah's treasures, food for the afterlife in the form of a licorice block and pictures of his royal relatives, transport and even slaves with white kilts. Amelia stared at them, paling to the whiteness of chalk. Paolo took her arm, worried.

'What were these children doing when you saw them yesterday, Bert?'

'Trying to wrap up an old girl's cat as a mummy,' chuckled Bert. 'They had all the bandages but the cat wouldn't play.'

'Jim, tell us what you were playing here when Mr McNaughton caught you.'

'Pyramids,' whispered Jim. 'We took the tyre down and Mickey was up the tree. We was hauling the stones up like the pictures said. It worked bonzer, too. We had four stones for each side of the square, and we almost finished it when...'

'Exactly. Why was the deceased wearing street shoes? He saw from his drive a gaggle of street children desecrating his sacred turf. And after he had strictly forbidden his daughter to allow them on the property. What did he do? He strode across here and bellowed in his most terrifying voice that they should clear off. Mickey was up in the tree, holding the rope to which the top stone was attached. The deceased halted directly under him and Mickey was so terrified that he let the stone go. Then he fell off the tree and ran for his life. Is that right?'

Jim nodded. Mickey began to howl. Bert, who had been expecting this, thrust a huge toffee apple into the gaping maw.

'The kids all ran away as fast as they could go. Eh, Jimmy?'

Jimmy grinned, remembering that flight over the fence and down the valley, into the safety of their favourite box-thorn.

'So, you see, the blow was delivered by a more powerful force than man. It was gravity that murdered McNaughton. That pitcher weighs about twenty pounds and it fell some three feet. Enough to cave in any skull. So McNaughton dies as he had lived; a mean old cuss.'

'How did the tyre get back, then?'

'Ah. In the house, Miss Amelia is told that her brother has been pacing about uttering threats against her father before stamping off down the valley. She goes to look for him. There is her father, lying in the grass, perfectly dead. She does not understand the significance of the stones. She leaps to the conclusion that her brother has killed her father. She takes the bluestones and dumps them over the wall, with the tomb treasures. She unties the rope and throws it away. She is wearing soft house shoes so she leaves no footmark. Then she takes a new piece of rope and rehangs the tyre. The children's pulley has fallen naturally into the groove carved in the bark by the swing, so there is no other sign of their presence. She intends to discover the body the next day, but Daniel the spaniel is not going to be denied. Danny knows a dead body when he sees one. So the death is revealed sooner than she expected. Is that what happened, Amelia?'

Paolo gave her an affectionate shake.

'Why did you not tell me, foolish one? I would have helped you. You must not carry stones—you will spoil your fingers.'

Bill, congested with emotion, said, 'Amelia! Is this true?'

'Yes, Bill.'

'Sporting of you, old girl,' he mumbled. Amelia smiled. Mrs McNaughton, who was a little slow, finally reached her conclusion.

'Then it was an accident.'

'Yes, Mother.'

'Bill didn't kill him.'

'No, Mother.'

'In fact, no one killed him!'

'That is right, Mrs McNaughton,' agreed Detective-inspector Benton. 'Much as I hate to admit it.'

'Good. I also have a witness to Bill's walk. It can be confirmed by consulting the daybook in Kew police station. You should have checked. This is she—Miss Wilson.'

Margaret Wilson was a sturdy, tanned, straightforward young woman, who had clearly never lied in her life.

'I passed Bill on that path at four,' she stated. 'He has met me before, but I must have made no impression on him, which is a pity.'

Bill protested incoherently. 'No, Margaret, don't think that. I had a lot on my mind. I was in a mood. Don't think that I...' He trailed off and blushed.

Miss Wilson took his arm.

'Well. Is this the end of the game?' asked Paolo.

'Ask the detective-inspector,' said Phryne.

'Is it?' Paolo hugged his fiancée close. 'Are you going to arrest the girl for loyalty to her brother? Surely that would not be a good deed. And he died by his own act. Had he not ambushed these children he would be alive today, which would not be a good idea.'

'No charges will be laid against Miss McNaughton or the kids,' said the detective-inspector glumly.

'Then I would like to announce that Miss McNaughton has agreed to be my wife and I trust that we shall see you all at the wedding, including you, *scugnizzi*. If you wash your faces first. Since my wife will not have any money from the estate of her father no aspersions can be cast at us.'

'That's what you think,' commented Jillian. 'That clause is invalid. Void for being contrary to public policy. She will get the money without the condition, as will Mrs McNaughton. I know the solicitor who drew up that will. Poor thing. He told the old man all about what would happen if it was challenged, but all he would say was, "They'd never dare". Unpleasant person. So if I feel like casting the odd aspersion at you, Paolo, I shall cast them.'

'Under the circumstances you are welcome, *Signorina Avvocata*. Shall we also invite this so-tedious policeman to our wedding, *cara*?'

'Yes,' said Amelia. 'I want to paint him.'

They all went to lunch, well and truly satisfied.

'Have another cocktail,' suggested Phryne to the detective-inspector. 'Theories are like that. At least I didn't expose you through my old friend who works for "The Hawklet", did I?'

The policeman paled, and gulped the cocktail.

The street children were seated at the buffet, with all their favourite foods within reach. Lucy had uncorked Mickey from his apple and was feeding him cream cake while she ate a fat chocolate bar in neat, mouselike nibbles. Jim and Elsie were up to their eyes in rainbow jelly. Janey was applying raspberry vinegar to her face and the front of her frock. The violent death of McNaughton did not seem to be haunting them.

Bert lifted his beer in a toast to Cec, who could not move because Amelia was sketching him and asking if he had a Scandinavian grandparent. Phryne had snared a lamington out of sheer nostalgia and was wondering if Margaret Wilson really wanted Bill McNaughton, in view of his lousy heredity.

Someone seized her arm in an iron grip.

'Damn you, Phryne,' hissed Jillian Henderson. 'You've gone and lost me my murder!'

Murder on the Ballerat Train

Chapter One

There was a beetle sitting next to the goat:
(it was a very queer carriage full
of passengers altogether)
Alice Through the Looking Glass,
Lewis Carroll

Fortunately, the Hon. Phryne Fisher was a light sleeper. She had dozed for most of the journey, but when the nauseating odour of chloroform impinged on her senses, she had sufficient presence of mind to realize that something was happening while she still had wits enough to react.

Reaching over the slumbering form of her maid and companion, Dot, she groped for and found her handbag. She dragged it open, moving as though she were five fathoms under water. The clasp of the handbag seemed impossibly complex, and finally, swearing under her breath and gasping for air, she tore it open with her teeth, extracted her Beretta .32 with which she always travelled, and waveringly took aim. She squeezed off a shot that broke the window.

It shattered into a thousand shards, spattering Phryne and Dot with glass, and admitting a great gush of cold air.

Phryne choked, coughed, and staggered to her feet. She hung out of the window until she was quite certain of her sobriety, then hauled the other window open. The train was still moving. Smoke blew back into her face. What was happening? Phryne reached into the picnic basket, found the bottle of cold tea, and took a refreshing swig. Dot was out to the world, slumped over her travelling bag, her long hair coming loose from its plait. Phryne listened carefully at her maid's mouth, with a cold fear in her heart. But Dot was breathing regularly and seemed only to be deeply asleep.

Phryne wet her handkerchief with the remains of the cold tea and opened the door of the compartment. A wave of chloroform struck her, and she had to duck back into her compartment, take a deep breath and hold it, before running into the corridor, tearing open a window and leaning through it. There was not a sound on the train; not a noise of human occupancy. She sucked in a breath and rushed to the next window, repeating the procedure until all the windows were as wide open as the railways allowed.

There were four compartments in this first-class carriage. She had noticed the occupants as she had sauntered along before supper; an elderly lady and her companion in the first, a harassed woman and three diabolical children in the second, and a young couple in the third. Phryne and Dot had occupied the fourth, and that probably explained their relative immunity, as the smell got thicker and harder to bear as Phryne neared the front of the train.

The engine halted; she heard the whistle, and an odd bumping noise at the front of the first-class carriage. There was a rush of steam, and the train began to move again, almost precipitating Phryne onto her knees, as she was still rather shaky. Still coughing and retching, she opened the window of the young couple, then the mother and the children. Finally she approached the first compartment, and the smell was strong enough to sting her eyes. She applied the wet handkerchief again, staining her face with tea, dived in and stood staring.

The companion lay flat on the floor with a spilt cup by her hand, but the window was already open and the old lady was gone.

Phryne then did something that she had always wanted to do. She pulled the communication cord as hard as she could.

The train screeched to a satisfying halt, and a porter came running, slapping open the door to the dining-car and immediately beginning to cough.

'Did you pull that cord, Miss?' he asked. 'For the love of Mike, what's been happening here?'

'Chloroform,' said Phryne. 'Help me get them out into the fresh air.'

The porter shouted, and several more liveried men crowded into the carriage, before they began to choke and tried to run out again.

'Idiots!' gasped Phryne. 'Put a wet hanky over your silly faces and come and help me.'

'I'll handle it, Miss,' said one rather tall and charming conductor. 'You'd better come out too, until it clears a little. Give me your hand, Miss, and down we go.' Phryne, who was feeling very unwell, allowed herself to be carried down the step and off the siding. She sat down unsteadily in cold wet grass and was delighted with the sensation. It seemed more real than the hot, thick darkness of the train.

The tall conductor laid Dot down beside Phryne, and the old woman's companion beside her. Dot turned over in deep sleep, her face against Phryne's neck, sniffed, croaked 'Nuit D'Amour', sneezed, and woke up.

'Lie still, Dot dear, we've had a strange experience. We are quite all right, and will be even better in a minute. Ah. Someone with sense.'

Phryne accepted a cup of hot, sugared tea from an intelligent steward and held it to Dot's lips.

'Here you are, old dear, take a few sips and you'll be as right as rain.'

'Oh, Miss, I feel that sick! Did I faint?' Dot supped some more tea, and recovered enough to sit up and take the cup.

'In a way, Dot, we all did. Someone, for some unknown reason, has chloroformed us. We were in the end carriage and thus we inhaled the slightest dose, though it was quite enough, as I'm sure you will agree. And when I get hold of the person who has done this,' continued Phryne, gulping her tea and getting to her feet, 'they will be sorry that they were ever born. All right now, Dot? I mean, all right to be left? I want to scout around a bit.'

'All right, Miss,' agreed Dot, and lay down in the dank grass, wishing that her head would stop swimming.

The train had come to a halt in utter darkness somewhere on the way to Ballarat. All around the pastures were flat, cold, and wet; it was the middle of winter. She regained the train as the guards were carrying out the last of the children, a limp and pitiful bundle.

'Well, this wasn't on the timetable!' she exclaimed to the nearest conductor. 'What happened? And who caused it to happen?'

'I thought that you might have seen something, Miss, since you were the only one awake. Though you seem to have caught a fair lungful of the stuff,' he added. 'You sure that you feel quite the thing, Miss?'

Phryne caught at the proffered arm thankfully.

'I'm quite all right, just a little wobbly in the under-pinnings. What are we going to do?'

'Well, Miss, the train-conductor thinks that we'd better put everyone on board as soon as they have recovered a bit and take the train on to the next town. There's a policeman there and they can send for a doctor. Some of them kids are in a bad way.'

'Yes, I expect that will be the best plan. I'll go and see if I can help. Give me an arm, will you? Do you know any artificial respiration?'

'Yes, Miss,' said the middle-aged man, glancing admiringly at the white face under the cloche hat. 'I learned it for lifesaving.'

'Come on, then, we've got lives to save. The children and the pregnant woman are the main risks.'

Phryne found, on examination, that the youngest child, a particularly devilish three year old on whom she had been wishing death all day was the worst affected. His face was flushed, and there seemed to be no breath in the little body. She caught the child up in her arms and squeezed him gently.

'Breathe, little monster,' she admonished him, 'and you shall dance on all my hats, and push Dot's shoes out the window. Breathe, pest, or I shall never forgive myself. Come on, child, breathe!'

In, out, the chest rose and fell. The child gulped air, choked, fell silent again, as Phryne jogged his chest and he dragged in another breath, with nerve-racking intervals in which she heard the other passengers groaning awake. The pregnant woman was retching violently, and abjuring her comatose husband to awake. A small hand clutched Phryne painfully by the nose and the child's strong legs flexed and kicked. The whole child seemed to gather himself for some final effort. Phryne held her breath. Was this a death tremor? Johnnie took his first independent breath.

'Waaaah!' he screamed, and Phryne began to laugh.

'Here, you take him,' she said to the nearest guard. 'But be careful, he'll be sick in a moment.'

The guard was a family man, and took the resultant mess philosophically. They were all awake now; the woman and the children, the pregnant lady and her husband, and Dot. All except the companion to the elderly lady, and she was burned about the nose and mouth and very deeply drugged, though her heart pounded strongly under Phryne's hand.

'All back on the train,' ordered the conductor. 'This way, ladies and gentlemen, and we'll soon have you comfortable. This is some sort of silly joke, and the Railways will be responsible for any damages. Might I offer you a hand, Miss er...'

'Fisher. The Hon. Phryne Fisher,' said Phryne, allowing herself to lean on the arm. 'I really am not feeling at all well. How long to Ballan?'

'About ten minutes, Miss, if you'll excuse the guard's van, there being no room in the rest of the train.'

Phryne and Dot sat side by side on the floor, next to a chained dog and a cage full of sleepy chickens. The lady-companion was laid beside them, and the rest of the first-class passengers sat around the walls, surveying each other with discomfort.

'I say, old girl, you look as if you'd been pulled through the hedge backwards,' opined the young husband in a feeble attempt at humour, and his pregnant lady rocketed into hysteria.

It took Phryne the ten minutes to Ballan to induce in the lady a reasonable frame of mind, and at the end of it Phryne was a rag.

'If you have anything else to say that you think is funny, I'll thank you to keep it to yourself,' she snarled at the husband, catching him a nasty accidental-on-purpose crack on the shins. 'I've got other things to do than calm the heeby-jeebies. Now we are at Ballan, Dot, I hope that we can get to the overnight things, for we really must have a hot bath and a change of clothes, or we shall catch our death.'

'There's a hotel in Ballan,' said the mother, catching little Johnnie as, much recovered, he poked his fingers in among the chickens, 'Come away, Johnnie, do!'

'The Railways can pay for it, then,' suggested the young man, with a wary eye on Phryne. 'I haven't got the cash for an overnight stay.'

'I can advance you enough,' said Phryne. 'Not to worry. Here comes our nice conductor to release us from durance fairly vile.'

The conductor had clearly done wonders in a very short time.

'If the ladies and gentlemen would care to break their journey for awhile, they may like to bathe and change at the hotel,' he suggested. 'The guards will bring your baggage. The hotel is about a hundred yards down the street, and we will carry the sick lady.'

Phryne took one child, Dot another, and they trailed wearily down the road to the Ballan Hotel, a guesthouse of some pretension. They were met at the door by a plump and distressed landlady who exclaimed over their condition and took charge of the children.

'Room two, ladies, there's a bath all ready for you. I'll send the man with the baggage when he arrives. I shall have tea ready directly, and I've sent for the doctor, he should be here soon.'

Dot and Phryne gained their room and Phryne began to strip off her wet garments. Dot located the bath, and gestured to it.

'You first—you were worse affected,' insisted Phryne, and Dot recognized inflexibility when she saw it. She took off her clothes in the bathroom and sank into the tub, feeling the aching cold ease out of her bones. She heard the door open and close as she lay back and shut her eyes, and presently there was Phryne's voice.

'Come on, old dear, you don't want to fall asleep again! I've got the clothes and I've got some tea.'

'In a minute,' promised Dot, and exchanged places with her mistress.

They were dressed in clean clothes and thoroughly warmed when the conductor returned to advise them that the chloroform vapour was all gone and they could resume their journey, if they liked. Phryne was ready to go, and was called in to rouse the companion of the elderly lady.

The woman was much scorched or scalded about the nose and mouth, and the doctor seemed worried about her. She had not begun to rouse until the injection of camphor had been made. Then she opened her eyes all of a sudden, and hearing Phryne's voice, asked, 'Where's Mother?'

And Mother was gone.

After that, there was no further chance of getting to Ballarat, and Phryne turned to the landlady.

'There was another lady on the train, and she has definitely gone. We must call the police—perhaps she fell out the window. Is there a police station in Ballan?'

'Yes, Miss, I'll send the boy around now. What a terrible thing! We'll have to rouse out some of the men to go searching.'

'Dot, are you better?' asked Phryne of her maid.

Dot replied, 'I'm still a bit woozy, Miss. What do you want me to do?'

'Go and make some tea.'

'I can manage that,' agreed Dot, and went out. The doctor was applying a soothing cream to the stricken woman's face.

'What burned her? Chloroform?' asked Phryne, as she took the jar out of the doctor's insecure hold and held it out for him to dip into. 'Does it burn like that?'

'Certainly. She has had a chloroform soaked cloth laid over her face, and if you hadn't woken them all up and got her out of the train, she would now be dead, and even so there may be permanent damage to her liver.'

'What about the rest of us? Would we have all been affected just by the chloroform in the first compartment?'

'No. The gas is heavy, much heavier than air, and very volatile. Someone must have poured it into the ventilation system. Someone wanted you all asleep, Miss Fisher, but I have no idea why. There now, you may stopper the jar. Poor woman, a nasty awakening, but she's slumped back into sleep again. Can you watch her for an hour? I should go and see how those children are getting along.'

'By all means,' agreed Phryne, her conscience still tender in the matter of little Johnnie. 'I'll stay here. If she wakes, can I give her tea?'

'If she wakes, Miss Fisher, you can give her anything you like,' said the doctor, and hefted his black bag in the direction of the children's room.

An hour later, at three in the morning, the woman awoke. Phryne saw her stir and mutter, and lifted her to moisten her lips with water.

'What happened? Where's Mother?' came the cracked voice, prevented only by bodily weakness from shrieking.

'Hush, hush now, you're safe, and they are out looking for your mother.'

'Who are you?' asked the woman dazedly. She saw Phryne's expensive dressing-gown, edged in fox fur, her Russian leather boots of rusty hue, and an aloof, pale, delicate face, framed in neat, short black hair and with penetrating green eyes. Next to this vision of modish loveliness was a plain young woman with plaits, dressed in a chenille gown like a bedspread.

'I'm Phryne Fisher and this is Dot Williams, my companion. Who are you?'

'Eunice Henderson,' murmured the woman. 'Pleased to meet you. Where is Mother? What is happening? And what's wrong with me? I can't have fainted. I never faint.'

'No, you didn't faint. We are in the Ballan hotel. Someone chloroformed us—the whole first-class carriage. I knew that I should have motored to Ballarat, but I do like trains, though I'm rapidly going off them at the moment. Luckily, I was in the last compartment, and I am a very light sleeper. I broke the window, and then opened all the others and dragged everyone out. You I found lying on the floor of the compartment, with a spilt glass near your hand, and there was no one else there, I can assure you. The window was open—could she have fallen out?'

'I suppose so—she is a thin little thing, Mother. I can't remember much. I was asleep, then I heard this thump, and I felt ever so ill, so I got up to get some water, and…that's all I can recall.'

'Well, never mind for the moment. There's nothing we can do until the searchers come back. They have roused the railwaymen and they've all gone walking back along the track. They'll find her if she is there. Why not go back to sleep? I'll wake you if anything happens.'

Eunice Henderson closed her eyes.

'Miss, she must have been the Eunice that the old lady was nagging all the time on the train,' whispered Dot, and Phryne nodded. The journey had been made unpleasant not only by the children, but also by an old woman's partially deaf whine in the forward compartment, as unceasing as a stream and as irritating as the mosquito which had caused Phryne's sleep to be so light. She had reflected during the journey that the mosquito was the lesser hazard, because it could be silenced with a vigorous puff of Flit.

'Eunice, the window is shut—you know that I hate stale air!' 'Eunice, the window is open—you know that I hate a draught!' 'Eunice, I want my tea!' 'Eunice, you are so slow!' 'Eunice, when do we get to Ballarat?' 'Eunice, are you listening?' 'Eunice, where's my novel? No, not that novel, you stupid girl, the one I was reading yesterday. What do you mean, you didn't bring it? What other mother has to endure such a stupid, graceless, uncaring daughter? At least you'll never marry, Eunice, you'll be with me until I die—and don't think you'll get all my money—don't frown at me, girl! No one loves a poor, deserted old woman! Eunice! Where are you going?'

Phryne thought that if Eunice had finally tipped Mother out the train, she could understand it. But it did not look as though she had. Surely Eunice would not have drugged the whole train—or burned herself so badly.

Under the burns and the soothing cream, Eunice was rather good looking. She had strong, clean features, rather masculine but well-formed, and curly brown hair kept firmly controlled under bandeau and net. Her eyes, Phryne remembered, were a rich brown, and she was long limbed and athletic. Why should her mother have been so sure that Eunice would never marry? Admittedly, there was a shortage of young men, and a super-fluity of women, the War to End All Wars having slaughtered the manhood of the Empire, but they were there if one tried. Perhaps Eunice had never had the chance to try. Mother was a full-time career.

Dot poured herself another cup of tea and began to twist her plait into a knot, which meant that she was thinking.

'Miss, could she have…?'

'I don't think so, Dot, because of the burns. She didn't need to go through all this pretence. All she had to do was boost Mother out of the window, wait a few minutes, then stagger out into the corridor and faint. The train would be miles away by the time she 'recovered' and then all she had to do was gasp that Mother was looking out of the window, lost her grip and fell, and that would be that. No old lady would survive a fall from a fast moving train, at least, its unlikely. No. Someone altogether other has contrived this, and a clumsy attempt it is.

The previous theory at least has the virtue of simplicity. This one is too elaborate and should not prove too hard to solve, if it is murder.'

'If it's murder, Miss? What else could it be?'

'Kidnapping? Some frolic that went wrong? I don't know, Dot. Let's wait until we see what develops. Would you like to take a short nap? I can watch for a while—I'm not sleepy.'

'Neither am I,' said Dot. 'I don't want to ever sleep again!'

◇◇◇

They watched until four in the morning, when a respectful, soft-footed maid came to ask if the Hon. Phryne Fisher could spare Sergeant Wallace a word.

Miss Fisher could. She rose from her seat on the floor and wrapped her cream dressing-gown around her and followed the maid into what looked to be the hotel's breakfast-room. Phryne was too tired to be hungry, but thought longingly of coffee.

Miraculously, the policeman had before him a full percolator and several cups. He poured one for Phryne and she sat sipping gratefully and breathing in the steam.

This sergeant was one of the large economy-sized policemen, being about six-and-a-half-feet tall and several axehandles across the shoulders. The Australian sun had scorched his milky Celtic complexion into the hue of council house brick. His light grey eyes, however, were bright and shrewd.

'Well, Miss Fisher, I'm Sergeant Wallace and I'm pleased to meet you. Detective-inspector Robinson says to give you his best regards.'

Phryne looked at this country cop over the edge of her coffee cup. He grinned.

'I telephoned the list of passengers to the central office an hour ago, Miss Fisher, and Robbo was on duty. He recognized the name. Thinks a great deal of you, he does. We went to school together,' he added. 'Geelong Grammar. I won a scholarship, however. How are you, Miss? Feeling more the thing?'

'Yes. But Miss Henderson is still very unwell—and worried about her mother. Have you found her?'

'Yes, Miss, we've found her all right.'

'Dead?'

'As a doornail. We brought her into Ballan a few minutes ago. Did you see her, Miss? To identify, I mean?'

'Yes, I saw her,' agreed Phryne. 'I would know her again.' She thought of the tiny, wizened figure, her thinning white hair carefully combed and dressed in a bun, her fingers laden with many emeralds.

'Would you do it, then, Miss? I'm only asking to spare Miss Henderson, and they have no near relations. And Robbo, I mean Detective-inspector Robinson, has a high opinion of your courage, Miss Fisher.'

'Very well. Let's get it over, then. Lead the way.'

The huge policeman shouldered his way out of the breakfast room into a cold yard, and thence into a stable smelling of dust and hay and horses.

'We put her in here for the moment, Miss,' he said solemnly. 'We'll take her into the Coroner's later. But I want to make sure that it's the right woman.'

He lifted the lamp high, casting a pool of soft golden light.

'Is this her, Miss Fisher?' he asked, and drew back the blanket from an untouched face.

'Yes,' said Phryne. 'Poor woman! How did she die?' As she spoke her hands touched the skull, and felt the terrible dent where consciousness had been crushed. The skin was clammy and chill in the way that only the dead are cold. The eyes were shut, and someone had bound up the jaw. Mrs. Henderson wore no expression now but peace and faint surprise. There was nothing here to shock Miss Henderson. Phryne said so.

'Maybe not from the face,' said the sergeant grimly. 'But have a look at the rest.'

Phryne drew off the blanket and stepped back a pace, astonished and sick. Such a fury had fallen on the old woman that scarcely a bone was whole. She was covered in red clay. Her limbs were broken, even her fingers twisted out of true, though no part of her seemed to be missing. She laid the blanket back over the wreck of a human creature and shook her head.

'What could have done that? Did a train run over her?'

'No, Miss. The doctor has a theory, but it's not a nice one.'

'Tell me, while we go back to the hotel,' she said, taking the sergeant's arm. He closed the stable door carefully and waited until Phryne was seated with a fresh cup of coffee before he said, 'The doctor reckons she was stamped on.'

'Stamped on?'

'Yes, Miss, by feet.'

'Ugh, Sergeant, I hope your doctor is wrong. What a dreadful thought! Who could have hated her that much?'

'Ah, there you have me, Miss. I don't know. Now tell me exactly what happened this night, from the time you got on the train.'

Phryne gathered her thoughts, and began.

'I boarded the train at six o'clock at Flinders Street Station with my companion Miss Williams, a bunch of narcissus, a picnic basket, a trunk, a suitcase, a hatbox and three novels for railway reading, intending to go to Ballarat to visit some of my cousins—the Reverend Mr. Fisher and his sisters. I believe that they are well known in the city and they were expecting me, so you can check with them, and tell them that I shall be along as soon as I can. We were seated in the fourth compartment of the first-class carriage. We saw to the baggage, then had a cup of tea and a biscuit from the dining car. There I made the acquaintance of Miss and Mrs. Henderson, and the woman with the children.'

'Mrs. Agnes Lilley, that is, Miss, and Johnnie, Ernest, and George.'

'Quite. Those children were the most pestilential set of little nuisances who ever afflicted a train. Mrs. Henderson found them particularly annoying, I thought. I had a few words with that poor old lady on the subject of modern children and how they should have all been drowned at birth, and then Dot and I went back to the compartment. We had some tea in the thermos and we didn't need to stay in the dining car. I noticed that the couple—'

'Mr. Alexander Cotton and his wife, Daisy,' put in the sergeant helpfully.

'Yes, she seemed ill and nervous, and he was bringing her a cup of tea. A clumsy young man. He spilled it all over a passing child and I refilled it from my flask so that he didn't need to go back to the dining car and doubtless spill it all over again. That sort of young man can continue being clumsy all night, if pressed. I also noticed that his wife is very pregnant, because I find expectant women uncomfortable travelling companions. I hoped that she wasn't going to deliver in the train, which I believe is not uncommon. Can I have some more coffee?'

'There's none left.' The sergeant pressed a bell, and the landlady came to the door.

'Could we have some more coffee, Mrs. Johnson? Is Doctor Heron still here?'

'Yes, Bill, the doctor's watching over one of them kids. He's worried about the youngest. I'll get some more coffee in a tick—shall I fetch the doctor?'

'No need at the moment, just catch him if he looks like going home. Thanks, Mrs. J.'

'I was reading one of my novels and Dot was asleep, and I dozed off over the pages with my light on, then I smelt chloroform. I woke up, and broke the window.'

'Why did you wake up, Miss Fisher? Everyone else just seems to have got sleepier.'

'I hate the smell of chloroform,' said Phryne, lighting a gasper to banish the remembrance. 'That sweet, cloying stench—ugh! I must have inhaled quite a lot, though, I could hardly move.'

'How did you break the window, Miss?'

'I hit it with my shoe,' lied Phryne, who was not going to disclose the presence of her pistol unless she had to. 'And I damaged the heel, blast it. A new shoe, too.'

Should the sergeant search, he would find Phryne's high-heeled shoe with window glass in the leather and glass damage to the heel. Phryne had carefully ruined the shoe on the way to Ballan. She believed in being just as truthful as was congruent with sense and convenience.

'Yes, and then what happened?' asked the sergeant.

'I staggered out and opened all the windows, and I pulled the communication cord.'

'Yes, Miss, that was at 7:20 p.m. The guard looked at his watch—Railways policy, evidently—and how long do you think that opening the windows took?'

'Oh, about ten minutes. I felt the train stop for a while when I was letting in the air.'

'Ah, yes, Miss, that times it. Water stop for three minutes at 7:15 p.m.'

'There was some sort of bump—I thought it came from the front of the train—but I was getting very wobbly by then.'

'I'm sure you acted very properly, Miss Fisher. If you hadn't broken that window, the whole carriage would have been gassed, and the doctor says that some of them kids would have been dead before the train got to Ballarat. A terrible thing, and Mrs. Henderson dead, too.'

'Can she have fallen out of the window, do you think?'

'Fallen or been dragged,' said the sergeant grimly. 'Here's the coffee. Thank you, Mrs. J.'

Mrs. Johnson withdrew reluctantly—it was not often that anything interesting happened in Ballan—and the sergeant poured more coffee for Phryne.

'What did you see, Miss, when you opened each compartment door?'

He got out his notebook and licked his pencil.

'In the compartment nearest me were Mr. and Mrs. Cotton. They seemed to have fallen under the influence together, for he had his arms around her and she had her face buried in his shoulder. They were half-conscious. Then there was Mrs. Lilley and her frightful children—she was stirring and moaning, but the children were all dead to the world…what an unfortunate metaphor, I beg your pardon. In the first compartment the window was open, Mrs. Henderson was gone, and Miss Henderson was lying on the floor, prone, with a cloth half-over her face.'

'What was she wearing?'

'A skirt and blouse, and a woolly shawl. She had a spilled cup near her hand, as though she had dropped it where she fell. The smell of chloroform in that confined place was awful, it stung my eyes until I could hardly see.'

'And then what did you do, Miss?'

'I pulled the communication cord and the guards came, and we got everyone out of the train. Where is the train, by the way? You can't have left it sitting on the line all this time, not if you haven't closed the rail link altogether.'

'No, Miss, we haven't closed the line, not now we've found the body. The rest of the train has gone on to Ballarat, but the first-class carriage is still here in the siding, in case we can find a clue. You didn't happen to notice anyone you didn't know walking through the train, did you, Miss? After you came back from the dining car.'

'Only a rather good looking young guard, blond, he was, with a very nice smile.'

'A young man, Miss? I saw all the guards on that train, and there was none of 'em under forty.'

'Are you sure?' demanded Phryne, who had a clear recollection of a rather ravishing young face under the cap; unlined, smooth, tanned, and certainly not more than twenty-two or -three years old.

'Quite sure,' responded the sergeant. 'Would you know this man again, Miss?'

'I think so,' temporized Phryne. 'Perhaps. But you'd better start looking for a blond young man, Sergeant, because I think that he might be your murderer.'

Chapter Two

Then a very gentle voice in the distance
said, 'She must be labelled "Lass, With
Care", you know—'

Alice Through the Looking Glass
Lewis Carroll

There was nothing to be done for the rest of the night but to recruit as much strength as possible. Phryne curled up in an armchair, and Dot went to lie on her bed. Miss Henderson awoke at intervals, was reassured, and lapsed back into sleep. Gradually the cold, before-dawn grey light seeped into the room, and Phryne dozed off.

Her dreams were most uncomfortable, and she was glad to wake. All through and around a peculiar series of events constructed by her bewildered subconscious was the picture of the old woman as she had last seen her; the broken limbs, the pathetically twisted fingers, bare and broken…Phryne said, 'Rings!' and woke herself up.

'Thank God for waking, I could not have stood that dream much longer. Her rings! All those emeralds, and they are gone. I must tell that nice sergeant, but first I must have a bath and some breakfast and find some clothes. I wonder how long we shall have to stay here? And how is Miss Henderson?'

Phryne bent over the patient, and found her sleeping normally, her face still and peaceful under the burns. Her heartbeat was strong and regular. Fairly soon she would have to know that her mother was dead, but with any luck Phryne would not be the one to tell her.

Phryne tiptoed into the room allotted to herself and Dot and found that her maid was awake and had run a bath, set out Phryne's clothes, and was herself washed and dressed.

Phryne shed her cream velvet and fox fur dressing-gown gratefully, pulled off her silk pyjamas, and subsided into the steam, scented with Phryne's favourite bath oil, 'Rêve du Coquette'.

She dried herself thoroughly, as though she could scour the memory of death off her skin with the hard hotel towelling, and dressed for what looked to be a cold, nasty winter's day in trousers of black fine-loomed wool, a silk shirt in emerald green, a jumper knitted with rather amusing cats, and the black cloche. She pulled on her red Russian boots and took a red outer coat of voluminous cut with deep pockets.

Dot was dressed in a long warm skirt and a woolly jacket in fine undyed fleece. She had a wheat coloured shirt and thick lisle stockings, but was still pinched and shivering.

'You should wear trousers, Dot, they are the only sensible clothing for this sort of weather.'

'Oh, no, Miss,' was all that Dot would reply through chattering teeth, so Phryne gave up and led the way into the breakfast-room. It was eight-thirty in the morning, and someone should surely be stirring.

The breakfast-room (which Phryne was sure would double as the dining-room) was a large room with bay windows, now looking out onto miserable cows and battered scrub. Every leaf was hung with dew, as the early fog condensed, and it was grey and chill, a suitable morning for the aftermath of a murder. However, the chafing dishes were set out next to a tall coffee-pot and all the makings for tea, and a scent of toast and bacon was in the air. The room was decorated in pink-and-black, jazz colours, and tall vases of gum leaves lent the air an outback scent.

It was modern and stylish without being so *outré* that it would be out of fashion in a year.

Miss Fisher was pleased to approve, and to load her plate with eggs and bacon and toast. Dot joined her, equally hungry, and they were drinking their second cup of tea before they had time to speak.

'You know that they've found the body, Dot?'

'Yes, Miss, that cop told me. How did she die?'

'I'd say a massive fracture of the skull, but she was extensively damaged, Dot, I hope and trust after she was dead. And her rings are missing—all those emeralds.'

'Robbery?' asked Dot.

'Murder, Dot. Robbery was probably an afterthought. No one would go to all that trouble just to rob an old woman, rings or no rings—at least, I don't think so. People are strange. Have some marmalade, it's excellent.'

'When do you reckon that cop will let us go?' asked Dot, taking some marmalade. Phryne was right—it was excellent.

'Have to be fairly soon, Dot, after all, they've found the body and none of us could have killed her…except me, of course. I wonder if he suspects me!'

'Suspects you, Miss!' Dot was indignant. 'You wouldn't go through all this mucking about if you wanted to kill someone. Like a play, this is, not like real life.'

'You are very acute, Dot. That is exactly what it is. Just like a play. Elaborate, theatrical and stagey. Hello! Here comes our policeman now. Who has he with him?'

Sergeant Wallace came into the breakfast-room, leading a girl by the hand. She was about twelve or thirteen, with two long plaits of brown hair and a skimpy, too-tight dress in shabby winceyette. She was carrying a battered leather attaché-case and a felt hat, the elastic of which was frayed by chewing. The sergeant led her over to Phryne's table and said:

'Well, Miss Fisher, Robbo said that you have a talent for mysteries, and here's one that I can't solve. This young woman was on the train, that's clear enough, for she had a ticket to Ballarat in her pocket, done up with a safety pin. She was found standing on the platform at Ballarat. No one came for her, and no one knows her, and she can't remember her own name. She can't tell us anything at all about herself, and I don't mind telling you I'm stumped. Perhaps you'd do me the favour of taking charge of her for the moment, until we can get the Welfare onto it?'

At the mention of the word 'Welfare', Dot had gone pale, and Phryne did not fail to notice this, feeling rather the same herself. In her childhood of straitened circumstances, the Welfare, who took children away so that they were never seen again, was a hideous phantom.

'No, no, there is no need to trouble them,' she said hastily, taking the girl's hand and sitting her down beside Dot. 'We will be delighted to look after the poor little mite, won't we, Dot?'

Dot nodded and went to fetch a fresh cup and a plate for the girl. The sergeant was about to leave when Phryne seized his arm.

'There's something I forgot to tell you,' she whispered. 'Her fingers were bare, weren't they? And when I saw her first, they were loaded down with rings—valuable ones—mostly emeralds and diamonds.'

'Thanks, Miss Fisher, that is a help. Robbery might be the motive, then, though I can't imagine how that advances matters. How is the daughter?'

'I left her sleeping peacefully. I'll send Dot to help her with her toilet as soon as she's finished breakfast. Dr. Heron had better see her again before she gets up, she was very deeply drugged.'

The sergeant agreed and went away. Phryne came back to her table to find that the girl had been helped to eggs and bacon and toast and tea and was eating as though she was famished.

'Slow down, old thing, there's plenty more,' she said, and the girl looked up, smiled, and laid down her knife and fork to take a gulp of tea.

Phryne let her eat in peace as she observed her. Neat table manners, someone had taught her well; and if she had plaited her own hair, she was a tidy creature. She could not help the winceyette dress, which had been made for someone less coltish and thinner, and Phryne resolved to get rid of that dress as soon as possible. Though she had not spoken, she had understood what Phryne had said. Therefore she spoke English, which was a help. There were permanent blue shadows under the eyes which spoke of childhood illness, but she seemed sturdy enough. The nails on the large well-formed hands were bitten to the quick.

The girl finished her breakfast, pushing back the plate with a satisfied sigh, and Phryne poured her some more tea.

'I'm Phryne Fisher, and this is Dorothy Williams. What's your name?' she asked quietly, and the girl's brow puckered.

'I can't remember!' she said, and began to cry.

Dot hastily supplied her with a handkerchief and a hug, and Phryne said quickly, 'Never mind. We'll call you Jane. Would you like to come and stay with me for a while, Jane?'

Jane stopped crying and nodded, drying her face. Phryne smiled.

'Good, that's settled. Now I have to go and talk to that nice policeman again, so why don't you find yourself something pleasant to pass the time. There are books and games on that shelf. Dot will help you. See you in an hour or so, Dot.'

Phryne slung her red coat around her shoulders, checked that cigarettes and money reposed in her pockets, and sauntered out into the chilly yard to find the sergeant.

She found him staring mournfully at the stable door, whence two well-dressed men were carrying a stretcher.

'Going for autopsy in Melbourne,' he said in answer to her question. 'I hope she was dead when all that happened.'

'So do I. And I haven't got far with the new puzzle, either.'

'No? She don't remember?'

'She don't. I have called her Jane. Was she definitely on that train?'

'Why, yes, Miss, she was seen on it, second carriage from the end. Second-class ticket, single. Nothing on her to identify her, so the Ballarat people shipped her back, thinking that the two mysteries must be connected.'

'That is not necessarily the case,' said Phryne. 'She could have nothing to do with it.'

'And that's true too,' agreed the sergeant, in deepest gloom. 'Well, they've taken the body away, and now I have to break it to Miss Henderson. Hang on a tick. It would come much better from a woman. I don't suppose that you...'

Phryne sighed. She had thought that this might happen.

'All right. I'll tell Miss Henderson if you take me to see the scene of the crime.'

'Deal,' agreed the sergeant, and Phryne returned to the hotel.

Miss Henderson was sitting up in bed and taking a little toast and tea when Miss Fisher arrived. Dot had taken the child Jane into the bathroom and was abjuring her to wash behind her ears. Miss Henderson took one look at Phryne's solemn face and said, 'Mother's dead, isn't she?'

'Yes, I'm afraid she is.'

'You know, I thought she must be.'

Miss Henderson began to cry, in a helpless way, seeming to be unaware that she was still holding a piece of toast in one hand and her cup of tea in the other. Phryne took away the cup and the toast and gave Miss Henderson a handkerchief, three of which she had prudently provided.

Miss Henderson wiped her face and leaned forward, grabbing Phryne's wrist in a fierce grip.

'You are a detective, are you not? I read about that case of the unspeakable little man you caught in Queenscliff. And the Spanish ambassador's son's kitten. You're clever. You can catch him for me.'

'Catch whom?' asked Phryne, fighting the urge to free her hand. 'Calm yourself, Miss Henderson.'

'The murderer, of course.'

'Do you really want to hire me? Think about it. I may find out the truth.'

'That's what I want you to find,' said Miss Henderson firmly. 'I know that Mother was a nuisance. I have quite often felt like killing her myself, God forgive me, but that does not mean that I did it or contrived it. Murder is such a monstrous thing. And why? Why? The person she injured most was me—hounding me, nagging me, day after day, hour after hour, until I thought

I'd go mad! If anyone had reason to kill Mother, it was me, but I didn't. And now I don't know what to do or where to turn.'

She sobbed for a few minutes, then took control of herself again, putting down the handkerchief.

'So I want to hire you, Miss Fisher, to find whoever killed my mother. Find out the truth.'

'All right,' agreed Phryne, sitting down on the end of the bed. 'On condition that you drink the rest of that tea and don't get up until the doctor has seen you.'

'I'll be good. Miss Fisher, tell me—did she suffer?'

'No,' said Phryne, thinking of the great blow the old woman had taken to the head—surely no awareness could survive that. 'No, I'm sure she did not suffer.'

'How did she…die?'

'She was hit on the head very hard,' said Phryne. 'One heavy blow. But her body was much damaged after she was dead—the fall from the train, possibly.'

'Can I see her?'

'No, the body has gone to Melbourne for *post mortem*. You can see her later. She looks fine. Her face is quite untouched. She will not shock you.'

'She shocked me enough when she was alive,' commented Miss Henderson wryly. 'I doubt that she'll shock me that much now that she is dead.'

Phryne left Eunice Henderson to her tea and found Dot, who had Jane's clothes over her arm.

'Well, any name tags or laundry marks, Dot?'

'Nothing at all, Miss. I tell you one thing, she's a cleanly little madam, but she ain't used to a bath. She's been cat-washing since she was a baby, I reckon.'

Phryne recalled cat-washes, because she had taken them herself until the death of some young men had dragged her upwards into the world of running water and bathrooms. One obtained a bowl of hot water, and standing on a mat and removing one article of clothing at a time, one washed first face and hands, then the upper body, removing the shirt, then the lower body, removing and replacing the skirt, until finally one stood both feet in the basin (assuming that they would fit) having washed the whole person in about two pints of hot water, or one kettle-full. It was satisfying in an economical sort of way, but was nothing like the joyful sensation of sinking into a hot, scented bath. Phryne almost envied Jane the pleasure which she must be experiencing.

'What about the clothes themselves?'

'Hand-me-downs,' said Dot without hesitation. 'See—hem's been let down twice, and the colour's faded with a lot of washing. Homemade,' she added, exhibiting the inside collar where no label had ever been attached. 'And not very well, either. Her singlet and bloomers are wool, but old and scratchy, and thin enough to put your fingers through.'

'Well, she can't put those back on,' commented Phryne. 'Can you find something of mine that will fit?'

'No, Miss, I'll go out directly and buy her some suitable clothes,' said Dot, shocked that this waif should be clothed in Phryne's silk underwear. 'That would be better, Miss.' Phryne gave Dot enough money to purchase clothes to last Jane until she got back to Phryne's own house, and dragged herself away to find the sergeant yet again. He was still standing in the yard, gloomily smoking a cigarette and communing with the crows who were gathered on the milking shed fence.

'Well, I've told Miss Henderson and it's time for you to keep your part of the bargain,' she said brightly. The crows, alarmed by the extreme redness of her coat, rose flapping in a body, making raucous comments.

'Very well, Miss Fisher, I've got a car, come along. It's not far,' added the depressed sergeant. 'And blessed if I can see how she was got out. I've walked every inch of the line, both with a lantern and in daylight,' he said, helping Miss Fisher into the battered Model T and cranking the engine into a sputtering semblance of life. 'And there isn't a footprint or a mark of where she fell.'

Chapter Three

So young a child,' said the gentleman
sitting opposite to her, (he was dressed in
white paper) 'ought to know which way
she's going, even if she doesn't know her
own name!'

Alice Through the Looking Glass,
Lewis Carroll

'That's where they found the body,' said the sergeant as they
stood beside the track. 'A good ten yards. She can't have fallen
that far, and there is not a mark, Miss Fisher...look for yourself.'

Phryne stepped away from the track and surveyed the ground.
The water tower with its wooden scaffolding stood about fifteen feet high, with the cloth funnel that fed the train hanging
down. The ground was firm but moist red clay, the consistency
of an ice-cream brick, and certainly there was no sign of anyone
walking on it. Further away, along the path, were the multiple
tracks of the searchers, the clay reproducing their bootmarks
and even the round indentation where someone had set down
a lantern, and the cup-shaped prints of knees next to the body.
There were multiple marks there, but the ground was all cut up,
churned and confused by the searchers so no individual print
could be discerned.

'She was trodden into the mud,' said the sergeant. 'They near had to dig her out. Over there, Miss Fisher, you can see.'

'Yes, what a mess! No chance of finding anything there. Have you walked along a bit further?'

'Yes, Miss, a good half mile, but this is where she landed, however she got out. A bit further back I found the glass where you broke your window, and that must mark the beginning of the whole thing. Before that, Mrs. Henderson was alive.'

'Hmm, yes. Has anyone climbed the water tower?'

'Yes, Miss, I thought of that, but the canvas funnel isn't long enough to catch, and the train-men were using it to refill the boiler. There's nothing unusual up there, Miss.'

'It was just a thought. Well, we might go back to Ballan, then, Sergeant, and have a look at the first-class carriage.'

'All right, Miss. Er...how did Miss Henderson take the news of her mother's death?'

'She was very distressed; not that I think that she liked her mother at all, indeed, the old lady was fretting the life out of her, but she has hired me to find out who killed her, and I don't think that she did it, I really don't.'

'Hired you, Miss? Will you take the assignment?'

'Oh, yes, I think so. I want to find the murderer too. I don't like having my journeys interrupted by chloroform.'

The Model T made the short journey to the rail siding without shedding any of the more essential of its parts, and they shuddered to a halt. A very large constable was on guard next to the train. He stood up hurriedly when he saw the sergeant and endeavoured to hide his doorstep cheese sandwich behind his back.

'Anyone been about, Jones?' asked the sergeant, elaborately not noticing the sandwich. 'All quiet?'

'Sir, that Mrs. Lilley came and collected some of the children's clothes, but I made sure that she only went into her compartment, sir.'

'And that's all?'

'Yes, sir.'

'All right. You can go and get some breakfast—take half an hour, you must be hungry.' The sergeant smiled laconically, and allowed Phryne to precede him onto the train.

'The smell's almost gone,' she commented. 'Thank goodness. Here's where I was sitting, and Dot. Nothing there. Here is the lair of those awful children. Mr. and Mrs. Cotton were here… tell me, has anything been touched?'

'No, Miss Fisher, except when Miss Henderson was removed. Why? Something missing?'

'The cloth, the one that was laid over her face. It isn't here. Perhaps they took it with Miss Henderson. Otherwise it looks just as it did. Now, see, Sergeant, look at these marks.' The sergeant came fully into the compartment, which had two long padded seats. Both ladies had evidently been reclining, almost or fully asleep. A woolly rug was flung from the seat nearest the engine and was crumpled on the floor. The shawl on the other seat was thrown to the end, as though the sleeper had arisen hurriedly.

'See, they were both lying here, heads to the outside wall, with the window open like that. At least I suppose the window was open. I must ask Miss Henderson. I heard her mother complaining about the window quite a lot, but she didn't seem to have a preference really. She was just doing it to irritate. "She only does it to annoy, because she knows it teases".'

The sergeant, who was evidently unfamiliar with *Alice in Wonderland,* looked blank.

'Then,' continued Phryne, bending close to the windowsill, 'see? Those scrape marks. She was pulled out the window after she was drugged—I hope—and…'

'And?' prompted the sergeant with heavy irony, 'carried up into the air by angels? Lifted up by aeroplane?'

'Yes, that is a problem, I agree, my dear police officer, but it's clear she was dragged. Look at the marks! Plain as the nose on your face.'

'Yes, that is what they look like, as though something has been pulled through that window, and even a little of her hair has caught, Miss, I believe you are right. But what happened then I can't imagine. She was thrown a long way, Miss.'

'What if the murderer were on the roof of the train?' asked Phryne suddenly. 'Has it rained since last night?'

'Well, yes, Miss, there was a shower at about five, quite a heavy one, that's why everything is so soggy.'

'Blast! That will have washed all the marks off the roof.'

'But you could have something there, Miss! If he was on the roof that would account for the marks, and even for where the body was found. She was a light little thing.'

'And the injuries?'

'Maybe the doctor was just indulging a diseased imagination. Not much happens in Ballan, you know.'

'So she could have been that damaged by such a fall?'

'I reckon so, Miss. That train builds up speed. She'd hit the earth with a fair old thump.'

'Well, there's not much else to see in here,' commented Phryne, noting that the old lady had a lurid taste in reading matter. Next to her place was an edition of *Varney the Vampire* which Phryne remembered from her youth to be fairly blood-chilling. Miss Henderson had been beguiling the journey with *Manon Lescaut*, in French, the unexpurgated edition. By the bookmark she had nearly finished it. Phryne reflected that the woman who chose *Manon* and the woman who preferred *Varney* were hardly likely to be soul mates.

Most of the hand-baggage had been taken to the hotel, but Phryne picked up one parcel which seemed to contain paper and was addressed to Miss Henderson. She weighed it in her hands and put it down again—just paper.

The sergeant escorted her out of the train to the hotel. The constable was returning from what, to judge from the crumbs which he was brushing off his uniform, had been a very good breakfast.

'Keep watch for a bit longer, lad,' said the sergeant, and looked hungrily toward the kitchen. Phryne interpreted the glance correctly.

'Good heavens, man, have you not eaten? You can't deduce things on an empty stomach. Mrs. Johnson makes an excellent omelette,' she added, and gave him a push.

She then walked back to her own room to see if Dot had extracted any information from the unknown girl.

She had been comprehensively washed and was enduring a punitive combing of her long hair, and bearing it pretty well, it seemed. Dot had obtained a very plain skirt and blouse in a depressing serge dyed with what appeared to be bitumen, but even in these unpromising clothes the girl was rather pretty.

As Phryne entered, the hair was at last drawn back from her face and Jane sat up and sighed with relief.

'I always hated having my hair dressed,' commented Phryne. 'That's why I cut it short as soon as I could. How do you feel, Jane?'

'Very well, Miss,' said Jane calmly. 'But I still can't remember anything. It's like there's a hole in my memory. As though I was just born.'

'Hmm. There are several things about you that we know. One is that you are an Australian; the accent is unmistakable. You speak English. And there are things that you have not forgotten: how to eat with a knife and fork, how to read, how to converse. I therefore conclude that you will get your memory back in time if you don't worry at it.'

Jane looked relieved. Phryne left her to play a quiet game of solitaire, which she also remembered, it seemed, and drew Dot aside.

'Dot, those clothes!'

'Yes, Miss, I know, but that's all they had in the general store, and I had to dress her in something. You would have liked the other clothes even less than these. They don't have no style in the outback,' said Dot, to whom all places more than four miles from the GPO were country. Phryne smiled and forebore to comment.

'Never mind, they will last her until we get back to the city. How does she strike you?'

'I reckon that she is telling the truth,' said Dot twisting her plait. 'Every time she tries to think about who she is she starts to tremble and to sweat, and you can't fake that. Why she can't remember is more than I can tell. She's healthy, though skinny, and I reckon she's about thirteen. There's no bruise or mark on her and I couldn't find a lump on her head. Her eyes are clear so I don't think that she's been drugged.'

'If we can rule out trauma and drugs then I think it has to be shock, and that is something that wears off, it can't be broken through. Like Mary's Little Lamb, we leave her alone and she'll come home, bringing her tail behind her. Meanwhile the mystery deepens. I can't imagine how Mrs. Henderson was got out of the train—at least, she was dragged out of the window, but all the signs seem to indicate that she was dragged up, and unless the murderer was on the roof of the train, I don't know how that can be. Any ideas, Dot?'

'No, Miss, not at the moment.'

'Very well, let's have a brief chat with the others who were on the train and then I think that we shall go back to Melbourne. There's nothing more to do here and somehow I've gone right off trains, and Ballarat, too.'

'Me, too,' agreed Dot. 'Next time, can we take the car, Miss?'

Phryne smiled. At last, her nervous maid had been converted to the joys of motoring. But it had taken a murder to convince her.

The surviving passengers were all grouped in the pink and black breakfast-room. The pregnant woman looked washed-out and leaned on a husband who had lost all of his bounce. Mrs. Lilley's appalling children had been stuffed with so many sweets and cakes by a distracted mother and a sympathetic cook that they sat, bloated and queasy, quiet for the moment. Miss Henderson had risen and dressed and was the calmest of the group. The burns had blistered during the night and she was obviously in pain. Mrs. Johnson had served tea and coffee and Miss Henderson was sipping milk through a straw.

Phryne took her seat and accepted a cup of coffee from the hovering landlady.

Sergeant Wallace came in, a massive presence which seemed to fill the doorway, and everyone looked up, falling silent. He raised a hand, embarrassed.

'Nothing new, ladies and gentlemen, but a couple more questions and then you can go on, or go back, whatever suits you. First: did anyone notice a young guard?'

Mrs. Lilley looked up.

'Yes, a blond young man, rather good looking? He passed me twice. The first time he stopped and said hello, then the next time that I saw him he seemed to be avoiding me, but I didn't think anything of it.'

'Why not, if he was pleasant the first time?'

'Johnnie bit him,' admitted Mrs. Lilley shamefacedly. 'He was being a dog and the young man wouldn't pat him, so he bit him—I don't know why my children aren't like anyone else's!—so after that, of course, I wasn't surprised that he didn't want to talk to us again. It would be different if my husband hadn't died,' said poor Mrs. Lilley. 'And he had shell-shock so he couldn't discipline them. But oh, dear, I wish I had stayed home!'

Mrs. Lilley burst into tears. The children, shocked, clustered around her and patted her, Johnnie delivering a fierce hack to the ankle of Sergeant Wallace, whom he perceived as a persecutor of his mother. The sergeant, to his credit, winced in silence and merely held the child in a tight but comforting grip.

'You take a hold of yourself, young feller-me-lad,' he admonished. 'You be nice to your mum, now, and don't drive her mad with all your pranks. Mrs. J, perhaps you could come up with some sal volatile. Anyone else see this guard?'

Mr. and Mrs. Cotton shook their heads. They had been involved, it seemed, in an engrossing quarrel over whose duty it was to lock the back door, and this had kept them going until they had both fallen asleep. They had not noticed the young guard.

Mrs. Johnson had produced the sal volatile and Mrs. Lilley appeared to be recovering. She was, it appeared, taking her little demons to her relatives in Ballarat, and Phryne fervently hoped that they were prepared for the invasion.

'Now, if you will all give me your names and addresses and a telephone number if you have one, you can all be on your way. I've hired the station taxi to take all the stuff and the Ballarat train will be through in an hour.'

'Miss Fisher, can I ask you a question?' asked Mr. Cotton. 'Did you see this guard? And do you think that he was the murderer?'

'Yes, I saw him, and I think he might have been the murderer,' answered Phryne carefully. 'And I have a question for you. Has anyone seen this girl before?'

She nodded toward the door, where Dot was escorting Jane into the room. All the passengers looked at her narrowly, and she blushed and hung her head.

'I call her Jane,' said Phryne, making a broad gesture. 'She can't remember who she is. Can anyone help?'

The Cottons shook their heads. Mrs. Lilley looked up from her sal volatile to sigh. Little Johnnie, however, gave a whoop of joy and ran forward to embrace as much of Jane as he could reach, which was about knee-level. Jane's face lit up, and she lifted the child and embraced him.

'Johnnie!' she cried. 'Your name is Johnnie!' Then the young brow clouded, and she bent her head, as though the weight of her hair pulled it down. 'But I don't know any more,' she mourned.

'Mrs. Lilley, did your children leave the first-class carriage?' asked Phryne.

Mrs. Lilley shrugged.

'They were running around all over the place, dear, for quite a while, especially when I was changing the baby. I lost Johnnie for quite half an hour, I believe, when we got onto the train. I don't know where he was, it was dark, and I was worried, but he turned up as good as gold, like he always does, bless him. He might have got out of the carriage. I'll ask him.'

'Johnnie,' she began in a calm voice. 'Tell Mummy where you met the girl.'

Johnnie, clinging tight to Jane, shook his head and shut his mouth tight.

'Johnnie, Mummy won't be angry if you went out of the carriage. Tell me, where did you meet the girl?'

Johnnie unlocked his lips long enough to say, 'No,' firmly.

'I'll give you this cake if you tell me,' bribed Phryne, and Johnnie repeated, 'No,' in a deeply regretful tone. 'Has someone told you not to tell?' persisted Phryne, and Johnnie nodded.

'A man in a uniform?' asked the sergeant, and Johnnie nodded again. 'Well, I'm a policeman, and you always have to tell policemen the truth, you know that, don't you?' Johnnie nodded again.

'Well, where did you meet the girl?' asked Sergeant Wallace, and Johnnie said, 'Dark,' and grabbed for the cake.

Phryne swung it up out of grasping distance and said, 'Dark where?'

'Paddock,' said Johnnie. 'Train stop. In paddock. She put Johnnie back on train. Chuff, chuff, chuff,' he commented. 'Cake now.'

Phryne gave him his cake. She felt that he had earned it. But the puzzle had become worse.

'Cryptic infant,' she commented as Johnnie ate about half of the chocolate cake and smeared the rest evenly over his countenance. 'What do you think he meant, Mrs. Lilley?'

'Oh dear, Miss Fisher, he's such a clever little boy, there's no telling what he meant—I mean, he may be telling the truth, but he does make things up, I'm afraid.'

'What sort of things does he make up?' asked Phryne. Mrs. Lilley blushed.

'Well, he said that there was a bear under his bed, and there simply isn't room,' she added, sounding imbecilic even to her own ears. 'And he said that his father came and tucked him in and said good night, when his father has been dead for eight months.'

'Did so,' affirmed Johnnie. 'Daddy came. Scared away the bear. More cake?' he asked, with an unexpectedly charming smile.

'Well, perhaps his father did come back to the precious pet,' commented Dot, unexpectedly maternal. Johnnie turned his face confidingly up to Jane.

'Girl in the dark,' he reiterated, as this had yielded cake before. 'In the paddock. Outside the train. Johnnie climb down. Girl lift me up. Johnnie was scared.'

'Of the bear?' asked the policeman, gently. Johnnie blushed, resembling his mother for the first time.

'Bears in the dark,' he agreed. 'Girl put Johnnie back in the light. No bears. Nice girl. Johnnie likes girl. Down now,' he requested, and Jane put him on his feet. He ran to his mother and buried his face in her skirt.

'Jane, you must have got off the train for some reason, found Johnnie there, and put him back, that's what he means by "into the light", I expect. Does any of that ring a bell?'

For a moment the girl's face had an intense, concentrated look, as if she were listening to a distant sound, but it died away. She shook her head.

'Never mind—it will come. Now, who's coming back to Melbourne with me? Miss Henderson?'

Miss Henderson looked pained.

'I would be grateful for the company,' she said with difficulty. 'Mother and I have a house, you know, but it is all shut up for the winter.'

'Good. The Melbourne train is in half an hour. Dot will help you to pack. Is there an account to pay, Mrs. Johnson?'

'No, Miss Fisher, the Railways is taking care of all that.'

'Good. Here is my card. If you recall anything that might help, then please call me on this telephone number.'

She distributed a number of her own cards: 'Miss Phryne Fisher. Investigations. 221B, The Esplanade, St. Kilda'.

She had reached the door and was leaving when she remembered something, and beckoned to the sergeant. He joined her.

'Did you find the cloth?'

'The one with the chloroform? Yes, Miss. It's in the station. Want to walk over there with me?'

Phryne laid one hand on his arm and he escorted her down the street to the small wooden building that housed the police station. It was bare but tidy, with ledger and telephone and desk.

The sergeant produced a cardboard box, from which emanated a strong stench of chloroform. He held it out. Quickly, holding her breath, Phryne shook out a strip of common white pineapple towelling, such as is supplied in public toilets and at cheap hotels. It had a faint blue thread running through it that indicated that it had belonged to someone who had their laundry commercially done.

'Cheap and nasty, and he hasn't even used the whole towel,' she commented, handing the rag back. 'I think that shows a really unpleasant form of economy. Nothing there, Sergeant. Are you going to keep this case, or will it go to CID in Melbourne?'

'Probably to CID, Miss, which is a pity. I would have looked forward to working with you,' he said, greatly daring, and Phryne took his face between her hands and kissed him soundly.

'I would have liked that too, my dear Sergeant Wallace, but I'm afraid that I must love you and leave you. Farewell,' she breezed and left to catch the train to Melbourne, abandoning a deeply impressed policeman without a backward glance.

'If she's a flapper,' mused the sergeant, wiping Passionate Rouge lipstick off his blameless mouth, 'then I'm all for 'em, and I don't care what Mum says.'

Chapter Four

'She'll have to go back from here as luggage!'
Alice Through the Looking Glass,
Lewis Carroll

Phryne caught the train with seconds to spare, as Johnnie had seriously objected to parting with Jane, and had to be placated with yet more cake. Dot, with customary efficiency, had loaded all Phryne's belongings, Miss Henderson, Jane, and herself aboard ten minutes before, and was in a fever lest Phryne should miss this train and have to wait for the next, which was a slow one, stopping at all the intervening stations. Miss Henderson smiled wryly through her blisters and remarked, 'She must be a sore trial to you.'

Dot immediately bridled. No one criticized Phryne in front of her and got away with it.

'She's the dearest, sweetest, cleverest mistress any woman could get,' she declared. 'She's only late because she's stopped to soothe that crying child. She's been very good to me and I won't hear a word against her.'

'My apologies,' muttered Miss Henderson, rather taken aback. 'I did not mean any insult.'

Before Dot could reply, Phryne herself came running, flung herself aboard the train, and sat down panting.

'Whew!' She fanned herself. 'I thought I'd never bribe that small monster to silence. He's going to be as fat as a little pig if someone doesn't take him in hand.'

The train started with a jerk, and Phryne found the novel which she had been reading, and handed to Miss Henderson her copy of *Manon Lescaut*. She accepted the book, nodded her thanks, and opened it. The carriage was silent all the way to Melbourne.

<>·<>·<>

Phryne had telephoned ahead, and Mr. Butler was at the station to meet them. Phryne's houseman was proudly at the wheel of the massive and elegant fire-engine red Hispano-Suiza, Phryne's prize possession. Even she did not like to think of what she had paid for it, but it was worth every penny. The coachwork, applied by a master, had been lovingly polished, and all the brass and chrome glittered in the still, cold air. Jane drew in an audible breath at the sight of the magnificent car.

'Is it not lovely?' asked Phryne dotingly, as Mr. Butler climbed out to pile the luggage in the back, and to seat the ladies. Jane nodded, awed. Even Miss Henderson seemed impressed.

'Soon be home, ladies,' said Mr. Butler bracingly. 'Mrs. Butler has a nice small luncheon on the stove and your rooms are all ready. Nice cup of tea as soon as you get in,' he added, as he was convinced that the cure for almost all feminine woes was a nice cup of tea.

'I've rung Dr. MacMillan as you asked, Miss,' he said in an undertone to Phryne, who had seated herself in the front seat, consenting to be driven for this time. 'She'll be along directly, she says, and she can come to lunch.'

'Very good, Mr. B., you've done well. Sorry to land back on your hands after promising to be away for a week,' she said, and Mr. Butler grinned as he started the big car and moved away from the kerb.

'Oh, that's all right, Miss. It's too quiet without you around.'

'You know that we have had a murder?' she asked, and the grey head nodded, his eyes on the road.

'Yes, Miss, them newspaper reporters were around this morning, looking for a story. I told 'em you weren't here, and they slunk away, but they'll be back, though perhaps not tonight. It's in all the papers, Miss. I've bought 'em, as I thought you'd like to see 'em.'

'Excellent. Quite right. But we might keep them away from Miss Henderson. It was her mother, you know.'

Mr. Butler whistled.

'They're up in your sitting room, Miss,' he said. 'Mrs. B. thought as how you might be bringing the poor lady home.'

They arrived at Phryne's bijou residence somewhat shaken and partially frozen, and did not see much of the house as they were ushered inside to a blazing log fire and the cheering scent of hot buttered muffins, cinnamon toast, and pot pourri, of which Phryne was very fond. She had two big Chinese bronze bowls, encircled with dragons, and these were filled with rose leaves and petals, verbena and orris root. Beside the fireplace was a tall famille rose jar filled with wintersweet.

'Come in, my dears, and sit down,' said Phryne solicitously, ushering her guests into the salon and taking their coats.

'A bitter day for tragedy and train journeys! Mrs. B. will have some tea made instantly. Sit down, Jane, warm your hands. Miss Henderson, perhaps you'd like to lie down.'

'No, dear, I would hate to miss this fire. What a quantity of wood. And what a heat! Oh, I do love a fire. It makes even winter bearable.'

This was the first sign of enthusiasm which Phryne had seen from Miss Henderson, and it seemed genuine. Mr. Butler, having helped the ailing lady into the house, went out to park the car and assist the boy in bringing in more wood for the house. Miss Fisher was not afraid of expense in a reasonable cause and she had purchased a pyramid sized heap of dry, split wood.

The seating provided was in the form of large, overstuffed leather armchairs and a big club settee, drawn close to the fire. The overwhelming blues and greens of the room were set off by the red light. Phryne had dropped her red mantle and kicked off her shoes, flinging herself into one of the armchairs and holding out her frozen feet to the flames.

'Gosh, I think that all my toes would have dropped off if that ride had lasted another ten minutes. Ah. Tea,' she added with deep appreciation, as Mrs. Butler brought in the trolley loaded with the big silver tea pot and further plates of goodies. A glass of brandy and milk had been provided for Miss Henderson, and she sipped it decorously through a straw.

Jane took a cup of tea, added three sugars and a lot of milk, and was given a plate and free range among the edibles. Restraining a small cry of delight, which Phryne found very touching, she took a wedge of toast and a muffin to begin with.

A ring at the doorbell announced Dr. MacMillan. She bustled in, shaking water off her rough tweed coat, and was provided with tea and muffins.

'Oh, Lord, what a nasty day!' she exclaimed. 'Cold as a Monday morning in Manchester, so it is.'

'Miss Henderson, Jane, this is Dr. MacMillan, an old friend of mine. I've asked her here to have tea, and also to take a look at you both, because I am rather worried about your condition. Miss Henderson has been chloroformed, and Jane can't remember who she is.'

'Well!' The patients surveyed the doctor as she looked them up and down. Dr. MacMillan was a stout, ruddy woman of fifty, vigorous and brave, with pepper and salt hair and a weather-ruined complexion. She was dressed in a tweed gentleman's suit with formal white shirt, collar, tie, and waistcoat, and she had large, capable hands, now cradling the tea-cup. She saw a thin, frightened girl with long plaits and a bluish cast to a pale countenance, and a stately and well-dressed, intelligent woman with a burnt face, calmly sipping her drink. The doctor finished her tea and muffin and slapped down the cup.

'You first, my bird,' she said to Jane and gave her an encouraging grin. 'Lost your memory, eh? There have been times, ay there have, when I've wished that I had the losing of mine. The front room, Phryne?'

'Yes, it's all ready,' answered Phryne. Dr. MacMillan escorted Jane out.

She was back in a quarter of an hour, and Jane was, it seemed, rather relieved than otherwise by the examination. Miss Henderson arose and crossed the room under her own power, and the doctor closed the door again.

'More tea, Jane? What did Dr. MacMillan say?'

'She said there's nothing wrong with me that time won't cure, and that I should drink lots of milk and sleep and my memory will come back. Isn't she lovely?' asked Jane in a hero-worshipping trance. 'Could I be a doctor, I wonder? Not a nurse, but a doctor—like Dr. MacMillan?'

'I don't see why not, but it depends on how hard you study,' said Phryne. 'We've got it easy, compared to Dr. MacMillan. She had to fight the whole medical establishment to become a doctor—in her day they wouldn't allow women interns into the wards, in case they should see something which would shock their delicacy.'

'I think…I think I'm quite good at school,' faltered Jane.

Phryne scanned the bookshelves and gathered an armload of texts.

'Here, take one of these in turn and read aloud,' she instructed, and Jane opened *Origin of Species* and began to read with some fluency. Phryne was impressed. When the girl reached *Alice in Wonderland*, she flushed, and dropped the book.

'I've read this before,' she exclaimed. 'But I can't recall how it ends.'

'Jane, I have a high opinion of your brains. If you never get your memory back, it does not matter. If we can't find your family, I will send you to university if you want to become a doctor. So don't worry. I don't care if you never remember. Why not read the rest of Alice and see how it comes out?' Phryne left Jane lying on the hearthrug, eating cinnamon toast and dripping happy tears onto *Tractatus Philosophicus*.

'Dry old tome, anyway,' muttered Phryne, and went to find Dot.

Phryne had renovated her house extensively, and one thing of which she was rather proud was the conversion of a dull sitting-room on the ground floor back into two neat little guest rooms. Both had electric fires, and one still had the original grate. Phryne had allotted this one to Miss Henderson as soon as she had observed that lady's love affair with fire. The rooms had been washed a pale peach, with bright curtains and bed-spread in one and furnishings of a deep and soothing green in the other. Phryne hoped that Jane, who seemed to be a studious child, would not object to the grass-green, pink and black stripes which wriggled across her bed.

She made a brief check for clean towels and new soap, although she was sure that Mrs. Butler would not have tolerated a fold out of place. She was correct. Everything was in order and a small but hot fire burned in the grate in the peach and green room.

The door opened, and Mr. Butler entered, carrying Miss Henderson with apparent effort, and Dr. MacMillan turned back the bed.

'Find her a nightdress, Phryne, the poor woman's worn out with shock and pain. Thank you, Mr. Butler,' she added, and that invaluable man left the room. 'I've written a prescription for a cocaine ointment which should help. There's nothing more consistently painful than a burn, and I've given her some Chloral so she should sleep for a few hours. By then she will be feeling better, I think, but she should keep to her bed for at least a week. Are you prepared to keep her, Phryne?'

'Certainly, poor woman, she can't go home to a bare house and no care. We can look after her, Dot and me. What should we look out for?'

'I'll come each day to dress her face, we must be careful that she does not break the blisters by scratching, or she may have a scar. Otherwise she will be sleepy and sad, and will need a warm bed, plenty of liquids, and light nourishing food, which I dare say your admirable Mrs. Butler can manage. There, I'll just tuck her in, and we'll leave her alone. Is that fire safe?'

Phryne accompanied the doctor back to the sitting-room, where Jane had mopped her tears hastily and was now studying Glaister on Poisons. Dr. MacMillan observed this with pleasure.

'You're a keen study,' she commented. 'But you'd better read *Alice* while you have the chance.'

'Have you read *Alice in Wonderland?*' asked Jane, astonished, and Dr. MacMillan laughed comfortably and took a scone.

'Certainly I have, and recently, too. A fine book to keep your perspective.' She bit into the scone. 'Child, could you go into the kitchen and ask for some more tea? I'm parched with all this work.'

Jane went out, delighted to do something to help. Dr. Mac-Millan laid an urgent hand on Phryne's shoulder.

'You must keep that child safe,' she whispered, spattering Phryne with crumbs. 'She's been molested, and I fear that is why she lost her memory.'

'Raped?' asked Phryne, turning sick.

'No. Mishandled, however, and attempted, I'd say, and not too long ago. Maybe a week.'

'I'll keep her as my own rather than let anything like that happen to the poor little thing.'

'Good. That is what I hoped to hear.'

'But what if she recovers her memory?'

'You must find the man,' said Dr. MacMillan. 'I think she may have come from an orphanage. They send their girls out when they are twelve or thirteen, and rape or worse is the fate of many of them. Perhaps she should be photographed. Someone should remember her.'

Jane came back with more tea, and they read *Alice in Wonderland* aloud until it was time for a brisk walk before dinner.

Chapter Five

'I was very nearly putting you out of the window into the snow! And you'd have deserved it, you little mischievous darling!...now you can't deny it, kitty!'

Alice Through the Looking Glass,
Lewis Carroll

Five hours of sleep, and Miss Henderson awoke in pain and in fear, gasping for air.

'Where am I?' she whispered, and someone leaned over and turned up the bedside light. Dot helped Miss Henderson to sit up against her arm and found the little jar which Dr. MacMillan had instructed the pharmacist to compound.

'Don't you try and talk yet, Miss, until I can put some of this stuff on your mouth. Doctor says that it might make your face a bit numb but that'll be an improvement, eh?'

Dot smeared the cocaine ointment freely over the burns, using the little spatula supplied for the purpose, and then helped her patient to a drink.

'There, that's better, isn't it? You're in the Hon. Phryne Fisher's house, and I'm Dot.'

Dot wondered fleetingly if Miss Henderson, too, was losing her memory, but this did not appear to be the case. The woman swallowed the barley water and smiled crookedly.

'Yes, of course I remember, how nice this all is! What a lovely room, and a fire and all. And that is my favourite shade of peach.' Miss Henderson took a little more of the cooling drink. 'I can sit up on my own, really.'

'All right, Miss, is there anything I can get you? Are you hungry?'

'Why,' said Miss Henderson, 'I believe that I am hungry. Indeed, I don't think I have had anything to eat for ever so long. Can you fetch me something?'

'Yes, Miss. How about a nice omelette, now? A little toast?'

'That would be lovely,' sighed Miss Henderson, relaxing into a pile of feather pillows—in all her life she had never had more than one pillow, as her mother had considered it unhealthy—and smiling a creditable smile.

Dot obtained an omelette and Mrs. Butler set the tray daintily, including a napkin in a ring and a vase of flowers.

'She'll likely be overset, poor thing, with her mother killed and all that, not to mention being hurt,' she fussed. 'Don't you drop that tray, now, Dot!'

'I'll be careful,' promised Dot, and carried it steadily. She watched her patient eat, removed the plate, and brought in a small cup of custard and a pot of tea.

'I did not mean to insult you when I said that Miss Fisher must be a trial,' explained Miss Henderson. 'I was very fond of my mother, and she was a trial. How old do you think I am?' she went on, and Dot shook her head.

'It's hard to tell with all them burns, Miss. You sound young.'

'So I am. I am twenty-seven. Younger, I guess, than your Miss Fisher, but Mother was convinced that I would never marry. "You'll be with me until I die, Eunice," she used to say—and now it's true, poor Mother, though she never meant it like that. She was furious when Alastair came on the scene and wanted to marry me, and she did her best to get rid of him, but he proved to be of sterner stuff than the rest. She told him that she knew that he was marrying me for my money, and he just smiled and agreed with her.'

'So you've got money, Miss?'

'Oh, a modest competance. It yields me three hundred a year, and the house is mine now.'

'More tea, Miss? Do you want me to call this Alastair, then? We are on the telephone.'

'He must be frantic,' gasped Miss Henderson, her hand flying to her mouth. 'And he wouldn't know where I am! Oh, lord, Dot, please, can you call him at his rooms, and tell him that I am quite safe and he can visit me? How could I have forgotten?'

'It's been a tiring day, Miss,' said Dot, writing down the telephone number. 'I'll ring him, Miss, don't you worry. You all right to be left? I'll do it now.'

'Yes, yes, please do it now,' begged Miss Henderson, and Dot went out and closed the door.

Dot conveyed the message through the medium of a phone which appeared to be in a fish-and-chip shop somewhere in Lygon Street, Carlton. A young man's voice came on the phone, breathless.

'Hello, hello? Damn this instrument! Hello? Are you there?'

'This is Miss Williams. I am calling for Miss Henderson,' repeated Dot patiently for the fourth time. 'Are you Mr. Thompson?'

'Yes, Alastair Thompson here, Miss Williams, where is Eunice?'

'Take down the address,' said Dot. '221B, The Esplanade, St. Kilda. Call tomorrow about three.'

'Is she all right?' bellowed the voice. Someone in the background was shrieking in Italian.

'She's burned her face with that chloroform and she's upset about her mother. Come at three,' yelled Dot and hung up.

Phryne had largely cured her of her dread of telephones but she still thought them a clumsy means of exchanging ideas. She went back to Miss Henderson and advised that the young man would call the next day, and Miss Henderson looked even more alarmed.

'I can't let him see me like this!' she wailed.

Phryne, having finished dinner, walked in at this point and heard the whole story in three minutes.

'Simple, my dear, you shall have a veil. Perfectly proper and it will stop you from alarming your young man. What does he do, Miss Henderson?'

'Please call me Eunice. He's in final year Medicine, he will be on the wards next year. He's twenty-five,' she said simply, 'and he wants to marry me.'

'Very nice,' said Phryne. 'Here's your medicine, Eunice. Drink it up like a good girl and I'll see you in the morning. How do you feel?'

Eunice patted the pillow, luxuriating in more comfort than she had ever enjoyed and shocked at herself for being so pleased.

'I feel fine,' she sighed, swallowed her Chloral Hydrate (which tasted foul) and fell instantly asleep.

Dot allowed Phryne to drag her into the sitting-room.

'Come into my parlour,' said Phryne, grinning wolvishly. 'And tell all. Who is this young man?'

'He's her intended, Miss, and her mother didn't like him. That's all I know about it. Give over pulling me, Miss, I didn't get no more out of her, except that she seems to have had a fair old time with her mum. Not a nice old lady, Miss.'

'No, she wasn't. However, the plot thickens. I shall be delighted to meet this excellent young man. Care to play a game of cards, Dot? It appears that our Jane also remembers how to play chess, though she won't beat Dr. MacMillan.'

'No, thanks, Miss, I want to have a bath and go to bed. It's been a long day and I think I've a cold coming on.'

'Poor Dot! Get Mrs. B. to make you a whisky toddy, and take a really hot bath. I shall read, then—there's a new novel I haven't even glanced at, the bookshop really is hopeless—I don't even recall ordering it.'

Dot climbed the stairs to her bathroom with her whisky toddy steaming in her hand. The last she saw of Phryne for the night was her concentrated, Dutch doll face bent over a book. But it was not the latest novel. It was Glaister, on Poisons.

⟨⟩⟨⟩⟨⟩

Jane slept soundly for about three hours, and then awoke to hear a small, odd sound. She lay frozen, gripped by a fear which was all the worse because she could not tell why she should be afraid. Something was scratching at the window. Jane, trembling, was in such an agony of fear that she could not bear to lie still any longer. She threw back the quilt and put her feet to the carpet, hoping that the bed would not creak. It creaked. She froze again. The room was as cold as ice. Nothing happened. Then the scratch came again, and an odd sound like an unoiled hinge. Was someone trying to open the window? That was too much. She leapt at the window and snatched back the curtain, unlocking the latch and thrusting at the frame. The window grated open with a gush of cold sleet and something small, cold, and black half-fell into Jane's lap. She shut the window again and locked it, cradling the creature in her arms. It was a kitten, perhaps six weeks old, thin as a little bag of bones and almost as cold as the weather. Jane clutched it to her bosom, shivering and laughing under her breath.

'Oh, kitty, you gave me such a fright! You're as cold as ice. Come on, kitty, you can come back to bed with me, and then we shall both be warm.'

Still trembling, Jane carried the icy bundle of wet fur back to her brightly patterned bed with the peach sheets, the Onkaparinga blankets, and the quilt and replaced herself in the small hollow in which she had formerly lain.

The kitten, warming into life, began to wash itself with precise licks, curled under the blankets, nestling under Jane's chin. It was an unobservant animal, or it might have wondered why its rescuer cried herself to sleep.

⟨⟩⟨⟩⟨⟩

Miss Eunice Henderson, tended by Dot, was washed and breakfasted by the time Phryne came in with a selection of veils and an armload of nightgowns.

'That's a perfectly sensible gown you've got on, Eunice, but you will need a change. Perhaps you'd like to borrow some of mine? And I've brought a few hats. We should be able to cobble something together.'

Eunice touched the fabrics reverently. Crêpe de Chine, silk, satin, all the luscious delicacy and flowing draperies of a whole harem-full of houris. Eunice tried to imagine herself in one of these extravagant garments and utterly failed.

'I can't wear any of these beautiful things, really, Phryne, I just wouldn't look right in them.'

'Oh, yes you would, you have a lovely figure—do you swim?—long legs and a swan neck. Something with a high neck, I think, to show off that jaw line, especially since we are going to conceal your face. What about this?'

She exhibited a satin robe and gown, cut in a rather medieval line, with high neck and flowing sleeves. They were edged in white rabbit fur, and were of a deep, mossy green.

'They are beautiful,' said Eunice. 'All right, I will borrow them if you don't mind.'

'Of course I don't mind, old dear. Now what about this hat? It matches the gown, and it has a nice long chin-veil.'

The hat was a Paris model, made by a *couturière* who actually liked women, and it was small and plain, but superbly made. In the gown and the hat, Eunice Henderson was astonished at how…well…really…how beautiful she looked. So was Phryne, who had not expected such an excellent result.

'You really do look smashing, Eunice. I think you should stay in bed,' said Phryne. 'Dr. MacMillan said so, and I have a great deal of respect for her opinions. Wait until she has dressed your face, and then we shall don the glad rags for your young man. Good morning, Jane. What have you got?' Jane entered, still clad in the bitumen serge, and carrying something small and alive. She held it out to Phryne.

'He came to my window last night. Can I keep him? Mrs. Butler said that she needs a cat to keep down the mice, and he won't eat much. Please.'

'Of course you can keep him, Jane. He actually came to you? That is a great compliment.' She took the kitten, which was so light that she feared it might float away. 'If Mrs. B. will have a cat, then he can stay. Take him out to the kitchen and give him a lot of food. Poor little creature is all skin and bone.' The kitten, which Phryne had been stroking, purred and gave her thumb a quick lick, then walked off her hand onto Jane's shoulder, where he perched, holding onto the plait and balancing with his absurd scrap of a tail.

'Isn't he a pretty one,' commented Miss Henderson. Jane beamed.

'He will need a bath and a collar,' said Phryne. 'We will buy one this morning in town. We are going to get you some clothes, for I cannot stand that dreadful suit a moment longer. Mrs. B. will look after the kitten. Have you given him a name?' Jane paused at the door, the familiar listening look on her face.

'I think he should be called Ember,' she said, and vanished in the direction of the washing up and the milk delivery, in both of which Ember took a deep professional interest.

'She's coming along,' commented Miss Henderson. 'Poor child. Still, she's fallen on her feet, finding you. As have I. There must be some cat in my family after all.'

⟨⟩⟨⟩⟨⟩

Phryne left Dot and Mrs. Butler to look after Eunice Henderson, and spent an interesting morning in the shops with Jane. The girl had good, if restrained taste, and seemed to prefer grey and dark blue, which certainly set off her brown-blonde hair and her brown eyes. Phryne bought two suits, shoes and stockings, and sufficient underwear and shirts for a week's wear. Phryne's laundry was sent to the Chinese every week. She laughed when Phryne suggested donating her black suit to the poor, and was still chuckling when Phryne stuffed the offending garments into the hands of a woman begging on the street corner near the station.

'See, that earned us a blessing,' said Phryne. 'Giving things away is a good way of acquiring merit, and not too hard on the purse. Here's our train, now, have we got everything?' She checked over the parcels. The collar and the flea-soap for Ember; the chrysanthemums, the unspoilt product of a hothouse, for Dot, who doted on them; the small vial of expensive 'Lalla' perfume and a box of 'Rachel *poudré riz*' for Phryne; the suitcase and all the rest of the clothes were to be sent on by the shops.

'Yes, that's everything, and here's the train.'

They found a corner seat and Phryne talked amiably with the girl all the way home, reflecting that good clothes make a great difference to an adolescent. Her gawkiness had been concealed by fine tailoring, and now she was such a refreshing sight that an elderly gentleman opposite them could not take his eyes off her all the way to St. Kilda, and on their way out of the train offered Phryne compliments on her sister.

Phryne laughed, linked arms with Jane, and walked along the sea front. The wind was cold but Jane was warm inside her new woollen topcoat, and her new shoes hardly hurt her feet at all.

'Miss Fisher?' asked Jane, tugging at Phryne's arm.

'Mmm?'

'Why are you doing all this for me?'

'What? For you? Well, there are several reasons. Because that nice policeman asked me to mind you. Because I would not hand a dog over to the Welfare. Because you are a mystery and mysteries interest me. Because you are intelligent and I am interested in establishing a scholarship for intelligent girls. Because you rescue black kittens. Also,' said Phryne, stopping and turning to face the girl, 'because I was very poor, as poor as I think you must have been, and I was rescued, and I think that I should return the favour. Does that answer your question?'

'Yes,' said Jane, much relieved, and followed Phryne into the house, where luncheon was on the table.

Chapter Six

'I'm quite content to stay here—
only I am so hot and thirsty!'
Alice Through the Looking Glass,
Lewis Carroll

Three o'clock was approaching, and the house was tense. The only one who seemed unaffected by it was Jane, who spent the afternoon consoling Ember after his bath, which he had not enjoyed at all, and endeavouring to persuade him to accept the collar as a mark of respect, instead of the instrument of feline torture which was his first impression. She was not succeeding very well, to judge by the number of times Phryne heard her say, 'Now you have put all your paws into it again, you bad cat!' There would be a pause while she disentangled the kitten, an interlude while they played paperchase or had one of the light meals which Mrs. Butler served to him, and then the litany would begin again. When Phryne looked in at three, both Jane and Ember had fallen asleep on Jane's bed. Phryne threw the quilt over the two of them and closed the door.

Mrs. Butler was worrying about the milk, which might be on the turn, and the dairy had not come today. Dot was worried about the laundry, which had unaccountably lost three socks and one of Phryne's cherished moss-green pillow cases. Phryne was tense on behalf of Miss Henderson, and Eunice, having surveyed her damaged face in a mirror for the first time, had burst into tears and taken to her bed, refusing to come out from under the covers until Dr. MacMillan had threatened that she should not see her young man at all.

This was enough to drag Eunice out from under the sheets, and when she had been anointed and dressed and veiled, she really was stunning. Phryne hoped that this young man was worth all this trouble, while reflecting cynically that no young man ever was.

The doorbell rang. Mr. Butler announced, 'Mr. Thompson and Mr. Herbert'. Aha! Perhaps the young man was as nervous about this visit as Eunice had been. If so, it showed a nice spirit. It would be up to her to entertain the friend, and Phryne sighed. She had sometimes questioned the ways of the All Wise Providence in His construction of young men. She would, however, entertain the companion, however taciturn or even spotty, with as good a grace as she could muster. After all, this was a murder inquiry, and she had deliberately chosen this profession. 'I could have stayed in Father's house and arranged flowers for the county,' she reminded herself, and swept forward to greet the visitors.

To her surprise and delight, they were very good looking. Both young men of medium height, with blond hair in an Eton crop, blue eyes, the fashionable flannel bags and the anyone-for-tennis blazer, the loose white 'artistic' shirts and the innovative wrist watches. Phryne had not seen one of these before. Both of them were as athletic and as sleek as otters. The lithe lines of the shoulder and hip spoke of smooth muscle and hidden power; these were not rowdies, but they were sportsmen of some sort.

They were dressed rather casually for a visit to a lady's house and the first young man eagerly explained.

'Miss Fisher? An honour to meet such a famous Sherlock. I'm Lindsay Herbert and this is Alastair Thompson. We apologize for our attire but we were training and the coach just wouldn't let us off, even though we explained about Miss Henderson.'

'Quite all right, gentlemen—do come in. Training for what?' asked Phryne casually, leading the way into her parlour and indicating seats before the fire. Lindsay sat down, but Alastair hovered.

'Dot, could you take Mr. Thompson to Miss Henderson, please? Just a moment, Mr. Thompson. Miss Henderson has gone through a terrible experience. You must be gentle with her and not ask her a lot of questions. She can't talk easily because of the burns, but she will not be scarred. Do you understand?' The young man drew himself up haughtily.

'I am a medical student, Miss Fisher, and I know how to talk to the sick. You have no need to be concerned.'

He followed Dot, and Lindsay laid a hand on Phryne's arm.

'Don't be angry, Miss Fisher, he doesn't mean to be so rude. He's been worried sick about Miss Henderson.'

'Yes, a terrible thing,' agreed Phryne. The hand on her arm was long and strong, and warm, even though it was sleeting again outside. She smiled at Lindsay, and patted the hand.

'Will she really be all right? And is she badly hurt?'

'The burns are not too bad, but the doctor is afraid of damage to the liver. Are you a medical student, too?'

'Lord, no, I'm a humble lawyer. Got to pass this year, you know, or the Pater will cut off supplies. I've been up at the Shop for five years, and this is the sixth.'

'Oh?' asked Phryne, scanning the perfect muscular curve of shoulder and throat. The firelight became him.

'Yes, I just could not get the hang of Contracts, and then I had to repeat Trusts, because I couldn't get the hang of them, either. In any case I'll be articled next year, and I'm most interested in crime. I shall go to the bar when the Pater can be convinced to stump up, and I shall specialize in crime. Fascinating. That's why I asked old Alastair to bring me along. I wanted to meet you.'

'Well, now you have met me,' said Phryne, leaning back in the leather armchair, 'what do you think?'

'Well, Miss Fisher, I'd heard you were good at puzzles, and I'd got it into my head that you were an old maid with a bent for detection—I never thought that you...that you...'

'That I?'

'Would be beautiful,' concluded Lindsay simply, and kissed the hand which lay along the top of the settee.

'Thank you. I'm glad that you came even when you thought I was an old maid. That shows dedication. What do you think of our little murder, then?'

'She was a really nasty old woman,' said the young man slowly. 'But it is a terrible thing to kill someone. A human, I mean, however horrible or superfluous, a breathing creature; a terrible responsibility, to take someone's death on yourself.'

'But that's what most murderers are like,' said Phryne. 'They are always sure that they are right, and that gives them the moral force to take on that burden. Or sometimes it is simpler; this person is in my way, and therefore they must die; because they are in my way, they do not deserve to live. I've heard that tune often enough.'

The young man appeared disconcerted at the vehemence of Phryne's discourse, and she changed the subject. One did not wantonly disconcert young men on whom one might be having designs in future.

And she might well have designs. A very pretty young man indeed, and predisposed by his odd interest in crime to be receptive.

'Training, you said?' Phryne poured the young man a drink— a weak brandy-and-water, at his request—and he took the glass and waved it enthusiastically.

'Rowing, Miss Fisher—on the river.'

Phryne suppressed the retort that she didn't think that it was on the land.

'I'm in the eight which might make the University team, Miss Fisher, but we have to keep up to the mark, so we are training all through the winter. You might like to come down and watch us. Our coach is a tartar, old Ellis.'

'Where do you train?' asked Phryne.

'Melbourne University boathouse, Miss, I can show you where it is, and we have some fine parties there, too.'

'Indeed?' Phryne was not concentrating. She was worried about Eunice, and caught herself agreeing to come and watch him training on the morrow before she realized what she had done. I really must start listening to what I am saying, she told herself firmly, but by then it was too late.

'Have you known Mr. Thompson long?'

'Lord, yes, we were at school together—Melbourne Grammar. I was quite a new chum then, coming from London, and the other fellows would have ragged me to death had it not been for Alastair. He's a good chap. I owe him a great deal,' said the young man solemnly. 'And he's very clever. A real shark at school for all those mathematics—I couldn't get the hang of them, either—and now they say he might win the surgery prize this year. He'll be a good doctor—sort of trustworthy, you know. But a nasty temper when aroused. We were playing football once, just a friendly game, and one of the forwards copped him one on the nose, and he gave a roar and pounced, and it took three men to pull him off the bully. But the nicest, kindest fellow you could meet,' he said hastily, 'a very good friend to me. I reckon there's nothing he couldn't do if he set his mind to it.'

Phryne replenished the brandy-and-water and asked her guest to show her his wrist watch. He exhibited it wrist and all, forcing Phryne to take his hand.

'It's a good watch, the Pater sent to New York for it—they are all the rage there, I'm told—and it keeps good time.' The hand and arm were now lying across Phryne's breasts, and her breathing jogged her nipples. 'I just have to be careful to keep it…out of…the water…'

His face was close, the mouth opening on a soft lip, his skin smelling of yellow soap and masculine sweat. Phryne abandoned herself and the arms circled her, the mouth closing on hers with emphasis and skill.

Phryne had retained her deep devotion to the male sex. She took care of her body, and her virtue took care of itself. The young man was sleek and strong, an intriguing combination, and had the promise of being a very fair lover indeed. But she did not have the time to indulge in spur-of-the-moment indiscretions on couches, and she detached herself gently, putting aside the hot mouth that kissed and clung.

'No, no, not now. Come back some time, my pretty young man, and I shall be delighted to receive you—but I'm too old to be seduced in front of a fire at four in the afternoon. Oh, you are lovely.' She kissed him again, just below the ear, where his hair curled enchantingly. 'Quite lovely.'

'Oh, Miss Fisher,' gasped Lindsay, dropping to his knees in front of her and burying his head in her shoulder, 'I think I've fallen in love with you!'

'Quite possibly,' agreed Phryne briskly. 'But it will wear off. I will come and watch you train tomorrow, as I promised when I wasn't myself, and then we may make some arrangements. But I am not toying with your heart, Lindsay—just your body. It is useless to fall in love with me—I do not want to damage you. Do you understand?'

'No,' confessed Lindsay, rubbing his face against her neck. 'But whatever you say, Miss Fisher.'

'I think,' conceded Phryne, 'that you had better call me Phryne.'

Mr. Herbert gulped his drink.

<>◇<>

Eunice Henderson, safe behind her veil, surveyed her lover with doting eyes. He was not tall, just the right size, and had delightful blue eyes, which were at present clouded with worry. He was worried about *her*! The thought was intoxicating. He, in turn, was struck with how elegant his fiancée looked. The green gown revealed the long, swooping line from hip to knee, the small waist, and the light curve of her small breasts. He sat down on the chair next to her bed and took her hand. It was hot, and he wondered what her temperature was.

'How do you feel, Eunice? I'm horrified by all this.'

'I feel much better. Miss Fisher has been very kind to me. She is also going to find out who killed Mother.'

'Oh. What about the burns, Eunice? I didn't know that chloroform would burn skin like that. Poor girl! What does the doctor say?'

'She says that it will heal without a scar if I don't scratch, though that is very hard, for it itches like fury. However, it doesn't hurt any more, and it really was painful. Ally, I thought I'd never bear the train journey to Melbourne. I only managed it because I was reading *Manon* and I could hide my face. I've got some ointment and the doctor says I should stay in bed for a week yet. I do feel weak. Were you worried about me?'

'My dear girl, can you doubt it? I was just about to storm Police Headquarters when the girl rang and told me where you were.'

He kissed the hand he was holding.

'Lindsay has gone to talk to Miss Fisher, he wanted to meet her, he's a crime buff. I bet he wouldn't like murder so much if he ever saw a corpse. What happened on that train, Eu? I've only read the press reports, and they are very highly coloured.'

'I don't know. I didn't wake until it was all over. Someone drugged the train, and dragged mother out of the window, no one knows how, and then she was found dead quite thirty feet from the track, and no one knows how she got there, either. It's all a terrible mystery. If it hadn't been for Miss Fisher the children on the train would have been dead, and the doctor still doesn't know if I'll have permanent liver damage. Can we talk about something else?'

'Oh, Eu, I had no idea that it was so bad! What would you like to talk about?'

'Us,' whispered Eunice. 'Now we can marry.'

'Of course we can, as soon as you are better. Let's put the notice in the paper tomorrow. The engagement is announced between Alastair, only son of William and Charlotte Thompson, of Right Street, Kew, and Eunice, only child of the late Walter and...' He faltered, and Eunice finished the notice:

'The late Anne Henderson of South Yarra. We can't put that in the paper, can we, with Mother not even buried? After the funeral, when I am up and about again, then we can marry. Unless you've changed your mind?'

'Oh, Eunice!' exclaimed Alastair Thompson, and embraced her with sufficient fervour to convince even the most obdurate lady that her swain had not changed his mind.

<><><>

Phryne, who was not obdurate, was swapping kisses and confidences with the second pretty young man in her house. Lindsay was ardent; his breath scorched her face; his lips were demanding and could prove engrossing; but Phryne's mind, which was seldom involved with her body at all, was ticking over nicely, and she was extracting much interesting information from Lindsay in between embraces.

'So you live in the same house as Alastair? What a comfortable arrangement. Who does the housekeeping?'

'Oh, a woman comes in every morning to make the beds and cook us some dinner to re-heat,' said Lindsay, insinuating a supple hand down Phryne's back. 'What involved undergarments you wear!'

'I shall teach you how to remove them,' promised Phryne. 'You will find that skill useful in years to come. But not now. Have you no sense of timing?'

'That's what the coach always says,' chuckled Lindsay, removing his hand. 'Very well, Miss Fisher, let us be proper. Alastair hasn't got much cash, see, his people are poor—respectable, I mean, his father's a doctor—but not much lettuce, so he lives with me. Pater gave me the house, and he pays for the housekeeper, and I like the company, so it all works out well. Amazing fellow, Alastair. I'm uncommonly fond of him. You know, even when he's strapped, he's never bitten me for a fiver till Thursday? None of the rest of my acquaintance have showed that restraint. Some of them look on me as a money tree…I like this fabric, it's so smooth. What is it?'

'Silk,' said Phryne, pulling down her skirt so that it almost reached her knees. 'It is supposed to be smooth and I'm glad that you like it. I think that it's about time that I flung you and your friend into the snow, Lindsay. I'll see you tomorrow. What time?'

'Nine in the morning,' said Lindsay, reluctantly releasing Phryne. 'At the boathouse. Why are you throwing us out? Have I lost my charm, already?'

'No, my dear, you have all the charm you came with. But I have to go and read a *post mortem* report, and talk to a policeman.'

'Can I come too?'

'No. I'll see you tomorrow.' She rang the bell. 'Mr. Butler, will you see the gentlemen out? And bring the car around. I've got to go into Russell Street.'

Lindsay collected his friend and left, not without a backward glance.

'Well, what did you think of them?' she asked Dot.

Dot grinned. 'Lindsay is all right, Miss, if you like Tom cats.'

'You know that I do,' agreed Phryne.

Chapter Seven

'You'll be catching a crab directly,' said Alice.
Alice Through the Looking Glass,
Lewis Carroll

Phryne steered the red car into the city. Detective-inspector Robinson (call me Jack, Miss Fisher, everyone does) had taken over the investigation and was anxious to interview her. He had promised the *post mortem* report and any more information that came to hand.

She parked her car in the police garage and ascended the dank stairs to the small bleak office which Jack inhabited. He looked up as she entered; an undistinguished youngish man with mid-brown hair and mid-brown eyes and no feature which one could remember more than three minutes after he had gone. It was this anonymity which had made him a relentless shadow of some of Melbourne's most wary crooks. They were now languishing behind bars, wondering how they had been detected, still not recalling the ordinary man on the street corner who had followed them doggedly for days. In private life he was a quiet man with a doting family who grew grevilleas and rare native orchids in his yard. He would talk learnedly of mulch unless instantly and firmly dissuaded.

'Ah, Miss Fisher. I hope that you are well? How nice to see you again. I won't offer you police-station tea, because I'm sure you've tasted it before. I want you to tell me all about the murder on the Ballarat train.'

'Delighted,' said Phryne promptly.

As usual, she told her tale with dispatch and not an unnecessary word. Detective-inspector Robinson took notes attentively.

'Dragged through the window, eh?'

'Absolutely. I'm almost sure that she was pulled up, because of the hair caught in the crack in the sill, but where the murderer was, I cannot tell.'

'And the blond young guard. Describe him.'

'About five-ten, blue eyes, a pleasant smile, looked well built but slender, no distinguishing marks except a scar on his forehead. A cut along the brow line. All healed over. I think he was about twenty-five but he could have been younger, the cap is very disguising. I didn't pay much attention,' apologized Phryne. 'I was rather tired.'

'I could hope that all the witnesses that I interview weren't paying attention like that,' said the detective-inspector. 'What about motive?'

'The daughter had the best motive.' Phryne crossed her legs and tugged her black skirt down, lest she should distract the policeman. 'But I don't think that she did it. She could have shoved her mother out of the train and then doped herself. She might not have known that chloroform burns skin. I met her fiancé today, and he didn't know, and he's a medical student.'

'What did you make of him, Miss Fisher?'

'An arrogant young man, but most doctors are like that. About medium height, with pale hair and blue eyes, as was his pretty friend, they could be twins. Both strong, I should say, and active. It might be an idea to ask the attentive Mr. Thompson where he was on the night in question.'

'You didn't take to him, Miss Fisher?' asked the detective. 'What about the other one, his friend?'

'Lindsay Herbert. A very nice, if rather gushing and naïve, young man. I took to him, and he took to me, and stuck to me like glue, almost as if he had been instructed to do so.'

'What, Miss, did the young hound try to take advantage of you?' gasped the detective-inspector, and Phryne chuckled.

'If there is any advantage to be taken, Jack, you can rely on me to take it. I can cope with Master Lindsay. I didn't really have a chance to talk to Thompson. Perhaps you will have more success.'

'Perhaps. I shall certainly do so, and that at the earliest. Where do they live, these students?'

'In digs in Carlton, I fancy. But I know where they will be at nine tomorrow morning.'

'Where?'

'Rowing. I am going down to the boathouse to watch them practice. Perhaps you would like to come too?'

'Yes, Miss Fisher, I think that I might.'

'Good. Now, the autopsy report.'

Phryne scanned the buff folder critically, attempting to translate the medical terms into something that might relate to the broken body of the old woman. It seemed that all of the gross fractures had been inflicted after death, including the massive blow which had cracked the skull. The cause of death had been...

'Hanging? That's what that means, isn't it, Jack? Fracture of the cervical vertebrae?'

'Yes, Miss. Hanging it is. The hyoid bone in the throat which is always broken when there is a death by strangulation was fractured but the doctor says that it was a broken neck. That's how you die if you are hanged, Miss. The sudden jerk.' He mimed the rope pulling taut and the sickening flop of the broken neck, and Phryne shuddered.

'Don't, Jack, please, it's too awful. What could have happened? The first bit is clear. Someone doped the carriage and sent us all to sleep, and perhaps we were meant to sleep forever. Then no one would be able to tell when the body was removed, or how, but I woke up too soon. How that murderer must be disliking me, for I foiled his little plan proper. All right, the carriage is full of people all asleep, and the old woman is dragged out—with a rope around her neck?—suspended, and dropped.'

'Don't forget the Ballan doctor's theory.'

'The man is deranged, it's too ghastly to contemplate.'

'And how is the girl, the one who lost her memory?'

'Jane? I call her Jane, she hasn't remembered. I shall have a photographer take some pictures of her, and perhaps you can have them distributed among the stations and your staff. Someone must have lost her. I'm keeping her anyway, she's been molested, and if that is what triggered her off, then I am going to skin the man alive if she remembers who he is. She's a very clever girl and I expect to have her recalling her past any day now.'

'Sexually molested?'

'So Dr. MacMillan says.'

'Poor little thing. You'll let me in on the arrest, Miss Fisher, as usual?'

'You will have to be quick,' said Phryne grimly, and Jack Robinson nodded.

'You didn't kill that child-molesting bastard we arrested in Queenscliff,' he said gently. 'Even though you did shoot him a bit.'

'That's because I promised to deliver him to you in a plain brown wrapper,' said Phryne reasonably. 'This one is all mine.'

Wisely, the detective-inspector decided not to pursue the subject, and returned to the matter of murder on the Ballarat train.

'I've checked up on all the guards and railway employees on that train, by the way, and Wallace was right—not one of them under forty. You are sure that it was a young man?'

'Positive,' said Phryne, recalling the smooth, unlined throat and chin.

'I shall see you tomorrow, then, Miss Fisher—at the Melbourne University boathouse,' and the policeman escorted Phryne out of the building and down the steps. She was restless, aroused by the ardent young man's attentions, and decided to pass some blameless hours in the museum and art gallery. There she spent some time before the Apollo, a copy of the Belvedere, and tore her salacious mind away with some difficulty.

Phryne was home in time for a pleasant dinner and a bath, then put herself to bed early, sober and alone.

<>‹›<>

Dot woke Phryne with a cup of Turkish coffee at eight-thirty, and informed her half-asleep mistress that it was a nasty damp chill morning, but that it was not actually raining. She added that Mr. Butler had taken Jane to the photographer and that Miss Henderson was still asleep. Phryne absorbed the coffee, which was as close as one got to neat caffeine, washed, and dressed in boots, trousers, and a heavy jacket. Dot found a suitable hat and an umbrella and gloves and assisted Phryne to start the huge car.

'I must have been mad to agree with this,' she commented. 'Steady she goes, Dot. Thanks, go inside quickly before you freeze to the spot. Back directly,' she called, and put the Hispano-Suiza into gear.

She drove without haste, threading the traffic through the city and out onto the road which circled the gardens, finding the turn without backing more than enough to ruin the temper. The track down to the boathouse was rough, but not too muddy, and the big car negotiated it with ease. She stopped and got out, and the first thing that she saw was a long wooden shell with eight pairs of legs, locomoting down to the water.

A further glance showed her that this was a racing boat being carried by its crew. She waved, and a forest of hands waved back; evidently the crew were not used to being watched while training, and appreciated the company. A small man, thin, with a red face and fanatic's eyes, was climbing onto a very new and shiny bicycle.

He gave Phryne a disapproving glare in passing, and wobbled down onto the towing path. The crew had dropped their boat neatly into the water, where it seemed to float as light as a leaf, and then they all hopped in with scarcely a ripple, oars extended. Phryne saw the beautiful Lindsay and Alastair, who was rowing stroke. He still looked nervous and strained. Phryne heard the command: 'Racing start! Three quarter!' and the boat slid quickly into the stream. 'Half!' and the oars feathered and dipped with speed. 'Three quarter and go!' and the boat was moving swiftly down the waterway, the coach toiling alongside on his bicycle. They were under the bridge, and Phryne had to strain her eyes to see them. By one of those freaks caused by the combination of sound and water, she heard the command 'Bow and two!' and the boat spun on its axis and sped down the river towards her. It seemed to be travelling quite fast, and the coach was toiling over his handlebars. This did not interrupt his breath in the slightest, and he was shouting opprobrious epithets like a sergeant-major.

'Jones, pull your stomach in! Get your hands round that oar, Hoskins! You aren't stirring soup! What's the matter with you, Herbert, dreaming about your lady friend? Put your back into it! Catch! Finish! Catch! Finish!'

He roared to a halt and glared as the crew regained the boathouse.

'You row like a lot of schoolgirls! How do you row?'

'Like schoolgirls, sir,' came the obedient chorus, and Mr. Ellis grunted, seeming to breathe fire through his nostrils. 'That's right! That so-called racing start was slower than a nurse and a pram! So we do it again! And if you are still thinking about your lady friends,' here he gave Phryne a furious look, whiffling the ends of his bristly black moustache, 'or your breakfasts, you'll never make the team! All right! Racing start! And this time, keep your minds on what you are doing!'

The crew lifted the oars again, and Phryne wandered away from the bank and found a seat and lit a cigarette. She had a book in her pocket and was just wondering whether Lindsay would be mortally offended if she read it, when she glanced up and saw the sight of the year, which more people claimed to have witnessed than would have fitted on the bank, even standing on each other's shoulders.

The choleric coach, aroused to apoplexy by some fault in the crew's performance, raised his megaphone to curse them heartily and found that there was a dip in the towing path. With a final, full-throated cry of 'schoolgirls!' he careered down the bank, losing control of the bike but retaining his grip on the megaphone, and with a muffled 'Argh!' was seated on the bicycle and clutching the megaphone in seven feet of water. The boat swept past, full of rowers so paralysed with shock that they did not know how to react, and so appalled that they did not dare to laugh. They turned at the bridge and came back, extending an oar for Ellis to hang on to, but he had struggled to the shore by then and was standing by the boathouse, muddy and dripping, dredging river weed from his megaphone.

'Be here tomorrow, and be on time,' was all he said, and stalked away, while Phryne bit her finger to still the hysteria which threatened to choke her. The crew carried the shell out of the water and stowed it and the oars, by which time the coach had disappeared around the corner. Lindsay howled with mirth, followed by all but the serious Alastair.

'Oh, oh, my ribs will crack!' protested Lindsay, hanging on to Phryne's shoulder as she wiped her eyes. 'He'll never live it down, never. Poor old Ellis! Schoolgirls! Well, Miss Fisher, you can't say that we aren't amusing company. I'll just have a shower and change, and then I'll be at your service. If you don't mind waiting?'

Phryne inclined her head, and was instantly the centre of a vocal group. It appeared that her reputation as a detective had gone before her.

'Would you come along and talk to some of the fellows, Miss Fisher?' asked an eager young man. 'We'd love to hear about your experiences.'

I bet you would, thought Phryne. But you aren't going to.

'I am talking to the fellows,' she temporized, 'and you should get an introduction to a real detective. I'm just an amateur. Are you all students?'

'Yes, Miss Fisher, but in different faculties. Edwards and Johnson are Music, Herbert and Tommy Jones are Commerce, Thompson and Connors are Medicine and the other Herbert is Law. I'm Arts, unlike all these blundering oafs. Just now we are pondering whether it would be better to request the ladies to join us in song and beer, but mostly song, as our glee club is running out of glees which sound good with only tenor and bass.'

'The trouble with scoring the Elizabethan stuff for the male voice is that it all sounds so Russian,' complained one of the music students. 'And a little of that goes a long way, you know.'

'I agree entirely. What's wrong with asking the ladies to join?'

'Well, it seems silly, but we are all friends together, and we get drunk together and no one minds, and we tend to sing rather rude songs, and the ladies...'

'Shall we make a little bet?' suggested Phryne. 'Put your groups together for some madrigals, and I'll bet you five pounds to a row down the river in a real boat that they know much ruder ones.'

'Bet,' said the Arts student instantly. 'My name is Black, Miss Fisher, Aaron Black, and I'm by way of being convenor of the Glee Club. We'll ask the girls, because we want to do the Brahms *Liebeslieder*, and we shall have a bit of a sing in the boathouse on—say, Friday? Yes? And will you come, too? I know that the ladies would love to meet you—and I'm sure that you can sing. Unlike Tommy over there, who is tone deaf.'

'Yes, I can sing,' agreed Phryne. 'What time? And shall I bring anything?'

'Some beer would be nice,' said Aaron Black. 'You will come, then?'

'If that place has any heating, yes.'

'It shall be heated, if I have to bribe the furnace man with gold,' said Aaron. 'Till then, Miss Fisher.'

Alastair passed her on his way into the boathouse, but he did not say a word. Phryne went back thoughtfully to sit in the car and was presently joined by Lindsay, clean and dressed in old flannels and a cricket jumper.

'I never thought that you'd really come,' he said quietly. 'I am honoured, Miss Fisher.'

'Get in,' invited Phryne, 'I'm freezing here. What nice fellows your crewmates are. They've invited me to a sing-song in the boathouse on Friday. Are you coming? Can you sing?'

'Yes, and yes,' agreed the young man, slicking back his hair. 'Nothing would keep me away from you, Phryne. And I carol a very neat stave, if I do say so myself.'

'Sing to me,' requested Phryne. 'Shall you come home with me?' she added, with such hidden emphasis that Lindsay's admirable jaw dropped.

'Yes,' he stammered, and Phryne started the car.

As they negotiated the muddy path, the young man began to sing, in a pure, unaccented tenor:

Since making whoopee became all the rage,
It's even got into the old bird cage,
My canary has circles under his eyes…

Chapter Eight

'I never put things into people's hands—that
would never do—you must get it for yourself.'
Alice Through the Looking Glass,
Lewis Carroll

'I should like a word with you, if you please,' said an undistinguished man courteously, flashing a badge. Alastair was leaving
the boathouse in search of any vehicle which was going to Carlton when a hand fell on his shoulder. 'I'm Detective-inspector
Robinson, and I'm investigating the murder of Mrs. Henderson.
I gather that you know her daughter.'

'Yes, I do, we are engaged to be married. I don't know anything about the murder.'

'Just for the record, sir, where were you on the night of the
twenty-first of June?' asked the policeman, taking out a notebook.
'Perhaps we might sit down on this seat here, you look tired.'

'I'm not tired,' snapped the young man. 'And I'm not telling
you anything. I don't have to tell you what I was doing.'

'No, sir, you don't have to tell me, but if you don't then I will
have to find out, and it would be easier all round if you told
me,' said the detective easily. 'That was the night of the murder,
and I will be asking all of the persons involved what they were
doing. Just for elimination, you understand. Were you at home?'

'I suppose so,' agreed Alastair grudgingly. Detective-inspector Robinson made a laborious note.

'I see, and was anyone with you?'

'No. My room-mate was out. All night. I don't know where he was, either. You'll have to ask him.'

'I don't see what business it is of mine, as he isn't involved with this matter at all.'

'Oh, isn't he? I tell you one thing, that female harpy has got her claws into him. She collected him like a parcel and he's gone off with her in her big red car.'

'Well, that's not my affair either, is it? Or yours, sir.' Robinson did not correct the young man, although he knew that harpies are always female. Robinson had been to a public school.

'That's none of my concern. What were you doing, at home and all alone? Did anyone call?'

'No. I was quite alone all night and I can't prove it. So put that in your pipe and smoke it,' added the young man fiercely. 'I don't have to answer to you! And unless you want to arrest me now, I'm going home.'

'I'm not arresting you,' said the policeman calmly, 'yet.'

'Then I'm going,' said Alastair defiantly. He walked a few paces, stopped and glared, as if defying Robinson to make a move, then strode away.

'Well, that may be the product of injured innocence, and it may not,' mused the detective-inspector. 'A little more inquiry should settle it. And Miss Fisher has taken the other one home with her, has she?' he chuckled. 'Pity I can't use her methods of interrogation. I'm sure that they would be more fun.' He went back to his police car and drove decorously back to Russell Street.

On arrival, he found a packet of photographs on the desk, with a note from Dot.

'Dear Mr. Robinson,' he read. Dot still did not like policemen, but she did like Robinson, so she did not use his title. 'Miss Fisher said to send these to you. She also wants me to tell you that the girl is five feet tall, weighs six stone, and has brown eyes and brown hair. She has no distinguishing—' Dot had taken several tries to manage this word—'marks or scars except a brown mole on her right upper arm. She says that she has had the pictures taken in the old frock she wore on the train, and hopes that you can find out who lost her. Yours truly, Dorothy Williams (Miss).'

The photographs showed a thin, pale young woman with long hair. Anyone who knew the girl ought to recognize her from them. The detective-inspector called up his minions, sent out the negative plates to be copied and distributed, and also ordered a discreet watch on the angry medical student. 'Just,' he said to himself, 'in case.'

<>< ><>

Phryne arrived home, found that Dot and Jane had gone back with Dr. MacMillan to the Queen Victoria Hospital to observe casualty, and Miss Henderson was ensconced for the day in her bed with a new novel. Mrs. Butler was expecting the dairy-boy and the baker, and so was relieved of her anxieties in the matter of the milk. Phryne put in an order for hot chocolate and raisin toast and led the bemused young man up the stairs to her private chambers.

These were decorated in her favourite shade of green; curtains and carpets were mossy, and even the sheets on her bed were leaf-coloured. It was a little like being in a tree, the young man thought, as he sank down onto a couch which yielded luxuriously to his weight and seemed to embrace his limbs.

Lindsay Herbert had seen many movies, and he was reminded forcibly of Theda Bara in *Desire*. She, however, had reclined on a tigerskin rug, and Miss Fisher had only common sheepskin.

The fire was lit, the room was warm, and Lindsay was alert, aroused, and tense. Had she brought him here only to tease him, to raise him to an unbearable pitch of desire and then to disappoint him? He had known such women. He hoped that Phryne was not one of them, but he was neither sure nor certain, and sipped his hot chocolate suspiciously.

He began to realize that she was in earnest when she dismissed Mr. Butler, told him that she was not to be disturbed, and threw the bolt on the door. Now these three rooms were cut off from the rest of the house, although household noises could be heard through the floor; the voice of Mrs. Butler giving the dairy-man a piece of her mind in reference to the soured milk of yesterday, and the noise of Mr. Butler using the new vacuum cleaner on the hall carpet.

Lindsay put down the cup and stood up, and Phryne put a record on the gramophone. She wound it up with some force and placed the needle on the spinning disc, and there was Bessie Smith, the thin, feline voice, lamenting, 'He's a woodpecker, and I just knock on wood…'

Phryne slid into Lindsay's arms and whispered, 'Let's dance.' They began to foxtrot slowly to the woman's lament. Lindsay was keenly alive to the scent of Miss Fisher's hair, the smoothness of her bare arms, and when she raised her head, he laid his mouth to her throat and clutched her close.

'Oh, Phryne,' he breathed and her voice came, cool and amused.

'Do you want me?'

'You know I do.'

'Well, I want you, too,' she returned, her hands dropping to the buttons of his shirt. The song ground to an end and the gramophone ran down. Phryne peeled off the young man's shirt and caressed the shoulders and back, smooth and lithe and muscular, unblemished, young. Here were no hard lumps of football muscle, but the long sinews of a runner. Lindsay, striving to control hands that trembled, undid the hook at the back of Miss Fisher's beautiful woollen dress, and then fumbled his way down until the dress dropped, and she was revealed in bust-band and petticoat and gartered stockings. He noticed that she had jazz garters, all colours, as she sat down on the couch and extended her legs for him to remove them. As he rolled the silk, trying not to snag it, he relished the smoothness of her naked skin, and saw that she, too, trembled at his touch.

The petticoat, it appeared, came off over her head, and the bust-band undid at the back.

Phryne took her lover by the hand and led him to her big bed, in the warm room, and lay down. Her body seemed almost luminous against the dark-green sheets, and Lindsay, for a moment, was overcome and thought that he might faint. Her scent was musky now, female and demanding, and he was afraid that he might hurt her.

She wriggled a little, and was underneath him; he was not sure how she had got there. He felt the delicate bones, overlaid with fine skin, at her hip and her chest; ran his hands down her sides as she thrust up her breasts to his mouth.

As the lips closed, Phryne gave a soft cry, and Lindsay was inside her, the strong but liquid, blood-heat tissue and muscle clutching and sucking, and Lindsay realized that she did not mean to cheat him.

All previous half-frightened, half-bold encounters in bushes, which had been the pitch of his sexual experience before, vanished before this bath of sensuality. The woman was strong and as lithe as a cat; she twisted and moved beneath and above him, stroking and kissing; she loved the touch of his hands and body in the same way as he loved the contact of her skin on his own. He detected the ripple of her desire as it reached its climax; he fell forward onto her body as she flexed and gasped and was clutched close in her arms.

Lindsay Herbert buried his face in Phryne's shoulder and began to weep.

Phryne, assuaged, held him close, his tears pooling in the hollow of her collarbone, until he sniffed and shook his head, and then she said gently, 'Are you regretting the loss of your innocence, my dear?'

The young man raised a glowing, wet face to hers and said, 'Oh, no, no, it was just so lovely, so lovely, Phryne, I couldn't bear it to end…I mean…'

Phryne released him and he rolled away to dry his eyes on the sheet. He laid a calloused hand on her thigh, and laughed. Phryne sat up.

'If that is the joy of conquest, my sweet darling, then I can't approve of it. Come and lie down again. I like the feel of your body, Lindsay—you are an intriguing mixture of smooth and strong.'

He stretched out beside her and yawned.

'I thought that you were a vamp,' he said artlessly, and was mildly offended when Phryne began to laugh. 'No, don't laugh at me. I mean, vamps always lead men on, and arouse them, and then abandon them.'

'Well, I certainly aimed to arouse lust,' agreed Phryne, gurgling with suppressed laughter, 'but I had no intention of leaving you unsatisfied. And there's no hurry, my sweet. We can stay here all day. Unless you have something else to do?'

Lindsay pulled a grim face.

'You realize that you've made me miss three lectures,' he reproved, and Phryne pulled him down into her arms again.

'And I shall make you miss another three,' she said, sealing his protesting mouth with her own. Lindsay knew when he had met a determined woman. He submitted.

<>◇<>

Miss Henderson, on inquiring as to the whereabouts of Miss Fisher, was told by Mr. Butler that she was in conference and could not be disturbed. Mr. Butler's face was perfectly straight. He was pleased that Miss Fisher had dropped the painter who had been her last lover. The painter had left partly-finished canvases all over the place and had washed his brushes in Mrs. Butler's pristine kitchen sink. A law student, Mr. Butler reflected, was likely to be much cleaner around the house.

<>◇<>

Awakening from a light sleep, Lindsay turned over with a muttered curse, loath to leave the most ravishing dream he had enjoyed for...well, for all of his life. His face came into contact with Phryne's sleeping breast and he woke, and kissed her.

'Oh, Phryne, so you weren't a dream!'

'Quite real and indeed palpable,' agreed Phryne. 'But I must get up, Lindsay darling. I've got things to do.'

'Yes, I know,' said the young man, holding her firmly and pinning her down with one knee. 'Later.'

'Later,' Phryne succumbed, laughing.

〈〉〈〉〈〉

Lindsay was in the bathroom, wondering which of the golden dolphin taps would yield hot water, when there was a thunderous banging at the front door, and he heard the admirable Mr. Butler open it.

'I must see Miss Henderson,' he heard Alastair say, in a muted roar which meant that he was very angry indeed. Phryne pulled on a robe and joined him in listening.

'Very well, sir, if you would care to wait I will ascertain if she is at home,' Mr. Butler replied.

Alastair yelled, 'You know she's at home!'

Mr. Butler said crushingly, 'I meant, sir, that I would find out if she is at home to you.'

There was a silence, during which they could hear feet pacing to and fro across the tiles of the landing. The door to Miss Henderson's room opened and shut.

'Miss Henderson will see you, sir.'

The feet ran down the hall. Phryne heard the door crash open.

'Eunice, have you had the infernal nerve to call in the police?' shouted Alastair, and Phryne swore.

'Hell! Has the man no heart? What did I do with my clothes?'

She dragged on some garments and ran down the stairs, with the half-naked Lindsay close behind her.

'Mr. Thompson, I must ask you not to make such a noise!' she said icily, and he turned on her a face white with fury.

'You traitorous bitch! What have you done with my friend? All you women are alike—all betrayers and whores!'

He swung back his arm, meaning to slap Phryne across the face, and found himself on his knees with a terrible pain in his elbow. Miss Fisher's face, calm and cold, was three inches from his own, and he could smell the scent of female sexuality exuding from her skin. It turned him sick.

'Make one move and I'll break your arm,' said Miss Fisher flatly. 'What do you mean, storming into my house like a bully? Call me a traitor, will you? Here is your friend. I haven't hurt him. I have pleased him—and perhaps that's more than you could have done, hmm? Go on. Try to hit me again.'

Lindsay, aghast, had stopped on the stairs when he realized that Phryne did not need any help. The fight was going out of Alastair. At the same time, Dot and Jane came to the front door, Miss Henderson started to cry, Mr. Butler picked up the telephone to call the police and Mrs. Butler appeared from the kitchen with the poker. Alastair stood up slowly, glared at Phryne, turned, and walked out of the house.

'The fun's over,' said Phryne, pushing back her hair. 'Come down, Lindsay. Mr. B., shut the door, and serve some drinks. Don't distress yourself, Miss Henderson, it's just a brainstorm of some kind, he'll be better tomorrow. Dot, Jane, how nice to see you. Come in and I think I will open a bottle of champagne, Mr. B. It has been a very good day, otherwise.'

Phryne sank down on the couch and set about dispelling the sour aftertaste of Alastair's violence with vivacity and Veuve Clicquot.

Chapter Nine

*'Although she managed to pick plenty of
beautiful Rushes...there was always a
more lovely one that she couldn't reach.'*

Alice Through the Looking Glass,
Lewis Carroll

Phryne woke from an uncomfortable dream—not precisely a
nightmare but certainly not a delightful reverie—and found that
during the night she had pulled a pillow over her face, which
probably accounted for it.

Next to her, sleeping like a baby, lay the beautiful Lindsay, as
sleek as a seal, and utterly relaxed. Phryne picked up his hand,
and dropped it. It fell limply.

'Out to the world,' she observed, and went to the bathroom
to run herself a deep, hot, foaming bath, scented with 'Rose de
Gueldy'. Then she sat down on the big bed and looked at her
lover, finding herself unexpectedly moved by his beauty and
his gentleness. Her motives in seducing him had been mixed,
to say the least; among them lust and the desire to hammer a
wedge between him and his friend Alastair predominated. He
had been an engrossing, untiring, eager lover and an apt pupil,
and she almost envied the lucky young woman whom he would

marry. Like Janet in the old ballad of Tam Lin, 'she had gotten a stately groom'.

He sighed and turned over, revealing the ordered propriety of bone and muscle that was his back, and Phryne was about to slide down beside him again when she bethought herself of her bath, and went to take it, getting to the taps seconds before it overflowed.

She soaked herself thoroughly, and only rose from the foam like Aphrodite when Mr. Butler tapped at the door with the early morning tea.

'Good morning, Mr. Butler,' she said, accepting the loaded tray, and the houseman smiled at her.

'Good morning, Miss Fisher, you are looking well, the young man has done you good. I've brought the papers, Miss Jane's photograph is in them.'

'Thank you, Mr. Butler,' and Phryne shut the door, woke Lindsay with a cup of tea, and sat down beside him to survey the news.

Jane's photograph occupied a column of page three, with the caption, 'Do you know this girl?' Phryne thought that it had come out uncommonly well, and should produce results. Lindsay sat up sleepily and drank his tea, and Phryne settled back comfortably against his shoulder.

'I don't know if I dare go back to my digs,' confessed the young man who had done Miss Fisher so much good. 'How can I look old Alastair in the eye?'

'Mmm?' asked Phryne and Lindsay tried to explain.

'You see, we've known each other almost all our lives, and we've always done everything together—we used to climb together, but Alastair had an accident with another climber. He was killed by a falling rock, and Alastair thought that it was his fault, though it wasn't, of course, rocks can happen to anyone, then we were in the school play together—he was a good actor. I remember him doing Captain Hook, limping around waiting for the crocodile…tick…tick…with his face all scarred.'

'Oh? How did he do that?' asked Phryne, who was not really listening.

'Glue, Phryne—just glue. You must have noticed how it puckers up your skin if you spill it. A line of glue on the face and there's your scar. Perfect. Then we joined the Glee Club, and because we couldn't climb anymore, he suggested that we take up rowing, and we've always done everything together, except…'

'Except this,' said Phryne, kissing him on his swollen mouth. 'But it was bound to happen, Lindsay. Didn't you feel left out when he took up with Miss Henderson?'

'Well, no, she never seduced him, and I always thought her a very dull girl, with that frightful mother. I could never understand what he saw in her, really. A very good girl, of course, but no conversation. She used to just sit there and adore him and her mother would sit there and abuse him, and I refused to go there again, I just couldn't see the amusement in it. But he seemed devoted, though he never talked about her. Then again, words could not express what I feel about you, so there it is. And I must get up and go to training,' said the young man reluctantly. 'Shall I see you again?'

'Do you want to?'

'More than anything else.'

'Then you shall. But not tonight. I shall see you Friday at the Glee Club singalong, and you shall come home with me again, if you like. Today's Wednesday. That should give you time to recover.'

'I'll never recover,' declared Lindsay Herbert gallantly, and escorted Phryne down to breakfast.

Lindsay was just about to leave when the doorbell rang and Mr. Butler allowed a crestfallen Alastair to enter. The student was bearing a huge bundle of out-of-season roses and did not even start when he came face to face with Lindsay and Phryne.

'I came to say how sorry I was about that scene yesterday,' he said in a low voice, thrusting the flowers at Phryne. She sidestepped neatly.

'Take them to Miss Henderson, she's the one you have hurt.' Phryne's voice was cold. 'You didn't do me any harm.'

'Lindsay, old man, I'm sorry,' said Alastair, and Lindsay took his hand and shook it warmly.

'That's all right, Alastair. I'll wait for you and we shall go to training together.'

Lindsay sat down in the hall and Alastair went to make peace with his fiancée.

From the cry of delight which Phryne heard from outside the door, where she was unashamedly listening, it seemed that he had succeeded. He came out five minutes later, collected Lindsay, and went off down the path, a picture of humility.

Dot wondered that Phryne shut the door behind them with such a vindictive slap.

The phone rang as she was walking down the hall, and Phryne took the call herself.

'Yes, this is Miss Fisher…yes, the Honourable Phryne Fisher,' Dot heard Phryne say impatiently. 'A missing girl? Where was she last seen?' She was scribbling notes on the telephone book. 'I see, outside Emily MacPherson? Someone actually saw her go? Good. A description of the abductor please…yes. Portly but respectable…all right. Do you have a photograph of her? Good. And some idea of her destination? Oh, dear. I see. Gertrude Street, eh? She has been seen there? By whom? Never mind, I suppose that I don't need to know that, really. Send me the photograph and I'll do what I can. Yes, Mr. Hart, I will reassure her that you still want her…of course. Send the photograph as soon as you can. You shall have her home soon if that is where she is. Goodbye.'

'What is it, Miss?'

'Troubles rarely come singly, Dot. That was a Mr. Hart who wants me to retrieve his daughter Gabrielle from a brothel in Fitzroy, whence she was enticed from outside the Emily MacPherson School of Domestic Science by a portly but respectable gentleman. And her father wants her back, convinced that she has been mesmerized. It sounds highly unlikely to me. However, I shall take the photo and do the brothel rummage with Klara. She knows everyone on Gertrude Street. Nothing I can do until the picture arrives. Now who is calling, for God's sake?'

It was the estate manager. Phryne stamped into her salon and awaited him with scant patience. She was not in the mood for business.

Phryne spent an irritating morning arguing with Mr. Turner who wanted her to buy more shares. Phryne was acquiring land, and selling off her speculative shares, sometimes even at a loss. The only ones she consented to keep were beer, tobacco, and flour.

'I don't care,' she finally shouted, out of all patience with the man. 'I don't care if shares in some Argentinian gold mine are going cheap. They can't be cheap enough for me. I want houses and I want government stocks, and that's all I want, except perhaps some more jewellery. That is my last word, and if you do not carry out my wishes, I will find a solicitor who can. Mr. Butler, see Mr. Turner out!'

Mr. Turner left, taking his hat more in sorrow than in anger, and Mr. Butler shut him out. Mr. Turner turned back on the porch, as though he had thought of yet another stock which Miss Fisher might find more acceptable, but Mr. Butler had locked the door. He was sorry that his mistress was in such a tiz, and put his head around the kitchen door to warn his wife that lunch had better be early and good, because Miss Fisher was going to need a drink.

Miss Fisher, however, did not get the chance. Another caller hung on the bell, and this time Mr. Butler was faced with a tall, raw-boned woman, who demanded, 'Where's my niece?'

Mr. Butler was about to tell her to drink beer next time, because gin obviously gave her the heeby jeebies, when she flourished a photograph torn out of a newspaper. It was Jane's photograph.

'Perhaps you should speak to Miss Fisher, then, Mrs....'

'Miss,' she snarled. 'Miss Gay.'

Mr. Butler went regretfully to Phryne to warn her that someone had come to remove Jane. Phryne came out into the hall
with outstretched hand, at the same time as Jane emerged from
her room, with Ember riding on her shoulder.

'There she is. My niece. I want her back!'

'Do you?' asked Phryne unpleasantly. 'I see. Jane, do you
remember this…lady?'

Jane had shrunk back against the wall, frightened by the
strident voice and the clutching hand.

'Of course she remembers me!' shrieked Miss Gay, who
seemed to be singularly badly named. 'I'm her Aunt Jessie and
she's my niece Jane Graham, and if you didn't know her name
why did you call her Jane?'

'I plucked a name out of the air, and I don't think she recalls
you, do you, Jane?'

Jane shook her head, numbly. Phryne turned Miss Gay by
the sleeve.

'Leave me your address, and some proofs that she is your
niece, and I'll have my lawyer look them over. I really can't release
Jane into your custody until I am sure that she is your relative.
And possibly not then. What were you about, to let her get that
thin, and be on a train to Ballarat all on her own?'

'I pinned her ticket into her pocket, and she was lucky to get
the job, going as a skivvy in a doctor's house, she was, though I
suppose they've got someone else for the job now. Don't listen
to her if she says that I mistreated her…I treated her like one of
my own, so I did, when her mother died, and then her grandmother died…'

'Yes, thank you, Miss Gay, what is your address?' asked Phryne,
and wrote it down. 'I'll be in touch with you in due course, or my
solicitor will. You are the girl's legal guardian, I assume? Appointed
by a Court? No? I thought not. Good morning, Miss Gay.'

Phryne stepped back as she gave the woman a shrewd push
and shoved her out of the house in mid-sentence.

'Quick, Mr. Butler, shut that door, bolt it and bar it, don't
let anyone in. I am not at home to anyone, not even a long lost

relative or a man telling me I have won Tatt's. Gosh, what a morning! Jane? Where are you?'

Jane was crushed into the corner of her bed, with an indignant Ember in her arms, and Phryne did not touch her. She sat down on the end of the bed and said casually, 'I'm not going to give you up, you know. That woman has no claim on you. Even if you are Jane Graham, and it's a nice name, I like it, she can't make you live with her. She isn't your guardian and she may not be your closest relative. So don't worry. I'll call my solicitor and have him draw up adoption papers at once. In fact, I'll call him now. Have you remembered anything?'

'Sort of. I began to remember when Ember scratched on the window. My name is Jane Graham. I recall my grandmother but I don't remember that woman at all. As far as I know, I've never seen her before. What's the address, Miss Fisher?'

'Seventeen Railway Crescent, Seddon.'

Jane shook her head again.

'No.'

'Not a bell?'

'No.'

'You can tell me the truth, you know. I've given you my word that you shall stay with me, and I am not forsworn.'

'Miss Fisher, I am telling you the truth. I don't recall the address and I don't know the name. I can remember everything up to my grandmother's death. Then it's all a fog.'

'What was in the parcel we took with us on the train?'

'Rachel coloured rice powder and Lalla perfume, a collar for Ember and some flea-soap, and…and…there was something else…the chrysanthemums for Dot. I think that's all.'

'There's nothing wrong with your memory, is there, Jane?'

Jane shook her head, so that the heavy plaits danced.

'No. I can remember everything that happened from the time I was on Ballarat station, but nothing of the past until my grandmother's funeral.'

'I know who we need,' said Phryne briskly. 'We need Bert and Cec. I'll go and call them now.'

'Bert?' asked Jane, bewildered but uncoiling from her defensive crouch.

'And Cec,' agreed Phryne, on her way to the phone. She dialled, and asked the operator for an address in Fitzroy.

'Bert? It's Phryne Fisher. I've got a bit of a job for you. Are you on?'

The telephone quacked, seeming to expostulate.

'No, no, nothing rough, or illegal, just a spot of investigating. Excellent. See you in an hour,' and Phryne rang off. She smiled at Jane.

'There's just time for lunch, and then we shall send out the troops. Don't look so downcast, pet. You are staying with me, come Hell or high water. If you remember anything else, anything at all, tell me. Now—lunch.'

Because of Mr. Butler's warning and because of her own culinary pride, Mrs. Butler served up a *riz de veau financiére* of superlative tenderness and flavour, followed by a selection of cheeses and a compôte of winter fruits. Phryne had two glasses of a nice dry Barossa, which she was trying for a vintner friend, and was in an expansive mood when Bert and Cec arrived in their shiny new taxi.

They came in and sat down, uneasy in Phryne's delicate salon, and were introduced.

'This is Jane Graham, or at least, we think she is. Have you seen the papers today?'

Bert nodded. Cec grunted.

'Jane, this is Mr. Albert Johnson, a staunch friend of mine.' Jane looked at Bert. He was short and stocky, with shrewd blue eyes and a thatch of dark hair, thinning at the crown. He was wearing a threadbare blue suit and a clean white shirt, evidently newly donned. He smiled at Jane.

'And this is Mr. Cecil Yates, Bert's mate; you should get on, he loves cats.'

Ember gave a mute vote of confidence by leaping up onto Cec's knee and climbing his coat. Cec stroked him gently. He was tall and Scandinavian looking, with a mane of blond hair and incongruous deep brown eyes like a spaniel. He nodded at Jane.

Bert gave the kitten a polite pat and said, 'Well, Miss, what's the go?'

'Jane was given to me to mind, because she was found on the Ballarat train in a skimpy little dress I wouldn't have clothed a dog in, with a second-class ticket in her pocket and no memory of who she was or how she got there. Today a frightful woman arrived and demanded her, saying that she was her niece, and she has left me papers that seem to prove that this is true. I'm keeping her anyway, because she was misused in that woman's clutches, and I'm adopting her. However, I have a good reason for wanting to know exactly what happened to her in Miss Gay's house—was ever a harridan worse named—and I want you to find out.'

'You say you got a reason,' said Bert slowly. 'Can you tell me what it is?'

'No. But it has to do with the murder I'm investigating.'

'What, the murder on the Ballarat train? You was on the train, Miss?'

'I was. And I've got the victim's daughter here, too. She has hired me to find the murderer, and so I shall. However. Find out all you can about dear Miss Gay. Who lives with her—especially men—who visits her, all of her background. Can you do it? Usual rates,' she added.

'The question is not, can we do it, but will we do it,' observed Bert. 'What do you think, mate?'

'I reckon we can do it,' agreed Cec, and Bert put out his hand.

'We're on,' he said, and Phryne poured them a beer to celebrate.

<>‹›‹>

Phryne took a nap that afternoon, and passed a quiet evening playing at whist with Jane and Miss Henderson, who had greatly recovered. Her blisters were drying, and Dr. MacMillan had hopes that her liver was not damaged after all. Jane showed an unexpected ruthlessness, and won almost seven shillings in pennies before they broke up and went to bed. Jane took Ember with her, as usual, and he slept amicably on her pillow.

◇◇◇

Lindsay Herbert lunched at the 'Varsity, went to his Torts lecture where he learned more than he thought that he needed to know about false imprisonment, and went home to dine with Alastair, who seemed subdued. His outburst in Phryne's house had profoundly shocked him, and when the young men had stacked the dishes in the sink for Mrs. Whatsis to clean in the morning, he lit a nervous cigarette and tried to expound.

'I don't know how to apologize to you, old man, for that appalling bad show at Miss Fisher's.'

'That's all right, old fellow, think no more of it.' Lindsay was sleepy with remembered satiation, and disinclined to listen to self-pity or even explanations.

'But it's not all right. I lost my head completely—just like those fellows in the Great War—shell-shocked, they used to call it.'

'Why, what shocked you?'

'First there was Eunice—poor girl, her face is all burnt, she looks dreadful—then you taking up with Miss Fisher and just wafting off without a word—then a policeman had the infernal nerve to ask me—me!—where I was on the night of the murder.'

'Well, I could scarcely say, "sorry, old boy, must rush, I'm being ravished by a beautiful lady", now, could I? Especially if I wasn't sure if she was going to ravish me or not. I mean, a fellow would look a fool, wouldn't he? And I suppose the police chappie has his job to do. Where were you, anyway?'

'Here,' snapped Alastair, butting out his cigarette as if he had a grudge against it. 'Did she?'

'Did she what?'

'Ravish you?'

'Old man, since the beginning of time, few men have been as completely ravished as I have been.'

'Hmm,' grunted Alastair. 'Are you seeing her again?'

'Friday night.'

'Well, ask her how she is going on the murder. She's taken possession of my fiancée and my friend, but she won't solve the murder by sex-appeal. No, Miss Fisher,' commented Alastair savagely. 'Not as easily as all that.'

'Well, well, I'll ask her,' said Lindsay peaceably.

'If you can spare the time,' snorted his friend, and stalked out to go to bed, slamming the door.

Chapter Ten

*'Then two are cheaper than one?' Alice said in a
surprised tone, taking out her purse.*

*'Only you must eat them both, if you buy two,'
said the Sheep.*

*'Then I'll have one please,' said Alice... 'They
mightn't be at all nice, you know.'*

Alice Through the Looking Glass,
Lewis Carroll

Bert and Cec found the large and imposing house at Railway
Crescent, Seddon, without much difficulty. It was in a fine state
of studied disrepair. The iron lace which decorated the verandah
was both unpainted and broken, and the bluestone frontage had
been whitewashed by some past idiot. The distemper was now
wearing off in flakes and tatters, and no maintenance had been
done on the roof since the Father of All was a callow youth. The
gate sagged on its hinges, the front garden was a wilderness of
hemlock and slimy grass, and the bell-pull, when pulled, emitted
a rasping screech and fell off in Bert's hand.

A sign had been painted over the whitewash next to the door.
It said 'Rooms to Let. Full Bord' in red lead. Bert had an idea.

'Quick, you get down the path, Cec, and I'll ask for a room. I don't want her to see you.'

Cec caught on and retreated into the bushes, and a scatter of footsteps announced that someone was coming.

The door creaked open on unoiled hinges, and a small and slatternly girl answered, 'What do you want?'

'I want a room,' rejoined Bert roughly. 'The missus at home?'

The girl nodded, knotting an apron stained with the washing up of several years, and swung the door wide.

'Come in,' she parroted tonelessly. 'It's ten shillings a week, washing extra, and no drink or tobacco in the house.' In a small voice, she added, 'But you'd be better to go elsewhere.'

Bert heard, grinning, and patted the girl on a bony shoulder. 'I got my reasons,' he said portentously, and the girl's eyes lit for a moment with an answering spark.

'What's yer name?' asked Bert, and the small voice said, 'Ruth. Don't let her know I been talking to you.'

There was such an undercurrent of fear in her voice that Bert did not reply aloud, but nodded.

'Who's at the door, girl?' demanded a screech from the back of the house. 'I don't know, girls these days can't do a good day's work, not like it was when I was a girl. Twelve hours a day I used to work, and hard, too. Now they snivel and fall ill if they're asked to serve tea. Well? Who is it?'

'Please, Missus, it's a man,' faltered Ruth. 'He wants a room, Missus.'

'Oh does he? Have you told him about it?'

'Yes, Miss, I told him.'

Ruth's eyes implored Bert not to say anything critical, and he began to feel a strong sense of partisanship with this overworked skivvy. Poor little thing! The woman was evidently a tartar.

'Yair, she told me. So, have you got a room or haven't yer? I ain't got all day.'

Miss Gay emerged from the kitchen, wiping her hands on a dirty teatowel. Bert looked her up and down and classified her instantly as Prize Bitch, filthy class. Prize bitches came in two classes, the fanatically clean, who smelt of bleach, and the slatternly, who smelt of old, boiled cabbage. Miss Gay was also redolent of yellow soap and sour milk. She was not a prepossessing sight, clad in down-at-the-heel house slippers, a faded wrapper in what appeared to be hessian, no stockings and a yellow cardigan draggled at the hips. Bert smiled his best smile and was rewarded with a slight softening of the rigid jaw and mean, thin lips.

'Here's me money,' he offered, handing over a ten-bob note that vanished into the unacceptable recesses of her costume. 'Show me the room.'

The small maid accompanied them up the unswept stairs to a room which had once been fine. The ceiling was high and decorated with plaster mouldings, and the walls had been papered with Morris designs. A plasterboard partition had been erected, cutting off the window, and the room contained a single iron army cot with two blankets, a dresser which had originally come from a kitchen, still equipped with cup-hooks, a table with one leg shorter than the others and an easy chair so battered that its original form could hardly be guessed. Bert concealed his loathing and said easily, 'This'll do me, Missus. What about meals?'

'Breakfast at seven, and lunch at twelve, if you come home to it. Dinner at six. If you want a packed lunch, tell me the day before. Put anything to be washed in that bag and it goes out on Monday. Washing is extra.'

'Latch-key,' suggested Bert, and one was detached from Miss Gay's jingling belt and handed over.

'No alcohol or tobacco in the rooms, and lights out at ten. No women, either. Visitors are to stay in the parlour. Board is due every Friday, at twelve noon, sharp. Anything you want, ask Ruth here. She's a stupid, worthless girl, but I can't abandon my own flesh and blood.'

Ruth twisted her dirty apron around a grimy hand and gulped back a sob. Miss Gay sailed away down the stairs, and Bert felt in his pocket.

'Here, take this,' he whispered, pressing half-a-crown into the girl's chapped hand. 'And not a word to a soul, eh?'

Ruth nodded. Her brown eyes were bright and shrewd.

'You ain't one of her usual lodgers,' observed Ruth curiously. 'What are you doing here?'

'Go downstairs and get a broom and sweep this floor,' ordered Bert in a loud voice, and Ruth scurried down and returned with an article which could technically be called a broom, though it had scant three bristles left. With this, patiently, for she was a diligent girl, Ruth began to sweep the floor, while Bert explained what he was doing in a fast undertone.

'There's this girl, see, her name is Jane Graham. The Hon. Phryne Fisher has got this Jane in her care, because she's lost her memory—I mean, Jane has. Your Miss Gay turned up there this morning and demanded Jane, saying that she was her niece. Now my Miss Fisher reckons there is something wrong, and she sent me to investigate it. Do you know Jane?'

'Yes. She's my best friend, Jane is. She was here for about six months, after her grandmother died. First her mother died and then her grandma, and her father's a sailor, and he ain't never come back from his last voyage, so Missus took Jane.'

'Out of kindness?' asked Bert artlessly. Ruth laughed, a small slave's laugh.

'Kindness? Her? You're joking. She took Jane like she took me, for the work she could get out of us. But Jane was funny.'

'How, funny?'

'She had nightmares,' said Ruth. 'See, her grandma hanged herself, and Jane found her, in this house, it was, by the window upstairs, I durstn't go there. Then there was the mesmeric man.'

'The who? Look out, she's coming back. Hookit, Ruthie,' warned Bert, and shoved the girl out of his room.

'Come back with a broom that sweeps,' he said roughly, and Ruth ran down the stairs, passing the Missus. Miss Gay slapped at her, but Ruth was quick, and the blow missed.

'Girls!' snorted Miss Gay. 'Everything all right, Mr....'

'Smith,' said Bert. 'Bert Smith.'

'I've brought your rent book, Mr. Smith.'

'Thanks. Send up that girl with a real broom, will you? There's plaster all over this floor—a man could break his neck.'

Miss Gay departed, and Bert shut the door. His room had no outlet except the doorway, and he felt stifled. At some time a leak had started in the roof, and water had trickled down the wall, leaving a great rusty stain like a grinning face.

'A real palace,' observed Bert sardonically, and sat down gingerly on the army cot to wait for Ruth.

It was half an hour before she returned, this time with a reasonable broom, and she had been crying. Bert observed the marks of tears on the child's face and said, 'She been knocking you about?'

Ruth nodded.

'She told me not to talk to you, but I'm going to,' she said defiantly. Bert shut the door and leaned on it, occluding the keyhole in case Miss Gay should decide to eavesdrop.

Ruth took the broom and began to sweep noisily, and Bert asked, 'What was this man?'

'The mesmeric man, the hypnotist. On the halls, he was. At the Tivoli. He tried to hypnotize me, but I just pretended. He mesmerized Jane lots of times. He could make her think that ice was a red-hot poker, and after he touched her with the ice a red blister would form on her arm. He made her think that she was talking to her grandma, and telling her how the missus beat her, and then the missus would punish her when she came round. It was horrible,' confessed Ruth, sneezing in the plaster dust. 'But I was glad it wasn't me.'

'He still here?' asked Bert, shocked, and Ruth nodded.

'He's her fancy man,' she said gravely. 'That's what the lodgers say. He's got the best room and the window and all, and he gets all the good food—bacon and eggs and rolls and that.'

'You hungry?' asked Bert. 'Where did she get you?'

'From the Orphanage. I'm *not* her flesh and blood! She adopted me. My parents are dead. I wish she hadn't,' said Ruth sadly. 'I liked the Orphanage. The nuns were letting me teach the younger kids their ABC. I didn't want to leave, but she took me...There,' she added in a loud voice, 'I've swept up all the plaster, Mr. Smith.' Ruth's hearing, sharpened by pain, had picked up the approach of Miss Gay before Bert had heard her. He opened the door, and Ruth went out, carrying the broom and the dustpan. Bert emerged into the passage.

'I'm just going out for a couple of hours, Missus,' he said flatly, and walked down the stairs and out at the hall door. Bert felt that he had been dipped neck-deep in sewage.

He found the cab, with Cec in it, around the corner in Charles Street, and Cec started the engine.

'To the pub,' ordered Bert. 'I never, in all my born days, saw such a place as that. It's filthier than a pigsty and God alone knows what would happen to a girl.'

'So, we don't go back,' said Cec, stopping the cab outside the Mona Castle, and Bert shook his head.

'Oh, yes we do,' he said grimly. 'Something nasty is going on in that place, and I'm going to get to the bottom of it.'

'What was Miss Fisher not telling us?' asked Cec, when they had glasses in their hands, and Bert rolled another smoke.

'I don't know, but I'm beginning to guess, and I don't like what I'm thinking, Cec, I don't like it one bit.'

Bert told Cec what he was thinking, and they bought another beer.

'So I've taken a room there, Miss,' reported Bert on the pub telephone. 'And I gotta go back tonight. I want to meet this hypnotist chap.'

'Yes, you do want to meet him,' agreed Phryne. 'But be careful, won't you? They sound like very unpleasant people.'

'So am I,' growled Bert, baring his teeth. 'Me and Cec is very unpleasant people, as well.'

'All right, my dear, but keep in mind that I want to know all about the man before you pulp him. You have guessed about Jane, haven't you?'

'Yair Miss, I guessed. As soon as I heard about the mesmerism.'

'So I want him alive,' said Phryne urgently. 'He might be able to give her her memory back!'

Bert reluctantly accepted the justice of this.

'All right, Miss, I see what you mean. Me and Cec will be gentle with him. And there might be another waif, Miss. Orphan called Ruth. That bitch don't treat her right—beg pardon, Miss.'

Phryne sighed. Suddenly her life seemed to have become over-populated.

'Oh, well, one more won't make any difference, bring her along. When?'

'Termorrer, Miss, if we can manage it, and you might have your tame cop standing by.'

'Perhaps,' said Phryne, and Bert felt a chill go through his spine, the remembered over-the-top thrill.

'All right, Miss, I'll see you then, goodbye.'

He hung up, paid the publican for the call, and returned to Cec.

'She said that we can take the little girl as well,' he commented. 'Your shout, mate. No alcohol allowed in me new place of residence.'

⟨⟩⟨⟩⟨⟩

Phryne stared at the photograph which had been delivered. Had this man mesmerized Gabrielle Hart? It was time that Miss Hart was found. She would go to see Klara in Fitzroy.

⟨⟩⟨⟩⟨⟩

Bert went back to Miss Gay's house, and found that dinner was on the table. Cec had returned to their own lodging house to explain Bert's absence to their excellent landlady.

The dining vault was as cold as a Russian military advance and not as well provisioned. The great table, which was made of mahogany which had not been polished in decades, was laid with a spotted off-white cloth and a harlequin range of dishes. Quite of lot of them were cracked or chipped, and the silverware was Brittania metal and not clean. Bert observed that one place was set with clean, new dishes and real silver, and in front of it was the cruet, the bread, and the butter.

The five other occupants of the house were already seated. They seemed a forlorn collection, with all the spirit crushed out of them by a combination of life, circumstances, and their landlady. Bert thought of his own Mrs. Hamilton, all dimples and a dab hand with pastry, and envied Cec his dinner. Two old men, vague and possibly senile; a young man in the last stages of consumption, who was as thin as a lath; a labourer or small tradesman with a missing arm, who seemed to retain some individuality; and a sleek and roly-poly gentleman in spotless evening costume, waistcoat and white tie and probably evening pumps, though Bert did not look under the table. His manicured plump white hands cut the bread and buttered it as though there were no starving men at the same table. He had brown eyes like pebbles and that thick, pale skin which speaks of too much greasepaint at an early age. Miss Gay came in, bearing a tureen of frightful soup (which the gentleman did not take) and Bert was introduced.

'This is Mr. Smith,' announced Miss Gay, dispensing pig swill. 'Mr. Brown, Mr. Hammond', she said gesturing at the old men, who made no sign—'Mr. Jones' to the young man—'Mr. Bradford' to the tradesman, who nodded and spooned up his soup as though he was used to the taste. 'And allow me to introduce Mr. Henry Burton.'

'I saw you once,' commented Bert, pinning down an elusive memory, 'on the Tivoli. You were on the same bill as that Chinese magician, the one who used to catch bullets in his teeth.'

Mr. Burton bowed.

'The Great Chang; he died, poor fellow, doing that bullet trick, a few years later.'

Miss Gay served what smelt like a tasty chicken soup to Mr. Burton, from his own small saucepan. The other lodgers lacked the spirit even to glare at this arrant favouritism. Mr. Burton had a wonderful voice; rich, deep, persuasive, a vocal instrument perfectly wielded. Bert remembered the act which he had seen; a man behaving like a chicken, a woman stretched stiff as a board between two chairs. It had been very impressive. What was the great man doing in a dump like this? Surely he could not dote upon the appalling Miss Gay?

Ruth came in to remove the soup plates, and to hand out dinner plates, which were also mismatched and chipped. Miss Gay brought in congealed gravy, fatty, depressed roast beast of some sort—Bert suspected horse—and potatoes as hard as bullets. The lodgers munched their way uncomplainingly through this detestable repast, while Mr. Henry Burton dined on a pheasant in redcurrant jelly and winter broccoli.

Pudding was a floury suet thing with very little gooseberry jam. Even the old men could not eat it. Mr. Burton had water biscuits and stilton cheese. Bert drank a cup of hot water in which three tealeaves had been steeped and went up to bed. Most of the lodgers did the same. Bert reflected, as he lay down in the creaking cot, that he had been more comfortable on the hills among the dead men and the Turkish snipers.

‹›‹›‹›

Phryne dismissed her taxi in Gertrude Street and emerged into the cold, wrapping her furs around her and snuggling her chin into the sumptuous collar of red fox. She was uncertain as to where she should begin in this rough place, in search of Gabrielle Hart.

She had a photograph of the girl. She looked again on the thin, unsensual, plain face, beaky nose and deep eye-sockets, a generous mouth. This young woman was not pretty, and would be consequently easy to seduce by flattery. She was sixteen.

By arrangement, Phryne met the unsettling Klara in a tea and sly-grog shop on the corner.

'Phryne! Come and buy me some tea,' called Klara. She was a small, thin woman dressed in a gym slip. Her hips and breasts had never developed adult curves; she looked like a pre-pubescent schoolgirl. She was twenty-three, lesbian, and very acute.

Tea was purchased. Phryne liked Klara, but found her company worrying. No one hated the whole male sex, absolutely and without exceptions, like Klara. She was a very successful whore, and her tax returns usually came in above three thousand pounds a year.

The tea-shop was cold. Klara was wearing only her gymslip and a ratty overcoat; her skinny legs were bare and muddy. Phryne huddled into her coat.

'Aren't you cold, Klara? Have some of this disgusting tea.'

'Oh, I'm cold all right, but that's what the punters pay for, ain't it? I'll be warm enough when I get home. Show me the photo.'

Klara drank the luke-warm tea and considered.

'I ain't seen her, but that don't mean she ain't here. We'll start at the end of the street and work our way down. Lucky it's such a crook night; no one'll be out pounding the pavements if they can avoid it. You equipped for trouble, Phryne?'

Phryne nodded. Her little gun was loaded and in her pocket.

'All right. Come on, love. Bye, Jack!'

A figure shining with grease looked up from the chip fryer and grinned.

'This is the first. The other two only deal in chinks. Hello, Alice. Got a friend with me tonight. Seen this girl?'

'Hello, Klara,' said the big woman in purple satin uneasily, shooting a sidelong glance at Phryne. 'No, I ain't seen her, she ain't one of mine.'

A languid girl, wearing only a stained silk petticoat, looked in on the mistress.

'The gent in number four is passed out,' she said casually. 'Better call the boys and put him out. I don't like his breathing; he's gone purple and is puffing like a grampus. Hello, Klara! What are you doing in this abode of vice?'

'Hello, Sylvia. Looking for this girl.'

Sylvia pushed back a mop of bleached curly hair and considered Phryne.

'You don't look like one of them Soul Rescue people,' she commented. 'What do you want her for?'

'I want to take her home,' said Phryne. 'Her father is worried about her.'

'Jeez, I wish I had a father to worry about me.'

'Do you know her, Syl?'

'Is there a reward?'

'There might be.' Klara consulted Phryne with a look.

'Yair. Well, she's the new one in Chicago Pete's. Better watch out, Klara. They ain't nice people. Saw her this arvo. Seemed dazed. She ain't been there long. Chicago Pete's girls always look like that.'

'Drugged?'

Syl shrugged admirable shoulders under the drooping silk. 'Maybe.'

Phryne folded a five-pound note and thrust it into Sylvia's hand. She and Klara regained the street.

'Chicago Pete?'

'Yair. A yank. They say he was a gangster, but they'll say anything on this road. Come along, there's the entrance.'

Phryne and Klara lurked, surveying the respectable darkstone entry of a two-storey house.

'How do we get in? And can we get her out?'

Klara grinned, showing unexpectedly white teeth between blistered lips. She felt in her shabby pocket and produced a knife.

'Even Chicago Pete knows not to muck about with me,' she hissed. Phryne wondered what elemental force she had let loose on Gertrude Street and decided that Gertrude Street could look after itself.

'Which way shall we go in?' asked Phryne.

'Front door,' decided Klara, and led the way up the respectable stone steps to a thick, closed door.

On this she knocked what was evidently a coded series of taps and it creaked open. A flat-faced individual was behind the door and stared unspeaking at the guttersnipe and Phryne in her furs.

'Well?' he asked in an American rasp.

'You new?' asked Klara scornfully. She came up to his second waistcoat button.

'Yeah, I just got off the boat, why?'

'I'm Klara, get Chicago Pete for me, willya?'

'Now why should I do that?'

'Because if you don't know me, Pete does, and he'll knock your block off if he misses me; we're pals, Pete and me.'

The doorkeeper let them into a well-kept hall and lumbered off up the stairs.

'Pals?' asked Phryne, noticing that the street-side windows were barred.

'Yair, pals. He says I remind him of his little sister. He's as queer as a nine dollar bill, Pete is. Here he comes. Gimme that photo and let me do the talking.'

Chicago Pete was a ruin; huge, damaged. His face might originally have been comely, but it had been beaten and twisted out of true as though an angry child had wrung a wet clay head between temperamental fingers. His eyes were dark, and as flat and cold as a slate tombstone.

'Klara! Why haven't you been here for a week, little Miss?' The voice was lovely, soft and rich with a Southern accent.

'I been busy,' said Klara. 'I got a proposition for you, Pete, and I want to do you a favour.'

'Come in here.' He ushered them into a room which was frilled and shirred in pastel shades, like a Victorian boudoir. 'I know you don't drink, little Miss, but I have lemonade. And maybe a good Kentucky bourbon for your friend, eh?'

Phryne accepted a glass and Klara sat on the edge of a table, exhibiting her thin legs splashed with mudstains. They affected Chicago Pete strangely.

'Why don't you wear some of them nice clothes I bought you, Missie? You make me sad, looking so bare.'

'Business,' snapped Klara. 'Listen. We want to buy one of your girls. This is my friend Phryne; she's acting for another party, and we don't want no trouble.'

'Which one?'

Klara handed him the picture. Chicago Pete's eyes narrowed. 'Her? You can have her. The cook reckons she's under a spell.'

'What, that black monster in your kitchen? What would he know?'

'You mind your tongue, Miss. The doctor, he's a New Orleans man, a jazz-man, a voodoo priest. He knows a spell when he sees one. She ain't worth nothing, that doll. And I paid...'

He stopped, calculating what the market might bear. Phryne smiled. She did not mind what she paid. Mr. Hart could afford it. And she was interested in the spell.

'Dope?' she asked, and Chicago Pete shook his awful head.

'No. Or if it is, it ain't like no dope I've ever seen. I'll get them to bring her down. Wait a moment.'

He stepped to the door, gave an order to the doorkeeper, and said to Phryne, 'She ain't been used much. And she ain't been damaged. Much. What will you offer?'

'How much did she cost you?'

'Ten bills.'

'Twelve.'

'Twenty.'

'Fifteen.'

'Nineteen. Here she is. Say hello to the nice lady, doll.'

The girl was limp, her gaze vacant. She was dressed in a nightgown far too big for her and her feet were bare. She was bruised over all of her body that Phryne could see.

'She must have had clothes,' commented Phryne. 'Can someone bring them? We'll dress her again, and then I want to see your jazz-man.'

'If you want him, he's in the kitchen. But I don't think...' Klara pointed, and Phryne went out, past the doorkeeper, into the back of the house where she could smell cooking.

'Shrimps and rice and peas,' said the thin black man, pointing into a pot. 'Very nice. What you want, Miss?'

'I want you to take the spell off Gabrielle Hart,' said Phryne, and repeated it in French. The old man grinned and took off his apron, then reached for a cloth bag and a handful of feathers.

'We had *poulet Orleans* for dinner.' He took a little dish that seemed to be full of blood. 'You know voodoo?'

'A little. I have been to Haiti. Can you do this?'

'*Oueh*,' he grunted. 'You pay me ten silver florins and I do it. Little doll will remember.'

'Who put on the spell? Another voodoo priest?'

The old man shook his head.

'Ain't none of my magic, but strong magic. Strong,' he repeated, hefted the loaded tray, and followed Phryne into the pink-and-blue sitting-room.

The girl had been clad in her own street clothes again, and Klara had combed her tangled hair and plaited it. She looked now like the schoolgirl she had been when someone snapped his fingers and told her to follow. Her eyes were still glazed. Klara had planted herself on Chicago Pete's knees and he hugged her very carefully, as though she might break.

'I don't like this,' he said uneasily, and Klara patted his cheek.

'It's worth nineteen bills, Pete,' she soothed. The priest set down the tray, and stared at the girl, then picked up her wrist and allowed it to drop.

'Strong magic,' he commented, setting out the blood and the feathers and laying down a white tablecloth over the Chinese carpet. He removed his shirt and began to anoint himself with the blood, muttering under his breath. Gabrielle stared at him. Her attention had been caught, for the first time.

Around the old man's neck swung a bright gold coin. Her eyes fixed on this as he began to dance.

Three times around the girl the old man moved; then he lit the bundle of feathers and cried out, 'Erzulie! You captured this soul! You possessed this girl! Erzulie! You took her! I call for the third time, and you release her. You give her back to the world: Erzulie!'

Neither Chicago Pete nor Klara had moved. The smoke from the chicken feathers filled the delicate room with a farmyard reek. Phryne almost fancied that dreadful, elemental things moved and squeaked in that smoke; she shook herself and pinched the back of her hand hard.

Gabrielle Hart flinched as from a striking thunderbolt and began to wail. Klara ran to her and hugged the shocked face against her skinny bosom. The old man straightened up, shiny with sweat, and held out a bloodstained hand to Phryne.

She poured the coins from her purse, and added one extra.

'You come on a Saturday,' he said to Phryne as he bent to collect the instruments of his magic. 'We got good jazz. Best in the city.'

'For the love of Mike,' cried Chicago Pete. 'Get out of here! And take all that heathen stuff with you!'

The priest folded the tablecloth and went out. Klara released the girl.

'All right, Mr., er…here is the money, and we must be going. Can your doorman call us a taxi? Thank you so much,' said Phryne graciously.

The doorman was dispatched for a cab. Gabrielle Hart sat in her chair and cried and cried.

'You sure you want her?' asked Chicago Pete, and Phryne smiled.

Klara and Phryne left the respectable house and waited for the taxi on the front steps. Gabrielle had stopped crying and was now asking questions, some of which Phryne could answer.

'What am I doing here? Who are you? Where am I?'

'I am the Hon. Phryne Fisher, and this is Klara. You are in Gertrude Street, Fitzroy, and only God knows what you are doing here. You had a brainstorm, my dear, and we are taking you home.'

'No, no, someone else said that to me…someone else said that they were taking me home…and they didn't…they *hurt* me!'

'Oh, Lord…all right. Calm yourself. You shall tell the driver where to go. Oh, thank God, it's Cec.'

Cec smiled his beautiful smile from the driving seat of the taxi.

'I'm on me pat,' he told Phryne. 'Bert's still about that… er…business with the boarding house. Poor old bloke. They said you was out on a case in Gertrude Street and I thought…'

'You thought right. This young woman is Gabrielle Hart, and she will tell you the address. Take her there and deliver her into the care of her father only. If he isn't home, wait, but I think that he will be there soon. Give him my card and tell him I shall call on him tomorrow. Hang on to this girl, Cec, don't let her get out until you are at her house. She's a little disordered.'

'All right,' agreed Cec, opening the door. 'Come on, Miss.'

Gabrielle Hart moved to the taxi, got in, and gave Cec the direction. He looked over at Phryne.

'What about you, Miss?'

'We'll get another taxi. She's scared of us. See you later, Cec.'

'We might as well walk down to the rank,' suggested Klara. They had only gone about three paces before the attack came.

Two men came quickly, out of an alleyway. They disregarded Klara, brushing her aside, and both grabbed for Phryne. She dropped to her knees under their weight; she heard her stocking tear and felt her knee graze. They had one arm each, and she could not reach her pocket. They did not say a word. Phryne's breath scraped in her chest. They were taller and heavier than she.

A Master-at-Arms had once spent three weeks teaching Miss Fisher the elements of unarmed combat. She was not afraid, only very angry that she should be taken thus off guard. She allowed her fury free rein.

'Crack' the first one's knee as she kicked back, hard, then rammed her high-heeled shoe down on his other foot. He let go. With the impetus from that Phryne flung herself at the other attacker. Her elbow caught his ribs; her knee came up with all her force, and he fell to his knees, dropping a cosh. Phryne, fast and lethal, retreated a pace and kicked again, and felt a rib or two break with a curious, dry sound.

'Bastards!' panted Klara, standing on the other attacker's stomach with one foot on his throat. 'Pete musta changed his mind about the girl.'

'No, not Pete, I think.'

Phryne kicked over one man and dragged his head up by the hair.

'Who sent you?' she hissed. The man looked up glazedly into blazing green eyes and winced.

'Who?'

Phryne shook him and bashed the skull against the ground a few times. 'Tell me or I'll kill you.'

The knife was at the attacker's unsavoury collar. He blinked.

'I just reckoned you'd be rich, dressed up like that,' he croaked, and fell out of consciousness.

'Fitzroy is so bad for the nerves,' sighed Phryne. 'Leave him alone. I owe you a good dinner and a night out, Klara. What shall it be?'

'The Bach concert on Tuesday, and dinner at the Ritz,' decided Klara. She dusted off her hands and pulled down her gym tunic. 'I prefer Johann Christian, but I can put up with Johann Sebastian. We can get a taxi at the rank. You all right, Phryne?'

'Fine,' agreed Phryne, pulling up her torn stocking. 'I'm fine.'

Chapter Eleven

*'Give your evidence,' repeated the King angrily.
'Or I'll have you executed, whether you are nervous or not!'*

Alice Through the Looking Glass,
Lewis Carroll

Phryne woke on Thursday morning knowing who had murdered Mrs. Henderson, and wondering what she was going to
do about it. The method was obvious, the motive transparent,
and even the face of the blond guard was beginning to resemble
one which she had seen in real life.

'How shall I do this? It will break poor Eunice's heart.'
Phryne took her morning bath without appreciating the scent
and dressed in haste.

It had to be Alastair Thompson. He was used to disguise. He
had a terrible temper. He had no alibi for the night in question.
All that he had to do was to chloroform the people, sling a rope
around Mrs. Henderson, and cast a line over the water tower.
He was a rock climber. Then he could haul her up, and himself,
and leave no tracks. Whether he dropped her or trampled on
her did not matter. All he had to do was to get rid of the mother
and Eunice would fall into his arms and give him all her money,
of which Phryne supposed that there must be a fair amount.

Phryne decided to call Detective-inspector Robinson, and when she had established contact with him, found that he had reached the same conclusion.

'I'm bringing him in for questioning today,' he assured Phryne. 'I'm of the same mind, Miss Fisher. I'll let you know.'

Phryne decided that there was no need to worry Miss Henderson with any news until she could say something positive, and closeted herself with her solicitor, who had drawn up the adoption papers.

'But Miss Fisher, you have kept the girl from her guardian's care,' he protested. Phryne grinned and shoved Miss Gay's 'documents' at him.

'She has no legal guardian. Miss Gay is her aunt, but no adoption proceedings were ever taken. Here's her birth certificate and all. Poor little thing. Have you sorted it all out?'

'Yes, Miss Fisher. If you will just put your finger on this seal and repeat after me, "To this adoption I hereby put my name and seal"—just a legal form, Miss Fisher, you understand—and it is all completed.'

Phryne complied.

'She's mine, now?'

'After the judge has approved this, yes.'

'Excellent. When can you get it into court?'

'In due course, Miss Fisher.'

'That won't do. "In due course" means at least six months.'

'It is a practice court application, so I can probably get it into the list for next week,' said the lawyer, shocked yet again by Miss Fisher's disrespect for the law. He bundled up his papers and took his leave. Jane tapped at the door of the parlour.

'Miss, I've recalled something.'

'Good. What is it?'

'I remember Miss Gay. She took me and Grandma to her house. It was a horrible place. Grandma…something happened to Grandma.'

'It will come back. Nothing more about the train?'

'No. Was that your lawyer, Miss Fisher?'

'Yes. I just signed the adoption papers. You're mine now, Jane, and no one can take you away.'

Phryne told herself that she should have known better than to say things like that. Jane began to weep, threw herself at Phryne and held her tight, and Ember scratched his way onto her upper arm, balanced like a small black owl, and glared.

'You are quite right, Ember,' Phryne told him. 'It was a very silly thing to say. Never mind. Jane, my dear, here is a hankie, and I think that we should sit down. All this emotion is wearying, isn't it?'

<><><>

More emotion was expressed by a horrified client on the telephone.

'Miss Fisher, I must first thank you for retrieving my daughter.' He began with deceptive calmness. 'But do you know what they have done to her, those hounds?'

'I have a fair idea,' admitted Phryne. 'She has certainly been beaten.'

'Beaten, and…and…assaulted, and the doctor thinks that she may have a…venereal disease.'

'Yes.'

'Who were they?' he screamed. 'Tell me their names!'

Mr. Hart dropped any pretence of control.

'I don't know their names, and if I did I should not tell you. Private vengeance is unsound, and moreover illegal. Leave them to me.'

Some nuance in her voice must have told Mr. Hart that he was talking to a very angry woman.

'You know them?'

'I shall know them. And they shall all be very, very sorry. I promise.'

'Is there anything I can do?' asked Mr. Hart, subdued.

'Nothing. They have ravished your daughter, and a thousand offences beside. Leave them to me. Your daughter needs you now. She is an innocent victim, poor thing. She probably won't remember anything about it, so don't remind her. I am sure that you can find her the best of care. Then take her right away from Melbourne for six months. Switzerland has some very pleasant scenery.'

'I put my confidence in you, Miss Fisher.'

'So you may, Mr. Hart.'

She hung up the phone. How was she going to find the abductor and avenge poor Gabrielle Hart? But now she was determined. She had given her word.

<><><>

Detective-inspector Robinson surveyed the young man in the clutch of two policemen with approval. He was a fighter, this one, and it had taken the combined strength of four officers to bring him in. Even now he was straining in the grip of the station's two heaviest and strongest officers.

'It is my duty to warn you that you do not have to say anything, but that anything you do say will be taken down and may be used in evidence,' he said quietly.

The prisoner demanded, 'What are you charging me with?'

'The murder at or near Ballan on the night of the 21st of June 1928 of Anne Henderson by strangulation,' said the policeman, and Alastair Thompson laughed.

'Then you've got another thing coming. I'll tell you where I was on the night of the 21st of June 1928.'

'Well, I'm glad that you have decided to tell me at last.'

'I was in the City Watchhouse,' sneered Thompson. 'Drunk and Disorderly. I was fined five bob the next morning. Cheap at the price, considering. Go on. Ask the watchhousekeeper!'

This was a surprise. Detective-inspector Robinson, however, preserved his habitual calm.

'Book him in, please, Duty Officer,' he requested civilly, and the young man was forced into a chair to be photographed, stripped of boot-laces, tie and braces, and placed with a certain celerity into a nice quiet cell.

'Get those developed and send across for the drunks book,' he snapped, and an underling carried off the camera and raced across the road to the Watchhouse, demanding the Cell Register for the 21st of June.

'You can't have it,' snapped the sergeant. 'It's my current book and I need it. Tell Jack Robinson to come and inspect it himself. What's all this about?'

'Murder suspect says that he was banged up on the night,' gasped the cadet. 'He'll skin me if I come back without it! Have a heart!'

'You can copy the page,' said the sergeant, relenting. 'And you can note at the same time the names of the officers what were on duty on the night of the twenty-first. Who was it?' He leaned ponderously over the counter. 'Aha. Sergeant Thomas and Constable Hawthorn. You can have Hawthorn, for all the use he is, but you can't have Thomas, he's on leave.'

'When will he be back?' asked the cadet, scribbling furiously with a spluttering pen on the back of a jail order. 'This nib is frayed, Sarge, I swear.'

'He's in Rye on his honeymoon,' replied the sergeant, grinning evilly. 'Didn't leave no address. There you are, son, and take Constable Hawthorn with you. Hawthorn!' he bellowed.

A faint voice echoed from the cells, 'Yes, Sarge?'

'Get across and see if you can identify a prisoner of Jack Robinson's, will you lad? And you needn't hurry back. Get some lunch.'

'But sarge, it's only half-past ten!'

'Get some breakfast, then,' snapped the Sergeant, and the cadet conducted Constable Hawthorn back across Russell Street to the detective-inspector's office, waving his jail order the while so that the ink would dry.

The cadet peeped up at Hawthorn. He was very tall, over six feet, and pale, and vague. His mouth had a tendency to drop open and his eyes had the dull, unfocused gaze which the cadet had previously only seen in sheep.

Hawthorn asked mildly, his voice as bland as cream, 'What's this all about, young feller?'

'Please, sir, the detective-inspector has a suspect for the Ballan railway murder, and he says that he was in the Watchhouse that night.'

'And he wants me to identify him?'

'Yes, sir.'

'Oh,' remarked the tall constable, and accompanied the cadet to Robinson's office.

The copy was laid down on the desk and Robinson scanned it irritably.

'You read it, boy,' he snarled at the cadet, and the boy read, 'John Smith, 14 Eldemere Crescent, Brighton.'

'He's an old customer...name really is John Smith, too, and no one ever believes him—has to carry his birth certificate around with him. Says he's never forgiven his father for it...no, that ain't him. Go on.'

'John Smith, The Buildings, East St. Kilda.'

'Now I don't know that one. Do you recall that John Smith, Hawthorn?'

'Yes, sir. About...er, well, smallish, and er...fair, with...er... blue eyes, I think, sir.'

'Could you identify him?'

'Oh, yes, sir,' said Hawthorn. 'I think so.'

Detective-inspector Robinson grunted, got to his feet, and led the way to the holding cells. A furious face glared up at the window-slot as he drew back the bolt.

'Have a look, son. Is that the man?'

'Oh, yes, sir,' agreed Hawthorn happily. Robinson gritted his teeth, and gave the order to release the suspect from detention.

'I didn't want to tell anyone that I'd got drunk, so I gave a false name. I believe that this is not unusual. May I go now?' asked Alastair, with frigid politeness.

'You may go, but you are on bail. You may not leave the state or change your address without notifying us of your where-abouts. Do you understand that?'

'I understand,' said Alastair, with a smile that showed all his teeth, and he turned and left the police station.

Detective-inspector Robinson lifted the telephone and requested Miss Fisher's number.

'I don't think that it's disastrous, but it certainly casts a lot of doubt on my theory,' said Phryne when the exasperated policeman reached her. 'Have you examined his handwriting?

He would have had to sign himself out. And are you sure of the police witness?'

'No, Miss, that I am not. Boy's a fool. However, identification is identification.'

'Wasn't anyone else there?'

'Yes, but the sergeant is on his honeymoon, I can't call him back.'

'No, but you can send him a photograph, can't you?'

'Yes, I'll do that. And I'd keep out of Alastair's way, Miss Fisher, if I were you.'

'I can look after myself,' said Phryne crisply. 'Get weaving with the photo. See you soon,' she added, and hung up.

The cadet was very impressed that the detective-inspector could swear for so long without repeating himself.

‹›‹›‹›

Bert in later years said that breakfast at Miss Gay's was the single most miserable experience of his whole life. 'Not sad, mate,' he explained. 'But down right starving mean stone the crows and starve the lizards dirt miserable.'

The table was laid, as before, with cruet and mismatched plates, and Mr. Henry Burton's special dishes.

They sat in a hungry circle around a vat of horrible porridge, as thin as library paste, scorched, and lumpy, while Mr. Henry Burton said grace in an unctuous voice. Bert refused the clag, but the others ate voraciously. Mr. Burton was breaking his fast on new rolls, hot from the oven, cherry jam, and butter. He had a pot of brewed coffee next to him. Bert accepted a plate of incinerated egg-powder and bacon so burned as only to be of professional interest to a pathologist. He tried to make a sandwich with his two pieces of stale white bread and marge, but the bacon broke as he touched it with the knife.

'Can't you give a man a feed?' asked the tradesman, holding out a plate on which reposed a four-days-dead egg and bacon of transcendant carbonization.

'I can't take your bacon back to the kitchen, Mr. Hammond,' snapped Miss Gay, slapping at Ruth's head as she passed. 'You've bent it.'

Bert drank a cup of tea and chuckled.

After breakfast, the workers departed, and Mr. Burton showed signs of going out. He took his hat and his stick, donned a fleecy-lined overcoat, and yelled for Ruth.

'Call me a cab, girl.'

Bert grabbed the moment.

'I'll get you one, sir,' he said civilly, and stepped into the kitchen, where Miss Gay kept the telephone.

'Ruthie!' he whispered, 'we're taking Mr. Burton. Here's a card. You go to this house if she hurts you again.'

Ruth nodded, stowed the card in her pocket, and Bert slipped back into the hall.

'At the door in a moment, sir,' he said, and went down the rickety front steps to look for Cec, who was due directly.

The bonzer new taxi pulled up, and Bert opened the door for the gentleman, closed it and jumped into the front seat.

'Here!' protested Mr. Burton, 'I didn't ask you to share my taxi!'

Bert grinned.

'It's my taxi—well, half mine. This is my mate, Cec. Say hello to the nice gent, Cec.'

Cec muttered 'hello' and kept his eyes on the road.

'Where are you taking me?' asked Mr. Burton.

'A lady friend of ours wants to see you real bad.'

'Which lady?'

'The Honourable Phryne Fisher, that's who.'

'Is she a fan? I hope that she does not want her fortune told. I don't tell fortunes, you know.'

'No, she wants some mesmerism done,' said Bert.

They were on Dynon Road and fleeing like the wind for St. Kilda. If he could keep this oily old bastard talking, that would be all the sweeter.

'Yair, some of that hypnotizing what you done on the Halls, they say you used to be great.'

'Used to be? My dear sir, I am the Great Hypno. You yourself have seen my powers.'

'Yair, I remember. You made sheilas as stiff as boards and laid 'em between two chairs. But I don't reckon you could put anyone under that didn't want to be,' said Bert easily, and Henry Burton bristled.

'Oh no? You, for instance?'

'Yair, me, for instance.'

'Look into my eyes,' said Henry Burton, 'and we will see. Look deep into my eyes.'

Bert looked. The eyes, which were brown and had seemed hard, were now soft, like the eyes of a deer or a rabbit; deep enough to drown in. They seemed to grow bigger, until they encompassed all of Bert's field of vision; the voice was soothing.

'You hear nothing but my voice,' said Burton softly. 'You hear nothing but my words, my voice, you do nothing but as I command you. You cannot move,' he suggested softly. 'You cannot lift your hand until I tell you.' Bert, terrified, found that he could not lift his hand. He was frozen in his half-turned position, seeing nothing but the eyes, and wondering vaguely why he could not hear the engine of the cab or any other noises. Bert began to panic and vainly struggled to move so much as a finger.

Cec stopped the cab outside Phryne's house and got out. He opened the door and commented in his quiet, unemphatic tone, 'If you don't release my mate, I'm gonna break your neck.'

Mr. Burton flushed, leaned forward, and snapped his fingers in Bert's face. 'You feel rested and refreshed,' he said hurriedly. 'You are awake when I count ten. Ten, nine, eight, seven, six, five, you are free now, four, three, two, one. There.

'Just a demonstration,' said Mr. Burton airily, and got out of the car and climbed the steps to Phryne's front door.

Chapter Twelve

'It's time for you to answer now,' the Queen said looking at her watch. 'Open your mouth a little wider when you speak…'

Alice Through the Looking Glass,
Lewis Carroll

'Ah, this must be the Great Hypno!' exclaimed Phryne, as Mr. Butler conducted her guests into the parlour. 'This is my companion Miss Williams, and we are delighted to meet you. Do sit down. Would you care for a drink?'

The Great Hypno smirked and bowed, gave his coat and hat to Mr. Butler and took a seat, accepting a whisky and soda.

'You wanted to see me, Miss Fisher? What about, may I inquire? It must be pressing, since you had me kidnapped. I am pleased that my fame is still strong, I have been retired from the stage for five years.'

'Yes, why did you retire? Bookings not too hot?'

The man bridled, tugging at his glossy forelock. 'Certainly not,' he said indignantly. 'I found another…er…line of work, which was so engrossing that it required me to devote all my time to it.'

'Yes, I have always thought that it must be a tiring profession, procuring.'

Bert, who had remained near the door, nodded as though he had had his suspicions confirmed. Cec watched the scene with a still face, but his fists clenched.

'You take the likely ones from orphanages,' stated Phryne. 'And the repulsive Miss Gay adopts them. Such a charitable woman! I've spoken to three institutions where she is well known. A lady with a social conscience, they said, those stupid people, a lady who takes on the hard cases and bad girls and finds them suitable employment. That is with the help of her tame mesmerist, who makes sure that the difficult ones don't raise any dust. Eh, Mr. Burton?'

'I have never been so insulted in my life!' huffed the stout man, fighting to get out of his armchair. Phryne laughed.

'Oh, come now, in all your life? You mustn't have been listening. Don't get up, Mr. Burton,' she added, revealing the dainty gun which she was aiming at him. Mr. Burton blanched. He dropped back into the chair and extracted a silk hankie and mopped his face.

'Come on, admit it and don't waste my time!' snapped Phryne. 'Or I shall have an accident with this little gun, you see if I don't! How many girls? Talk!'

'It must be…oh…thirty-five or so. Yes, thirty-five, if you don't count Jane.'

'Thirty-five,' said Phryne stonily. 'I see. Where did you sell them?'

'Various places. I supplied the country, mainly. They mostly came from the institutions well broken in, you know, little tarts in all but profession, and it wasn't necessary to hypnotize many—a waste of my Art, as I told Miss Gay. All it generally needed was to explain the situation, that they were going to make a lot of money, from something more pleasant than domestic labour, and most of them agreed.'

'And then what?'

'When the girl was in the correct frame of mind, we would arrange for her journey, wiring ahead to the buyer.'

'How much did you ask for each girl?'

'One hundred and fifty pounds. Good girls, most of them. Though I only got a hundred for that little bitch from the Emily MacPherson. Of course there was a certain wastage—always is in that profession—suicide, alcohol and drugs, mainly, and of course venereal disease, but all I sent were clean and relatively new, my buyers know that.'

Phryne swallowed. Dot stared, open mouthed. Cec reached for the nearest decanter and took three deep gulps, passing it to Bert. Mr. Burton, full-fed and shiny, sat back, amused by their reaction.

'Why are you so shocked? It is your nice society which demands that there should be whores and there should be nice girls. While there are nice girls there must be whores—all that I did was supply them.'

'Being a whore should be a matter of choice,' said Phryne. 'And what choice did you give them? Did you ask Gabrielle Hart if she wanted to be raped and drugged? Now, Mr. Burton, I have a proposition for you.'

'I thought that you might have,' smiled Mr. Burton.

'You remember Jane?'

'Yes, whining little scrap, with her books and her Ruthie and her grandma.'

'Yes. Jane. You hypnotized her, did you not?'

'I did. She was on the train to Ballarat to join a very exclusive house there, run by a generous friend of mine, but she never got there. I put her on the afternoon train, and she was found on the night train. She must have got off somewhere, but I can't explain what went wrong—she had explicit post-hypnotic instructions.'

'I want you to give her back her memory,' said Phryne quickly.

'And if I refuse?'

'Then I fear...' said Phryne, waving the little gun. Mr. Burton observed that her attitude was negligent and her purple silk afternoon dress positively decadent, but her wrist did not droop and her finger was on the trigger.

'Bring her in,' he said, coughing into the handkerchief. 'I will try. But she may not respond. I tell you, there has been another intervening event, a trauma of some sort.'

'Did you always have sex with the girls, Mr. Burton?' asked Phryne.

He answered absently, 'Oh, yes, Miss Fisher, it was part of the treatment, and part of the reason why I stayed in the business. There have to be some compensations for retiring from the stage. But this one, I recall, squealed, and then I recalled that the Ballarat brothel paid a fifty pound bonus for virgins, so I relented. I didn't like to hurt them, you know.'

Bert made a choking noise and wrung his felt hat to ruin. Phryne gave him a severe look.

'So the trauma was some other thing, not a sexual assault?' asked Phryne evenly.

'Oh, yes, something quite unexpected,' said Mr. Burton, unconscious of any irony. Dot went out and fetched Jane, who came in warily, not knowing Mr. Burton but not liking him, either. Phryne concealed the gun, and took the girl's hand.

'Jane, dear, you sit down here and look at this gentleman. You are quite safe. I am here, and I will not leave you.'

Ember stalked off Jane's shoulder and onto Phryne's lap, curled into a fuzzy black ball and purred. Jane relaxed. Mr. Burton leaned forward, placing one thumb on her forehead.

'You are sleepy, Jane, are you not?' The magnificent voice was as deep as organ music. 'Are you asleep, Jane?'

Jane's eyes were open, but her voice was cold and characterless, like the voice of a ghost. 'I am asleep.'

'What were this man's commands to you?' asked Phryne, and Jane twitched a little at the unfamiliar voice, but answered: 'To forget what he did to me.'

'Jane, that command is removed,' said Mr. Burton, eyeing the pistol barrel within a foot of his face. 'You are free and released from all commands, from me or anyone else. From the time that I count from ten you will begin to remember, and by midnight you will recall everything that has happened. Do you understand, Jane?'

'I understand that I am free,' repeated the mechanical voice, and even in deep trance it had a different quality. 'I understand that I am not under your command anymore.'

'Ten, nine, eight, stretch yourself, Jane, seven, six, five, four, blink, girl, you feel rested and refreshed and you will recover your memory slowly until at midnight it will be complete, three, two, one, awake!' He snapped his fingers in Jane's face, and she blinked, focused, and drew back into Phryne's embrace with a cry.

'It's him! The man who...hurt me. He scratched at the window and made me let him in. Oh, Miss Fisher, don't let him take me away!'

Phryne hugged Jane, and then transferred her to Dot, while Mr. Burton stood up and smiled his satisfied smile. Dot clutched a frantic Jane and was scratched by a frantic Ember, who blamed her for being dislodged from Phryne's knee.

'Well, Miss Fisher, I have done what you wanted, shall we discuss payment?'

Cec growled, and Bert took two steps forward.

'Payment?' he shouted. 'You filthy hound, I'll break your bloody neck!'

'One moment,' said Phryne, holding off Bert with a gesture. 'Are you willing to give yourself up to the police?'

'Really, Miss Fisher, are you joking? And if you let your hired ruffian lay a finger on me, I'll have an action for assault and battery. I am going to walk out of that door a free man, Miss Fisher. Do you know why? Because not one of those thirty-five would testify against me. They all love me like a father, the little fools, and in any case seven of them are dead.'

'You are *not* going to walk out that door, do you know why?' asked Phryne, smiling unpleasantly, 'because there is a rat in the arras. Did your shorthand writer catch all of that, Jack?'

'Yes, Miss, got it all down pat,' said the detective-inspector, stepping out from behind the curtain. 'I bet you weren't expecting to see me again, eh, Henry?'

'Robinson!' gasped Henry Burton. 'How did you get here?'

'I've had you on suspicion for years, you bastard,' The detective-inspector smiled his sweetest 'come-along-with-me' smile. 'I've got the testimony of nine of those little girls, once their trance wore off, but it wasn't enough, as there were great gaps in their memory. They couldn't remember how they got into the grips of a portly, respectable gentleman with beautiful eyes. Now I know that Miss Gay got 'em from the asylums, it won't be too tricky to connect it all up so that even my chief will have to believe it.'

Bert and Cec seized the Great Hypno.

'Just one punch,' pleaded Bert. 'Just the one.'

'No, I gotta get him back to headquarters. He's a mine of information. He knows all about the vice rings and all the white slaving in Victoria. I don't want him damaged!'

Diving under the arms of the struggling men as quick as a bird after a worm, Jane launched herself out of Dot's embrace and flew at Mr. Burton, fingers hooked into claws. She was mad with release and the intolerable rush of returned memory, and Ember, springing from her shoulder, clawed at whatever foothold he could reach as Cec restrained the struggling child and hauled her away from the ruin of Henry Burton's face.

Ember fled to Cec, as all cats did, and tucked his small spade-shaped head in the crook of the tall man's arm. Jane, her fury spent, buried her face in his shoulder, and he held her head down so that she should not have yet another horror to burden her memory.

Razor-sharp, kitten claws scrabbling desperately for a hold had done what no poor twelve-year-old whore had managed. They had dimmed Henry Burton's magical gaze.

Shocked, Bert released the man, and Mr. Butler, who had been an enthralled spectator throughout, telephoned for an ambulance. The room was silent, except for Jane's sobbing and the muted bubbling snuffle of Burton, who had clamped his hands over his face. The ambulance came in ten minutes, during which time no one moved or spoke, and Robinson and his shorthand writer and his prisoner went away. The front door shut. Still no one moved. Cec stroked the kitten and Jane with equal gentleness, and Dot drew a deep breath and stood up.

'Well, that's all over, and a very nasty end, and you can't say that he didn't deserve it, the horrible man. Mr. B., ask Mrs. B. for some tea, will you? Miss, you might like a brandy? Mr. Cec, can I offer you a drink? A cup of tea?'

Her brisk voice brought everyone to. Phryne rummaged for a light for her cigarette. Jane sat up and wiped her face on Cec's shirt. Bert sat down and rolled a smoke with hands that hardly shook at all. Cec smiled up at Dot.

'Thank you, Miss, I'd like a beer, and so would Bert, and then a feed. Poor bloke's been living on cabbage stalks and offal for days.'

It is an index to how much better they were all feeling after a few minutes that when Ember removed his head from the crook of Cec's arm and began to wash his front feet, no one shuddered at the thought of what he was washing off.

'Mate, mate, we was forgettin'!' exclaimed Bert, slamming down an empty beer glass. 'What about little Ruthie?'

'She's in the kitchen,' observed Mrs. Butler tartly, refilling the glass with ease and skill. 'She's been here for ten minutes, but I couldn't interrupt you. Such goings on in a lady's house! But it all seems to be over now. Ruth is well, Mr....er...Bert. She says that Miss Gay beat her again, and she has a beautiful black eye, poor mite—and she ran away to Miss Fisher like you told her. She's in the middle of a bath, or I'd call her in. Is this horrible business settled, then?' she asked in a worried undertone, but not low enough to escape Phryne. Mrs. Butler moved aside to allow Jane and Ember to rush to the kitchen. Cries of delight greeted them from the Butler's bathroom.

'This particular horrid business is over,' she said, patting her housekeeper on the arm, 'but the other horrid business is sent right back to square one. The person that had all the earmarks of being the murderer on the train has the best alibi of all—he was in police custody, so that puts him right out of the picture. Dear me. What a tiring day! Can you manage an early dinner, Mrs. B.? Poor Bert has been on a reducing diet lately. Then I think that we could all profit from an early night. Tomorrow I'm going with Miss Henderson to open up her house and help her clear out, and Dot and Jane are coming too. That will be exhausting enough, but then I've just remembered that the students' Glee Club is on at the boathouse tomorrow night.'

'Yes, Miss, an early dinner, I've got some fish that the boy swears was caught this morning, and I can easily make a few extra chips. Will that suit? And don't worry about your problem,' soothed Mrs. Butler, seeing that Phryne was white and strained. 'It will quite likely solve itself if you don't worry at it. More beer, Mr. Bert?'

Bert held out his glass and grinned.

'It's worth a man doing a perish if he gets one of your dinners, Mrs. Butler.'

'Go on with you,' sniffed that lady, and bustled back to her kitchen to fry up a storm.

Jane was sitting on the hearth, with a scrubbed-clean Ruth. Ember was on her lap. The kitten had quite recovered and was watching the flames with his ears laid back as though he was at his mother's breast.

'I'm remembering a lot more,' she said quietly. 'I remember getting off the train, at a station in the middle of big open paddocks. I didn't know who I was or where I was going but I knew that I didn't want to go there. I sat down on the station seat, then it got dark and a train stopped, and I heard a child crying, so I went to get him and I put him on the train again, then it seemed silly to stay where I was, so I got on the train too, and hid in the ladies. I stayed there until…something happened… then I was at Ballarat and I couldn't remember a thing. It feels like it happened to someone else, not me,' she explained. 'All cotton-woolly, as though it was a movie.'

'And, of course, there was no one on the station to meet you, because you were on the wrong train,' mused Phryne. 'It all fits, Jane.'

Jane looked up suddenly and laid a hand on Phryne's silk-clad knee. Her upturned face was very young.

'Am I still a good girl, Miss?'

Phryne, leaning down to embrace Jane with an unaccustomed catch at the heart, assured her that she was.

Chapter Thirteen

…and she was quite pleased to find that there was a real one blazing away as brightly as the one she had left behind.

'So I shall be as warm here as I was in the old room,' thought Alice.

'Warmer, in fact, because there'll be no one here to scold me away from the fire.'

Alice Through the Looking Glass,
Lewis Carroll

'Lord, isn't it cold in here? Never mind, Dot will soon have a fire lit. Did you have any servants, Eunice? If so they haven't left the old place in any sort of order.'

'No, I dismissed them, with notice of course, and I fear that they haven't complied with their employment conditions.'

Phryne, Dot, Jane, and Ruth had escorted Eunice Henderson to her home in case she should be overwhelmed by her memories as she climbed the front steps to the dull grey door. When it became clear that Eunice had a grip on her emotions they turned to the more pressing matters an unoccupied house presented them with.

The house had that musty chill which falls upon unoccupied houses, and depresses the spirits of all visitors. Dot hung
up her good blue coat on the hallstand and went to find the
kitchen, taking the girls with her, to light the stove and open
some windows. Dot carried her capacious basket well supplied
with a picnic, and tea and sugar and a bottle of milk. Phryne
helped Eunice out of her coat and elected to remain wrapped
in her sables.

Eunice ran a glove along the hall table and examined her
finger; it was coated with dust. The house was an elegant Edwardian family mansion, stoutly built and ornately decorated, but it
was unloved, overcrowded, and dilapidated. Phryne picked up
a vase in which lilies had died; they moved with a sad rustle in
their slime-green water.

'This will need an army of parlourmaids to set in order,'
sighed Eunice. 'When are your cleaners coming, Miss Fisher?'

'I told them ten o'clock, and that will be them now, I expect.
Admirable women; Mrs. Butler recommends them.'

Phryne answered a strident ring at the bell and ushered in a
small stout woman and a small thin woman, relieved them of
their coats, and pointed them toward the diningroom.

'There you are, ladies, I suggest that you make a start by
opening all of the windows and letting a nice fresh gale in. Miss
Henderson, this is Mrs. Price and Mrs. Cummings.'

'Glad to meet you, ladies,' said Eunice. 'Do you think that
you can manage? It's a frightful mess.'

The thin woman tugged at her hem, tied her apron strings,
and wrapped an enormous red and white bandana around her
head.

'Me and Maise'll manage,' she said. 'Done worse than this,
eh, Maise?'

Maise nodded, enveloping her head in a blue scarf.

'Hot water in the kitchen?' asked Adela Price, and Phryne
nodded. They squared their shoulders.

'I'll do the windows, Dell, and you open the flues and start
the fires,' said Maise, and Eunice led Phryne upstairs.

'I'm afraid that it has all gone downhill since Mother lost all her money,' she apologized. 'She used to be very well-off, you know, and she got used to luxury. It was all that I could manage to keep her in linen sheets, after the crash of the Megatherium Trust, you know.'

'Your mother had money in that trust?' asked Phryne, catching up on a dusty landing and following Eunice into a dark bedroom. The Megatherium Trust, a hastily put together fraud perpetrated by the Honourable Bobby Matthews, remittance-man of Phryne's acquaintance, had crashed resoundingly at the end of May 1928, taking all its investors with it. The Hon. Bobby had elected to seek the warmer and less indictable climes of South America. Phryne had not been sorry to see him go. Megatherium indeed! Many less-than-funny jokes had been made about prehistoric monsters after the crash.

'Oh, yes, all of her money was in Megatherium. She lost every penny that she had. Dear me, this carpet is sadly motheaten. Do you think that your friends will want such a sad relic?'

'Bert and Cec can find a home for everything, even if it's only the tip. Pardon me for asking, Eunice, but does your young man know this?'

'Why, no, the question never came up. I suppose that he assumed that I was wealthy. I am well provided for, of course, but entirely by my own labours.'

'Oh?' asked Phryne, her mind buzzing with theories, 'what labours?'

'You promise not to tell anyone at all?' pressed Eunice, stopping with an armload of dreadful dresses.

'Not a soul,' promised Phryne, crossing her heart.

Eunice opened a little door and slipped inside. Phryne had taken it for a powdering closet, but it was a study. There was a professional looking typewriter and a load of carefully numbered manuscripts. Phryne remembered the packet of foolscap paper she had picked up in the train.

'You're a writer!' she cried. Eunice Henderson blushed.

'Romantic novels for railway reading, and, dear, they are too, too terrible.'

'What are you working on at present?'

'Nothing at the moment, I have just been correcting the proofs of *Passion's Bondslaves*. It is quite the most disgusting drivel I ever read, so I am sure that it will be just as successful as *Silken Fetters* and *Midnight of the Sheik*. I sold a thousand copies of that in two weeks, and it's still in print. You won't tell, Phryne, will you?'

'Of course not, my dear, but I think that it is so enterprising of you! How did you begin?'

'Well, Mother always liked to read the things, revolting slop for the most part, and I learned typewriting so that I could do Mother's accounts. I was practising on the machine, and I thought I'd see if I could write the stuff, it seemed easy enough, and, my dear, it simply poured onto the page, I could hardly type fast enough to keep up. I never knew that I had such an indelicate imagination,' she confessed, throwing down the dresses in a rustling heap. 'So I sent it to a publisher who knew my father and could be sworn to secrecy, and there it was. I can write one every three months, and the market seems rather under-supplied with tripe than otherwise. So I could afford lavender-water for Mother, and handmade chocolates, and trips to Ballarat, and… oh, dear, I had forgotten all about Mother! How heartless of me!'

Eunice sat down on the brass bed and wept for five minutes, at the end of which she wiped her eyes, replaced her handkerchief, and went on with the conversation.

'It will catch me like that for awhile, now that my face is healed and I'm not doped with pain-killers,' she said sadly. 'Poor Mother! Who could have killed her?'

'For a while I thought that it was your young man, Eunice, God forgive me,' confessed Phryne, sorting shoes into a pile. 'But it can't have been him.'

'It can't?' she asked tautly.

'No, it seems that he was in police custody that night. Drunk and Disorderly.'

'How…how very unlike him.' Eunice flung three gloves onto the pile. 'I have never seen him touch alcohol…at least, very rarely. Never mind. I forgive your suspicions, Phryne, it did look black against him. Why did Mother keep seven unmatching stockings, do you think? What are we going to do with all this stuff?'

'We are going to put all the clothes and so on in a big heap in the upstairs hall, and Dot will sort from there. Some of the things will go to deserving causes and the worst will be dropped off at the rag-pickers by Bert and Cec. All we have to do is to decide what you want to keep.'

'All the stuff in here can go, and this carpet—it will probably roll if you can dislodge the corner…thank you.' They began to carry out a motley collection of old clothes, good clothes, handbags by the hundred, shoes ranging from the Victorian to the Edwardian, combs and boxes of caked powder, greasy hairpins, mob-caps and lacy petticoats. After two hours they had sorted out all the upstairs rooms and Phryne was ready for a cup of tea and a cigarette.

Dot, Ruth, and Jane were working at the clothing mound, packing the good things into teachests and the rags into chaff-bags. Bert, Cec, and the charwomen were removing the discarded furniture, knick-knacks, what-nots, and so on into Bert's disreputable van.

'It really is lovely to clean out all this old rubbish,' said Eunice as they passed the workers on the way to the kitchen. 'But are you sure that anyone would want all this stuff? Look at that glass bowl over Great-Grandma's wedding bouquet! What an excrescence!'

Cec, who had earmarked the glass bowl as a present for his sweetheart, commented, 'Real good glass, this. Made by a crafts-man,' and Miss Henderson smiled warmly.

'Take it and enjoy it,' she recommended.

Cec grinned.

Bert called from the door, 'Are you coming, mate? A man hasn't got all day!' and Cec grabbed the glass dish and went.

Phryne and Eunice had their cup of tea, and surveyed the sterling work which had already been done. The floors were swept clean, the windows open, the fires burning, and the house smelt pleasantly of wood smoke and furniture polish.

'It is very kind of you to help me, Phryne,' she observed. 'This will all be finished in one day, and I can sleep in my own bed tonight.'

'You won't mind being here on your own?'

'No, dear, what could harm me? I am exorcising the ghosts of all of my family, and I shall be quite happy alone. I'm only keeping the basic furniture, and all of those ornaments and feathers and dead birds and seashells and small tables can go. I am throwing out the firescreen made by Aunt Matilda, whom I always hated, and dear Cousin Nell's *petit point* chair, and Uncle John's butterfly collection. It's a fine empty feeling,' she continued, a little intoxicated by all that space. 'It's a nice house, if it wasn't all cluttered. And the curtains. I have always hated those heaped up lace curtains.'

'Don't throw them away, you need something to cover the windows,' objected Phryne. 'Cut them off.'

'Cut them off?'

'Yes, just snip them level with the floor.'

Eunice Henderson flung herself at Phryne and kissed her soundly.

'Oh, Phryne, why did I never think of that? In all that time when I hated the idea of all that lace lying around on the floor for the sole reason of demonstrating that you could afford to have lace lying on the floor, and I never thought of that! Quick! Where's the scissors?'

They snipped with a will, and the yards of superfluous lace joined a century's gleaning of costumes in the chaff bags. Dot claimed armloads of delicate undergarments for her own; Jane and Ruth found a store of satins from China and were allowed to keep them all; Bert took a fancy to a huge conch, and took it for a present to his landlady. It took eleven trips of the rickety van to various destinations before the detritus of seventy years was removed from the house, and Phryne marvelled that it still looked full. The linen room was bursting with Irish sheets, there were beds and tables and chairs and fire irons and paintings, but only one ornament remained in the entire mansion; a tall blue vase, quite unfigured, which some pirating ancestor had picked up in the Boxer wars.

'It's the only thing of Mother's that I wanted,' said Eunice, as they sat around the kitchen table sipping afternoon tea. 'I want you to have it, Phryne. It will go beautifully with your sea-green and sea-blue salon.'

'Oh, Eunice, I couldn't, it's much too valuable...'

'Yes, you could. Otherwise I shall break it. I don't want to see another ornament in my entire life. I shall have a study in the breakfast-room, which looks out onto the garden. I shall be very happy. And I am still employing you to find out who killed my mother.'

'Yes, I know, old thing, and I haven't the slightest idea at the moment. However, something will turn up. Are you sure you are all right to be left?'

'Perfectly,' asserted Eunice, as she stood bidding them farewell in her scoured, cold hallway. The wind had been from the west and the house smelled of the sea. Behind her in the swept-clean morning-room a bright fire glowed, and her supper was laid out on the one remaining small table. Phryne kissed Eunice goodbye, and allowed Bert to give her a lift home in the truck, in which she sat nursing the blue vase as though it was a child.

‹›‹›‹›

Phryne dined early with Dot, Jane, and Ruth. Jane was preoccupied, and between the egg-and-bacon pie and the chops Phryne asked her what the matter was.

'I've remembered,' said Jane. 'What sent me off—what broke his power. It was something I saw. You know about my gran? She hanged herself, my gran did, at the window of the upstairs at Miss Gay's.'

'What did you see?' asked Phryne. 'Don't tell me if you don't want to.'

'I saw an old woman hanged,' muttered Jane. 'She was pulled out of the window by her neck; just like my gran's, her head was.' Jane's head flopped sickeningly sideways in demonstration. 'It was bright moonlight, like it was the night my Gran died. That's what set me off. That's why I went queer.'

'Where was this, Jane?'

'By the tower, the thing that the trains get water from. And there was a man there, Miss Fisher, a man.'

'What was he doing?'

'Pulling on the rope. The body rose, and so did he; he climbed over her and onto the water tower, then he swung her and dropped her on the grass. It was horrible, and I hid my eyes. Then he jumped down…'

Jane broke off. Ruth caught Jane in her arms.

'Ruthie! It was awful!'

'You just tell Miss about it,' commanded Ruth, and Jane obeyed.

'He landed on her body and…'

'I know what he did, Jane. No need to go on. Then what did you do?'

'I was watching out of the window of the ladies, Miss, and I heard a terrible scream behind me, and then the train started again. I just stayed where I was, Miss.'

'Would you know the man again, Jane?'

'Yes, Miss. I expect so.'

'Good. Now you and Ruthie sit down and eat some chops and let's get on with the dinner, for I am famished.'

Ruth paused with a fork halfway to her mouth and asked the question that had been concerning her since her arrival.

'Miss Fisher, what are you going to do with me?'

'I'm not going to do anything with you, if you mean by that, something to you. What would you like me to do?'

'Jane says that you are sending her to school.'

'That is true.'

'And that you like intelligent girls.'

'Yes.'

'And you adopted her.'

'Yes,' agreed Phryne, wondering what was coming.

'I'm intelligent and I can work hard and I have always looked after Jane. What'll she do without me? You should take both of us, Miss, not just pick one like kittens out of a litter.'

Jane laid her hand on Ruth's shoulder and looked at Phryne. Ruth bit the end of one plait reflectively. Then she took up her fork and swallowed the piece of chop impaled on it, as though she was not sure when she would get another meal. Phryne smiled.

'Two are better than one,' she said. 'I was wondering how Jane would manage in this rackety house on her own. All right, Ruth. You too. Any relatives?'

'No,' affirmed Ruth, and took some more bread, thankful for the first time in her life that she was an orphan.

'I'll call that irritating solicitor tomorrow and get it all put through legally. But you will have to go to school, girls, through term, and you can come back here in the holidays. You can do anything you like, as long as you are willing to work for it. And you must never say anything about my cases, nothing at all, do you understand?'

Both heads nodded. They understood. Ruth grinned a huge grin and slapped Jane on the shoulder.

'No more Miss Gay, Jane, no more Seddon, no more of the Great Hypno, and best of all…'

'Best of all?' asked Phryne.

'No more dishes,' concluded Ruth, and hugged Jane so hard that Ember scratched her.

‹›‹›‹›

Phryne finished her dinner and went upstairs to change, wondering what she should wear to a Glee Club singalong. She decided on comfort, dark trousers and jacket, and her sheepskin overcoat, perfect for the chill, dark night which it promised to be.

She was coming downstairs when the phone rang and she picked up the receiver. It was Detective-inspector Robinson, evidently in an elated mood.

'Miss Fisher? Ah! Answering your own phone? This'll never do—I just rang to tell you about our scoundrel.'

'Oh? Which one?'

The policeman chuckled.

'Burton. He's out of hospital and helping us with our inquiries. He's singing like a canary, unlike that prize bitch of a wife of his.'

'What? Married to Miss Gay?'

'Indeed. The wounds to his eyes ain't serious—just scratches, but he seems to have lost his power. Tried mesmerizing one of my constables—you never had such a laugh in all your life.'

'Be careful of him, Jack, he's dangerous.'

'Miss Fisher, it's well known that you can't be hypnotized if you don't want to be. He's lost his fangs, all right.'

'His dentist will have to fit him with an entirely new set. Congratulations.'

'Thanks, Miss Fisher. And another thing, I got a reply from Thomas, you know, the sergeant down at Rye on leave?'

'And?'

'Can't say yes or no. Said he remembered the man, but couldn't say if that was him or not. Said it was an odd case—he didn't seem very drunk, but when the beat constable passed him by, he tripped him and then tried to steal his helmet. Young gentlemen will have their tricks, especially young university gentlemen.'

'Indeed. Well, that's about all that we can do at present. Oh, Jack, I forgot to tell you. I have an eyewitness to the murder, who saw what happened and can identify the murderer.'

'An eyewitness to the murder, Miss Fisher? Who?'

'Jane, I told you she had remembered. Listen.' Phryne told the story of Jane's grandmother and the manner of her death.

'It appears that the old woman hanged in a noose against a lighted window is what shocked the child out of the trance your harmless Mr. Burton had put her into, and she saw the man on the water tower.'

'She saw him?' exclaimed Jack Robinson. 'To know again?'

'So she says,' replied Phryne. 'I'll bring her tomorrow to look at photographs. All right?'

'Tomorrow,' agreed Jack Robinson.

Chapter Fourteen

'He had softly and silently vanished away…'
'The Hunting of the Snark,'
Lewis Carroll

Ruthie and Jane had so much to catch up with that Phryne suggested moving Ruth's camp-bed into Jane's room. She knew that they would talk all night but thought that they might as well do it in comfort. Jane was regaining her past in large chunks, and Phryne hoped that it would not prove too indigestible.

Ruth, Jane, and Ember partook of a light supper of bread-and-butter and hot milk, then they all snuggled into Jane's bed so that they could talk without being heard. It was a cold night, but the girls and the kitten were warm in their nest under the eiderdown with the jazz-coloured cover. Phryne looked in on them as she was going out.

'Good night, my dears,' she said, and heard the chorused 'good night, Miss Fisher' from the heaped covers. She smiled and closed the door.

'Dot, I'm going to this Glee Club do, only because I promised to bring the beer. Go to bed, old thing, and don't worry. Mr. B.! All the crates safely stowed?'

'Yes, Miss Fisher, all secure.'

'All right, I'm off—I may bring company home, but I shan't need you again tonight. Everyone can go to bed. We've all had too much excitement lately. All the locks and things up, Mr. Butler? Good. Well, sleep tight,' said Phryne, and sailed out into the night, a furry cap on her head, huddled in the sheepskin coat, and looking like a rather dapper member of the Tsar's entourage of female soldiers. She started the Hispano-Suiza without trouble, steered her carefully into The Esplanade, and turned her nose for the city. The wind whipped her face, tearing at her hair and she laughed aloud into the rainy dark. It was fine to be on the road with all this power at one's fingertips! She leaned on the accelerator, and the car leapt like a deer under her hand.

She rolled carefully down the unmade road to the boathouse, and it was obvious that there was revelry afoot. The boathouse, a rather rickety two-storey construction with a balcony, was lit with lanterns, as were several of the surrounding trees. There was a measured chorus of voices singing Blake's 'Jerusalem'. Phryne stopped the car and listened. It was perfect. The rain drifted softly down, the river ran with a slap and gurgle, and the voices, from highest sop to lowest bass, were blended as finely as a Ritz Hotel cocktail.

> Bring me my bow of burning gold
> Bring me my arrows of desire
> Bring me my spear, Oh! Clouds, unfold!
> Bring me my chariot of fire!

Blake really was an excellent poet, Phryne reflected, lighting a cigarette and leaning back on the leather upholstery, though regrettably mad, as poets so often are.

The song finished. Several people came out onto the balcony, and one girl exclaimed in a high-pitched voice, somewhat affected by gin, 'Oh, I say! What a spiffing car!'

'That must be Miss Fisher,' someone else commented. 'I hope she's remembered the beer!'

'I have remembered the beer,' she called up. 'But you'll have to carry it yourself.'

There was a clatter of feet, and several young men erupted out of the boathouse and down the steps.

'Oh, Miss Fisher, I'm so glad that you could come. Let me help you out, what an amazin' car! Very kind of you to bring some refreshments for the lads…and the girls, of course, I was forgetting. Connors, you and Tommy Jones get the beer, will you? Do you remember me, Miss Fisher?'

Phryne accepted the eager clasp and extracted herself from the driving seat, summoning up the name to match the bright, intelligent face.

'Of course I remember you,' she temporized. 'Aaron Black, that's who you are. Well? What about the bet?'

'You can call on me for a row down the river in a real boat,' he confessed, grinning. 'They know several much ruder songs than we have heard. But we are learning. We think that we should put the two societies together, Miss Fisher, I mean, silly, isn't it, in these days of equality, females all over the shop, I mean, women students in Medicine and even in Law; silly to have separate singing, when all parts in music are of equal value. What do you think of it?'

Phryne allowed herself to be led up the stairs by this charming young man, past a series of boats stored in racks like coffins, and up onto a plain dancing floor, with a servery in one corner and the balcony at the end.

'It's a bit of a crush,' apologized Connors, panting past with a crate. 'I always think that the balcony is not going to make it through another party, but it has managed so far.'

'Beer?' cried a huge young man, seizing the crate and extracting a bottle. He bit off the cap and gulped half the contents before his outraged friend regained possession.

'Beer!' he said with a delighted smile, and grabbed for the bottle again.

'Behave yourself, oaf! This is Miss Fisher, donor of all that amber liquid and some plonk for the ladies, so be civil.'

The huge dark young man took up Phryne's gloved hand with wincing delicacy and bestowed a respectful kiss.

'Madam, your kindness overwhelms us...can I have my bottle back now, Aaron?'

Aaron returned the bottle, seeing that Phryne was amused, and the chorus began on a sad tale of a young maid who was poor (but she was honest). Phryne sighted Alastair across the room, scowling, and the beautiful and diverting Lindsay near him, looking embarrassed. Then two young women claimed Phryne's attention and a bottle of her wine and she elbowed her way out on the balcony, where there was a wicker garden-seat.

'What do you think of this idea of putting the two societies together, Miss Fisher?' asked the blonde girl, gnawing at an ink-stained fingernail. 'They are pretty rough types, these Glee-ers.'

'Nonsense, Marion,' retorted her companion, who was thin and stylish and would be elegant when she started wearing stockings. 'They're nervous around us. Once they see that we aren't put off by the vulgarity they'll be all right. And we need some basses if we are to put on that B Minor Mass you're always talking about.'

'I suppose so. The world has a lot of men in it, doesn't it? It won't do just to pretend that they don't exist. Miss Fisher, we are devoted admirers of yours. We read all of your cases. Are you engaged in one at the moment?'

'Why, yes, I am engaged in the cases of the vanishing lady and the appearing lady; one died and one is alive.'

'Ooh, a riddle! Let's see if we can guess it. Do you want some of this wine? It's rather good,' said Marion. 'Let's get Alastair onto it, he's frightfully good at riddles.'

'Alastair!' shrieked the other girl, but Alastair did not seem to have heard her. He turned his back to the balcony and was arguing with Lindsay.

'What's wrong with him lately?' demanded Agnes. 'He's terribly shirty at the moment. Used to be a good enough chap, too, though a shark for the books.'

'I'm doing Arts,' explained Marion. 'Agnes here is doing Medicine. So is that Alastair chap, and he was rather fun, though over the last year he's been awfully dull. Does nothing but talk about money.'

Phryne accepted some of the wine, a good Traminer Reisling from the Hunter Valley which she had personally selected as being light and sweet enough for a student's taste. No glass being evident, she drank out of the bottle, sharing it with the two girls.

'I don't know that one,' remarked Agnes. 'What are the men singing?'

> Behind the door, her pappy kept a shotgun,
> He kept it in December and the merry month of May
> And when they asked him why the heck he kept it
> He kept it for a student who is far, far away

'Far away', carolled the tenors, 'Far away', growled the basses, 'He kept it for a student who is far, far away.'

'That's a good song, we must learn it. Look here, Agnes, I think you're right. It sounds much better with us all singing together. So much more balanced. Not shrill, like we used to sound.'

'Ah, and you should have heard us,' commented Lindsay from behind Phryne. 'We growled like bears with sore heads. Now the sound is quite perfect.'

'Not quite perfect,' disagreed Johnson, poking his head under Lindsay's arm. 'There is a lot of dissonance which can be removed by rehearsal. We need to knock the raw edges off and get used to singing in time with each other. Listen. One half of the room is out of tempo with the other half.'

This was true. Someone had started the old catch, 'My man Tom has a thing that is long,' which the girls also knew. 'My maid Mary has a thing that is hairy,' they replied, but somehow got irremediably out of synch, so it was hard to tell whose thing was long and whose thing was hairy. Eventually cacophony was reached and they broke off, laughing.

'Was that as indelicate as it sounded?' asked Phryne, and Marion blushed. 'It's a broom and a broom stick.' Phryne laughed and had another mouthful of wine. It was cold and dark outside, and the rain slanted down in sheets, but in the boathouse it was very warm, and the wine was delicious, and the singing was (occasionally) excellent. Phryne relaxed for the first time since she had left the bed with Lindsay in it and produced a flask of Cointreau.

This drink was new to many who tasted it, and it seemed to have a powerful effect. Edwards, the music student, suggested a negro spiritual, and they began to sing 'Swing Low, Sweet Chariot'. The battery of voices in that confined space, all trained to hit a note so that it went down and stayed down, was terrific. Phryne felt tears prick her eyes, as she joined in, and Marion was openly snuffling.

> I looked over Jordan, and what did I see?
> Coming for to carry me home
> A band of Angels coming after me
> Coming for to carry me home.

Before the impact of the song had time to die away, Edwards was pushed aside and the bespectacled madrigal enthusiast flourished a pile of sheet music.

'Sops on the right, basses on the left,' he ordered, and Phryne was left alone on the balcony.

She reclaimed her flask and sat staring out into the night, enjoying the rain, until she felt a hand slide up her calf to her knee and she covered it with her own.

'It's me, dear lady,' said Lindsay's voice from the floor, where he was lying out of sight of his fellow choristers. 'Have you forgotten me so soon?'

'No, dear boy, I haven't forgotten anything at all. Come and sit next to me, or do you like it there on the floor?'

'If they see me I shall be dragged off to sing—I like it better here—how smooth your legs are. Smoother than anything I can think of, except your thighs.'

'You are an impudent young man,' said Phryne, catching her breath. 'What were you quarelling with Alastair about?'

'Does it matter?' asked Lindsay, laying his head in her lap. 'Will you take me away and ravish me again tonight?'

'Perhaps, if you merit ravishing. What was the quarrel?'

'How tiresome you are, I shall be jealous of Alastair, you are so interested in him. If you must know, he wants to move out of my house, and he has packed up all his things. I was asking him where he was going to go, and he took me up uncommonly short and told me it was none of my business, which of course, it isn't.'

'When is he to go? Stop fooling, Lindsay, this is important.'

'Tomorrow,' replied Lindsay, hurt. 'I don't know where he's going but I think that it might not be unconnected with the not-so-blushing beauty and the money. Funny, you know, that was the night I spent in the jug.'

'You *what?*'

'Oh, I hadn't done anything wrong,' protested Lindsay. 'Old Alastair used to have spiffing ideas, you know, before he went strange.'

'Did he?' asked Phryne in a tone so compelling that Lindsay got up from the floor and faced her. 'What did old Alastair suggest?'

'Well, it was like this,' he stammered, staring into the face of a fury, cut out of marble, with eyes of green ice. 'He said that if I was going to be a lawyer I ought to understand about prisons, and the only way to really understand a prison is to be in one, and he said that I should get myself taken up for Drunk and Disorderly and be locked in overnight. Everyone gives a false name, you know. For God's sake, Phryne, what's wrong? What have I done?'

'Where's Alastair?' she asked through numb lips, and scanned the room; an easy thing, since Alastair should have been with the tenors, and he was not there.

'Come,' cried Phryne. She shinned down the verandah pole, leapt and raced for her car, with the young man behind and gaining fast. Phryne threw herself into the driving seat and jabbed the self-starter. The powerful engine turned over with a roar.

'Where are we going?' yelled Lindsay.

Phryne cried, 'We are going to prevent another murder—if we get there in time.'

Lindsay hung on as the Hispano-Suiza, howling on all cylinders, rocketed over the lumpy track and into the road.

Lindsay did not know that cars could go that fast. Phryne, when roused, could drive like a demon, having taken lessons from Miss May Cunliffe, the Cairo to London Road Race winner. Phryne had strong nerves and wiry wrists and the engine of the Hispano-Suiza had been built for racing. The rain drummed on the roof and the windshield; the lights smeared as though marked with vaseline.

Lindsay hung on, cheering, exultant; Phryne clutched the wheel and bit her lip and hoped that she had guessed where the murderer was going.

After ten minutes, Lindsay said, 'Phryne, we are going home, I mean, to your house, are we not? What do you think is going to happen there?'

'I don't know,' snapped Phryne, skidding around a slow trundling truck. 'Reach into the side pocket, will you?'

'My God, Miss Fisher, a gun?'

'Can you use it?'

'Yes,' agreed Lindsay dubiously. 'I've fired one before.'

'Good. Just try not to kill anyone with it. Now, listen. When we get to the house I want you to walk noisily down the left sideway, and I'll go down the right. Make a lot of noise. Sing, if you like. Be genial and drunken if he is there. Hold him until help comes. Can you do it?'

Phryne felt, rather than saw, the spine stiffen and the jaw harden. There was good stuff in the young man.

'I can do it. Why is he going to your house?'

'Because he's found out that Jane has seen him before.'

The car rolled to a silent halt in the cold street. Rain washed the cobbles and slicked the asphalt. Phryne buttoned her coat and pulled her cap down over her eyes, leaned over, and kissed Lindsay hard on the lips.

'Good luck,' she said, and got out of the car.

'Over the top,' said Lindsay, remembering a hundred woeful movies.

He tasted Phryne's kiss on his lips all down the dark alley at the side of the house.

Chapter Fifteen

'Somehow it seems to fill my head with
ideas,—only I don't exactly know what
they are! However, somebody killed some-
thing, that's clear, at any rate...'

Alice Through the Looking Glass,
Lewis Carroll

There were no lights in the house, and it was getting on for one in the morning. It was so quiet, except for the swish of the rain in the leaves, that Phryne could hear Lindsay on the other side of the house, singing in his pleasant tenor 'Swing low, sweet chariot' interrupted by the occasional hiccup. He really had a talent for acting, which his arrogant friend would never suspect. It was dark, and wet, and Phryne had not realized how many lumpy objects, just at shin height, were stored in her sideway. She banged into what seemed to be a spade, to judge by the clatter, and caught it up, using it to mark her steps and make as loud a noise as possible.

Perhaps she was wrong. Perhaps he had gone to call on Eunice, perhaps he had taken a female Glee-er into the bushes (though surely even students were not that lusty on a night like this), perhaps he had gone blamelessly home to bed. A branch struck Phryne across the face and blinded her; when she could see again she had been seized in a bone-breaking hold and there was a hand over her mouth.

She did not struggle, since this was futile; she gave a gasp and allowed herself to go limp. Her attacker was not expecting this; he had to change his grip to bear her up, and he grabbed her around the waist, leaving her hands and her mouth free. She was carried for a few paces, the strength of her captor surprising her. Phryne was a light weight, but this man carried her as if she weighed no more than a feather.

'Fainted, have you?' snarled a distorted voice. 'Miss fineairs Fisher, stealing my friend away like a poor dog to a flaunting bitch. I'll show you, Miss Fisher, who thinks you are so clever. Then I'll kill you, and leave you lying splayed for your lover to find. I can hear him, stumbling and singing, the drunken loon. Playing hide and seek, were you? First you, then him, then the little bitch, and the money is all mine.'

He dropped Phryne on her back and began to tear at the buttons of her sheepskin jacket. Phryne was cold with horror; the man was ten times stronger than she, and she had little time before she would be pinned like a moth.

Quickly, neatly, she rolled, drew up her legs, and kicked out with all her strength. She felt her heels sink into something soft. Her attacker gave a roar like a wounded boar and fell to his knees, catching Phryne's neck with his right hand. His agony was measureless, his grip like that of an ape, and Phryne tore at the fingers. His one hand was not wide enough to encompass her throat, but he had his thumb on the carotid, and the air began to redden before her eyes.

'Oh, there you are, Alastair, old chap,' burbled Lindsay, a little breathlessly. He had heard the shout and had broken the land speed record for running around houses in the dark.

'A fine night isn't it? Oh, I love these cool nights, to repose on the pale bosom of winter,' he carolled, lifting his full bottle, which he had found in the car. 'Have you seen Miss Fisher? Lovely girl. Oh, there she is.' He stared owlishly at Phryne's purpling face. 'Sorry, old chap,' he added, and brought the bottle down with all his force on his housemate's head.

The bottle cracked and broke, the scalp split, and blood blinded Alastair. He released Phryne, who crawled away, groping for the side of the house to haul herself to her feet.

'Alastair, are you dead?' asked Lindsay, bending low, and falling headlong as the strangling hands shot up out of the dark and fastened on his neck. He was dragged close to the blood-blubbered face, and did not have time even to cry out.

Phryne fired a bullet from the small gun and hit Alastair in the thigh. The body jerked, but he did not relax his grip. Lindsay thrashed, suffocating. Phryne raised the gun again and shot Alastair neatly in the forearm, disabling the wrist, so that she could pull the choking Lindsay away, and they stood embracing each other as the monster writhed on the leaf-mould.

'Go in, call the police, quick!' cried Phryne. 'Hurry!'

And Lindsay, coughing, stumbled away and she heard him pounding on the door. Lights went on in the hall. She could see the attacker clearly now. Alastair had been a good-looking young man; now he had the terror-mask of a beast, and Phryne retched when she looked at him. She held the gun unwaveringly, aware that it was glued to her hand with drying blood, and the moments crept on. More lights, and voices, and the 'ting' of the telephone taken off its hook. The thing on the ground stirred. Phryne backed, raising the gun.

'Kill me,' it muttered, blood bubbling from its nose.

'No,' she said, noticing that her voice trembled.

'Kill me. I wanted to kill you. I tried, and failed. It is the natural law. You must kill me.'

'No,' said Phryne. Her knees felt weak. If someone did not come soon, she would fall, and be within reach of that creature on the blood-spattered leaves.

'You killed the old woman,' she said, bolstering her courage.

'I did. She was useless. All women beyond childbearing are useless. She never trusted me, anyway. It was easy. I stole a uniform, got on the train, chloroformed Eunice and the old woman, then when the train stopped at the tower, I flung up my rope and a grapple, and there we were. She was no weight at all, really. And the power! I felt that I could rule the world. That's what murder does for you, Miss Bitch Fisher. It gives you the power of a god.'

'You came here to kill Jane,' said Phryne. 'She hasn't reached childbearing yet. Wouldn't that be a waste?'

Alastair heaved and thrashed, trying to sit up.

'Come and help me,' he demanded.

Phryne did not move.

'You're afraid of me, aren't you? And you should be. I am the superman.'

'I've heard of it,' commented Phryne.

'It would be a waste, but there is a lot of waste in nature. A million sperm to make one cell. A thousand little turtles hatched and only seventy reach the sea. Nature is prodigal. It would make more girls, and she had remembered. She was a danger to me… to me! No little tart could stand in the way of my destiny! All of those under protection shall flourish. All else shall be destroyed.'

'Eunice didn't flourish,' said Phryne, wondering if she had a fever or the night was getting hotter. 'You burnt her face.'

'A trifling error. I never used the stuff; it's old-fashioned, but I needed it because it is heavier than air, I wanted something that would drop down onto the faces of the sleepers. If you don't help me sit up, I'm going to choke on all the blood that is running down the back of my throat,' he added.

'Choke then,' said Phryne as Mr. Butler, Lindsay, and Dot rushed out of the house and she fell into Dot's arms.

'Better tell the cops to bring a doctor,' she gasped. 'Or his deathwish will be fulfilled.'

Dot bore her into the light, and Phryne caught sight of herself in the hall mirror. Her face was white, her eyes surrounded with black hollows, and there was no colour in her lip or cheek. She had, however, ample colour in the purple marks of fingers, so clearly delineated that Jack Robinson later suggested dusting her for prints. Phryne laughed at this, because they had taken away the unspeakable Alastair, strapped to a stretcher, raving, but alive, and she was contemplating a very stiff brandy and soda.

Dot had revived the parlour fire, and Lindsay cast himself down on the hearth rug and closed his eyes. He was smeared with leaf-mould and blood, and was as bruised as Phryne was, from the grasp of those terrible hands. Mr. Butler brought him a drink mixed to the identical recipe. When he had absorbed this and another, a little pink came back to his face and he was able to focus again.

He saw Phryne decorously divested of her jacket and trousers and dressed in a flowing woollen gown, grey-green as gum leaves, after Dot had sponged the mud and blood spatters from her face and hands. Lindsay was treated likewise by Mr. Butler, who washed his face as though he was five years old and still unreliable with chocolate. He gave up his tweed jacket, damaged (he feared) beyond repair, and his smeared trousers, and assumed a dressing-gown and slippers. He was back in his place before the fire, newly washed and dressed, feeling as he had when he was a child, and his nanny had brought him into the drawing-room for an hour before dinner.

Phryne cradled a steaming cup of strong black coffee in both hands, and Lindsay took his with a bewildered thankfulness, as though he had been woken out of a bad dream. A sip taught him that it was Irish coffee made with very good whisky. He drank a little, wondering why his throat was so sore, then became aware that Phryne was telling a story.

'He thought that Eunice Henderson's mother had a lot of money,' she was saying, staring into the depths of the cup. 'He was wrong, as it happens; the old woman was broke, she lost all her fortune in the Megatherium crash. Eunice has money of her own. She was supporting her mother. He read Eunice all wrong,' she added thoughtfully. 'She didn't like her mother—well, no one could—but she was content to wait until nature took its course. She didn't want to kill the old lady. I think that Alastair expected Eunice to be grateful, not mournful. He certainly didn't expect her to hire me to find out who killed her. That upset him. I thought he was just jealous of me because I seduced his friend.'

'Here, I say, Phryne!' objected Lindsay, waking up a little. Dot was smiling at him. Mr. Butler was refilling his glass. The policeman, who had evidently dressed in a hurry, as the bottoms of his pyjamas were visible beneath his trouser hems, was unmoved. Lindsay subsided. He was too tired, anyway, to worry about the rags of Miss Fisher's reputation.

'But I was wrong. He wasn't jealous—at least, not in that way. He was annoyed that any woman could take him on—could be so impudent as to attempt to fathom his motives! But I did. I caught sight of that guard's face, you know, and even with the scar and the cap I almost knew him. Then when he produced that alibi I was convinced that I must have been wrong, and then Lindsay exploded his Mills Bomb right under my chair. They are identical to a physical description.'

'You should have seen it,' said Lindsay sleepily. 'She swung down the boathouse porch like a monkey and drove back here like a demon. It was like riding the whirlwind.'

'Well, I didn't think we had time to spare.' Phryne drained the Irish coffee, touched her throat, and winced. 'And we didn't, either. Are the girls all right?'

'Yes, Miss, I checked, both as cosy as bugs in a rug, them and their cat.' Dot took one of Phryne's feet into her lap and began to rub it. She was sensible of the fact that while there were two sets of masculine arms to fall into, and one of them her current pet, Phryne had fallen into Dot's. Phryne's beautiful feet were colder than stone. Dot rubbed assiduously.

'I found out how he knew that little Jane knew him, Miss Fisher,' admitted Jack Robinson, vainly attempting to haul up his pyjama hem without seeming obvious. 'He overheard our conversation. My end of it, I mean, he was at the counter, signing the bail book, when I was talking to you. It won't happen again, I tell you,' he added fiercely. 'They will have to give me a phone in my office when I tell 'em about this. You could have been killed, Miss, not to mention the girls. What happened when you got to the house?'

'Well, I knew that he wasn't far ahead of us, because he'd been at the boathouse earlier, and I also knew that he could not get into the house. I had those windows fitted with strong diagonal bars, ever since Ember arrived and I realized how dark and little overlooked that sideway is. I thought that he would be prowling about the house, seeking whom he might devour.' She shuddered and swallowed painfully. 'And I thought that Lindsay and I would be a match for him. And we almost weren't, eh, Lindsay?'

'If you hadn't shot him,' opined Lindsay, 'he would have killed me. And I'm his oldest friend. Makes a man think, that does. Will he live, Detective-inspector?' Jack Robinson laughed grimly. Three o'clock in the morning was not his favourite hour, and he was not in the mood to mince words.

'He'll live to hang. Miss Fisher wasn't trying to kill him, so she didn't. He's got the constitution of an ox.'

At that moment, the telephone rang. Mr. Butler went to answer it. 'Miss Henderson, Miss Fisher,' he intoned. Phryne leaned on Dot's arm and staggered out to the phone.

'Hello, Eunice, what can I do for you?'

Phryne listened for a long moment; she thought that they might have been cut off. Then Eunice whispered, 'You know who killed Mother, don't you, Phryne?'

'Yes, my dear, I know.'

'I know too. It was Alastair, wasn't it?'

'Yes.'

'I knew his back, you see. I saw that blond guard, and I didn't recognize the face or the voice, but I knew his back. I've known all along, Phryne, and hoped it wasn't true.'

'Yes, Eunice.'

'Have they caught him?' The whisper was desperate.

'Yes, they've caught him.'

'Why?'

The voice was a wail. Phryne was too tired to think of a tactful reply, and talking hurt her throat.

'Money.'

'And Mother didn't have anything to leave but this house.' Eunice began to laugh. 'I would have given him everything I had.' There was a pause. 'Well, that's the end of that,' she said sadly.

'Eunice, have you no one to stay with you?' urged Phryne.

'No, dear, I don't need anyone. I shall be all right. I am on my own now—no mother, no relatives, no lover. It might be a rather interesting experience. I won't keep you in the hall on this cold night, Phryne. Thank you for everything.'

'Goodnight,' said Phryne, and Eunice hung up.

'That was Eunice Henderson,' she told her company. 'It seems that she suspected it was Alastair all along. Well, that's the end of that, as Eunice says. Give me some more of that Irish coffee, Mr. B., and then I think that we can all go to bed, again.'

'You'll be in touch, Miss Fisher? Have to make a statement about the capture of the felon,' said Jack Robinson. 'Nice work, Miss Fisher. We shall have to get you in the force, ha, ha.'

'Ha, ha,' agreed Phryne waspishly. 'Is it proved by evidence, Jack? Have some of the coffee, it puts heart into you. Are you all right, Lindsay?'

'Yes, I'm all right, just a little dazed by the pace of events.'

Phryne laughed. Jack Robinson accepted a cup of Irish coffee and said, 'Yes, well, they found the old woman's rings in his rooms. He escaped without leaving any traces, you know. He leapt down from the water tower onto the old woman's body, and thence to the track; there weren't no mud on him, so he didn't leave a mark. Then he coiled up his rope, walked down the track to the next station, changed his clothes and dumped the guard's uniform and the cap, peeled off his scar, and put on his own clothes again—he was carrying them all the time, in a knapsack like soldiers use. Relic of his climbing days, I assume. Then he took the train back to town. It was a good plot, though stagey. We might never have laid a hand on him if it weren't for you, Miss Fisher. I hope that you are not too uncomfortable.'

'Uncomfortable? No, not really, though I am going to be as stiff as a board tomorrow. Lindsay, my dear, you must have suspected him. You lived in the same house. He must have spouted all that guff about the superman to you.'

Lindsay woke up a little, blinking.

'Oh, yes, he did, Phryne, but I never paid much attention to it, I mean, one's friends often make asses of themselves, and it does not do to hold it against them. I thought that it was a phase he was going through—medical men are often odd, you know.'

'Yes, I know.'

'And what will happen to those two girls?' asked Jack Robinson. 'Shall I call in the Welfare?'

'No!' protested Phryne. 'They will be fine with me. I shall send them both to school, and they shall go to university if they wish. They're good girls,' she added quietly. 'Besides, Bert will kill me if anything happens to them. They will be fine. No need to worry about them.'

'Then I won't worry, and I will leave you,' said the detective-inspector. 'It's late and the missus will be worrying. Good night, Miss Fisher. Sleep well,' he added, with a wicked sidelong glance at Lindsay. Mr. Butler saw him out and doused the outside light. Phryne Fisher was not at home to any more visitors tonight.

Dot assisted Phryne to her feet. She held out a bruised hand to the beautiful Lindsay.

'Will you come and sleep with me?' she asked softly.

Lindsay attempted to leap to his feet, emitted a sharp gasp, and allowed Dot to drag him out of the chair.

Dot conducted the two of them upstairs into Phryne's boudoir, and put them to bed together neatly. She fetched an extra pillow for the young man and narrowly restrained herself from kissing his cheek as she tucked him in. Phryne was already asleep as soon as she lay down, and had embraced the young man, laying her head on his shoulder. He looked up at Dot, smiling drowsily.

'Good night, Dot,' he slurred, blind with fatigue, and this time Dot stooped and kissed him.

'Sweet dreams,' said Dot, extinguishing the light and closing the door.

She climbed her own stairs and found her own bed, but was not sleepy. She thought of the murder, the horrible transformation of the young man into a monster, and the tragic history of the two girls bedded down with their kitten in the guest bedroom. All the while, as she looked out to sea from her uncurtained window, the lights that were ships moved unfalteringly across the invisible water as if drawn by threads. Dot sighed, took off her dressing-gown and climbed into her own narrow bed.

There must be a reason in it all, thought Dot, and fell asleep trying to think of one.

To receive a free catalog of Poisoned Pen Press titles, please contact us in one of the following ways:

Phone: 1-800-421-3976
Facsimile: 1-480-949-1707
Email: info@poisonedpenpress.com
Website: www.poisonedpenpress.com

Poisoned Pen Press
6962 E. First Ave. Ste 103
Scottsdale, AZ 85251

CPSIA information can be obtained at www.ICGtesting.com
Printed in the USA
BVOW031022180413

318517BV00002B/103/P